Praise for THE DRAVENHEARST BRIDES

"A hauntingly beautiful gothic romance, Barrett's *Dravenhearst Brides* weaves a tale of love, obsession, and betrayal that had me spellbound from the very first page. The perfect next read for fans of Hester Fox and Diana Biller. "
—Jess Armstrong, *USA Today* bestselling author of the Ruby Vaughn Mysteries

"A beguiling, exquisitely disturbing treat of a novel, redolent with all the decadence of a Kentucky summer. Betrayal, loss, and generational trauma collide in a beautiful maelstrom of southern gothic horror that will have you leaving all the lights on. Glamorous and spine-chilling."
—Paulette Kennedy, bestselling author of *The Witch of Tin Mountain*

"In turns sensual, eerie, and deeply romantic, *The Dravenhearst Brides* enthralls from the first luscious page to its heart-stopping conclusion. As hazy and hot as summer in the Bluegrass—but with a gripping chill that keeps the suspense razor sharp—Lindsay Barrett's dark mystery is a true sensory indulgence. Clever plotting, glorious prose, and an incisive exploration of mental health breathe new life into a traditional gothic romance, all against the sweeping and swoony backdrop of Prohibition-era Kentucky."

—Erin Langston, *New York Times* celebrated author of *Forever Your Rogue*

THE DRAVENHEARST BRIDES

A Kentucky Gothic Romance

LINDSAY BARRETT

Cover design by Austin Drake | Bottle Cap Creative

Edited by Rachel Shipp

Paperback ISBN: 979-8-9925012-2-3

E-book ISBN: 979-8-9925012-3-0

Content Note from the Author

This story was inspired by asking the question, "What would happen if you introduced a woman who was already mentally unwell to the haunted manor of a gothic romance?" The chronic illness and mental health representation contained within—and the compounding synergy between them—are written based on my own personal experience.

Please note, this book contains and discusses: ableist language, depression/suicide, panic attacks, domestic violence, familial death, and infertility/miscarriage. There is a beautiful and healing love story that transcends the darkness within these pages, but please read with care.

To Scott,
whose infinite love and evening glass
of bourbon inspired all that follows.

1

Louisville, 1933

You are cordially invited to a formal
soiree at the Anderson residence.
Thirteenth of June, half past nine
402 Belgravia Court

THE NOOSE WAS TIGHTENING around Margaret Greenbrier's neck. It had been for quite some time—slowly, infinitesimally, but surely. As unstoppable as the current of the Ohio River outside her window. As steady as the hum of the cicadas on this sticky midsummer Kentucky eve. The sun would sink in the west tonight, rise in the east on the morrow, and the noose 'round her neck would be another crick tighter come dawn.

Margaret could scarcely breathe as she fastened a strand of plump pearls at her throat, fingers trembling at the clasp. Despite a plunging open back, the champagne silk of her evening gown was cloying. The pearls rubbed her collarbone, all softness and sensual luster. Was she imagining the tightness? Was she imagining, perchance, an insidious twist of smooth gemstones turning scratchy? A serpent twining around her airway...

Noose-like.

The pearls fell from her tremulous fingers, plummeting to the ground like shells ejected from a smoking shotgun. A flush rose on the back of her neck, beneath her pinned-up strawberry-blonde hair. This was how it always started, that damning, rushing flood of hot blood at her neck.

Tunneling vision came next.

Margaret's breath turned ragged, as distant to her ears as the rumble of thunder heralding a summer storm. The fallen pearls forgotten, she groped blindly for the safety of her bed, sinking onto the mattress, eyes tightly closed.

Vasovagal, the doctors called her, but that was only recently. Several years ago, when the episodes first started, she was labeled *anemic*. Low iron. Dietary adjustments were suggested—fish, spinach, the like—but when the fainting spells began to coincide with eruptions of tears and harsh guttural breaths that impeded speech and reason, the doctors branded her something else.

"Weak constitution, prone to fits of hysteria," they said, hushed, as though speaking filthy words. Had she not been the daughter—correction, heiress—of Kentucky cattle-ranching tycoon Samuel Greenbrier, a sanatorium, possibly even an *institution,* might have been delicately suggested. As it stood, she was prescribed laudanum, a drug her housebound and pinpoint-pupilled mother had known all too well.

Respite at their Bluegrass country manor, Greenbrier Estates, was also suggested. Fresh air, the physician was most certain, would do her good. But Margaret's feet remained firmly planted at her family's Louisville townhouse. Greenbrier Estates was far from bucolic; it was the root of her problems. This ascetic doctor with his crisp, patronizing speech and leather satchel full of scientific diagnoses...this man knew nothing of ghosts.

Margaret opened her eyes, her gaze tracing the sweeping folds of heavy maroon drapery flanking the bay window. For months on end, she'd sat on the cushioned seat of that window, watching through thick glass panes as life in Louisville unfolded without her. It was almost a comfort, learning the world didn't need her to keep turning. It made her feel small in a most reassuring way. Invisible. Half a ghost herself.

The flush behind Margaret's neck receded. She retrieved the pearls from the floor, then placed two fingers at her throat to check her pulse.

You're not hysterical, she reminded herself as gooseflesh broke out, hot sweat turning cold.

No. Margaret Greenbrier was *not* crazy. Being vasovagal was a legitimate medical condition, albeit one exacerbated by "distressing circumstances." Those were the careful words the most recent physician had used. Evidently, Margaret would rather flee her body—flee the conscious world altogether—than face trauma head-on. She'd been through enough.

"You are *not* crazy." She whispered the words, a talisman against the fear, and draped the necklace once more.

The pearls should have settled smoothly, but they rubbed like braided rope on the pale white, near-translucent skin of her throat. She didn't look in the mirror, terrified of what she might see. The sensation was real enough; she couldn't risk actually seeing a noose around her neck.

It would be awfully hard to prove her sanity if she started *seeing* things. Her mother saw things near the end, things most certainly not there. Elijah, for one.

But Margaret was not so far gone as that. No, ma'am.

She could—would—wear the pearls tonight. Everything was fine.

A knock on the door granted her deliverance. Margaret rose to her feet as her father entered. The warmth of his presence could chase away any ghost, for not even the occult would dare cross Samuel Greenbrier. A native Kentuckian through and through, Pa struck an indomitable figure in matters of both business and home.

"Margaret." His indulgent smile was broken by a hacking cough. He turned away, pressing a handkerchief to his lips, his chest heaving. When the fit subsided, he discreetly folded and secreted away the evidence.

But Margaret didn't need to see the blood to know it was there.

Samuel Greenbrier smiled again before extending his tuxedoed arm. "My beautiful gal, are you ready? Shall we?"

"We shall." She placed her hand in her father's.

Another night on the town. Another ballroom. Another promenade on Pa's arm, masquerading as the most prized of his cattle, healthy and whole.

Oh, the tangled web they'd together weave.

She allowed him to sweep her out of the brownstone, onto the dark streets of Louisville, and straight into a waiting motorcar. Its headlights pierced the night to illuminate the way.

Margaret leaned her head on her father's shoulder. They traveled in silence, but it was companionable, for there was no one in the world Margaret loved more than her darling Pa.

Even if he was responsible for the goddamn noose in the first place.

2

June 13, 1933

Samuel,

Enclosed you will find updated inheritance documents. They await signatures from both you and the new beneficiaries. Please note the addended marital clause, per your request. Once received, all copies will be notarized and returned.

Best,
Louisville Family Law Offices of Holland & Kirk

M ARGARET COULDN'T EVEN PRETEND to know whose miniature Victorian mansion on the outskirts of Louisville they were visiting tonight. Nearly every evening, Pa paraded her somewhere new, making endless introductions, hoping he might find one that would stick.

They never did. And time was rapidly running out.

At the age of twenty-two years—the last several spent as a recluse—Margaret was something of a mystery to polite society, reintroduced this season like a bolt from the blue. But while her softly curved, cherubic figure made short memories for the men, the women remembered perfectly well...

Three summers ago, her disastrous debut. The prolonged social isola-
tion—half self-imposed, half societally necessary—that followed.

No one could gossip like southern society women, and they had the
collective memory of a steel trap. They clustered in groups, whispering
behind hands like vultures pecking at a carcass. *There's something off about
that Greenbrier girl, something not quite right. Pretty enough, sure, but a bit
touched in the head.*

Margaret was not crazy. She was *not*.

But perception was reality, and all the money in the world couldn't buy
the illusion of sanity. Nor, apparently, could it convince even the most
red-blooded of men to get into bed with her.

Margaret kept her chin up, eyes level with those who sniped behind
closed fingers as she moved through the crowd. The judgmental stares were
like darts, a barrage of prickling attacks. A faint flush rose on her neck,
creeping higher with each step. Black spots dotted the corners of her vision,
closing in.

No. Not now. Not again.

There was so very much at stake.

"Ah, Alastair."

Pa's voice cut through her rising panic. The sight of the suitor before her
was enough to turn Margaret's scalding blood cold.

Alastair Pendry was a widower, agriculture titan, and old friend of her
father. Emphasis on *old*, all silver-streaked hair and fleshy lips. Lips that
curled in a cat-that-ate-the-canary smile as he gazed at Margaret.

"Samuel." Alastair extended a hand. "And Margaret—looking simply
grand this evening, as always."

His tone was above reproach. As was his gaze, pinned firmly on Margaret's cornflower-blue eyes, never drifting down the shapely curves of her
body, not even once. It was perhaps why her father considered Alastair a
respectable match despite the nearly thirty-year age difference. There was

also the simple but unavoidable matter of no other man offering, and their time had all but run out.

But prey always recognized predator, and Margaret was not fooled by Alastair Pendry. She knew this man would be the death of her. Her fingers drifted absentmindedly to the pearls at her throat, an instinctive tic.

Pa turned to her, expectant. Margaret was to play nice by acknowledging Alastair's compliment, perhaps even offer a warm smile or her hand for a kiss.

But she had no intention of spending a single moment with her soon-to-be fiancé. The discussion had occurred in her father's study only yesterday. The offer was made, and Pa intended to accept. He had no choice. Alastair would take care of her. She *needed* to be taken care of.

Margaret didn't want to hear it.

"Pardon me," she said to both gentlemen, prying her arm from her father's grasp. She fought to keep her steps unhurried as she walked away, cutting a course for the opposite side of the ballroom, to a spot near the wall with the other single women—the spinsters and widowed aunties—where she belonged. Fate was a devil who couldn't be bargained with. Margaret had learned that lesson long ago. The day Elijah died.

With each successive step, she moved faster, hands coiling in tight fists.

Then came the haunting taunt of the physician's voice. *Prone to fits of hysteria. Avoid distressing circumstances...*

Well. That was fine and dandy for him to say atop his clinical high horse, but this was Margaret's life. She *was* distressed. And feeling that way did not make her crazy or hysterical or any other ignominious label a man might slap across her forehead to silence and discredit her pain. First Eli, then Ma, had left her to face this mess alone. And now—

"Oof!" The exclamation tore from her lips, masking a rising sob as she collided with a powerfully built man. Margaret was sent reeling, the floor rushing up to meet her. She closed her eyes and stretched out an arm, bracing for impact. Felt the barest sweep of the man's fingers as he reached to catch her...

But no one had been there to catch Margaret in years. She hit the ground hard, twisting her wrist when she landed. The society crowd gasped, stunned by Margaret Greenbrier's latest faux pas.

"Oh, mercy." The man was aghast, eyes wide at the sight of her on the floor. "Are you all right? I'm simply..." His words dried up as his gaze swept her face.

Margaret stared at him in turn. The rational part of her mind recognized him as bourbon aristocrat Merrick Dravenhearst. A man who, much like herself, had curated a persona of recluse over the last several years. But whereas Margaret's malingering made her a social pariah, Dravenhearst's gave him an air of rakish mystery...helped along by the indisputable fact the man was handsome as hell. As handsome as the devil himself.

Merrick Dravenhearst's eyes were the same color as the bourbon his family was infamous for pandering. Eyes that, at first glance, were appreciative, but the longer he stared, twisted with something that looked an awful lot like horror.

Horror—at the mere sight of her!

"Beg pardon," Margaret murmured, lowering her lids in shame, cheeks coloring. "I was in a state, not looking—"

"The fault is mine." His voice was loud and confident, cutting through the whispers of the highfalutin crowd. The horror vanished from his eyes, replaced by something that looked quite appallingly like pity.

She preferred the horror, honestly.

"Are you all right, Miss...?" He let the question dangle and extended a hand to help her rise. The sharp line of his jaw was freshly shaved but shadowed with a hint of black. The kind of dusting that never truly went away, no matter how close the shave.

"Greenbrier." She placed her uninjured hand in his. His long fingers dwarfed hers, swallowing them. "Margaret Greenbrier."

"Margaret?" he repeated, his face twisting again, this time in an expression altogether unreadable. His fingers twitched within her grip, rough-hewn calluses apparent. It was wholly unexpected, such coarseness on the hands of a gentleman, but Margaret didn't linger to investigate.

"Yes." On her feet now, she turned away, seeking to disappear. "But I'm really no one...no one at all. I'm terribly sorry for the intrusion."

Gripping her wounded wrist in the opposite hand, she fled.

Margaret departed the ballroom through the same archway she'd entered not ten minutes prior. Tears fell down her cheeks unchecked. She dabbed them away, careful not to smear the paint on her face. She just needed a few moments alone to compose herself before rallying to face the jackals again.

Margaret slipped into a sitting room decorated in shades of green—heavy drapes the color of sage, a chesterfield sofa in deep emerald, pistachio-papered walls, and gilt-framed abstract paintings of forested game, heavy with hunter and evergreen brushstrokes.

She moved to close the door, but a foot jammed through the gap. A very shiny, polished, masculine foot.

"You are not all right."

For reasons most inexplicable, Merrick Dravenhearst had given chase after her panicked flight.

Margaret almost laughed because *of course* she wasn't all right. But no handsome man had pursued her from a ballroom before, so she held her tongue. This was quite a novelty.

"Are you hurt?"

"I'm fine." She answered automatically, but the tiniest part of her, the part positively aching to be seen, drew away from the door, allowing him to crack it open. She backed up slowly and sank into a velveteen club chair the color of a dill pickle, cradling her injured arm.

He hovered in the doorway. "You hurt your wrist."

"It's fine," she repeated.

"It's not."

"Are you a physician?"

"No."

"Then forgive me for disregarding your opinion on the matter." She offered a half smile. "Your chivalrous obligation has been met, Mr. Dravenhearst. My well-being ascertained, you may return to the party with a clear conscience. Please, go drink and dance with the other debutantes. You'll be missed."

He chuckled and stepped into the room. "There's not a single gal in there worth dancing with, and certainly nothing I want to drink, Miss Greenbrier...hasn't been since January 17, 1920." With a shifty smile, he produced a hip flask from under his jacket. "Which reminds me, physician or not, I've got the best cure around for that wrist." He unscrewed the cap and offered it to her, crouching on bended knee.

It was, she was forced to admit, a rather heady sight—this self-assured man on his knees before her. With closeness came sudden awareness of his sheer size, of the suit jacket pulling slightly at his shoulders, straining to contain the broad swell underneath. His shirt was the same, stretched just a hair too taut, catching on ridges of muscle upstanding gentlemen had no business having.

He needed a new suit, one that fit properly.

She recalled the coarseness of his hand in hers, cataloged the light crinkle lines around his tawny brown eyes. His black hair was thick and full, not a trace of balding or silver in sight. He was older than her but younger than Alastair. Significantly.

Margaret sniffed the air directly above the proffered flask, and the harsh burn of alcohol seared her nostrils. She coughed twice; whatever he was offering was *strong*. "You got a medicinal license for that?"

"Actually, Miss Greenbrier, I do. But of far greater import is your abominable dismissal of the finest bourbon in the state of Kentucky. You wound me."

Margaret narrowed her eyes and snorted, amused. "Is this the infamous Dravenhearst bourbon, then?"

"Ah." He placed a hand to his heart in mock-supplication. "You've heard of us?"

Against her best intentions, she let out a tiny giggle.

"Now then," he continued, smiling softly, "I'm almost afraid to offer again, since you've clearly no idea how to properly *sniff*, let alone sip, quality bourbon, but would you care for a taste?"

Hearing the dulcet drawl of his words, taking in the rakishly charming grin on his full lips, Margaret suddenly thought she just might. Her hand lifted, disconnected from her body and, most certainly, her mind.

The flask was warm in her grip.

Warm from the heat of his body, she realized. Her gaze swept over his domineering physique, so incongruous with his purported station and name. She gave a second sniff, this one small, dainty even.

"Notes of smoke and clove, upfront on your palate," he murmured, his focus darting between his flask and her lips. "With a smooth caramel finish."

It sounded delightful, like a sugar-and-spice childhood dream. Captivated, Margaret tipped back the flask and took a hearty pull.

"Whoa!" He grabbed for the bottle as the harsh burn flooded Margaret's mouth and nostrils. She fought the urge to spit it straight back out.

What a charlatan this man was, full of falsely honeyed words. She coughed violently as the bourbon scorched its way down her throat. This disgrace of a drink had just singed her tastebuds for the next week!

"You're a filthy liar," she managed between gags.

He released a half-suppressed chuckle. "Oh, am I now?"

"Indeed, sir, you are."

"First you impugn my family's lifeblood—our heirloom bourbon recipe—next you malign my reputation?"

"I'm sure it's hardly a first for either."

"Well." He leaned back on his haunches, a move perhaps intended to give her breathing room. But her eyes swept over his powerfully built thighs, and she lost her breath as quickly as it returned. "You may be right on the second count, certainly not on the first. Our bourbon, at least, is above reproach."

"I cannot honestly say I agree."

"It's an acquired taste. Perhaps I can convince you to take a second sip? Much smaller this time." He tilted his head. "Your wrist will thank you for it, if nothing else."

Margaret had limited experience with alcohol. Prohibition had begun when she was only nine, but she and Elijah had snuck a taste or two of their parents' moonshine on occasion, enough for Margaret to know it was of the second sip she had to beware. The second always went down smoother than the first. The second led to a third and a fourth, until suddenly you were rolling around on the basement floor, giggling with your twin brother, not a care in the world...

"Margot, are we flying?"

"We're a pair of blue jays!" She laughed, spreading her arms.

"Miss Greenbrier?" The handsome devil with the sweet bourbon eyes placed a hand on her knee.

Not Eli at all.

"Margot, catch me!"

She blinked, disoriented. "Forgive me." Against her better judgment, Margaret tossed back another sip, letting the burn in her throat overtake the one in her heart.

She was better prepared, but she'd still swear on her brother's grave there wasn't a trace of caramel to be found in this travesty of a drink. Her lips puckered.

"What's the verdict?" Dravenhearst leaned in. His hand, she realized, remained lightly perched on the tip of her knee. "Have I converted you from a dry to a wet?"

Margaret smirked. Drys were those who supported the temperance movement, the wets those who fought it. Frankly, she'd never given much thought to either side, nor had anyone ever asked her opinion. Alcohol had been outlawed as long as she could remember, simple as that.

Before she could formulate an answer, footsteps echoed in the hallway. The door creaked before slamming open as her father and Alastair strode into the room.

"Margaret?" Pa's brow furrowed with concern.

"What in blue blazes is going on here?" Alastair demanded.

Dravenhearst remained on his knees, his traitorous hand still resting on her thigh.

Oh, gracious, what a mess. If only she cared.

A deliciously rebellious smile rose on her lips, stretching muscles Margaret had nearly forgotten she possessed.

"Alastair." Dravenhearst rose to his feet and nodded, his hand vanishing from her leg. The spot quickly grew cold.

The introduction she thought she'd need died on her lips as Alastair's face curdled with open contempt.

"Merrick." Alastair nodded in turn, a sharp jerk of his head. His eyes, glimmering possessively, flicked to Margaret.

She detested his presumption with every fiber of her being. A fire kindled to life inside her, one that hadn't been lit in years and years.

Simply because she sensed it would cause quite a reckoning, Margaret stood and slipped her hand into Dravenhearst's. His fingers jerked with surprise, but bless his heart, he held fast.

Pa's face flickered with confusion, Alastair's with rapidly rising irritation.

"Miss Margaret," Alastair began, his voice low. "Shall I escort you back to the ballroom now?"

"Miss Greenbrier and I were not done conversing." Dravenhearst saved Margaret from a response. "I am, most assuredly, capable of seeing her safely back myself."

"Certainly." Alastair nodded. "Forgive me, though, if I'm hesitant to leave my *fiancée* in your notoriously dissolute company, Merrick."

Dravenhearst's fingers flinched again within her own, compelling Margaret to speak. "Beg pardon, sir, we are *not* affianced."

Alastair narrowed his eyes. "That's not the impression your father has given me."

At this, Samuel Greenbrier started to cough. All eyes in the room watched him withdraw a handkerchief and give three bellowing hacks into its folds. "Margaret..." he said, wiping his mouth.

His tone—weathered and beaten and defeated—was a slap to her face. It was not a tone Samuel Greenbrier used often, if at all. Margaret drew back, hiding behind Dravenhearst's shoulder, not wanting to hear another damning word.

"Is the matter indeed settled?" Dravenhearst asked, shifting from foot to foot, looking at Margaret rather than her father.

She blinked twice, disarmed.

"It *is* settled," Alastair interjected.

"If I was asking for your grandiose shyster's opinion, Alastair, I would have said as much," Dravenhearst replied, his eyes never leaving Margaret.

Her face burned, unused as she was to such single-minded consideration. She looked away first.

"Shyster?" Alastair cackled. "Takes one to know one, eh, Merrick?" He turned to Samuel. "The only *shyster* in this room is Mr. Dravenhearst. I suggest we gather Margaret and return to the ballroom posthaste. Do not entertain—"

"The matter is *not* settled," Pa interrupted, his attention focused on Dravenhearst, assessing. "But it will be. Imminently. If you've something to say, boy, the time has come."

The temperature in the room skyrocketed. Margaret's heart stuttered.

Dravenhearst licked his lips. He couldn't possibly have anything to say, Margaret could tell that much with the barest glance. It almost hurt more, to have this carrot dangled before her at the eleventh hour. Her desperation had never been higher.

A slow grin spread across Alastair's face. "Cat got your tongue, Merrick? I suppose not even the Greenbrier fortune and a pretty face can get those bachelor legs of yours down the aisle."

"Margaret." Pa stepped forward, prepared to take control of the spiraling situation. "Do you even know this man?"

She wasn't certain what prompted her to lie, but fib Margaret did. Straight through her teeth. "Of course."

"But you...you've never mentioned..." Pa rubbed his chin. "Where did you meet?"

Margaret was quick. "At the Collingsworth party, was it not?" She turned to Dravenhearst, her eyes wide, pleading.

"Indeed it was." A lazy grin overtook his features. The bastard was enjoying this. "I remember the evening well. You wore a midnight blue gown and this very same necklace, if I'm not mistaken." He brushed a finger over the pearls, and a shiver ran through Margaret, straight to her toes.

How did he...?

"We met again at the Feinstein home," he added. "You wore emerald green that evening, a stunning complement to your red hair." His gaze traced her face. A flicker of intimacy passed through his eyes, there and gone in a heartbeat.

But Margaret had seen. It puzzled her, this game he was playing. She couldn't even begin to ascertain his motives.

Dancing with the devil, she realized suddenly. *That's what I'm doing.*

"Yes," she murmured, unable to manage anything more. Because she *had* worn midnight blue and pearls to the Collingsworth gala, and emerald to the Feinstein's. But how on God's green earth did this man know that?

Alastair roused himself for a final parting shot. "Samuel," he said, his voice low and earnest. "We're old friends. I understand the situation you find yourself in, but you've always said your greatest fear was a fortune hunter seeking claim to your daughter. You've said it since the day she was born and placed in your arms." Alastair's gaze was steady as it flicked to Dravenhearst, then back. "I'm telling you, on my honor, there is one standing in this room today, make no mistake. I implore you, as your friend and as someone who loves Margaret dearly, to refuse to consider his impertinence."

"If the man intends to ask for my daughter's hand," Pa said, "he may do so anytime. *Properly.* We'll be accepting calls tomorrow." His eyes flitted to Dravenhearst's with significance. "For now, Margaret and I will take our leave."

Margaret lowered her lashes as she slipped past Dravenhearst. His gaze burned into her spine as she crossed the room, but she hadn't the courage to look back to meet it. She could ask nothing more of him. Tonight's game had gone far enough.

As she departed on her father's arm, Margaret's ears picked up hushed tones.

"You're a damn fool, boy," Alastair murmured. "You can't bring that girl to Dravenhearst Distilling as your bride, and you know it."

"I never said I was going to," came the cool response.

"See that you don't. The only thing more foolish than *me* courting Margaret is *you* courting her."

3

June 14, 1933

Xander,
I have been delayed. Unexpected business opportunity. A few
days at most.

More soon,
Merrick Dravenhearst

T HE NEXT DAY WAS interminable. Margaret had tossed and turned
in bed all night and risen with the sun at dawn. Time passed the way
hot molasses drips in an hourglass on a winter day, tantalizingly unhurried
and tainted with the sugarcoated sweetness of illicit anticipation.

He wouldn't come. She was certain.

And yet...and yet for the briefest of moments last night—the moment
when his eyes unflinchingly met her own while Alastair blustered around
them—she'd thought perhaps...perhaps...just maybe...

Margaret did quite a lot of pacing. Quite a bit of feigned eating and
distracted window-watching as well. She watched and waited until the sun

cast long shadows across the sidewalk. Until dusk settled, yawning its jaws in a quiet gasp over Louisville.

That's it then. She rose from her seat. *He's not coming. Whyever dare dream he might? A man like that...*

The laudanum was right there on her bedside table, ready and waiting. As familiar and comforting as a best friend, more so even. Margaret hadn't received any real friends at the Louisville townhouse in years. There was shame in that. Shame in knowing when her darkest hour had struck, no one showed up for her. She wasn't worth showing up for.

Even still, today, in the deepest, darkest, most vulnerable corner of her damaged heart, she had, perhaps, *hoped...*

Hope. A thing more dangerous than all the burning coal in Kentucky. A flash of Dravenhearst's amber eyes flared in her memory, the warmth of his hand on her knee.

Margaret winced at her longing. She should have known better.

The phantom grip of the noose slithered around her neck again, cinching tight. The laudanum winked from the table. She need only take two steps and reach for it.

She knew she would in the end. She always did. She was, after all, her mother's daughter. After Elijah's accident at their country manor in the Bluegrass, Vivian Greenbrier hadn't wasted any time pretending; she reached and drank, reached and drank.

Margaret didn't reach. She buried her face in her hands, shoulders arched forward like the broken wings of a fledgling bird.

"We're a pair of blue jays!"

Child Margaret's shoulders shook with giggles, grown-up Margaret's shook with restrained sobs.

"Margot, catch me!"

The thunderous pound of hoofbeats in her mind was replaced by a distant but solid sound of knocking. Her head snapped up, tears drying in their tracks, hand flying to her mouth.

Flying.

"Margot, are we flying?"

She shook her head to silence Eli's ghostly memory as a second knock, loud as cannon fire, reverberated. The boom echoed through the silent tomb that was the Louisville townhouse, rattling her very bones. Hinges whined as the front door opened.

Margaret couldn't help herself. She dropped to her knees and, like a child, crawled into the upstairs hallway. She inched forward until she could poke her head through the balusters of the banistered mezzanine overlooking the entry hall.

She made it just in time to spy a dark-haired, broad-shouldered gentleman cross the foyer before disappearing down a hallway. The one to her father's office.

Dravenhearst.

Her heart stopped, disbelief and anticipation warring in her mind.

"Why, Miss Margaret, whatever are you doing?"

The voice came from behind her. Margaret knew it well—Brigita, one of two maids employed by her father. Her arms were full of linens, her brow furrowed as she gazed at Margaret on hands and knees, rear end in the air like a bobber at the end of a fishing line.

Brigita clicked her tongue. "What in tarnation are you doing on the floor? Have you taken ill?"

Margaret could nearly hear the "again" Brigita so clearly longed to tack on the end of her question.

"No, er...it's only..." Heat rose in her cheeks. "I've lost an earring."

Yes, that would do. She combed her fingers across the carpet, pretending to search.

"But, Miss…" The divot between Brigita's brows etched deeper. "Both earrings are already in your ears, safe and secure."

"I'll be jiggered…are they really?" Margaret moved a hand to her right ear, smiling with feigned relief while tugging the pearl. "Oh, Brigita, you've found it! You're simply brilliant." She rose to her feet and squeezed the maid's arm in gratitude. Brigita tensed beneath her touch and withdrew, a wary look in her eye.

Crazy Margaret. Cuckoo Margaret. Mad Margaret. She'd heard it all before. Brigita didn't need to say a single word.

"Thank you, Brigita. I best be off to find the other one now." Margaret injected her tone with false sing-song cheer and smiled as she departed, leaving a dumbstruck Brigita in her wake.

When people think you're mad, Margaret thought wryly, *you can get away with so very much.* It was as inescapable a fact as it was convenient. In truth, Margaret had grown quite used to it. So much so that, at times, she wondered who she would be without this crutch.

"Lean on broken reeds, Margaret Greenbrier, and one day, you'll get a face full of swamp mud," her mother had always preached.

But as she closed her bedroom door, an unvarnished laugh escaped Margaret's lips. More of a cackle really. Witchy and wild and wanton.

Because broken reeds or not, Margaret had two earrings in her lobes, and *he came.*

The foolish devil actually *came.*

Her laughter began anew. She tipped her head back and sagged against her bedroom door, awash with relief and something that, goldarn it, felt an awful lot like hope once more.

Perhaps she was as mad as they said after all.

An hour later, Margaret drifted back to the mezzanine. She curled her fingers around the ivory balustrade and gazed into the marble foyer, waiting.

Footsteps trod in the hall, soft and steady. Margaret tightened her grip on the rail as Dravenhearst came into the entryway. He moved to the door with smooth purpose, glancing back only once before departing. He did not seem surprised to see her watching overhead. On the contrary, the left corner of his mouth lifted in amusement.

She cocked her head, her jaw open, a question hanging in the air. But her voice eluded her. Stolen from her lips along with the breath from her lungs, lost somewhere in the cavernous expanse of cold marbled space between her and this mystery of a man.

He came...but *why*?

Before Margaret could make sense of it, before a single word was exchanged, Dravenhearst tipped his hat and disappeared into the summer night.

Margaret blinked twice, unsettled, as the phantom of his imagined breath, his voice, whispered along the back of her neck.

Your move, Miss Greenbrier.

Pa leaned against the mahogany desk in his office with a heavy sigh. "Well, my darling, shall I start with the good news or the bad?"

Margaret shifted in the wingback chair. She imagined the imprint of Dravenhearst's body in this very seat mere minutes ago, for she'd pounded down the stairs and strode straight into her father's office before the cushion had even gone cold. "The bad, I suppose."

She braced herself for a death blow, one that would squelch the tiny ember of hope burning in her chest.

"He's unquestionably a fortune hunter, my darling. Most assuredly." Pa tilted his head, considering. "Though I'll say this for the man, at least he's honest."

"How do you reckon?"

"He didn't dance around the fact, came right out with it. He's a third-generation bourbon aristocrat, and Prohibition has wrung his empire plumb dry. He has barely two coins to rub together."

Margaret swallowed. Put in those terms, it made perfect sense. She nodded. A beribboned piggybank she was to be then.

"The good news," Pa said, crossing his arms, "is the man has a backbone made of steel. He's kept his head above water whilst most have drowned. And he's been watching the tide—five states have voted to ratify the Twenty-First Amendment to overturn Prohibition. Four more have votes scheduled next week."

Margaret sniffed. "Five is far from a majority. The temperance movement still grips the nation, has for more than a decade. The states are locked up tighter than a Baptist virgin. As are Dravenhearst's coffers, no doubt."

"A betrothal to a Dravenhearst, even a plumb broke one, is nothing to scoff at, Margaret," Pa continued, his voice soft. "His name carries weight, and though his estate is nearly defunct today, it might not be tomorrow. Particularly if it's combined with our assets."

She remained silent, stubbornly so. Men spoke of matches like picking horses at the Derby—clinically detached, all genes and odds. Was she wrong to desire something more? To want to fall for more than a family name? To be given the same consideration in return?

"You'll not ask for my opinion, but I feel obliged to give it nonetheless. And I..." Pa trailed off, dragging one hand along his desk as he walked around it, then sank into his chair with a tired sigh. "I only wish I could offer you more time." He reached into his pocket for his handkerchief and tossed it on the desk between them.

Margaret winced. It was streaked with blood.

The doctor had delivered his verdict almost five months ago: carcinoma of the lung, too advanced for any hope of cure. He gave Samuel his own prescription for laudanum and a projection of decline over six months, a year at most.

The physician's parting shot had been the final nail in the coffin. Margaret could hear the words even now. "It would be prudent to get your affairs in order sooner rather than later."

She'd been reintroduced to Louisville society barely a week later, suddenly the most prized of all the cattle her father owned. Samuel Greenbrier had an extensive portfolio of assets to secure, one his fey daughter could not possibly manage alone. It was Elijah, after all—the *son*—who had been groomed for the job. But when they'd put Elijah in the ground eight years past, it had never once been suggested Margaret learn, that she be taught in his stead. God forbid she be educated beyond eligibility.

Her father wished for more time. Margaret wished she could *turn back* time. She would do so very many things differently.

She cleared her throat. "What is it then?" she asked. "Your opinion."

"Alastair Pendry will make a fine husband, a fine partner." Pa hesitated when she pulled a face. "Let me finish, Margaret. I understand your reluctance—I do. The age gap is significant."

"He has *children* older than me."

"He does. But he also has wisdom and life experience, and whether you believe it or not, he cares for you. Deeply. Perhaps not the way you, as a young woman, wish to be cared for. But fondness and respect are not bad places from which to build a marriage."

Margaret squirmed in her seat, hating how reasonable her father sounded. "And Dravenhearst? A fortune hunter...you suspect he will suck Greenbrier Estates—and me—dry?"

Pa shook his head. "That man has found avenue after avenue to balance his accounts, no matter the personal cost. He's smart and sparing. He siphoned off what bourbon he could to the George T. Stagg distillery—they've a pharmaceutical permit. And to fill in the cracks, he pivoted."

"Pivoted to what?"

Now it was Pa's turn to fidget. "It's best you go into it knowing everything," he murmured, rubbing his jaw. "He pivoted to horses. He's a horseman, Margaret. Rides every day, races too."

She swallowed, her throat suddenly dry. Hoofbeats roared in her ears. The back of her neck prickled with heat. She closed her eyes.

Blasted Kentucky men and their horses.

"Of course," Pa was quick to continue, "Alastair is as well. You've always known that. I believe that's the source of the bad blood between the two. There's been some swapping of trainers and sire deals gone sour. Not to mention, Alastair has always been staunchly dry, and Dravenhearst is inarguably wet."

"I see," she managed, lids fluttering open.

"Dravenhearst had the Kentucky Derby winner three years ago, Gallant Fox. Quite the boon, that colt—they called it the Triple Crown, the three races he won. Earned Dravenhearst a windfall."

"Horses and hooch," Margaret grunted, sinking lower in her seat. "He's a regular philistine."

"A philistine perhaps, but one with a respectable lineage who's asked for your hand," Pa said. "I won't force you into a decision, Margaret, and to be frank, I don't know enough about this man to make any false assurances. He's got a good head for business, yes, but I cannot vouch for his character the way I can for Alastair. Perhaps you can fill in those gaps yourself. He says you've spent time together at several social events?"

Margaret thinned her lips, sucking them over her teeth. It was a lie. And in Margaret's experience, where one lie lay, more were likely buried alongside. Even still, she threw her own log on the pyre.

"We have."

Pa nodded warily.

"He really offered?" Margaret asked, wanting to be sure.

"He did."

Her heart stuttered.

The temptation to accept any man other than Alastair was strong. Dravenhearst was young, attractive, had his own estate—a bankrupt estate, perhaps, but that was nothing her own fortune couldn't change. She liked the appearance of the package, tied up with a nice symmetric bow. She focused on that package rather than the undercurrent of unease in her gut.

A shyster, Alastair had called him.

If my eyes are wide open, she reassured herself, *I'll not be played. It's a business arrangement for both of us. I can maximize my profits as much as he can.*

She already knew her answer, had known it the minute Dravenhearst walked through the door. It was like the laudanum on the nightstand—inevitable. Reach and drink.

Margaret drank.

"I choose him. The philistine," she whispered.

"You're certain?" Her father's gaze was penetrating, inscrutable.

"I am."

Pa rose from his seat. Margaret stood on the wobbly legs of a fawn, hesitant and brand new in the world.

"I'll send word to him this evening." Pa offered a weak smile. "Congratulations, Mrs. Dravenhearst."

She laughed, wholly uncomfortable, and turned to depart. "That will take some getting used to."

"In time, I'm sure it will suit. If I may give you one final piece of advice?"

Margaret hesitated, one foot already in the hallway. Her fingers curled around the door as she looked back. "You may." *Please.*

Her heart ached at the figure her father cut in the lamplight. Sunken, shadowed cheeks. Blue-bruised, veiny hands. His smooth voice now gravelly, permanently hoarse from the never-ending coughing fits that seized him every hour of every day. The currency value of her father's word skyrocketed the day she learned she would soon lose him.

"Marriage, especially in the early days, is ne'er easy. Tiptoeing around each other, fitting into a new household...these are difficult things." When her father swallowed, his Adam's apple bobbed prominently. His shoulders seemed small, frail beneath the now ill-fitting jacket. He'd lost more weight. "Love takes *time*, Margaret. In the early days, when it seems but a distant dream, I've found friendship is a very good place to start."

Friendship.

Margaret was starved for it. She hadn't felt a connective thread tie her to anyone but her father in so very long.

She swallowed thickly. "I'll remember, Pa."

4

June 17, 1933

Margaret,
See you at the altar.
I hope you like the flowers.

Yours,
Merrick Dravenhearst

IN THE YEARS LEADING to Margaret's debut, Vivian Greenbrier had talked incessantly—between swigs of laudanum—about her daughter's wedding. She'd hoped for early spring, a cloudless day under the dogwood blossoms. She said the church doors would be thrown open, overflowing with society guests. Margaret would have a dress with a train seven feet long—seven feet for biblical divinity, the bedrock of any upstanding debutante marriage. She made Margaret practice ruthlessly for every one of those seven feet, tacking a bedsheet to her backside to demonstrate how to turn without entangling herself. How to walk, straight-backed and tall, up the aisle with posture rigid enough to balance a book atop her head. Even near the end, when the laudanum was truly overcoming her faculties, her mother could somehow always straighten to balance that damn book, hypnotized with delirious fervor at the prospect of Margaret's fairytale marriage.

Ma said Margaret's wedding would be the happiest day of her life. But *whose* life Margaret often wondered—her own or that of her aging, disillusioned mother? A woman who shrank deeper inside herself every passing year, vitality fading to bone fading to shadow, then near the end, to naught more than a whisper.

Nevertheless, Margaret had been raised to believe her wedding would be the stuff of daydreams. But on that fateful morning, when she rose from her bed and opened the curtains, it was not the giddy anticipation of a blushing bride that she felt, but immense trepidation instead.

She did not slip into her wedding gown in a room full of giggling attendants. Her mother did not do up the buttons over her silk-covered back. It was Brigita who carefully pinned the veil in Margaret's red locks before dropping it over her face without a word.

It was a scorching summer day when her father took her arm outside the chapel, not a single dogwood blossom in sight. The sanctuary doors swept open, the pews inside empty. Barren.

Margaret looked down the aisle through the disorienting lens of her white veil and saw him there, her groom, tall and rather imposing in his black cutaway coat and tails. She focused not on his face as she approached, but on the white magnolia pinned to his lapel, a match to the cascading bouquet in her trembling hands.

"He chose magnolias," Pa had said when he handed her the spray of flowers with a handwritten note outside the chapel. "It's the flower of his estate."

Her father had given her mother a bouquet of blue hydrangeas on their wedding day, plucked from the bushes that surrounded the sprawling country mansion at Greenbrier Estates. Ma showed Margaret the pressed trimmings once, carefully tucked and dried between the pages of the Book of Psalms. A gilded memory preserved with tenderness and care.

As the ceremony began, Margaret continued staring at Dravenhearst's lapel, at the magnolia near her eye level. She wondered faintly if she should preserve cuttings from her own bouquet? If she dared believe this moment, these flowers, might one day mean something *more*.

She blinked in surprise when Dravenhearst's fingers brushed her veil, lifting it over her head. It was time for the vows. Margaret was so nervous, she could hardly focus. She raised her eyes to her groom's face. His pupils were dilated, black almost overtaking brown.

"I, Merrick," he began, "take you, Margaret, to be my wedded wife." He paused to swallow, his tongue darting out to lick dry lips. It was the only hint betraying possible nerves, for his voice was deep and smooth, his hands warm and steady where they held hers. "To have and to hold, from this day forward, for better, for worse, for richer, for poorer, in sickness and in health, until death do us part."

He did not blink once as he spoke, simply held Margaret's gaze, pouring deeper and deeper into her with every line. She knew not if he meant a single word, but it certainly *felt* like he did. He was as hypnotic as the devil himself, whispering sacred honeyed promises beneath the apse of the sanctuary. It was shockingly intimate, the room around them blurring at the edges, a hazy rainbow prism of stained glass. The spell broke only when his lips stopped moving.

Margaret lowered her lashes, abashed.

It was her turn. She lifted her eyes, dropped them again, unable to pour herself into him as he had into her. She whispered her vows to the marbled floor and hoped he would forgive her cowardice.

She felt vaguely sweaty, heart hammering when she finally finished. Then came a whiff of the old familiar fear, the phantom spirit of a flush rising on her neck. The anxiety was always there, lurking in the wings. Was she growing dizzy, her vision tunneling?

Mary, Mother of God, she prayed to a statue of the Holy Mother in the corner, just over her groom's shoulder, *give me strength.*

The preacher's drone buzzed remotely in her ears. Her breast continued to heave, the flush on her neck rising, becoming fully realized. She feared she might...

The world snapped into crystal clear focus when he touched her. Dravenhearst's fingers lifted her chin, curled around her jaw and cheek, almost gentle save for the rough-hewn texture of his calloused skin. Gooseflesh rose on her arms.

When she met his eyes, her mind errantly skittered to what would undoubtedly happen later this evening. The feel of these workworn fingers on her bare limbs. Her mouth dried at the thought. She knew little of the mechanics—for all the pontificating about her wedding day, her mother had stayed quite mum on *that* matter. Margaret had never even been kissed, how on earth was she supposed to—

His lips were approaching.

Her mind short-circuited, bursting like fiery hot filaments inside a worn-out Edison bulb. His hand was still on her cheek. She felt the barest pressure and yielded, letting him turn her head to the side, just so. His lips landed somewhere near the corner of her mouth, half on her cheek. It was over quickly, featherlight and horrifically proper. He pulled away in a hurry and dropped his hand.

Margaret's lips parted in surprise as something akin to—dare she admit it?—*disappointment* rushed in. She wasn't sure that abysmal happenstance even counted as a real kiss.

Mind scrambling to catch up with her legs, Margaret was paraded through the church on Dravenhearst's arm. Her husband was stiff, as stoic as a pallbearer in a funeral march.

Just before the church doors opened, just before she was blinded by the bright light of the Kentucky summer, she was assaulted by a vision—her white silk wedding gown turning black, dripping in ebony rivulets until she was shadow-clad from head to toe. Over her head bloomed a weeping veil, heavy with black lace spun from a spider's web. She was, in that final moment within the chapel walls, not a bride, but a woman marked for mourning. For death.

According to her mother, Margaret's wedding day should herald a new dawn, a new beginning...

"Mrs. Dravenhearst," her husband drawled, gesturing to the open-top roadster waiting on the street. The corner of his lip turned upward in a shifty half-grin. "Shall we?"

Margaret hesitated, grounding her runaway mind with facts.

Her gown was white, not black.

The veil bridal, not weeping.

Her name was Dravenhearst, no longer Greenbrier.

And so Margaret was the same, but also, somehow, irreparably different.

Mrs. Merrick Dravenhearst.

Her mother was right, this felt like a beginning. The beginning of the end.

5

June 17, 1870

Dear Diary,
A woman's worth will never be higher than on her wedding
day. She depreciates every day thereafter.

—Excerpt, the diary of Eleanor Dravenhearst

T HE DRIVE TO DRAVENHEARST Distilling began in silence. After
opening her door, Dravenhearst slipped behind the wheel of the
sporty roadster himself. The beast of an automobile roared to life, and
suddenly, Margaret was waving mechanically over her shoulder to Pa as the
wheels churned clouds of dust.

As her father disappeared from sight, Margaret knew a moment of
panic. When would she see him again?

Would she see him again, hearty and hale?

Margaret moved her hand from its stilted wave to her head, feeling the
pull of her bridal veil in the rising wind. Her other hand encircled the
magnolia bouquet in a death grip as the roadster whipped around a sharp
turn.

Gracious—where did this daredevil learn to drive?

She peeked leftward, stealing a glance. Dravenhearst exhaled, long and slow. The wind rumpled his black hair as the vehicle gained speed. With every passing mile, his fingers loosened on the wheel. Unclenching.

Margaret only wished she could do the same.

"How far to..." She could not bear to say *home*. "To your estate?"

"Not terribly far." He flashed a wicked smile. "I drive fast."

Yes, I can see that. They'd be lucky to survive the trip.

"The manor actually isn't far from Greenbrier Estates." His gaze flicked briefly to her. "It'll take a little over an hour."

She nodded. He lived near Frankfort then; her father had failed to mention *that* lovely tidbit. Margaret turned her head to watch the familiar streets of Louisville pass. She swallowed her discomfort as city faded to country.

"It's...it's quite hot today, is it not?" she offered weakly.

"Reckon so, midsummer Kentucky," he grunted, his focus never leaving the road.

How foolish they were—married yet barely able to string two meaningful sentences together. Any southern debutante worth her salt excelled at small talk, could charm the morning dew straight off a honeysuckle.

But Margaret was clearly not one of them. She forcibly withheld an unhappy sigh.

Dravenhearst shed his jacket, tossing it to the backseat. The sight of his black suspenders against his white shirt was intimate, as was the relaxed, near-rakish drape of his body across the seat. Legs spread. One hand on the wheel, the other dangling in open air, catching wind in his fingers.

In contrast, Margaret sat prim as a pilgrim, her back ramrod straight, with one hand clutching the seat cushion for dear life. She began to fan herself, feeling terribly, overwhelmingly anxious.

Margaret had not left Louisville in eight years, the majority of that time spent sealed inside the four walls of the brownstone with her increasingly agoraphobic mother. After Elijah's accident at Greenbrier Estates, Margaret and her mother had been in agreement they wanted to leave the countryside, but once in Louisville, her mother took to the city streets less and less frequently with each passing year.

The soft hills of the Bluegrass were much as Margaret remembered from childhood, but she was surprised by the degree of both development and dilapidation that had occurred through the years.

"The road…" she began, her voice scratchy from disuse. "The condition is quite good, is it not?"

He shot her an odd look. "Indeed."

"But many of the farms," she continued, licking her windburned lips, "seem to be in poor straits." She cataloged the passing of ramshackle barns and broken fences. Several fallow fields of dried-out crops—haphazardly plowed, if at all. Rail-thin animals grazing in empty pastures…this was not the way she remembered it at all.

Dravenhearst's grip on the steering wheel tightened, but he didn't meet her eyes. "I suppose inside the walls of your gilded townhome and socialite parties," he replied, his tone measured, "the depression gripping the majority of the state within its merciless clutches has seemed a distant enemy. A monster under someone else's bed, ne'er your own. But I assure you, for those of us living in the Bluegrass, it is a very real adversary."

Margaret started as though he'd struck her. It was a rather horrible thing to say, clearly delineating her as "other" and, worse still, spoiled. Sheltered and privileged and ignorant.

How dare he!

Wealthy or not, Margaret had been born on a Kentucky farm. That spirit ran in the blood of her veins. She'd spent the first half of her life running amok with Elijah through the fields of Greenbrier Estates. Milked her first cow at age seven, learned to shoot a gun by ten. She had as much claim to the Bluegrass as this entitled goldbrick beside her. A bourbon aristocrat he was, not some workworn farmhand or coal miner slaving deep and hard in the trenches of the backcountry.

But as she opened her mouth to say as much, Margaret remembered his roughened hands. The dire fiscal circumstances that had coaxed Dravenhearst to the altar alongside her today.

The corners of her mouth turned down, uncertainty rising in place of anger.

"Not long now," Dravenhearst murmured, half to himself, half to her. When the blue-green ribbon of the Kentucky River sprang up beside them, he steered the automobile off the main road. Their course turned bumpy, winding along a narrow, heavily rutted path, passing in and out of the shadow of trees.

Dravenhearst whipped the wheel to the right, directing the roadster to an entrance hidden amongst overgrown vegetation. He cast a sidelong glance at her, his eyes flickering with something she thought might be apprehension. "Home sweet home."

Margaret straightened in her seat, keen. The roadster passed through a crumbling brick-and-iron gate. A long straight drive lined with six towering magnolia trees stretched before them, three to a side, evenly spaced.

"Oh," Margaret breathed. They were simply beautiful, the trees in bloom. She forgot the vestiges of her earlier anger and turned to her husband. "I see why you chose magnolias." She lifted her bouquet and offered a tentative smile.

He nodded, fingers frozen tight on the wheel, gaze focused straight ahead.

She tried again. "It's a beautiful arrangement. And I noticed, er, a sprig of myrtle tucked within." It was a nice touch, thoughtful. Myrtle was reputed to herald good luck in love and marriage. She wanted him to know the gesture wasn't lost on her.

"That was Evangeline, our groundskeeper. She made the bouquet."

"Oh. I see." Margaret was struck silent yet again, stymied by his curtness.

As they cleared the final pair of magnolias, the manor rose before them. Brownstone in style, akin to the Louisville townhouse but far grander in scale. Easily thrice as big. The length of the exterior glowed with warmth in the late afternoon sun. The brick was crumbling and soot-stained in places, but in a rather well-loved way. A way that implied the place had stood through a fair breadth of history and held stories worth knowing.

Flanking the western front was a magnificent square turret and to the east, a rounded rooftop cupola, complete with a beautifully carved oriel window. A front portico stood central with a Tudor arch and a stained-glass window above the front door, a balustraded balcony overtop. Rectangular mullioned windows, several open to air, were spaced with perfect symmetry along the manor's length.

"Golly," Margaret murmured, slightly slack-jawed. "It's...it's beautiful...splendid, even. You didn't say—"

Dravenhearst snorted softly beside her. "Yes, if you enjoy splintered wood that warps in midsummer humidity and crumbling brick that lends to drafty winters, then *splendid* is precisely the word I'd choose. Not to mention the dust of centuries preserved carefully within."

"Surely—"

"I'll introduce you to the staff." He swung open his door, cutting Margaret off. "You'll be something of a novelty, no doubt. They, er, were hardly expecting me to return from the city with a bride." He rubbed the back of his neck and stole a glance at her. His gaze swept over her wedding gown, lingering ever so slightly on the generous swell of her chest, ineffectively restrained by scraps of bridal lace.

Embarrassed, Margaret looked away, peering at the small lineup clustered before the steps of the portico. One man, two women.

Her car door opened. The moment her feet touched estate ground, a tremor rocketed outward. She wobbled and gripped the automobile, smashing her bridal bouquet against the roadster.

"Gracious!"

"Are you well?" His eyebrows raised in alarm.

The marrow of Margaret's bones quaked, then steadied, as did the ground underfoot. She watched the soft vibration sweep away, rippling outward through the grass. It was subtle, so subtle she might have imagined it. Neither her husband nor the staff seemed to notice anything amiss. Overhead, a curtain on the second floor twitched, as though dropped from a parting hand. Margaret squinted but saw no one within.

"Forgive me, I'm merely stiff after the drive," she answered. She fell into step as her husband began to move.

"Down this southern hill to our right, you'll see the distillery rickhouses." Dravenhearst gestured to a group of brick buildings. "We have six, but one is sealed up, unusable. I'll ask you not to go wandering there, consider the rickhouses off-limits. The rest of the property, however, is at your disposal. Down the eastern slope, just there, you'll find the paddock and stables. I ride every morning. Do you?"

Margaret's mouth ran dry as her gaze rolled down the hill. Several horses grazed in the distance, their tails flicking sporadically. Unsettlingly.

"Er...what?" She turned a pair of wide doe eyes to Dravenhearst.

"Do you ride?" he repeated, slowly this time.

With every passing second she stared, mouth gaping, Dravenhearst's eyebrows rose closer to his hairline. He must think her mad. Or at best, a simpleton.

Say something, you ninny. Anything.

"No," she finally managed. There was a story, but it died on her lips. She felt no closeness, no warmth for this man, nothing to encourage her trust.

"Pity." Disappointment followed by dismissal flickered through his eyes.

I did, a small voice inside screamed. *I did ride. I can. Quite well. Once...*

"Margot, catch me!"

She swayed on the spot and whipped her head to the right. She was used to the ghostly voice in her mind, but she'd heard it aloud this time, clear as day. Hoofbeats too, fast approaching.

"What's wrong?" Dravenhearst turned to her, worry brewing in his amber eyes. Just over his shoulder, cresting the gentle hilltop, a horse appeared. First a pair of pointed ears, then beady eyes, a nickering snout, gleaming chestnut body. Strong, powerful.

Deadly.

"H-h-horse." She pointed.

"Oh." He turned, the worry in his expression transforming into a crinkled smile. "That's Omaha, our Derby prospect for next spring. He's magnificent, no?"

Not quite the descriptor Margaret would have chosen.

"That's Julian astride. He's training to jockey."

"Indeed?" Her response was faint. She barely cast Julian-the-jockey a glance, so focused was she on the beast. With every step the horse neared, Margaret pulled back. "Perhaps...please, shall we meet the household staff?" She dragged him away.

An ancient-looking man with spotty tufts of white hair growing from the most improbable places on his head stepped forward. The hand he extended to Dravenhearst was covered in liver spots and had an unmistakable tremor.

"Merrick, many happy returns." The man's voice was gravelly, a bit garbled even. "And ye've brought Babette?" His milky eyes gleamed as he turned to Margaret. "Wherever have you been, your ladyship? Reckon you must be tired. I've prepared your room, just as you prefer it—"

"Xander, no," Dravenhearst hissed. "This is Margaret, my wife."

"Yes, yes...*Margaret*. Precisely," the man chirped, eyes alight with fervor.

In the background, the two female staff members raised hands to their mouths in synchronized surprise.

Margaret leaned in and tipped her lips toward her husband's ear. "Happy returns? Is your birthday upcoming?"

"No." He turned helplessly to her. "Margaret, this is Xander Kent, our head of household. He's been at the estate for nigh on sixty years, since he was a boy." He lowered his voice to a pitch for her ears alone. "And his memory comes and goes a bit these days, easily confused."

"I see." She tilted her head, fascinated by the tiny outcroppings of hair spurting from the man's knobby ears, not to mention the absolute riot of his overgrown and tangled eyebrows. "Pleasure to meet you, Mr. Kent."

"Oh, Babette, surely—"

"Xander, sugar?" A diminutive woman with wiry, tanned forearms and a thick mane of silver hair stepped forward and wrapped an arm around his shoulders with care. The endearment had dripped from her lips with such a thick southern twang it sounded more like *shugga*. She continued, her voice deep and throaty, "This is Merrick's new bride, remember? *Merrick*, not Richard."

Dravenhearst's lips tightened and thinned. The beastly horse gave a soft snort, and Margaret blew out a nervous exhale. The sun beat down on the back of her neck, hotter than hot.

The silver-haired woman turned her warm eyes to Margaret. "Hello, I'm Evangeline, Xander's wife. I tend to the gardens and grounds of the estate."

"Oh." Margaret half-heartedly raised her bouquet, her grip on the stems sweaty. "Mr. Dravenhearst...er, Merrick..." She floundered, unsure what to call the man standing beside her and feeling quite embarrassed.

I'm so hopelessly out of my depths here.

"Merrick," he whispered, staring pointedly at the dirt.

"R-r-right." Margaret's voice shook. She swiped at the sweat beading across her upper lip, then the prickles at the back of her neck. "He mentioned you made my bouquet. The magnolia and myrtle...it's beautiful. Perfect."

"I'm glad you think so," Evangeline murmured, her hand running gently but possessively up and down Xander's arm.

Between the groundskeeper's falsely cheery smile and the butler's dazed eyes, his mouth half-open in bewilderment, a most unsettling feeling took over Margaret. It started in her toes and ran like a live wire straight to her gut. Something wasn't right. Sick to her stomach, she turned to Dravenhearst and was met with yet another weak smile. A blatant facade.

What is going on here?

"A *bride*, Merrick? Really?" The final member of the staff stepped forward, her stride powerful enough to lightly fan the few stubborn wisps that dared escape her tight blonde chignon. She wore jodhpurs, riding boots, and a tone dripping with disdain. "And one who looks a near replica of—"

"Ruth, not now."

The woman—Ruth—narrowed her eyes. They were lined in kohl, blue and sharp. "When then? After she's settled into the house, comfy and cozy and—"

"Goddammit, Ruth," Dravenhearst growled. "I said *not now.*" His voice took on a new tenor, an icy cold Margaret hadn't imagined it could hold. The snap of a shotgun being cocked and aimed.

Suddenly, the heated flush of the sun on her neck became too much. Tiny black spots appeared in her vision.

No. Please.

She moved a fluttering hand to fan herself. A futile effort.

"Ruth, you're being rude," Evangeline whispered, warning.

Ruth laughed, all pearlescent teeth and dimples, and thrust her hand forward. There was such confidence, even imperiousness, to the gesture, Margaret was unsure whether she was worthy to take it. She hesitated, her vision tunneling. She was so very hot.

"I'm Ruth Auclaire, the equestrian trainer."

Equestrian. Horses.

A faint whinny beside her.

"I'm..." Margaret gasped, her hand jolting forward even as her vision blacked out. Her next breath came in a halting, shuddering gasp as full panic set in. "I'm...I'm..."

Margaret.

The world disappeared. It was almost merciful when it went.

The last thing Margaret heard before she surrendered was a shocked gasp and a strangled cry from her unassuming husband's lips as she went down in a flurry of bridal skirts.

The magnolia bouquet fell from her slackened grip, crushed unceremoniously beneath her knees into the dirt.

6

May 4, 1901

My darling Richard,
Today we write the first page of our happily ever after.
Today I finally get to call you my husband.
And I, your Dravenhearst bride.

—Excerpt, a letter from Margaret Babette to her husband
on their wedding day

"WHAT THE HELL AM I supposed to do with her?" A loud voice penetrated Margaret's sleepy haze.

"What do you mean?" A shrill retort, unmistakably female. "You *married* her."

A striking *thud*. A fist hitting a wall.

"I didn't want to marry her, but the money—"

"I would have gotten us the money come spring. Omaha has gold in his bloodline. He's a champion."

"We wouldn't have made it to spring! I would have lost the house—the *distillery*—by October."

"The goddamn distillery? Really? You Dravenhearst men are all the same. Your precious bourbon, no matter the cost. And there is a *cost*, Merrick. A steep one." Her voice lowered almost to a whisper. "How could you?"

"Ruth, I—"

"That girl doesn't belong here. You swore you wouldn't...you *swore*. Never another Dravenhearst bride."

"There's no curse, Ruth."

"That's not what you said a decade ago. That's not what your mother—the last *Margaret*, the last Dravenhearst bride—believed."

Silence. Upon hearing her name, Margaret stirred, her eyelids fluttering.

"You've made a terrible mistake," Ruth said. "I won't forgive you for it, and neither will she, not once this place sinks its claws into her. I can't stand to be in this mausoleum even a second longer. When you're ready to admit what you've done, you know where to find me."

Thudding booted footsteps. The slam of a door.

The sounds echoed in Margaret's brain, pushing her away from consciousness again. She sank deeper into herself, pulling down the shutters and locking the doorway to her mind once more.

She wasn't ready to face it all.

Not yet. Maybe not ever.

Margaret awoke to a moist prodding against her palm. Snuffling. She sat bolt upright with a screech, frantically looking for a horse.

A yelp, followed by the *thump-thump-thump-thump* of four paws scampering away. A small black dog with fluffy fur and enormous brown eyes stared up at her, affronted.

"Beau?" Dravenhearst strode into the bedroom. The dog collapsed sideways, paws up, belly exposed for rubbing.

Dravenhearst dropped to his knees. "Getting into mischief, buddy?" His gaze moved from the dog to Margaret. "This is Beau. Apologies if he frightened you. He's always sticking his nose where it doesn't belong. It's the spitz in him, I'm afraid."

Spitz. An unusual breed. Black fur and a fox-like face, pointy ears, and an exceedingly bushy tail...she'd never seen a dog quite like him before.

Margaret fidgeted, then swung her legs over the side of the mattress. The bed was a four-poster with a filmy canopy and a lavender duvet, light and feathery. The room had an airy quality with its ivory paneled walls, helped along by wide-open French doors leading to a balcony. She could just make out the tips of the white magnolias in the distance.

Dravenhearst rose to his feet. The ticking of a clock echoed faintly from the hallway outside the bedroom.

Tick, tick, tick.

The metronome of time roared in Margaret's ears. Her cheeks heated as, with every passing second, she became more embarrassed and flustered by her inability to connect, to simply speak. To fill the silence between them with charming words or a winsome smile.

A new beginning here, that was what she'd hoped for. But how could she possibly start fresh when she was still the same old Margaret?

Tick, tick, tick.

He cleared his throat. "Are you feeling better?"

"I am. Thank you."

Tick, tick, tick.

He nodded slowly. "It's...it's quite warm today. I'm sure it's overwhelming for you, coming here with me. It all happened rather fast. I'm sure you were overcome—"

"Please stop." She simply couldn't bear it. "It wasn't the first time, nor do I expect it shall be the last."

"What do you mean?"

It was almost comical how his dog mirrored his movement, head tilted, lips slightly parted.

She focused on Beau instead of her husband and took the plunge. "I have a...condition. Perhaps I should have warned you. I'm vasovagal—my blood pressure drops, and I...I faint."

"You're...you mean you're unwell? Is it very limiting?"

She hated him a little for this response, for his quick rush to judgment. "It needn't be. Not usually. The physicians, they say it's triggered by...distressing circumstances. Nerves." She forced out a laugh and wrung her hands together. "And today has been...I've been a bit..."

"I understand."

"I'm not unwell," she maintained, hating the word.

"Of course not." His answer came too quick. It sounded false to her ears. *Tick, tick, tick.*

Margaret stared at his shoes. They were polished to a shine. "I'd hoped for a fresh start here," she admitted, "but it seems I've already made a mess of things, haven't I?"

The longer the silence stretched, the more intimidated and exposed Margaret felt. Just when she thought she could stand it no longer, he spoke.

"If you'd like a fresh start, how about a new name?"

"What?"

"My mother's name was Margaret," he said, his toe tapping three times in short succession. "Though amongst company, she often went by Babette, her maiden name."

"Was?"

"She died. Many years ago." He crossed his arms and scowled. "But people 'round here still remember her, so is there another name perhaps? A nickname? Xander is so easily confused these days."

And it's painful for you, Margaret surmised. She could hear the unspoken words even though he was not brave enough to say them. Haunted by loss...

There are ghosts in this house. The thought came unbidden, sudden. As though planted in her mind by someone else.

"Marge? Margie, perhaps?" he suggested.

She blinked.

"Maggie? Midge? Martha?"

She couldn't help it; she wrinkled her nose.

"Martha?" he repeated. "Not to your liking?"

"Not particularly," she whispered.

"What was that?" He stepped closer. "I'm an old man. You're going to have to speak up." His tone was close to teasing.

"You're not that much older than me."

"You think so?" He closed the remaining distance between them in two quick strides. When she, instinctively, looked downward, his knuckle was on her chin, tilting it back up. "How old do you think I am?"

He was standing very close. Margaret couldn't blink or look away if she tried. He'd been clean-shaven this morning at the altar, but shadowy black stubble had grown in around his jawline. The muscles there were tight, his teeth clenched.

And his eyes...those *eyes*. Hypnotic. Deep, churning amber. The most tempting melted butterscotch. The only flaws were tiny frown lines etched underneath.

They undoubtedly came from scowling so much.

"Care to guess?" he asked, his voice soft.

Margaret estimated thirty, so to be safe, she said, "Twenty-nine?"

He released her. "Thirty-one," he grunted, turning away. "And you're what? Twenty?"

"Twenty-two," she corrected.

"Perfect. Nearly a whole decade of life between us. Just goldarn perfect." His hands were on his head as he moved away from her.

Margaret snorted quietly, unsure why this seemed to bother him. Alastair had been nearly *three decades* her senior. Nine years, by contrast, seemed easily surmountable. Most men married women significantly younger anyway, better chance for children that way—

"Peggy? Marie? Greta?" He spoke the nicknames to the wall, hands still on his head.

Margaret couldn't help it, she giggled. His histrionics were certainly amusing. She wondered if he was like this all the time. *So dramatic.*

"I'm running out of options." When he finally turned to face her, a small smile tilted one-half of his lips from their pout.

A swooping, soaring sensation took root in Margaret's gut. Maybe she didn't mind the scowling so much. Not when a grin like that could break through the clouds.

"Margot, are we flying?"

She'd known what she would tell him from the first second he asked. It had felt wrong for so many years. No one had used the name since Eli.

A new beginning, her mother said.

A fresh start, Margaret hoped.

But could one ever truly start fresh? The past was always there, bleeding into the present. Tainting all it touched. Perhaps the best she could hope for was to come full circle. To work on becoming whole again.

And so, being either very brave or very stupid, she invited her own ghost into the house.

"You can call me Margot."

As they descended the stairs together for dinner, Margot Dravenhearst took inventory of her new home.

The two-story entry hall was cavernous, the grand staircase curving in sections around two walls of the room. The banister was carved from wood so dark it could only be ebony. The balusters were equally somber and elaborate, twisting in a serpentine design that proved disorientingly undulous when viewed in succession. Margot trod with near-silent steps over the worn wood as they slowly, so slowly, circled the room in descent.

The central chandelier must have once been grand, but its gold limbs and finials slept beneath heavy tarnish now. A layer of film coated its crystals, light unable to penetrate the thick shroud of dirt and cobwebs clinging to each pendeloque. Multicolor dust motes circled through the air, reflecting the fading rays of daylight from the large stained-glass window above the front door. Margot stared at it as they approached. Weaving, curling sprigs of purple flowers with soft yellow centers...

"Are those violets?" she asked.

"They are," Dravenhearst confirmed. "My mother had the window installation changed when she came here as a bride. My grandmother Eleanor had marigolds there. That color seemed fitting—quite close to the bourbon the distillery makes—but my mother...er, I'm told she didn't like it much."

"The flowers or the bourbon?"

"Well, I suppose...neither. If I'm being honest."

"Oh." *Interesting.*

He gestured to the window. "If you don't care for violets, we could commission a new installation. This is now your home as much as mine."

"No." Margot shook her head. "I'm sure you're quite attached—"

"I'm *not.*"

She was surprised by the vigor in his tone, the bite. "Okay. I...I'll think about it."

The hallway leading to the dining room was dark, illuminated by flickers of candlelight in ornamental gold wall sconces. Curiously, only every other pair was lit.

Inside the dining room, heavy drapes partially concealed the windows. The table was set for two—she could see that much in the flickering candlelight of yet another pair of long tapers.

"The house is wired for electricity, is it not?" She looked at the mahogany paneled wall and spotted a light switch. "Ah."

"Of course it is."

She walked several paces and reached for the switch.

"Er, is that necessary?" Dravenhearst moved to stop her.

"Necessary?" she repeated, confused. "Well, I do quite like to see what I'm ingesting for dinner."

"It's only..."

"Only what?" Her finger hovered beside the switch, itching to flip it.

"Electricity costs money."

Margot wasn't sure what she'd expected but most certainly not this. "Electricity...costs money?"

He shifted from foot to foot, then walked to the bar. It hosted an impressive lineup of decanters and carafes. He poured out a large glass of amber liquid. Bourbon, no doubt.

"Shall I make you a drink?" He tossed the offer over his shoulder.

Margot frowned. "No, thank you."

Perhaps her stiff tone alerted him, for he turned to her. "Are you certain? I know your first foray was cursory, but it's an acquired taste—"

"You assume I desire to acquire it."

"I assume nothing of your desires," he murmured, eyes pinned on her as he took his first sip.

Margot swallowed and crossed her arms. "What I'd rather discuss is your absurd concern we can't afford a side of illumination with our meal."

"I can see just fine," he said. "Perhaps you need your vision checked. I can summon a physician if need be."

"Which would cost a damn sight more than simply flicking a light switch."

"Ah, but a physician would be a one-time expense, and there is no greater priority than one's health. But electricity...are you planning to turn on lights all over the house every evening?"

"Only enough to watch where I step in this ghastly place. Wouldn't want to walk into a suit of armor, would I?"

At this, he cracked a smile. "We've no suits of armor, but it is rather ghastly, isn't it?" He tipped his chin upward to examine the coffered ceiling.

Each square was heavily carved with ornate depictions of foliage and vines. Central to each was a bearded centaur, their horse-like bodies stretched mid-gallop or rearing wildly, human heads tilted heavenward, mouths gaping in perhaps a war cry or benediction. But the longer Margot stared, the more convinced she was of their silent screams.

She shivered and looked away.

"Ghastly," Dravenhearst repeated. He gestured to the table. "Shall we?"

Margot took her seat and frowned at the lit tapers.

"Consider it romantic," he suggested, dragging his own chair out with a jarring scrape. He undid his cufflinks and folded up his sleeves, exposing strong forearms with a thick dusting of dark hair. "It's our wedding night after all."

"I suppose it is." Margot released a nervous breath at the reminder. There was simply no way she'd be able to eat. Not a single bite.

The meal progressed in silence. A shaky-handed Xander brought in a platter of roast beef and cooked vegetables. She could do little more than push the food around on her plate, mixing it up to make it appear she'd eaten. Her husband spent an inordinate amount of time separating and cutting each item into meticulously even, minute pieces. Only then did he begin to eat, one bite at a time in an even rotation around the plate. Carrot, meat, potato, onion. Carrot, meat, potato, onion. Carrot, meat, potato, onion...

His rigidity was perversely fascinating. What sort of sociopath had she married?

The scent of spun sugar overtook the air as dessert was brought in. It was a generous slice of spongey vanilla cake with finely detailed frosting—white flowers accented with rounded dollops of crimson extract—and a band of jam-like sauce separating the two layers.

"Who made this?" she asked, her mouth watering.

"Xander. It's one of his specialties. German buttercream with raspberry amaretto jam. He only makes it in the summer, using fresh preserves from Evangeline's garden."

"Xander?" She couldn't hide her surprise. The bumbling butler with the trembling hands created something this detailed, this exquisite?

"Yes, he likes to bake. He's a damn sight better at baking than he is at cooking. Since the meat didn't appear to your liking, perhaps this will suit better?"

So he'd noticed her subterfuge. Margot blushed and eyed the cake, tempted.

"It tastes as good as it looks, I assure you." Dravenhearst chuckled from down the table.

"You mean it isn't poisoned?" She meant the words as a joke, but as they left her mouth, they rang with a seed of buried, paranoid truth.

His jaw dropped. "Is that why you didn't eat dinner? Why on earth would I poison you?"

"We both know I'm worth far more to you dead than alive."

He pushed his chair back from the table in disgust. "That's a horrible thing to say. What kind of man do you think I am?"

"One who marries a woman he's just met for her money."

He fell silent. To punctuate her point, Margot sliced off the tip of the cake and lifted it to her lips. He watched, mesmerized. She gave it a delicate sniff before taking a bite. Raspberry exploded on her tongue.

As she chewed, he spoke again, his tone flat. "Your father didn't discuss the terms of his estate with you, did he?"

"I'm an only child, Mr. Dravenhearst—"

"Merrick."

She halted. It felt so intimate, his first name.

"My name is Merrick," he repeated. "It's going to be an awfully long lifetime together if you insist on using my surname for the entirety."

Merrick. She rolled the name around in her mind, tasting before she released it. "I'm an only child, *Merrick*. With a rapidly ailing, exorbitantly rich father. I know what I stand to inherit, as do you. We needn't pretend otherwise."

He leaned back in his chair, placing both hands on the armrests. Slowly, he drummed his fingers, one by one. When he finally spoke, his voice was deathly serious. "You know, I once stood to inherit an awful lot myself. Amazing how quickly things change." He gestured toward the window and the distillery beyond it. "I had more than fifty men in my employ thirteen years ago. On January 17, 1920, I sent them all home. Jobless. I—and they—learned very quickly how money can disappear." He snapped his fingers. "Just like that."

Margot sighed, sufficiently chastised. "I didn't mean—"

"You know what?" He rose from his seat. "It's been a long day. I'm sure you're tired. I know I am."

He looks it, she realized. The flickering candlelight cast his face in long shadows. His eyes pooled with depth, and he appeared a decade older than his thirty-one years. Infinitely more worldly than she in so many ways.

Margot's fears for the evening, for her wedding night, returned in full force. She nodded, barely able to summon words. "Yes," she whispered. "Yes, I'm quite tired."

"Shall we?"

Merrick took her arm as they left the room. His stride was purposeful, his grip on her elbow possessive. He steered her up the stairs, down the long hall to her bedroom.

Her hands began to tremble; she was certain he felt it against his arm. Dinner had not gone well, which was largely her own fault. She hadn't been trying to pick a fight. She wanted to find common ground with him. She wanted...

They reached her bedroom door. She paused, waiting for him to take the lead. The only sound in the hallway was the blasted clock.

Tick, tick, tick.

"Well." His voice came out as a low rumble that curled Margot's toes. "I suppose this is good night."

Good night?

She didn't move. Didn't breathe. There was only his slow inhale and the *tick, tick, tick* of the clock.

He stepped away from her. Infinitesimally but quite clearly.

She blinked, uncertain. Maybe she was supposed to *do* something? Say something? Her lips were glued shut.

"Good night, Margot."

It was too dark for her to make out the expression in his eyes. He was utterly unreadable.

"Where is your room?" she finally managed.

"Just there." He nodded at the door beside hers. "The rooms are adjoined, should you need anything."

She tilted her head. So she was supposed to say something after all. Now.

Margot summoned every ounce of courage. She was nervous, yes. She'd misstepped today. Several times. Badly. But she was filled with longing, pure and undiluted, for what her marriage could be. What she wanted it to be.

He doesn't have to be a stranger, she thought, running her eyes over his form in the dark hallway. Her gaze lingered on the strong swell of his shoulders. *He could be mine. This could be* something.

But only if she was brave enough to seize it. To make it so.

She reached for his wrist. Her touch was soft at first, ghosting over his bare skin. He twinged at the contact, but she refused to be deterred. She ran her fingers up the length of his sleeve, feeling the generous curve of biceps as her touch grew bolder. Gripping. Dragging. She nearly lost her breath at her own daring.

She inhaled shakily as her fingers settled atop his shoulder, barely brushing the nape of his neck.

"Perhaps," she breathed, her heart pounding, "you'd like to come in with me?"

Terror. Horror. Shock. Vulnerability.

All of it came rushing in at once, a dizzying medley that made her weak in the knees.

He bit his lip, then sighed and leaned in, whispering along the shell of her ear, his nose grazing her hair. "This is what you want?"

"Yes." Her back stiffened, but she lifted her chin, feigning confidence. Hoping the nervous tremor in her legs wouldn't betray her.

His fingers gripped hers, gently tugging her hand away from his neck.

"This is what you really want?" he repeated, brushing his lips over the inside of her wrist as he spoke. Pressing softly. A kiss made of breath as much as flesh.

A shiver coursed through her, shooting up her arm, down her spine. Her skin burned where his lips touched.

His gaze pierced her, searing through the darkness of the hallway. His lips parted before he spoke. "Because it's not what I want."

He stepped away, leaving her cold. Embarrassed. Confused.

Alone.

Margot was thunderstruck by his cruelty. Her vulnerability shattered, defensiveness rising in its place.

"You're wicked." She crossed her arms over her chest. "I'm just trying to do my job, to be a good wife."

"Exactly." He was scowling again.

"It's what I'm here for, isn't it? To shower you with newfound riches and give you a son who can take over your empire one day?" Her voice rang with fervor and frustration, the sting of tears, mortifyingly, rising. "I assume you didn't marry me simply to look on and laugh as I eat dessert every night."

"And you'd rather I sweep you up right now, pin you beneath me in my bed, and coldly impregnate you?" Color rose in his cheeks. "Is that really what you want?"

"No...I—"

"I don't understand you."

And I don't understand you, she wanted to scream. Instead, she swallowed the lump in her throat and spoke quietly. "I just thought that was what you wanted, what a husband expects."

"Well, it's not. None of this"—he gestured between them—"is what I want."

At those damning words, Margot's heart turned to ice. "I apologize for the misunderstanding. And for my forward behavior. It won't happen again."

He sighed, his eyes searching her own. For what, Margot couldn't be sure, but he would find no further vulnerability there. Not tonight. Perhaps not ever. All hope she carried for intimacy in her marriage, for companionship, and maybe—dare she say it?—even love, died then and there in that dark hallway.

Tick, tick, tick.

"Good night, Margot," he finally said. "Sleep well."

She nodded, unable to manage anything more. She stepped into her bedroom and shut the door with a very definitive *click*.

And then she was left alone. Left alone to remove her wedding gown herself. Left alone to hang it in a closet she realized was perfumed with faded jasmine and full of another woman's clothes. Left alone to slip into her bed.

A rumble of thunder echoed outside. A summer storm rolling in.

Margot had spent many nights alone in bed, and she'd never once minded before. But as she stared at the door between their bedrooms—closed and still and final and mocking—she found tonight, on her wedding night, she minded much more than she cared to admit.

7

June 18, 1933

My dearest Margaret,
The house was quiet this morning. Well, truthfully, it's been
quiet for years. But this morning was a different quiet. This
morning, the quiet was in the knowing. Knowing you are
gone. It is as it should be, for a daughter to grow and leave
her father's arms. But though you are gone from my home,
you are never gone from my heart.
Please write soon and tell me of your new life and family.

Forever yours,
Pa

A s SHE ALWAYS DID on Sunday mornings, Margot rose early. She hadn't lived near Frankfort for many years, but she recalled Sunday Mass began at half past eight, and God help the family who straggled in late. Father Simmons could send your soul straight to hell with a single look.

She slipped into the closet to select a suitable church dress and noticed her wedding gown had fallen to the floor. It rested in a crumpled heap near the corner of the closet.

How did that happen?

She reached for the clothes hanger, then strung up the gown once more. Margot cast a wary eye around the closet. She would need to go through this space and hang up her things today, lest they all become hopelessly wrinkled in her trunks. But the racks were already filled with clothes—day dresses and exquisite evening gowns—from another era. Another woman.

Merrick's mother, she realized, breathing in the perfumed jasmine in the air. The *other* Margaret, as she'd begun to think of her.

Margot sighed as she backed out of the closet. She dressed hurriedly in a periwinkle floral dress cut on the bias before pressing an ear to her husband's bedroom door. Naught but silence. Perhaps he was already awake and breakfasting? Yes, that'd be it.

Margot slipped into Oxford heels and church gloves, then hurried from the room. She was single-minded in her rush—so much so, she almost missed the oil portrait hanging atop the grand stairwell.

Almost.

She skidded to a halt. The painting was as tall as Margot herself and depicted a man and woman, both formally dressed. The man's countenance was stiff, as though he'd been forced into his tailcoat and disliked every minute of it. His hair was black and thick, the sharp cut of his jawline identical to Merrick's.

His father. Evidently, scowling was hereditary. *Which must mean...*

The woman, the *other* Margaret, was the real draw of the portrait. She stood beside her husband with one hand resting, casually possessive, on his chest. Her fingers dazzled with gemstone-heavy rings, sparkling even through painted oils. Her smile was close-lipped, the angle of her jaw tilted just so to set off her feathered hat, the plumes stained a deep plum to match the folds of her dress. Her skin was porcelain smooth, her eyes catlike and alert. Two locks of curling golden-red hair—the color identical to Margot's own—escaped the pins beneath her Gainsborough. And her stature—oh, her stature! Gossamer perfection with delicate wrists, a shapely bustled bottom, a full bosom, yet a waist so narrow, a stiff wind might simply blow her over. Margot leaned closer, envious. What witch had this woman bribed for a figure like that?

A flash of sudden movement, and she backed away. A trick of the light, perhaps...she thought she'd seen...no.

She stared deep into the woman's green eyes, searching for the twinkle, for the wink she'd surely imagined.

An abrupt *bang* echoed through the house. Margot jumped, her hand clutching her chest. The echo continued, reverberating like a slammed door. Breathless, she leaned around the corner, but no one was there.

A draft, perhaps? She shivered. Merrick had mentioned that, hadn't he? That the house was drafty?

Casting a final nervous glance over her shoulder at the portrait, Margot descended the stairs. She recalled Ruth, the equestrian trainer, mentioning a resemblance between her and the former lady of the house, but Margot didn't flatter herself to see it. It was the hair color, nothing more. She—the other Margaret—was the picture of vitality and perfection. *She* certainly hadn't been spurned on her wedding night. Not a chance in hell.

Babette. A voice rose, whispering the surname in Margot's mind as she hurried down the final steps. Her gaze moved to the stained-glass violets as she crossed the foyer. The aperture was dim, morning light just beginning to peek through.

When Margot entered the dining room, the table was set with fresh fruit and oatmeal. A bowl of the latter was placed before Merrick's empty seat, steaming as though he was expected any moment.

She heard footsteps before she saw him, heavy and steady in the hallway. She turned just as he rounded the corner.

"Oh," he cried, colliding with her. He grasped her arms to keep from stumbling.

"Sorry." She leapt away from his scalding touch. The specter of last night's rejection twisted her gut. She imagined her shame laid out before her as plainly as the breakfast spread. Margot knew it wasn't normal for a woman to sleep alone on her wedding night. Everyone knew it. And just once...oh, how she longed to be normal.

"The fault was mine," he said. "I wasn't expecting anyone...*you* to be up this early. And so well-dressed, to boot. Do we have a morning engagement I've forgotten?"

"It's Sunday," she said, confident it was answer enough. She stepped back to assess his attire. He wore exceedingly tight pants with leather inserts around the inseam. His equestrian jacket was unbuttoned to the waist, a loose shirt underneath. His hair was distinctly rumpled and windswept, his feet tucked into muddy stable boots.

The longer she looked, the deeper she frowned, certain this was not the attire of a man prepared to attend Sunday service with his wife, as any respectable Kentucky gentleman should. Those *pants!* They were downright sinful—so sinful Margot feared she'd not be able to tear her own sinful eyes away from his sinfully broad thighs. Or worse still, higher up...

She closed her eyes against the offending onslaught.

Forgive me, Father, for I have sinned—

"Do you find something amusing?"

When she peeped an eye open again, he was smirking.

"Amusing?" she breathed, gaze darting south, then promptly back up. "That's one word, I suppose, for your taste in breakfast attire."

He snorted. "I've been out riding. It's how I start every morning. If you'd ever like to join me, to learn—"

"But it's *Sunday*," she said, not wanting to answer his question about riding.

"Indeed." He raised his eyebrows. "You've mentioned that already."

"Sunday Mass begins in less than an hour. Unless you're so bold as to wear the devil's knickers"—she nodded toward his pants—"into a house of God, I suggest you change. Quickly."

He burst out laughing. "The devil's knickers?"

"You are *on display*," she hissed, averting her eyes again. "I suppose it'll give the old aunties in church the thrill of their lives—"

He laughed again, the sound deep and full. Unrestrained.

Margot's jaw slammed shut. Her mind raced as she tried to figure out precisely how to elicit that delicious sound from him again.

"That right there," he began, the vestiges of his laughter fading, "is the most tempting advertisement for church I've heard in years. Still not motivating enough to get me there though." He shouldered around her.

"You don't...you don't attend church?" She paled, her hand flying to her chest.

Merrick bit into an apple, chewing loudly. "Uh, no. Do you?"

"*Everyone* attends Mass." Her utter shock prevented a more sophisticated rebuttal.

You see? Her mother's voice chastised her in her mind. *This is the sort of thing you ought to have known about your husband* before *agreeing to marry him.*

Indeed. Horses, hooch, and a godless heathen, to boot.

"Not everyone." Merrick shifted on his feet, growing nervous under her scrutiny.

"Everyone of sound moral character."

"Ah. A fine distinction."

"Hell's bells, never you mind." She spun on her heel to depart. She didn't have the time or emotional countenance to argue with him. She would simply go by herself, that's all. No matter the twist of fear in her gut at the thought of striding into the church house unescorted and alone.

Alone. She sighed. She better get used to it. It was becoming something of a pattern since exchanging matrimonial vows.

"Where are you going?" Merrick called after her.

"To church." *Alone.*

His footsteps chased her into the entry hall. Full morning sun now streamed through the window, scattering speckles of lavender light across the wood floor.

"And how do you intend to get there?" The curl of his fingers around her arm stopped her momentum.

"I'll fly, of course." She huffed, staring him down. "On my witch's broom. Amazing how quickly a bride turns into a shrew, isn't it?"

"As quickly as her groom turns into an insensitive pig, I suppose." The crinkles around his eyes settled in a bemused frown. He sighed. "It's really that important to you?"

His acknowledgment appeased her. "It is."

Even during her darkest days—the endlessly dark days confined to the Louisville townhouse with her volatile mother—Sunday mornings had been sacred. Even when her mother had stopped going outside altogether, Pa paid a priest to hold private sermons in their home. It was routine, familiar, and in that way, a comfort.

Merrick sighed again, loosening his grip on her wrist. "I'll take you."

"You needn't. I'm fine going alone," she lied.

"If you'll just allow me a few minutes to change out of the *devil's knickers*," he said, a small smile breaking through, "we'll be on our way."

"Swell," she whispered. Her gaze lingered on his face, on the softening she saw there. His teasing was...not unwelcome.

As he turned to mount the stairs, every muscle in her husband's taut behind was on display. He vaulted upward on powerful thighs, skipping every other step. Another unexpected tease.

Margot blew out an exhale, trying to pretend she wasn't terribly, hopelessly, embarrassingly affected.

The devil's knickers indeed.

"You realize," Merrick whispered in her ear as they entered the church house, "religion is little more than a political tool for social control?"

"Hush." She silenced him.

"It's true. It's been used throughout history to great effect, most recently by those thumping moralizers behind the temperance movement, the ones who rallied for Prohibition and bankrupted my estate. Fucking Puritans—"

"Merrick!" she hissed, reaching to grip his hand. "*Language.* You are in a house of God."

"Not by my own volition." He glanced nervously around the room, halting his steps.

Margot quickly realized why, spotting a familiar face just up the aisle.

Alastair.

His gaze roved her from head to toe, settling on Margot and Merrick's joined hands. She couldn't read his expression, but he lifted his fingers in a stilted wave.

She pitched her voice for Merrick's ears alone. "Shall we be polite and say hello?" *Please don't make me say hello.*

"No. Old Kentucky blood feuds run deep. I have nothing to say to Alastair. Do you?"

She shook her head, relieved.

"Good." Merrick tightened his grip on her hand. It was comforting, a squeeze from an ally. "Then perhaps we should take our seats and wait for the show to begin."

Margot snorted as she stepped into the nearest pew. "It's not an opera or the ballet, Merrick. It's Sunday service."

He watched as she settled on her knees, folded her hands under her chin, and turned her attention forward.

"Oh, love." He chuckled. "You are woefully naive. This is the greatest show in town. And that man"—he nodded toward Father Simmons, stepping out of the vestibule—"is chief charlatan."

She sighed, gaze still pinned ahead. "Does it exhaust you?"

"What?"

"Being so ornery all the time."

"Horses are ornery," Merrick answered. "I'm merely pragmatic."

"I'd like to pray now," Margot said, her voice prim. She didn't want to fight with him. Not again. Not here.

"By all means." He gestured, quite magnanimously, to the altar. "May you bend the ear of Christ himself to make all your wishes come true. If that fails, we can try rubbing some of my grandmother Eleanor's antique bottles and lamps, see if we can't summon ourselves a genie."

She couldn't help herself. She whipped her head around and glared. *"What?"*

"Surely you've read *Arabian Nights*?" He widened his eyes as he sat back in the pew...sprawled, more like, his legs spread impudently wide. "It's a classic."

"Of course I—"

"Shh." He put a finger to his lips. "Father Simmons is ready to begin. I don't want to miss a single Machiavellian word."

Appalled, Margot turned to face front. "I'll pray a decade of the rosary for your black soul," she muttered under her breath.

"From your lips to God's ears, love," Merrick whispered back.

8

June 18, 1904

Jean-Philippe,
I'd like to commission a gown. I'm thinking...peacocks.
Do what you do best, darling.

Yours,
Babette Dravenhearst

M ERRICK RETURNED FROM MORNING services in a dour mood and made himself scarce, heading straight to the bourbon rickhouses. Margot was more than a little curious after his edict banning her from the distillery, but the glower on his face made her think twice about following.

Instead, she spent the afternoon quarantined on the floor of her closet, tossing the gowns, day dresses, and perhaps most flustering of all, *lingerie* of her predecessor into various piles on the floor and bed. Most were destined for donation, but she earmarked a select few to save. Several gowns were of such exquisitely detailed and ludicrous construction, it seemed a crime to part with them.

Margot stood with both hands on her hips and let out a tired but satisfied sigh as she surveyed her work. Seven piles earmarked for donation—truly a Herculean effort.

The door to her bedroom gave a whining creak.

"Gracious Lord in heaven above." The aging butler, Xander, poked his tufty head into the room. His face was aghast. "What in tarnation is going on in here?"

"Ah, Xander." Margot gave him a pleased smile. "I was just thinking of locating you for your opinion. I've been sorting through the closet, and—"

"The Chantilly lace mourning gown—this requires hanging to prevent creases." He sprang into action, pulling a black dress from a pile. "And gracious, whatever is the ermine cloak doing out? It's far too warm for this right now, m'lady." He scooped it up with his tremoring hands. "And is that the House of Worth peacock gown?" He positively shivered in fright. "Whyever have you removed the couture from its protective casing? The feathers aren't meant to be exposed to open air—they'll wilt and molt!"

"Wilt and molt?" She furrowed her brow. "But surely, on the bird itself, the feathers are exposed to open air all the time, are they not?"

"Babette, what has gotten into you?"

"I'm *Margot*," she corrected, looking directly at the butler. Did he truly not know who she was? Or was this merely a test, a perverse battle of wills against an outsider?

"Margot?" His brows drew inward. His confusion seemed genuine, but she was not reassured. Quite the contrary.

"Yes. Margot. Merrick's wife."

"Merrick...Merrick's wife?" Slowly, awareness dawned. Xander's bemused concern twisted into horror. "Why have you been touching Babette's things? What right have you?"

"It's my bedroom now," she said, instantly defensive. "My closet. I need to hang my things, *my* dresses."

Xander's jaw quivered as he looked around the room. "This is grave robbing, this is."

"Is there another place in the manor where we can store her gowns, perhaps?" Margot asked weakly, giving up all hope of donation. She simply hated confrontation. "I didn't mean to upset you."

"But you have." He was positively tremulous, gazing at the piled-up couture with sorrow. "You've disturbed her things without asking. It's not right. She'll be very upset."

"I'm sorry." Margot was wringing her hands, nearly as distressed as Xander. Her heartbeat pounded in her temples. How had this gone so wrong?

"We can just...perhaps we can put them back." He nodded. "That's what we'll do. We'll put them back very carefully, precisely as they were."

"But my things—"

"She won't like this at all." He lifted two garments with care and headed for the closet, speaking more to himself than Margot, stroking the ermine cloak like a lover, murmuring, "There, there."

Margot's vision began to tunnel as she recognized the dismissal. Dismissed from her own bedroom! As if she were an interloper, unwelcome. She was nearly in tears now. An embarrassed flush rose on the back of her neck, creeping ever higher. Her breathing grew ragged. She fled the suffocating room and collapsed to her knees in the candlelit hallway, out of sight of the horrible butler.

She closed her eyes, breathed in and out.

He's in the wrong, she told herself. *You're not crazy. You're not hysterical.*

The ticking of the grandfather clock roared in her ears. *Tick, tick.* She matched her inhalations to its rhythm, trying to slow her hitching breaths.

Xander is confused. It's your *closet,* she told herself.

"It's mine!" a vehement voice hissed. So very intense and close at hand, it raised shivers on Margot's neck. She sprang to her feet, whirling in a flurry of skirts.

A sudden chill overtook her.

The hallway was empty.

A draft blew down the corridor, whipping hair away from her face. Two doors along the passage slammed shut with jolting *bangs*.

Margot grew cold, cold to her very bones. When she exhaled, her breath was foggy. Her legs churned, propelling her backward.

A second gust blew down the corridor, extinguishing candles along the wall, one after the next. A black wave of darkness surged toward her. When the last taper guttered out, Margot stumbled. Her legs tangled in her skirt, then caught. She went down hard.

Her panting breath filled the air. Just beyond her feet, a floorboard creaked. Margot stifled a whimper, unable to see in the dark. She twisted to rise.

A hand grabbed her ankle. Icy fingers latching on, one by one, over her skin. Gripping. Dragging. So cold it burned.

Margot screamed and kicked ferociously. The hold of the vise broke, her foot swinging free. She lurched upright, then stumbled backward, eyes frantically searching the darkness for the threat.

Her spine slammed into a doorframe. She scampered over the landing and down the winding stairwell, yanked open the front door of the manor, and exploded into the fading rays of sunlight. The tear tracks frozen upon her cheeks melted instantly, becoming one with the midsummer humidity.

Deep breaths, she told herself. *Calm down.*

She shifted her skirt to examine her ankle. The skin was clear. No grip marks. No evidence of a frigid burn.

An imagined *frigid burn,* she told herself, exhaling mightily. She'd worked herself into a terrible state, let her distress get the better of her. How else could you explain—

"What's the matter, sugar?"

Margot spun to the voice. The estate groundskeeper, Evangeline, stood before her, a sharp trowel at her waist. Her hands were full of ripped-up weeds, the roots dangling freely.

Margot swiped at her tear tracks, but the woman had already seen.

"That house." Her voice was husky. She nodded over Margot's shoulder toward the manor. "It's no good for anyone, which is why I don't go inside. You shouldn't spend your days locked in there. You're always welcome to work outside with me."

Margot released a shuddering breath. "You...don't go inside?"

"I haven't set foot in that crypt for almost thirty years."

"Why not?"

Evangeline didn't answer, only puckered her lips and gazed over the gentle slope toward the distillery. A few crumbles of dirt and roots fell to the ground when she moved.

"Merrick told me I'm not to go in the rickhouses," Margot said, following the groundskeeper's sightline. "Not that there was something wrong with the manor itself."

"Yes. It's quite dangerous, the distillery." Her voice turned dreamy, at odds with her words. "There's a large sinkhole behind Rickhouse One"—she pointed to the nearest warehouse—"so it's best not to go wandering off. Wouldn't want you to get swallowed up when you've only just arrived."

Margot swallowed uncomfortably, eyeballing Rickhouse One. The brick was half covered with creeping ivy and unchecked wisteria, as though the earth was trying to swallow it whole.

"What a day it's been." Evangeline shook her dirt-laden fingers. "I've spent hours and hours weeding. It's an important task on an estate as long-standing as this." The pitch of her voice grew deep with promise, suspiciously so. "There will always be critters trying to creep in where they don't belong. Bold as brass, they are. Can you imagine?"

I'm the weed, Margot thought. *That's what she means, just as Xander implied.*

"Pruning, endless pruning." When Evangeline shifted her weight, the blade of her trowel caught sunlight. "Poison works nicely, for the most stubborn breeds. I blend my own with herbs and flora I grow here on the estate."

Margot paled, drawing a hand to her throat and stepping back. "Is that a threat?" she whispered.

Evangeline cocked her head. "Whatever do you mean?"

"You said...you just said...about weeds, creeping in where they don't belong. And pruning and poison," Margot rambled. Distantly, she sensed her paranoia running away with her, but she couldn't stop the words from coming.

Evangeline's brows pulled down, bemused. "Well, yes, weeds can quickly ruin a garden—the grounds of a whole estate—if left unchecked. Nature is one of the most ancient magics, and it must always be kept in balance. I consider myself a steward of that balance."

"A steward," Margot repeated. "You mean like a...a witch?"

Evangeline narrowed her eyes. "I prefer steward."

"O-of course," she stammered, glancing uneasily back toward the house. "I reckon I'll go back inside now. I'm feeling much better. Thank you."

"You shouldn't go in there just yet. Why don't you work in the garden with me?"

"No, it's getting late." Margot backed away. "Merrick will be expecting me for supper."

"All right, sugar. You newlyweds have a lovely evening." Evangeline waggled her long fingers as she turned to depart, causing a few more weeds to tumble to earth. The earth she'd unceremoniously ripped them from.

She'll do the same to you, given the chance.

The thought was sharp and crystal clear, but it had risen unbidden. Was it her own, or...was it the voice of someone else?

Margot eyed the manor with trepidation as she ascended the steps of the portico. She glanced back, but Evangeline had disappeared. Her gaze traveled downhill until it landed on the stables. Standing outside was the tall, lithe figure of the horse trainer, Ruth. A hand shaded her eyes as she stared up at Margot. The distance was too great to ascertain her expression, but Margot sensed coldness, that her presence was unwelcome.

The hinges of the front door whined as she pulled it open, wailing a warning to any who dared cross its threshold.

"It's nothing a good oiling won't fix," Margot said aloud, feigning cheerfulness. The hinges screeched again when she closed the door.

Evangeline had called the manor a crypt, Ruth a mausoleum. The memory was faint, buried deep from when Margot was half asleep, but it was there.

Why had both women said those things?

Perhaps oil would be superfluous. Perhaps the shrieking first impression suited after all.

9

June 18, 1933

Mr. Merrick Dravenhearst,
Same time. Same place.

—A

MARGOT'S SLEEP WAS FITFUL. She dreamed in black and white. Dreamed of magnolia trees and cobwebbed chandeliers. Of a color-bleached stained-glass window and moonbeams over mahogany floors. The train of a wedding gown slithering up a stairwell. A bridal veil disappearing around a corner. A lilting laugh in the distance.

Margot gave stuporous chase, possessed. The hallway lengthened with every stumbling step. Tunneling. Growing. Longer. Colder.

The walls closed in. Her legs churned faster, breath fogging as the temperature plummeted. She slipped on ice, the floor rushing up to meet her. She braced for impact, but it never came.

Hands gripped her shoulders, halting her fall. Yanking her up.

Frigid nails dug into her skin. Pain. Sudden and sharp and *real*.

A pair of black lips over sharp pearly white teeth. Lips twisting with derision as they spat, *"Who the* fuck *are you?"*

Margot jolted awake with a gasp, wrenched upright by the phantom yank. The tight press of invisible icy fingers still dug into her skin.

Beau stood in the open balcony doorway, silhouetted in moonlight and flanked by gauzy curtains blowing in the wind. His upper lip curled in a fearsome snarl, long hair standing on end down the length of his spine. He charged with a ripping growl. Margot's heart seized with terror, imagining sharp canines tearing into her throat.

Move!

But she was frozen, spellbound. Only when Beau's paws landed did the icy grip on her shoulders shatter. The force of the dog's tackle pushed her down in the bed.

Margot cried out. Her arms, bare beneath the thin straps of a summer nightdress, were embedded with deep, slicing fingernail marks. A rivulet of blood dripped down her pale skin.

Beau's canines vanished. He whined, pressing his muzzle into the trickle of blood.

"It's okay," she murmured, gently pushing him aside to strike a candle on her nightstand. She slid out of bed, light in hand, shivering.

There had been a woman in her room. She was sure of it. She'd heard her voice, felt the grip of her phantom fingers. Could smell jasmine on the air.

When Margot turned, her blood ran cold. Her wedding gown was draped over the foot of her bed. Lovingly. Deliberately.

She certainly hadn't placed it there. She *knew* she hadn't—it had been stuffed into the corner of the closet only last night. So how...?

She gazed at her reflection in the vanity mirror, searching for answers. Her shivering silhouette stared back. In the mirror, she watched her breath fog in the frigid air. Her candle snuffed out, trailing smoke.

Margot glanced down. The flame in her hand still burned. But in the looking glass, only darkness. And there, over her left shoulder, shadows shifted. Movement. Margot leaned closer, could just discern the shape of a woman's face. Watching her.

She spun.

No one was there.

A rumble outside shattered the stillness of the night. Margot rushed to the balcony. The roadster was pulled in front of the manor, headlights on and engine sputtering to life. A man's broad figure puttered around it. His face was illuminated briefly as he crossed in front of the hood.

Merrick.

Her night skirt rustled. Beau slunk to her side, his neck stretched out, watching his master.

Merrick climbed into the roadster. The engine turned over with a roar, and the motorcar shot forward, disappearing into the night.

"Beau?" She looked to the dog for answers, knowing he had none to give.

The mutt prowled away, down the length of the balcony. At the far end, another set of white curtains shifted in the breeze. The balcony connected her room to Merrick's.

Margot chewed her lip. Her husband had slipped out of his bed, out of their home, in the dead of night. Given his reputation, there was only one logical conclusion...and combined with the fact he refused to touch her, it was a damning realization indeed.

Merrick had a mistress.

She was such a fool. She spun on her heel and threw herself back into bed, no longer caring about the nightmare that awakened her or the puzzle of the wedding gown at the foot of her bed. Not any of it.

She cared only that her husband loved another. Was choosing another at this very moment. Committing adultery a mere day after exchanging vows.

She should never have married this devil of a man. What a curse it was, to be a Dravenhearst bride.

10

July 7, 1933

Dearest Pa,

*I hope this letter finds you well. I miss many things about
Louisville, but you most of all. It is strange to be back on a
country estate. The house is rather lovely, though I'm still get-
ting lost amidst its many rooms. Merrick has been attentive.
I've not seen the distillery yet, perhaps next week.
All is well, more soon!*

*Forever yours,
Margaret*

OVER THE COURSE OF the next few weeks, Margot fell into a routine. Her mornings began with a search for her roving wedding gown. One daybreak, she might open her eyes to find it strung up on the curtain rod over the French doors. The next, it would be draped over her cushioned vanity seat. Then there was the memorable morning Margot awoke with the dress clutched tightly in her hands, warm from the heat of her body, pulled to her chest while she slept.

She spoke of this mysterious morning game to no one, assuming she herself must be moving the gown during the night. Never mind she didn't recall doing so. She was preoccupied with the lackluster state of her marriage, that was all, and her wedding gown was a symbol of that, one her subconscious had clearly fixated on.

Since the night Merrick had snuck out of the manor, Margot had seen very little of him. He worked from sunup to sundown at the distillery. On one of the many days spent exploring the manor, she discovered the east tower, which featured a cozy little cupola with a wide-paned bay window framing a clear view of the bourbon rickhouses. She could sit on its cushioned seat for hours and watch Merrick stride in and out, Beau close on his heels, as he rolled barrels, moved equipment, took inventory, performed repairs, and went through his ledgers.

Just like back in Louisville, Margot learned much from window-watching. The distillery may be defunct, but that hardly stopped Merrick from working. He was endlessly preoccupied, and barrels were his prime fixation. Obsession, even. She'd never given them much thought before, but Margot soon realized barrels, like everything else in this world, were crafted by the hands of man. And watching her husband's hands shape wood...now *that* proved a mesmerizing affair.

The process began with large chunks of lumber, which Merrick sanded until smooth, then carefully cut into thin planks. He laid the planks side by side on the ground, moving them around as though slotting pieces into a puzzle. Once satisfied, he fitted the planks to the inside of a metal hoop, forming the bones of the barrel.

The interior was warmed over a small firepit while Merrick hammered more metal hoops around its length. This was Margot's favorite part, watching sparks shoot off from the intense friction, seeing the heat-softened wood bend in the hands of her iron-willed husband. The tight lines of his muscled body as he worked, full of tension and purpose.

Something from nothing, that was what he could create. The longer Margot watched, the more she ached for a closer view. To see his broad hands sliding along the wood's grain, feel the heat of sparks fanning her face. Hear his grunting exhalations of exertion, the *chink* of his hammer meeting iron. She'd thought she might question him about the barrels over dinner, but Merrick stopped showing up for meals altogether. If Margot didn't know better, she'd think her husband was avoiding her. And in his absence, the house became her constant companion.

Margot spent her days wandering from room to room, exploring labyrinthine passages and learning where the very best window perches were hidden. Aside from the cupola, there was a second-floor sitting room with a stunning view over the magnolia-lined drive.

And Margot fell in love with the solarium, with its glass ceiling and long wall of windows overlooking the back gardens. The furniture was made of wicker—perfect for soaking in sunbeams—save for an old oak escritoire tucked in the corner. Within its drawers, Margot found several groups of bound letters, with different but equally sweeping feminine penmanship lining the pages. Margot traced her fingers over the swirling ink and resolved to write her next note to her father from this very desk.

She stumbled upon the most opulent room in the house quite by accident. She'd been on her way to the solarium when she made a wrong turn from the main hall. She walked through a double-wide archway and lost her breath as the floor turned to marble.

The ballroom was immense, its ceiling pitched high and lined with elaborate crown molding and pilasters. Two crystal candelabra chandeliers, one at each end, were suspended overhead. The walls featured decorative raised panels trimmed with gold. Clusters of furniture gathered in corners, blanketed in white sheets and dustcovers. Most stunning of all was a lineup of mirrors running the length of the western wall. Mirrors with round edges, sharp corners, scalloped trim. All different shapes and sizes—rectangle, gilded rococo, convex, heavy baroque. Frames of gold and silver. As she paced down the room, a dozen reflections moved alongside her. If another transient form slipped in amongst them, that of a red-haired former mistress perhaps...well, Margot did not notice.

An honest to goodness ballroom, she marveled. Here—in her house!

She could only imagine the gatherings held when the estate was at its height of glamour and glory. Margot would dream of the parties at night—or try to, at least. Anything to block out the anticipation of staring at her husband's adjoined door, listening to the grandfather clock ticking down the minutes until unconsciousness claimed her. Alone.

Slumber always descended, in the end. Thick and deep. Inexplicably, there came a time every night when the temperature in her room plummeted. Margot's teeth would chatter. She would cling to the sheets, her eyes squeezed shut, counting the seconds until the unsettling freeze passed.

And it would always pass. Her muscles would unkink, thaw, grow languid with midsummer heat once more. And she would drift away.

Bang, bang, bang!

Margot's eyes sprang open with alarm, early morning rays of sunlight streaming into her bedroom. She was startled to realize she'd awakened standing upright, not nestled in bed. Her white nightdress was cool and silky around her legs. Abnormally so. As her vision slowly cleared, horror set in.

She wasn't wearing her cotton nightdress at all; she was wearing her *wedding gown.* Standing in the middle of her bedroom like a ghostly sleepwalking bride. Her hand flew to her mouth in shock.

Bang, bang! "Margot? Are you in there?"

It was Merrick, calling through the adjoining door.

Margot stifled a curse. Silence and avoidance from the blasted man for weeks, and *now* was the moment he chose to seek her out? Margot darted to the door, pressing her hands against it. She couldn't let him see her like this. He'd think she'd lost her mind.

Perhaps she had.

"Margot?" he called again, a bit impatiently. She imagined his fingers reaching for the doorknob.

"Y-yes," she managed. "I'm here. What is it?"

"May I come in?"

"No!" She pushed all her weight against the door in case he tried. "No, I don't think that's a good idea. I'm...I'm indisposed."

A creak of floorboards. She pictured him adjusting his stance, separated from her by the mere inch of wood beneath her palms.

"I just wanted to let you know that I'll be going to Greenbrier Estates today. At your father's invitation."

Greenbrier?

"He's going to show me around, teach me about the family business."

Margot nodded even though he couldn't see. "Thank you for telling me."

She looked at the recently finished letter to her father on her vanity, wondering if she might trust Merrick to bring it to him directly. There was nothing incriminating in it, just a few bland words about her new home, assuring her father that married life was treating her well...

A pack of lies.

Merrick cleared his throat on the other side of the door. "I was wondering if perhaps you might like to join me?"

"What?" She stepped back in surprise.

"I assume you'd like to see your father, maybe show me around Greenbrier yourself?"

Her heart rate skyrocketed at the suggestion. Her legs grew weak, and she sank to the floor in a puddle of silk.

Greenbrier...

No, the place was full of ghosts. She simply couldn't.

"Margot? Are you there?"

"I'm here," she whispered.

"I'll likely depart within the hour. Can you be ready?"

"No!" she cried, the word coming out far harsher than she'd intended.

"No?"

"I don't wish to go." *I can't.* She took a deep breath, trying to salvage the situation. "But...but I hope you have a lovely day. Give my father my best, will you?"

"I shall." He shifted his weight again. Now that Margot was on the floor, she could see the shadow of his feet beneath the door. They were bare.

"I suppose I'll just get ready then...look after Beau for me, will you? Keep him out of mischief."

She nodded, unable to speak. When she heard the floorboards groan, she swiped a hand up to her vanity, pulling down the letter. "Wait."

He paused.

"Would you give this to my father?" She slid the envelope beneath the door. "I was going to post it today, but since you'll be seeing him..." She trailed off.

"Of course. I'll give him your best."

"Thank you." Margot exhaled slowly through her teeth as his footfalls departed.

Merrick was going to Greenbrier today. The thought was enough to unspool her. She collapsed against the door and raised a trembling hand to her forehead. He was going to Greenbrier.

Her mind conjured images automatically. The whitewashed and sprawling country estate, its prim black shutters and open-air rooms. The blue hydrangea hedges—they'd be thick and full this time of year, guzzling water. The paddocks of cattle and the gentle rolling field where the horses were put out to graze. And beyond all that, near the edge of the estate bordering the Kentucky River, just past the sleeping eaves of Ma's favorite willow tree...the graves.

One for Elijah.

One for her mother.

She shivered, reaching for the cap sleeves of her wedding gown, yanking them down her shoulders. She wanted to shed this ghastly dress. She'd shed her very skin if she could, evaporate into thin air to float away, join with the clouds in the sky. Here, but also not...

Because Merrick was going to Greenbrier.

Which meant he might come back with questions.

Questions she wasn't prepared to answer.

11

September 1918

There are four things you must always remember, Merrick.
First and foremost, all bourbon is whiskey, but not all
whiskey is bourbon.
And all whiskey that's not bourbon is a waste of a barrel.

—Excerpt, a letter from Richard Dravenhearst's Last Will
& Testament

H ALFWAY THROUGH THE DAY, the realization struck—with her
husband away, the bourbon rickhouses were unattended. Margot
could steal away, look at those barrels he'd constructed up close, run her
fingers over them. Feel the wood for herself, examine the craftsmanship.

And figure out what in blue blazes he was doing with them. He couldn't
be making bourbon...could he? He said he hadn't made bourbon for years,
not since Prohibition made it illegal.

It was high noon when she set out, and the Kentucky sun was fierce.
Beau wilted quickly, his black fur amplifying the deadly effects of the midday heat. Margot directed her feet first to Rickhouse Two, where Merrick

ran his barrel cooperage. Beau pranced ahead to the doors, sticking his nose into the crack to nudge inside. The practiced expertise with which he conducted his break-in suggested this wasn't his first time.

Margot smirked, happy to be in league with such a smooth criminal.

As she neared the building, the scent of ash filled her lungs. The firepit was small, messy with burned debris and wood. A few planks with varying degrees of char lay about. She moved toward the rickhouse doors, glancing over her shoulder to be certain she wouldn't be caught. Evangeline was in the gardens today, Xander tucked inside the dusty manor, and Ruth...well, Margot had scarcely seen hide or hair of the equestrian trainer since she'd arrived.

It took several blinks for her pupils to adjust from the brilliant summer day to the dim warehouse, but once they did, Margot's jaw dropped.

"I'll be jiggered," she whispered, tilting her head to look up.

The warehouse was filled top to bottom with barrels. A central aisle ran straight ahead, splitting the interior in half. Rick shelves ran horizontally, row after row after row, each filled with barrels. On top of each rick was another rick, then another. And another. All filled with barrels. Always more barrels, endless barrels. Balcony walkways cut across the main aisle to access higher levels. Margot counted *five* of those. Five stories of barrels.

She paced down the center, utterly amazed. The scent of cedar and oak was all-consuming. With near reverence, she ran her fingers along the grain of a barrel, following the natural curve down its length. The wood was smooth and warm to the touch.

Curious, she rattled the barrel. There was no sloshing of liquid. She shook the one beside it and again came up empty. Margot looked skyward, amazed by the magnitude of her husband's enterprise. He *made* these barrels. With his own two hands. Enough to fill an entire warehouse.

She strode back to the door, her feet thudding solidly as she crossed the wood floor.

"Beau?" she whispered. "Where are you?"

It wouldn't do to leave without her partner in crime, but she had no clue where the mutt had slunk off to. The interior of the warehouse was hardly better than being outside. It was stiflingly hot from lack of airflow, the brick exterior baking in the sun all day, heating the space like an oven. Margot's skin dampened with sweat.

The temptation of a breeze stirred just ahead. Maybe Beau had already left? She called for the dog once more before slipping outside. Beside the firepit, she bent to pick up a charred and discarded plank. She breathed in its scent.

Positively intoxicating. Like burnt hickory.

Her fingers clamped possessively around the wood, intending to steal it. She loved it; she *wanted* it. Couldn't explain it, just knew she did.

Rickhouse One was next door. Was it also filled with barrels? Margot had to know. She walked toward the entrance. When she reached the doors, she yanked.

They didn't budge.

She gave a second pull before noticing chains wrapped around the handles. She ran her fingers along them, curious. They were bound tight, sealing the doors. She rattled them in annoyance, then sighed.

A hand clamped down on her shoulder.

Margot whirled with a startled screech, swinging her stolen plank in defense.

"Whoa, there." A tall man wearing a three-piece suit and a fedora jumped back. He released her shoulder and raised his hands in peace. "Didn't mean to startle ya, Miss...?"

The man had an oily look to him, finely dressed though he was, with his shiny shoes and T-bar chained pocket watch. He looked like a city rat, wholly out of place in the Bluegrass.

Margot was instantly distrustful.

"Greenbrier." A partial lie. She kept a firm grip on her plank, prepared to swing if necessary.

"Miss Greenbrier." The man's mouth twisted into a sunny grin, and he touched the brim of his hat. "Pleasure to make your acquaintance."

She lifted her eyebrows, unable to honestly return the sentiment. "And you are?"

"Hey!" A shout rang from the stables. A lanky, dark-haired man began to cross the property. For a moment, Margot fooled herself into thinking it was Merrick.

Beau emerged from the neighboring rickhouse and began to bark.

"Hey!" the man shouted again, gaining ground. "What'd Merrick tell you 'bout showing your face 'round these parts, Toni?"

"I was in the area." Toni snorted, then spit into the dusty ground near his shined shoes. Margot wrinkled her nose in distaste. "Is he around?"

"I'll tell ya the same as Merrick did—we got a telephone and a mailbox. They work jus' fine. Use 'em."

Toni frowned but began to back away. He touched the brim of his hat again and lowered his voice so only Margot could hear. "You'll tell him I stopped by, won't you, sweetheart? If you are who I think you are, it'll mean more comin' from you."

Margot's stomach twisted when he winked. Before she could reply, he turned tail and headed uphill.

"All right there, Mrs. Dravenhearst?" came a slow, drawling voice. The dark-haired man had finally reached her, his lips turned down, posture tight. The country burr of his speech was deep, but his eyes were young and unlined. Close to Margot's age, she'd venture.

"Reckon so." She straightened her spine as Beau settled by her side. "Or I will be once you tell me who in heckin' hell you are." Her grip tightened again around the wooden plank. It would make a decent weapon should this cowboy move even a single step closer before identifying himself.

"Goldarn it." He tossed his head back and laughed. "Tha's right. You hit the deck that day before we were properly introduced. I'm Julian—stable-boy and jockey most days, bourbon apprentice anytime your husband isn't too crotchety to have me."

"Oh. *Julian*." Margot's shoulders sagged with relief. She'd barely looked twice at the jockey on her arrival day, intimidated as she'd been by his mount. "I didn't recognize you."

"Clearly not. My apologies. I don't much fancy takin' a stave to the face for sneakin' up on a woman unprepared."

"A...a what?"

"They're called staves, that there wood you're carryin'. They're used to make bourbon barrels."

"Oh." She held the plank higher to look at it, abashed.

"That's pure American white oak you're holdin' there, Mrs. Draven-hearst. Real good stuff too. Merrick only sources the best."

"Yes, I've been so curious," Margot admitted, running a hand over the wood. She pointed toward the locked rickhouse, then began to walk around it. "I was just looking for—"

"Wouldn't chance explorin' back there if I was you," Julian interrupted. "There's a sinkhole 'round back. Didn't Merrick tell you?"

Margot shifted her weight. "He might've mentioned it." Or maybe Xander or Evangeline, Margot couldn't remember. She'd all but forgotten the warning.

"It's pretty dangerous. Would ya like to see?" Julian asked. "I know Merrick doesn't like people nosing 'round his rickhouses, but it's probably safer to show ya upfront, keep ya from tumbling unawares one day while you're out pickin' wildflowers...or whatever it is ladies of leisure do with their time."

She cracked a smile. "Show me."

"Beau, stay here," Julian commanded.

Margot tailed the young man around the rickhouse. The back wall was covered with rising vines of ivy and purple wisteria. The brick was crumbling badly back here, and a long crack ran down the length of the wall through the foundation.

"Watch your footing," Julian advised, reaching out to grip her arm. "One wrong step and it's curtains for us both."

The ground behind the rickhouse sloped gently downward to form a shallow basin.

"This is it. The sinkhole." Julian picked up a chunk of brick and tossed it ten feet into the nadir of the pit to demonstrate. It landed with a soft squelch, sinking halfway into the earth.

Kentucky was no stranger to sinkholes, something about groundwater drainage and soil composition...at least, that was what Margot recalled from the newspapers. Every year or so, they'd inevitably run an article whenever one cropped up in the state. Sinkholes could cause real damage, destroying roads and taking down houses. Margot glanced nervously at Rickhouse One, perched precariously at the edge.

"It looks ready to swallow the rickhouse," she observed. "Is the building secure?"

"Er, well..." Julian rubbed the back of his neck. "This here's Rickhouse One." He offered nothing more.

"Yes...Rickhouse One," she repeated. "Is it safe? Are there barrels inside? Bourbon?"

"Oh, there's bourbon in there." Julian chuckled. "Some real fine bourbon, been aging for goin' on twenty years. A real rarity."

"And...and you think that's wise?" Margot gestured to the crumbling foundation. "This building could cave in at any moment. Surely, if there's product of high value within, it should be moved—"

"Merrick hasn't told you about Rickhouse One?"

Margot folded her arms. "Is there something I should know?"

He laughed again, uneasy now. "You'll have to be askin' your husband about that, Mrs. Dravenhearst. S'not my story to tell, not my family skeleton."

So there was, in fact, a story.

Margot tilted her chin, trying to appear more confident than she felt. "I suppose I'll just ask him then." *Though I can imagine how that conversation will go.*

"Do that." Julian nodded, backing away. "Best wait until he's in a real fine mood. I'm not a married man myself, but seems to me, that's what pillow talk is for."

When Julian crooked a knowing grin, Margot blushed scarlet, embarrassed by the insinuation her nights in Dravenhearst Manor were consumed by her husband.

In reality, they were anything but.

She chuckled nervously. "I should return to the house."

He nodded. "Nice to properly meet ya, Mrs. Dravenhearst. And don't you worry on tellin' Merrick that grifter—Toni—stopped by. I'll handle it."

"I appreciate it, thanks."

"Oh, and if you ever want a tour of the stables, I'd be happy to oblige. We could get you set up with your own horse. Got plenty of real steady mares—"

Margot raised a hand to stop him. "That's kind of you, but I don't ride."

"I bet you ride just fine."

When he flicked his eyes appreciatively over Margot's curves, she bit her lip, uncertain whether they were still speaking of horses. Julian gave a booming laugh as he turned on his heel to depart, cutting a course for the stables.

Before Margot rounded the corner of the rickhouse, she looked back. The sinkhole had swallowed the brick. Erased its presence from history, simple as that.

Margot turned her discoveries over in her mind as she walked back to the manor. The chains on the rickhouse doors. The sinkhole...could that be it? Merrick had mentioned, she suddenly recalled, one of the rickhouses was sealed. He said it on their wedding day. He must've been speaking of Rickhouse One. Perhaps he sealed it because it was structurally unsafe?

"It's Margaret, yes?"

Margot startled as she crested the hill. The angle of the sun was intense, the glare obscuring her vision. She raised a hand to shade her eyes and saw Ruth, all tightly bound blonde hair and shining boots, towering before her. Gracious, the woman was tall, especially with an uphill advantage.

Margot took two steps to get on even ground. "Yes, but you can call me Margot. I've come to understand...Merrick mentioned his mother's name was also Margaret." She hugged her arms around her middle.

"So it was." Ruth frowned. "But those of us who knew her best called her by her maiden name, Babette. It suited her." She extended a hand. "I'm afraid our initial introduction got interrupted. I'm Ruth."

"I remember." Margot accepted the handshake.

Ruth's fingers, long and slender, gripped with surprising strength. What her riding jodhpurs and blazer lacked in ornamentation was made up for with exquisite tailoring. Combined with her conventionally angular features and military-straight posture, the woman reeked of the kind of confidence that came only from wealth and breeding.

"How have things been since your arrival? Have you been getting on properly—adjusting to the house?" Her words were perfectly pitched and appropriate, but it was her eyes that gave her away. A glimmer of intrigue buried in their blue depths.

Margot tilted her head but didn't respond, chewing over Ruth's peculiar word choice. *Adjusting* to the house.

"I'm sorry I didn't check in with you sooner," Ruth continued. "I've found myself otherwise prioritized. Training, you know. Our colt's Derby debut is less than a year away."

"How did you come to your position here?" Margot asked. "It's an unusual job for a woman, an equestrian trainer." To say the least.

"Quite accidentally." Ruth laughed. "I started as a hobbyist. Babette and I shared a love of horses. It wasn't until after her death I took on a more formal role, began experimenting with bloodlines and breeding. That's what horseracing is all about—bloodlines. Bad blood will always out, good will take gold."

Margot paused to assess the woman. It was almost impossible to pinpoint Ruth's age. Her skin was like porcelain, impossibly well preserved and without blemish. Her body was lean and fit. "You speak of Babette fondly," she observed. "Were you close?"

"We were. We'd been friends since girlhood and made our debuts together. Babette set her cap on Richard"—she nodded toward the manor—"early in the season. He never stood a chance. Anything that woman wanted, she got. I've never known anyone quite like her, before or since.

"They were a striking couple, a real fairytale match—both from blue blood families, attractive, wealthy as sin...but Babette was terribly young when she married, only eighteen. That's how I ended up here. I came with her as a companion. We ran the house together in the early years."

Margot started. "But what of your own prospects? That's quite a compromise to make for a friend."

Ruth snorted. "Unlike Babette, I didn't have stars in my eyes where marriage was concerned. I was in no hurry to wed. And I certainly didn't diminish my chances by moving here. Dravenhearst Manor was, at the turn of the century, the social capital of Kentucky. Babette and Richard threw legendary parties. The manor had a revolving door." Ruth gave a tinkling laugh. "I met my fair share of suitors, make no mistake. But I never married."

"Why not?"

Ruth's eyes misted, dancing with memories. "I found tremendous freedom when I moved here. Riding horses each morning, parties every weekend...no one to answer to but myself. It was the most..." She paused to inhale sharply. "*Exhilarating* time of my life. I think I made out better than Babette." She smiled at her own joke, then winced. "I'm sorry, that was in terribly poor taste. Of course I made out better. Babette died two decades ago, barely twelve years a bride. It was a...a devastating tragedy. They say the brightest stars burn out the fastest." She hugged herself and looked away, blinking.

A devastating tragedy...perhaps childbirth? Surprising herself, Margot reached over to gently grip Ruth's forearm. "I'm terribly sorry."

"It's not for you to be sorry about. It was half a lifetime ago, but the people on this estate have long memories. There's dark history here, and history seems to have a way of repeating itself." Her gaze was steady now, penetrating. "That's why I asked you about the house, about how you're getting on. Is everything truly all right?"

Margot bit the inside of her cheek. She was afraid. She didn't want to say what was happening at night, alone in her bedroom. The words, once uttered, could not be taken back.

Her mother had lost time near the end, unable to recall the things she'd done, uncertain even as to how she passed from one room to the next. She would move things, forget she moved them, then launch into endless paranoid tirades until she wore herself out. Until either Margot or her exhausted father would bring her laudanum. In the darkest depths of her heart, Margot began to think her mother crazy. It affected how she spoke to her, how she looked at her, and to this day, how she remembered her.

If she was being fully honest, it affected how she viewed herself as well. How others viewed her, especially after the horrific scandal of her debut. Mad Margaret, loony Margaret...she'd lived that life before. She wasn't willing to do it again. Not here, where she hoped to start over.

No. She'd not utter one complaint about the house. Everything was *fine*.

Margot kept her voice light. Pleasant. Forced a doe-eyed southern belle smile. "Everything is lovely. It's been perfect."

A flicker of uncertainty crossed Ruth's face before she offered a hesitant but relieved smile in return. "Well...good. Good. I'm glad."

Margot nodded faintly, keeping the silly grin on her face. She poked a thumb over her shoulder toward the manor. "Speaking of which, I best be heading back. Thank you for the chat. It was lovely."

As she turned to go, Ruth's fingers curled around Margot's forearm, gentle but insistent.

"Should it ever...not be *lovely*," she said, emphasizing Margot's word choice and biting her bottom lip, "come see me in Hellebore House."

"Where?"

"Just there." Ruth pointed. "The cottage beyond the stables, near the edge of the property. That's where I live." She cast a wary eye back to the manor, lurking over Margot's shoulder like a gargoyle. "I no longer keep a room in the main house. I prefer my own space."

"Of course." Margot wiggled her arm free. "I'll keep that in mind." She located the stone cottage in the distance, surrounded by flowering bushes. A small garden flanked the side, a veranda before the front door.

"Please do. Anytime, even if you'd just like to share a cup of tea in the afternoon. Babette and I did that often. She adored a good tea party...or gin rickeys on the porch in the summer."

"She sounds larger than life." Margot shifted her stance, the question on the tip of her tongue. "I'm wondering...how exactly did she die?"

Ruth's face fell still.

"I don't mean to be impertinent," Margot said, the words coming quickly. "It's only—"

"It's okay to be curious." Ruth's frozen features broke. "I'd be concerned if you weren't." A fleeting glance to meet Margot's eyes, then away. "Babette struggled after marrying Richard. She enjoyed the role of wife in theory, more so the role of hostess. She thrived as the center of attention. But in the moments between, the day-to-day management of the estate, stepping into her role as Merrick's mother...she floundered."

Ruth looked into the distance before continuing. "High as a kite one day, radiant as the sun, making you feel privileged just to stand in her light. But then the next...she'd be unable to get out of bed. Curtains pulled. Door closed. She called them 'fits of the sullens,' and she blamed them on many things—Richard, the house, the gin rickeys..." Ruth smiled, remembering, then shook her head. "Maybe it was everything. Maybe it was none of those things. Maybe there's a cost to shining so bright. If she was truly a star, she was a very fickle one indeed."

"I see." But Margot pursed her lips, unsure whether she really saw at all.

"No, you don't." Ruth's brows dipped. "But you will. Her death was a tragedy, but by her own hands. Babette died by suicide. She took her own life."

12

July 8, 1900

Ruth,
Don't wear pink tonight, but don something equally stun-
ning.
We'll be the brightest stars in Louisville.

Love Always,
Babette

T HERE WOULD BE NO sleep that night, Margot was sure of it. Not one wink. The humidity was oppressive, and her thoughts swirled with visions of Babette. Visions of Dravenhearst Manor lit not by sparse candlelight but the buzzing live wire of electricity. Glittering ballgowns and grand parties. The images played on the back of Margot's feverishly warm eyelids like a silent film at the picture shows.

A sharp sound cut through the night, a rumbling outside the manor. Familiar. Her eyes sprang open.

She dashed to the balcony just in time to watch the roadster pull an about-face in the circle drive, Merrick in the driver's seat.

Sneaking out. For the second time this week, third or fourth since their wedding. She'd lost count.

It felt like defeat, like the worst kind of shame. The soft depths of the bed called to her. The laudanum on the nightstand even more so.

But laudanum wasn't the only thing on the nightstand tonight. Dinner had been the usual solitary affair, but when Margot returned to her room, she discovered two surprises—an envelope with her name on it, presumably a return letter from her father, and a crystal vase filled with blue hydrangeas. She knew those flowers; they were from Greenbrier Estates. Only one person could have brought them.

Her darling, adulterous husband.

Margot crossed the room on sleepwalker's feet, then bent down to sniff the heavy blooms. They'd been Ma's favorite, these flowers, and against herself—against the ingrained impulse to have nothing in common with her mother—Margot had always loved them too.

It was unexpected of him to bring a bouquet back for her. Thoughtful. She'd been buoyed by the gesture, but those hopes were quickly dashed, run over by the roadster's squealing tires as her husband absconded yet again in the middle of the night.

Who is she, this other woman? It seemed critically important to know.

Margot grabbed recklessly for the laudanum as she tumbled back to bed. She tilted the bottle to her lips and drank deeply, relishing the bitter tincture on her tongue. It tasted like salvation. Like some goddamn peace and quiet.

She nestled into the sheets, wanting to disappear in the blissful abyss of unconsciousness. She certainly didn't want to remain here, her thoughts swimming with jealous resentment. Here she was, nearly a month a bride, her marriage bed cold. Unconsummated. Dying a slow death by neglectful asphyxiation, day after day.

Margot pictured the face of the mystery woman who shared nights with Merrick in her place. She would be beautiful, of course, striking and magnetic. Confident. She had to be.

Who is she? What does she have that I don't? Who? Who?

Through her rising opiate haze, Margot wondered if there was an owl on the balcony asking the question.

Who? Who? Who?

Then came the answer, her last conscious thought. A damning one, followed by eerie laughter, high and feminine.

Someone just like Babette.

The ballroom was aglow and hazy, rosy-hued in evening candlelight. Margot floated above the scene, drifting between the taper-laden chandeliers. Faces below blurred like the swirling brushstrokes of a Van Gogh painting, all movement, color, and current. All round edges. A feeling more than a reality.

She rolled over in the air, spinning lazily. Humidity sat like morning dewdrops on her bare limbs. Like water-laden crystals, glistening in the low light. Margot shimmered. Rolled her arms languorously, her gaze trailing across the scene below.

Like an angel, she descended. The skirt of her white nightgown billowed romantically, a peony in full bloom. Her bare toes pointed, then touched marbled ground. The cold hit her feet, icing them through. The sensation crept up her legs, rising like frost, as she began to move. Humid dewdrops turned to frozen crystals on her skin.

A ragtime reel was playing. Hands clapped to the beat, merry and sharp. The crowd fell away as two girls—a pair of doe-eyed, rosy-cheeked debutantes—stole center stage on the dance floor. One with soft red hair. The other, pale blonde.

Margaret Babette and Ruth Auclaire.

Their feet moved in perfect unison, punctuating every beat with a dance step. The clapping of the crowd increased, winding faster and faster. Challenging the girls to keep pace. To dance. To *fly*.

Only when it became untenable, only when their feet moved and tapped and twirled as mere blurs, did Babette break harmony, reaching for Ruth. The pair entwined their hands and leaned back, spinning like cherry blossoms falling to earth in springtime. Heads tilted up, curling strands of hair dripping down their backs, mouths open in joyous laughter. The sound rang louder in Margot's ears than the thunderous clapping. Rang like the pealing of church bells on Easter Sunday. The laughter of unbridled youth, of princesses in a room full of peasants.

Fascination and desire swelled in Margot's chest, shooting a current of warmth through her cold limbs, blazing all the way to the tips of her frosted fingers.

The two girls were a perfect pair of foils. Babette, the portrait of romance in a diaphanous dusty pink gown with ruffled gigot sleeves ending just above her elbow. Low cut to expose her flushed bosom, panting with exertion from the effects of the reel. And Ruth, a strikingly bold figure clad in black and white, art nouveau lines accenting curves down her bodice and lengthening the line of her legs. Her ears were weighted with succulent pearls, diamonds at her throat. Glittering with expense, dripping with it.

Together they consumed all the oxygen in the room.

"Louisville's own pair of Gibson girls," a watching mama announced. Curious, Margot reached for her, wondering if she could touch...but the woman drifted away, neither here nor there. Insubstantial.

"Indeed. Best for every other debutante in this room they make match- es quickly," her companion replied, staring right through Margot as she spoke. "Until those two dominoes fall, there'll be no room for the rest."

A dark-haired man in a crisp, narrow-cut tuxedo took to the floor. The music slowed. Ruth gave Babette a knowing, close-lipped smile, nodding over her friend's shoulder at the approaching gentleman. She leaned in to whisper something, pink lips nearly touching Babette's ear. Margot moved forward, dying to hear Ruth's words, but the music swelled, transitioning to a waltz. Ruth melted away as Babette turned straight into the man's arms and began to dance.

"You were saying," the mama said, nudging her friend's shoulder.

"Well, well, well. A Babette and a Dravenhearst. Wouldn't that be some- thing?"

"Mmm, yes. It's their fourth dance this week, second tonight. I daresay, that match is made."

Margot hardly breathed as she watched the pair, their bodies a hair closer than proper, eyes locked on each other. Gazes pooling. Swimming in each other.

Heat warmed Margot's core, between her legs, only from watching. Because if she slightly fuzzed her vision, it could be her and Merrick re- volving around the dance floor. Closer than close. A dark-haired devil and a strawberry-blonde cherub.

Oh, how she wanted to be held like that! To set every tongue in Louisville wagging for something so scandalously improper but undeni- ably *right*. To so clearly belong in another's embrace.

Margot raised her arms into the hold, imagining what it would feel like. Just before she gave into the music and began to move, the gentleman beside her shifted. She froze, wondering faintly if he might take her hands and dance. He was young and fit with soft brown hair and matching eyes, kind eyes.

But his hands didn't reach for her; instead, they clasped behind his back. A set of silver cufflinks twinkled in the candlelight, a pair of racehorses. When Margot's gaze traced up his arms, over his shoulders, across his face, she found abject longing. He stared straight through her with eyes for none but Babette.

Babette, who was twirling in Richard Dravenhearst's arms, seemingly enamored. Brushing her fingers on his neck, teasing, twining in the dark hair at his nape.

The man beside Margot flinched and turned tail. Only then did Babette's attention falter. Her gaze snapped like a magnet, watching the man's retreating back, like she'd known precisely where he stood all along. Her body continued to waltz, the crowd continued to gawk, but Margot was watching Babette's eyes—a single flicker, there and gone. Enough to give her away.

As the music faded, Dravenhearst leaned low to kiss Babette's curled fingers. She accepted her victory with smug delight, a princess ascending to the rank of queen. Murmurs buzzed through the room. Heedless, Babette took her leave, gently waving away another gentleman who extended his hand for a dance.

Margot gave chase through the crowd. She followed the swishing train of Babette's pink dress straight out of the ballroom and into a dark hallway. The temperature dropped several degrees. Margot shivered.

A closed door waited at the end of the passage. Babette paused, curling her fingers around the knob. Before she entered, she looked straight at Margot, her green eyes blazing with awareness.

She can see me, Margot realized. None of the others had noticed, but—

Babette winked. "Yes, Dravenhearst bride. I see you."

Margot jolted, the voice reaching her ears like wind chimes in the distance—airy, high, and melodic.

Babette's lips pursed. She blew Margot a playful kiss. "Watch this."

She turned the knob to slip inside, and Margot caught a glimpse of the brown-eyed man waiting within. Heard his voice, pleading, as she closed the door.

"Babette, please don't marry him."

The door clicked shut.

Margot's hands scrambled at the knob, twisting and turning, but it was futile. Locked. She pounded a hand on the wood in frustration, then pried at the keyhole. Twisting madly. She wanted to hear. To *see*.

A faint barking echoed down the hallway, but Margot was single-minded in her desire to open the door. She would not be distracted.

"Babette?"

She turned her head to the voice, but the hallway was empty. Suddenly, warm hands gripped her frozen arms, pressing.

"Babette, what are you doing?" The voice came from a great distance, as though underwater. Muted and muffled.

The barking grew louder, pounding in her head. She closed her eyes against the onslaught. The world tilted beneath her feet. When she lifted her lashes, the hallway had vanished, the Louisville ballroom worlds away, decades even.

Margot stood in the foyer of Dravenhearst Manor in her white cotton nightgown, her fingers gripping the handle of the front door. Beau had wiggled himself between her and the exit, nudging her away. She turned her head and gasped in surprise. The bulging, eerie blue eyes of the butler, Xander, loomed before her in the darkness.

"M'lady, where are you going? It's the middle of the night."

"I..." Margot released the handle in shock. "Nowhere."

"Babette, you should be abed. I'll escort you. Come."

Margot pulled back from him. "I'm *not* Babette." Never before had the distinction felt so crucial.

"Not..." Xander faltered, eyes searching. He shook his head. "Come. Richard will be—"

"I'm not Richard's wife. I'm *Margot*, Merrick's wife."

"Merrick's...wife?" Xander blinked twice, raising a hand to cover his gaping mouth. "*Merrick's* wife?"

"Yes," she breathed, folding her arms over her chest. Rubbing her hands up and down against the phantom chill still clinging to her limbs.

"No." He shook his head, voice raspy. "No, you can't be. No more Dravenhearst brides. He promised. We all agreed."

"What do you mean?"

"The curse," he whispered, eyes wide with reverence. With fear.

"What curse? Did something happen here, Xander? To the other wives?"

"Dead...two generations dead. First Eleanor, then Babette." His face crumpled. He dragged a hand over it, scrubbing hard.

"Ruth told me...she said Babette committed suicide."

"They *both* did. In Rickhouse One. Hung themselves from the rafters, dressed in their bridal gowns. The Dravenhearst suicide brides."

Jesus Christ. Margot stumbled back.

"The rickhouse has been sealed, but it matters not. Merrick shouldn't have brought you here. I..." He trailed off, looking sheepish. "I forget things, sometimes. I forget so many things, but I remember the important ones. I swear I do. I remember things that happened here. I remember what I did." He shivered. "You shouldn't have come. You should leave. Were you trying to?" He pointed to the door.

"No." Margot shook her head, finding her voice. "No, I was just...well, I don't know precisely what I was doing. I was asleep. Dreaming."

"Do you dream of her?"

She was almost afraid to ask. "Dream of who?"

"Eleanor."

"No. Not her."

"Not *her*?" Xander repeated. His eyes sharpened. "Then...Babette? You dream of *Babette*?"

Margot didn't answer.

"I'm only asking because I dream of her too," he whispered. "She's worse than Eleanor. Far worse. She is a true haunting."

A haunting. Margot shivered. *Is that what's happening to me?*

Xander closed his eyes for a long moment. When he opened them, he blinked slowly, stupidly. His irises were milky with the cataracts of age, almost glassy in the candlelight. "Babette? Whatever are you doing?"

"Wh-what?"

"You should be abed. It's terribly late. You know these late-night wanderings distress Richard." He reached for her. "Here, allow me to help—"

"No!" Margot cried, snatching her arm away, puzzled and terrified all at once. The Xander with the clear gaze and plaintive speech of the last several minutes was gone. She peered closely, uncertain. "Xander?"

"Yes, m'lady?" The slow tilt to his head was creepingly servile. His eyes were vacant. A light on, but nobody home.

Margot moved toward Beau, pressing her trembling leg against the dog for comfort.

"Come now, Babette," he continued, oblivious to her distress. He was but an old-time music box, playing the same tune over and over. "I'll see you abed. Come..."

13

July 9, 1933

Merrick,

Your copies of the notarized paperwork, as requested. I appreciate the consideration you've shown my daughter throughout this process. Of all the "assets" discussed herein, she is the most precious to me.

I know it is early yet, but it's my sincerest hope that one day you might agree.

Sincerely,
Samuel Greenbrier

I'M GOING MAD. IT'S *the only explanation.*

Margot needed to get dressed for church. She needed to procure her Book of Psalms, her handbag and matching gloves, then her husband, lest they be late.

Instead, she was staring at her wedding gown, strung up on the curtain rod by a length of rope.

A length of rope knotted around the neckline of the dress...

Noose-like.

It was a clear threat. A manifestation of her own subconscious, of the curse of the Dravenhearst brides. Tangible proof of the evil, the sick weakness, lurking within her.

Like mother, like daughter.

Margot's breathing grew ragged. Her fingers scrabbled at her neck, imagining the rough itch of tightening twine on her skin. Cutting off her air.

She stumbled to the bed, gasping.

Thunderous knocks battered the door.

"Not now," she whispered, clutching her head, trying to control her breath. She glanced at the dress, billowing in the morning breeze from the balcony. Another knock. Margot closed her eyes. It was all too much.

"Margot, are you nearly ready?" They were the first words her husband had spoken to her today, but he already sounded annoyed.

Margot stuffed her fist in her mouth, trying to muffle her panicked, gasping breaths. She didn't want Merrick to come in to investigate, couldn't afford to let him see the gown strung up on the curtain rod. Or worse, her on the floor.

Incapacitated.

Weak.

Hysterical.

"Wouldn't want to be late," her husband continued, his voice a bored drawl. "I'd hate to miss an opportunity to watch Father Simmons asphyxiate on his own doctrine of perfection."

The joke punctured her panic. She exhaled in a sharp snort.

"It's a beautiful day to be indoctrinated, don't you think?" His words were muffled by the door. "Or better yet, to take a midmorning nap. Reckon his holier-than-thou homily will do the job nicely."

Merrick's persistent irreverence brought a smile to her lips. She inhaled slowly, focusing on his voice, surprised to find how much it helped.

"Margot? Are you there?"

"Y-y-yes..." she called. She rose on trembling legs and gave a sharp tug on the wedding gown, pulling it down. "Yes, I'm here."

"Swell. Are you ready?"

"Almost," she lied, tossing the gown into one of the trunks in her closet and slamming the lid. She grabbed a lemon-yellow tea dress at random and shucked off her nightgown.

"If you'd prefer a lazy morning instead, I'm happy to oblige..."

"No, no," she called back, stepping directly into the day dress. God forgive her, there was no time to procure a matching chemise. "Sunday service is important. The whole community will be there, as will we."

Merrick mumbled something that sounded an awful lot like "a pack of zealots and fools."

A giggle rose unbidden to her lips.

"If you don't hurry, we're going to be—"

She pulled open the door with a flourish. "I'm all set."

Hardly. Her hair was unbound and loose around her shoulders, her body indecently wanton without proper structural undergarments, and her crocheted church gloves were nowhere to be seen.

"Oh." Merrick cleared his throat, taking in her disheveled appearance. "You look..."

"A bit undone." She laughed nervously and waved him off. "I've misplaced my gloves and—"

"Heaven forbid," Merrick teased. He reached for her hand, twining his fingers with hers. "A fine pair of sinners we'll make, you and I. Bare flesh in church and an atheist liberal on your arm. Holy water won't save you today, Mrs. Dravenhearst."

It certainly won't. That smile of his alone would be her demise. Godless, adulterous, a liar...oh, the list of his accolades went on and on. Yet here she was, a dog ravenous for any scrap of his philandering attention.

"We should go," Margot said quietly, casting her lashes downward. It was easier, perhaps, if she just didn't look at him.

But before they set out, her husband did something altogether unexpected. Something that made her traitorous, sinful heart somersault in exaltation.

Merrick leaned in and pressed his lips to her temple. "For what it's worth," he murmured against her skin, "I think you look quite beautiful this morning."

She started. Evidently, sleepwalking, hauntings, and a bit of morning madness agreed with her.

"Undone"—he tucked a stray strand of hair behind her ear—"suits you."

Nervous energy bubbled to her surface, releasing yet another giggle. Oh, how she loathed herself. "You've gone mad, like Alice's hatter in Wonderland."

"A high compliment if I've ever heard one. Can you keep a secret, love?" He brushed her ear with his knuckle as he quoted, "'We're all mad here.'"

Well, wasn't that the truth? A truth from which Margot—busy turning to vapor from the mere whisper of his touch—couldn't even pretend to be exempt. The riotous explosion of butterflies in her stomach and his iron-hot brand on her ear were evidence enough.

Love, he'd taken to calling her...

She shivered.

He isn't the mad one, she realized. *It's me. I grow madder and madder here by the day.*

Margot spent Sunday afternoon on her knees in the dirt.

When they returned from Mass, Merrick turned tail for the rickhouses. Margot let out a lengthy sigh, taking a long look at the manor. Her stomach soured at the thought of walking through the doors. Her noosed wedding gown was in there, waiting for her. Pulsing in a trunk upstairs, like Poe's tell-tale heart beneath the floorboards.

Margot stared at the house, and it stared back. Its mullioned windows were like the paned mosaic of dragonfly wings, glinting in the midday sun. Winking at her, drawing her in.

She crossed her arms, trying very hard not to feel silly. *Don't be a ninny.*

Evangeline walked by. She wore a pair of dirt-stained dungarees and wellington boots, her arms laden with gardening supplies. She followed Margot's uneasy gaze to the house before wordlessly offering a shovel.

Margot needed nothing more. She followed Evangeline down the hill to a plot of freshly tilled soil near the stables.

"Turnips, radish, collards, and pumpkin...fall harvest begins with mid-summer planting," Evangeline explained, handing off packets of seeds. "An inch deep, all in a row down this line."

And that was that. Margot dropped to her knees and set to work, reveling in the feel of soft dirt beneath her fingers, sunshine on her face, and a quiet, focused mind.

As she worked her way down the line, Evangeline followed, running her hands atop the fresh soil. Eyes closed, lips moving. Halfway through the planting, she noticed Margot staring.

"They can't talk back yet"—Evangeline nodded toward the ground—"but even seedlings can listen. What we exhale, nature inhales."

A bead of sweat dripped down Margot's nose, falling into the dirt. Evangeline smiled, pleased, then closed her eyes and resumed her benediction.

It wasn't until the sun began to fade that Margot rocked back on her heels and wiped sweat from her brow. She shifted in the dirt to look at the house atop the hill. With the sinking sun behind the building, the manor cast a long shadow. The two towers stretched toward her like greedy fingers, eager to repossess their quarry.

She sighed and rose to her feet, her gaze perusing the pasture. Julian was out there, holding the reins of a palomino. Beyond him, on the outskirts, Margot spied two men at the pasture fence, deep in discussion. Merrick was closer to her, his profile clearly visible. At first glance, his posture was relaxed, leaning forward over the rail. Casual confidence and power. But the longer she looked, the less comfortable she became. His broad shoulders were taut, stretching the planes of his white shirt to their limits, pulling at seams. And though his right hand dangled freely over open air, the fingers of his left were curled tightly around the pasture rail.

She recognized the stature of his silver-grayed companion.

Alastair Pendry.

What is he doing here? Her heart fluttered.

Alastair was speaking...ranting, more like. He gesticulated wildly over the fence at the grazing horses.

Julian turned, stretching the palomino's reins as he angled closer. Listening.

Alastair's mouth continued to move a mile a minute.

Ruth hovered nearby, the equestrian trainer's face half-hidden in the shadows where she lurked in the stable doorway. She stared at the pair with a murderous glint in her eyes. Her arms were tightly crossed, her toe tapping steadily. Her ice blue gaze flicked to Margot.

Ruth nodded pointedly at her, then toward the pair. *Get over there,* she seemed to say.

And do what?

Merrick cracked his knuckles over the railing as he listened, and the sight forced her into action.

"Merrick?" she called, beginning to move.

He startled, then held out a hand, signaling her to wait. He turned back to Alastair to say a few brief words, nodding as he spoke. Alastair's sour face lightened incrementally, appeased. He reached into his pocket and passed over three sheets of paper. Merrick scrawled something—presumably his signature—across the bottom of each page, then handed one back to Alastair.

Margot watched as final false pleasantries were exchanged, then Alastair turned and headed up the hill, departing.

She sighed with relief and continued walking. Merrick met her halfway, folding the papers and sticking them in his pocket.

"What was that about?" she asked.

He gestured uphill toward the house. "Shall we?"

"Merrick." She fell into step. "What did Alastair want?"

"Same thing he always wants, my distillery and my horses."

The horses she understood, but the distillery…the estate was bankrupt because of it. Bourbon was a poor investment these days.

"What sordid trouble have you gotten yourself into today?" he asked, eyeballing her dirty yellow dress, the mud caked under her fingernails.

"I'd hardly call gardening with Evangeline *sordid*," she replied. "Though I could ask the same of you." She indicated his smoke-stained shirt, undone at the collar to reveal a teasing glimpse of dark chest hair. Margot's cheeks flushed, and she lowered her gaze. His sleeves were rolled up to expose sooty hands and forearms, two fresh burn marks marring the skin.

"Don't know what you mean."

"You've been making barrels again today." She tweaked his nicked hand, and he flinched away.

"How do you know about the barrels?"

"You have warehouses full of them," she said. "All empty, gathering cobwebs. Why?"

"You're not supposed to be sniffing around the distillery."

"Julian offered to show me." Bit of a fib, but necessary.

"If you wanted a tour, all you had to do was ask." He ran a hand through his hair, rumpling it. Grumpy.

"You certainly didn't make it sound that way when I arrived. You all but forbade me from going near the rickhouses. I wonder *why*." She injected the final word with a touch of sarcasm. Thanks to Xander, she now knew precisely why, but she wanted to hear Merrick say it.

He held silent.

"And when would I have asked you?" she continued, picking up steam. "You've been avoiding me."

"I have not."

"You most certainly have."

"I most certainly have not."

She snorted. "You're a child."

"I'm not a child," he snapped, finally losing his composure. He jabbed two fingers toward the distillery behind them. "I'm a *man*. A man trying desperately to preserve a family business that hasn't turned a profit in over a decade. I'm a man busting his ass from sunup to sundown to do the work of twenty, *alone*. A man who has been on his own—managing an entire estate—since he was sixteen goddamn years old. Half my miserable life. So forgive me if I haven't paid you enough attention, *darling*, but the world does not, *cannot*, stop turning every time a debutante bride comes to Dravenhearst Manor." He finished in a wild huff, his eyes alight with fire and something Margot, with her own grief-seasoned gaze, recognized as pain.

She didn't have experience with raging men, but Margot did know what it was like to feel all alone in the world.

Half my miserable life, he'd said. *Alone.*

She took a deep breath. "I only asked about the barrels." Her voice was soft. "Will you tell me about them?"

"What?" His tone was still quite fierce. Unwilling to back down.

"I'd like to know about them. How you make them, why you make them, everything about them. They're magnificent."

They were outside the manor, on the portico before the front door.

"I..." His voice cracked. "I make them to remember. Bourbon spends years in the barrel, the distillate diffusing in and out of the wood's pores. We call it the devil's cut, the portion the barrel absorbs during maturation. But what remains, what *survives*, is stronger for it, sharpened and aged. Loss turned transformative."

"Transformative," she repeated softly. She'd never thought of loss in such a manner. "Who taught you how to make them?"

"No one taught me." His brows dipped, frown lines appearing. "I taught myself."

"Not your father?"

"He bought his barrels. I bought 'em too, before Prohibition. But then the money dried up, and I had to find another way."

"Well, there's plenty of money now." *It's why you married me.* "If you still need more barrels—though I can't imagine why—we can place an order for a shipment."

He shook his head. "I don't believe in paying another man for a job I can do myself."

It wasn't the answer she'd expected. She tilted her head.

"The tide is turning against Prohibition, Margot. Mark my words, I'll be making and selling bourbon by the new year. Which means I need to start filling barrels as soon as possible. That's what Alastair was doing here, trying to shake me down." He reached into his pocket and pulled out the papers, handing the top copy to her.

"What's this?" She skimmed the document, her head twinging at numbers and sums running up and down the page. She thrust it toward him, immediately disinterested.

"It's a bill. For a grain shipment from Alastair's farm," he explained. He pushed the paper back into her hands. "I need it to make mash. That's your copy."

"Why do I need a copy?" she asked, confused. *And what the hell is mash?*

Merrick stuck his hands back in his pockets and looked skyward, avoiding eye contact. "For your records. Because I'm going to repay you. Every cent."

Margot narrowed her eyes. "Repay me?"

"It's technically your money, not mine—which Alastair made damn sure I knew." His jaw ticked. "I don't have enough scratch left in my own accounts to kickstart the distillery into working order, but once we start selling bourbon again, the cashflow will follow. Consider this a start-up loan. One I intend to repay in full, soon as I'm able."

"Your accounts...my accounts..." Margot shook her head. "We're married. What's mine is yours. *Ours.* You don't have to ask for a loan."

"I want to." His eyes snapped to hers. "I'm not proud I have to, but I sacrificed my pride a long time ago to keep the distillery afloat."

He offered nothing else. No excuses, no pleas. Margot found she admired him for it. She could tell this was important to him, even if she didn't fully understand why. Slowly, she nodded. "Okay then. A loan."

"Thank you." He pulled the creaky door open for her. They walked up the stairs in silence, past the portrait of Babette and Richard.

It wasn't until they were standing outside their separate doors that Merrick spoke again, his voice barely above a whisper. "Margot? Do you know how many jobs Prohibition cost in this state?"

"I...what?" The question caught her off-guard. "I've no clue how many distilleries were shut down, but I'm sure hundreds of good men—"

"Hundreds?" He shook his head. "Try *thousands*. The distilleries are but the tip of the iceberg. What about the barrel cooperages? Bottle manufacturers? Farmers who supplied the grain for bourbon mash? Do you know how much money Kentucky lost in taxable revenue? How many state programs went underfunded before being cut?"

"I...I've never thought of it," she murmured, lowering her lashes.

"Most people don't," he whispered. "Most people say this economic depression started the day the market crashed, but a struck match won't catch ablaze without kindling. And the drys pushing temperance made sure there was plenty of it lying around in this state."

Margot nodded.

"That inheritance of yours?" He looked away, down the empty corridor. "It's a real privilege. I admire your father for everything he's built. You should too. I just..." He sighed and cut his gaze back to hers. "It's hard for me to hear the way you talk about it sometimes, how you take it for granted. God knows, I did the same, but if I could go back..."

Margot reached for his arm, suddenly understanding. She'd thrown her inheritance in his face more than once, testing him, perhaps seeking to hurt him. Not because she was ungrateful, but insecure. It was all she had to offer, the only reason a man like him might desire a woman like her. "You're right. I've been flippant. I apologize for that. It was never my intent."

He nodded and stuck his hands in his pockets. "Did you have a chance to review the papers I left you yesterday? On your nightstand?"

She frowned, thinking of the envelope beside the hydrangeas. In the midst of the tumultuous events that unfolded overnight and this morning, it was the furthest thing from her mind. "Er, no. That was from you? I assumed...a letter from my father."

"It's a copy of your father's will, freshly notarized, as well as our marriage contract."

She smiled. "Sounds dreadfully boring."

"You ought to read it."

She searched his serious eyes, uncertain. "I suppose I can make time—"

"If you look it over now, we can discuss it during dinner."

Margot shook her head. "I can't possibly have it read before dinner. I'll look it over before bed tonight, will that suffice?"

"Yes." He cracked open his door. "If you, er, need any assistance, just give a holler. I know you're likely used to having a lady's maid help you clean and dress for dinner. I'm sorry we don't...can't afford to staff one. It's been all I could do to protect Xander and Evangeline from unemployment these last few years."

Was that the hint of a blush rising in his suntanned cheeks?

"I don't need a lady's maid," she murmured. That was all going by the wayside these days anyway. Households were doing more with less, employing fewer staff. And he did seem to be terribly sensitive about money, her husband. She was only just beginning to understand the hardship hidden beneath his brusqueness. She eyed the flickering candles lighting the hallway with wry amusement. "But I will be turning on the lights in my room. Factor that into your electricity bill tabulations."

His soft smile and answering chuckle played on loop in Margot's mind for the rest of the evening.

14

July 9, 1933

Mr. Merrick Dravenhearst,
Tonight.

—A

T HREE BEAUTIFUL BUTTERFLIES, ALL in a row.
One silver, smaller than the others. One gold, near-translucent and difficult to see. And the final one, the largest, was the deepest shade of violet. The patterns on their wings were like mirrored inkblots—perfectly symmetric, whimsically chaotic. Glitter trailed on the breath of chilled wind beneath their wings.

Margot reached, mesmerized, but they slipped away, always beyond her grasp. Their pixie dust dispersed, like trying to capture smoke with her bare hands.

"Margot, catch me!" The tiny silver butterfly danced ahead.

Eli?

"Margot, we're flying!" His voice echoed, repeating a dozen times. Ripples on a lake.

The glitter-tinged world came into brassy focus, dripped in sepia, soft around the edges like film negatives. Margot was in a field at dusk, surrounded by golden wheat at the golden hour. The air was cold. Two butterflies danced ahead, weaving in and out of stalks. The violet butterfly paused, hovering before her.

"Watch this," it called, voice teasing. Familiar.

The butterfly zipped forward, flying loops around Margot's head and neck, sprinkling lavender fairy dust in her hair, over her bare collarbone. Margot breathed deeply, inhaling glitter. Shivering. The scent...sultry jasmine.

Margot raised her hands, palms open, as the silver butterfly came near. Tantalizingly close. Away. Close. Away. Again and again, ebbing and flowing like the tide.

"Please," Margot begged, silver tears running down her cheeks, freezing as they fell. "Eli, take my hand."

Pop! The soft scene burst like a soap bubble. The world sharpened. Stalks of gentle wheat turned pointed, razor-thin edges precise enough to draw blood. The gold butterfly flew right, soaring over the weapon-like wheat toward the towering magnolias at the edge of the field.

"Where is she going?" Margot asked.

It was the violet butterfly who answered. "She lives amongst the magnolias."

"Who does?"

A giggle. "Eleanor, of course."

The silver butterfly left next, flying skyward, disappearing into the heavens.

"And him? Where does he live?" Margot jumped to follow, flapping imaginary wings. Dreaming of an imaginary place and an imaginary brother who wasn't dead but, rather, waited for her with open arms.

I'd fly to the edge of the world for you, she vowed, flapping her wings. *I'd give anything—my life, my heart. I'd give it all up to reach you. Just once. Just for five more minutes.*

But her wings were only arms, her heart only human. And her two feet remained planted firmly and bitterly on the ground.

"The edge of the world?" the violet butterfly asked, wings winking.

Margot touched her lips. *Did I say that out loud?*

"If it's the edge of the world you're after, I can take you. Come."

Margot followed, leaving a trail of blood in her wake as the wheat stalks cut into her like jagged teeth. Deep ruby raindrops showered to the earth, the grain bending toward her as a flower tilts to the sun, hungry for more. The scent of jasmine mixed with iron hung heavy in the air.

At the edge of the field, a cathedral of stained glass rose before her. A lighthouse lit against the falling darkness, beaming color into the night. Margot tilted her head back in awe.

"In here." The violet butterfly landed on a purple pane, then melted through it, disappearing.

Margot pressed her palm to the cold window, but the pane didn't give. Her breath fogged the glass. "How?"

She tilted her head, studying the cathedral walls.

Only glass, she realized. Glass, which was made to be broken. Had to be, if she was to pass through. *Through the looking glass.*

She pressed two hands to the panes and bent her fingers, imagining claws. She raked her nails downward, leaving ten fissures. An earsplitting screech rent apart the night.

Margot liked it. She smiled and did it again. And again. And again. Chunks of multicolored crystal tumbled like jewels from a treasure chest onto the ground. Shards of sugary rainbow rock candy fell in clumps from the sky. The tears of angels, reflective and prismatic and pure, rained to the earth around her. And everywhere Margot looked...turning red. Blood streamed from her frozen fingers. Bled from the glass to the ground, forming a river.

"Margot, stop it!" A new voice. Gruff, insistent. Inherently male.

But nothing could stop her. She raked her nails down the glass again, chipping deeper. She had to get *in*. The edge of the earth. Elijah and Babette. They were all that mattered. They were there, and she—

"Margot, *wake up!*"

A stinging slap registered on her cheek. She blinked in shock.

And then she was falling.

Falling.

Falling.

Falling.

Through the looking glass she came. Whole and dazed and wild and awake. Her eyes fluttered rapidly as she tried to understand. Warm arms encircled her, holding her up.

"Margot?" It was Merrick.

Merrick's voice in her ear, his calloused hands gripping her bare arms. A strap of her nightdress slipped off her shoulder.

Her legs wobbled. She licked her lips, looking around. It was a foggy night, and she was outside Dravenhearst Manor. Outside and down the hill by the distillery. One hand scratched ferally at the wood of the sealed door to Rickhouse One. The other was wrapped in the iron chains barring the doors. All ten of her fingers, her nails, were ragged. Trickling with blood.

"Oh my God," she cried, her voice shaking. She released her grip on the door.

"It's all right."

It was very much *not* all right. Margot wasn't sure she'd ever been less all right in her entire life. "What's happening to me?"

"We'll get you inside and...and cleaned up," he said weakly, eyeing her bloody hands.

But when Margot looked at the fog-shrouded manor on the hill, her gut clenched with anxiety. The roadster was pulled around front, engine idling and headlights on. He'd been sneaking out again. That was why he'd found her. She should be grateful. Who knows what she might've done.

Yes, grateful...

But she wasn't sure she was.

Margot took a deep breath and pulled back. Far enough away to look directly into his amber eyes. "I think your house is haunted."

He didn't move. Didn't breathe.

She waited.

"Do you want to leave?" he finally asked. "You read the contracts, the will. You can go at any time."

She swallowed. She'd read them. Before bed, as she'd promised. Her father had done something extraordinary—he'd inserted a prenuptial clause. One that could only be voided with her consent, with her signature on a blank line. She could leave right now and take everything with her. It was a surprise, highly unusual to give a woman that kind of autonomy in her marriage.

Even more unusual, Merrick had signed it, agreed to the terms.

She tilted her head, her lips parted.

"Ask me," he said, his voice gruff. "Go ahead."

"Why on earth did you consent to those terms?" His answer mattered to her. It mattered immensely.

His arms still gripped hers. Her eyes searched, trying desperately to understand. As much as she'd wanted to break through the glass in her dream, that was how much she wanted his answer now. To hear the words she longed for from him.

"Because I'd hoped it wouldn't matter. Because I hope you'll stay."

15

July 10, 1933

Mr. Merrick Dravenhearst,
Where were you last night?

—A

*H*E DIDN'T DENY IT.

Margot paced back and forth in her bedroom the next morning.
It had been a dangerous thing to say. A statement that could, conceivably,
get her locked up in an asylum—talk of visions and ghosts and hauntings.

But he hadn't denied it.

I think your house is haunted, she'd said.

Do you want to leave? he'd asked in return.

She'd struggled with the question all morning, had packed and un-
packed her trunks a half dozen times in the last two hours, deliberating.

If she left her husband mere weeks into marriage, she'd be ruined.
She'd never marry again, never have a family. Her father's business, once
he passed, would rot into oblivion, and she'd be "mad Margaret" for all
eternity.

But it was even more mad to stay...wasn't it?

Margot paused her pacing to look in the mirror. For just a moment, a vision of Babette reflected back at her—eyes twinkling, hair burnished like the sunrise, the same as in the oil portrait. Margot blinked, once, twice, until her own image stared back. She shook her head, unsettled.

She should leave. They could have the marriage annulled. It would be shameful, yes, but Margot had been living with shame for years. She was the daughter who survived, not the son. It's what had landed her in this mess in the first place—her own weakness, inherent in both her gender and her constitution.

A knock on the door interrupted her thoughts.

"Margot?" Merrick called. "You in there?"

She contemplated remaining silent. It would serve him right, given his own propensity for brooding. But petty looked good on no one, least of all Margot. With a heavy sigh, she swung open the door.

"I was wondering..." Merrick paused and took a deep breath. "Uh, well, first of all, good morning."

Her forehead creased. "Good morning."

His next words came out quickly, all in a rush. "I was wondering if you might take a walk with me?"

"A walk?"

He licked his lips. "Yes. In the back gardens, perhaps?"

Margot chewed on her cheek, considering. His hands were in his pockets, but she could see them fidgeting, the material twisted and tortured beneath his fingers. She'd never seen him nervous before. Merrick always appeared quite unflappable—mysterious at times, but never unsure.

She bit her bottom lip. "All right."

"Yes?" He lifted his eyes hopefully.

"Yes. Is everything okay?"

"It is." The answer came fast, much too fast.

She tilted her head. "You're a terrible liar, you know. Which is odd. You do it so often, I'd really assume you'd be better at it."

He scowled as she fell into step beside him. "When have I ever lied to you?"

"You've done nothing but lie through your teeth since the night we met. Have you forgotten the bourbon—'hints of woodsmoke and clove with a caramel finish?' A load of malarkey!"

He laughed deeply. The formality of his posture loosened, his arm relaxing to brush hers. A swooping sensation settled in Margot's stomach.

"Malarkey or not, I recall you drinking it. Not once, but twice. So maybe I'm not such a bad liar after all."

"I did, didn't I?" It was her turn to laugh.

"Thought you were going to spit it out all over my shirt."

She laughed harder, lifting a hand to her mouth. "I nearly did."

"Well, you gulped it down like water. It's meant to be savored and appreciated. It's—"

"An acquired taste," she finished, looking at him with a smile. For the first time since coming to the manor, she felt a sense of budding familiarity.

*Perhaps...*she thought, her gaze tracing his face. *Perhaps there could be something here worth staying for after all.*

It was a beautiful morning for a turn outside. The flowerbeds and hedges were chaotic in the way of an unkept English garden, filled with wildflowers, vines, and an overflowing abundance of color. But the closer Margot looked, the more she realized just how intentional Evangeline had been with each placement—the tall fragrant lavender beside the low-lying dusty miller, the English rose bushes in irregular patches but always at the edge where they'd receive direct sun. Yarrow was mixed in with sweet peas. Hollyhocks climbed skyward on trellises.

Merrick didn't speak as he guided her deeper into the garden. The gravel path crunched softly beneath their feet. They came upon a stone bench amidst peonies, a creeping vine curling its tresses around the base.

Merrick gestured toward the seat. "I'd like to have a very honest conversation with you."

"All right." Her voice was breathy and false, very much unlike her own. As she settled on the bench, her pulse fluttered in her throat. Margot could feel it, just beneath the skin of her neck, thudding as fast as the feet of a rabbit in flight.

Merrick sat beside her. "It occurred to me last night that I haven't been fair to you. I'm not used to coexisting with someone, clearing my schedule with anyone, making plans to include another...I've been on my own for quite a long time.

"And where I've perhaps been most unfair," he continued, leaning forward with his hands clasped, "is leaving you to your own devices in my home. Without addressing the, er—perhaps we can call them idiosyncrasies?—the idiosyncrasies of my life and estate. And my family. I gather from your words last night, you've spoken to others about it?"

"Well, Ruth mentioned a few things about Babette...about your mother," she corrected. "And Xander said something about...a curse? The Dravenhearst suicide brides, he called it."

"*Xander* did?" He raised his eyebrows. "You must've caught him in a good moment."

Margot didn't particularly want to tell him the "good moment" came after an episode of her sleepwalking through the manor at midnight. What Merrick didn't know couldn't hurt him.

"What I don't understand though," he said, turning to look directly at her, "is why you didn't come straight to me and ask."

Margot blinked in surprise. "What?"

"If you had questions about things going on in my—*our* home, questions about my family, why didn't you just ask me?"

She was disarmed by the question, perfectly valid though it was. Why *hadn't* she simply gone straight to him and asked?

"B-because...I wasn't entirely sure what you would say. And honestly"—she flicked her gaze over him—"I wasn't certain you would tell me the truth. You've hardly given me a plethora of reasons to trust you." She cast her eyes down, thinking of his midnight jaunts in the roadster. She didn't dare bring those up. She couldn't. "And you haven't been around much."

"I'm here now. What do you want to know?"

"Is it true?" Her voice cracked. "Did both your mother and your grandmother kill themselves? In that rickhouse?"

"Yes."

"In their wedding gowns?" It sounded too sensational to be real, surely this part, at least, was—

"Yes."

She leaned back, eyes wide.

Merrick chose his words with care. "There has been a great deal of sadness in this house, particularly for the women who have lived here. I can't pretend to fully understand it, but Evangeline will no longer come inside, and Ruth hardly ever does. They feel something in the manor I don't. Have you felt it?"

She nodded, unable to speak.

He sighed, his fingers flexing. "I don't believe in curses. People have a choice in their fate, and my mother *chose* to kill herself. Saying a curse made her do it is providing her an excuse she doesn't deserve. But even I must admit a preternatural sadness hangs heavy in this house. It's something I never intended to bring a bride of my own into. You asked if my house is haunted?" He rubbed his thumb in tight, small circles on his opposite wrist. "I think it's possible. Cursed? No. Haunted?" He licked his lips.

"Possibly. It seemed unfair to expose another woman to that, suspecting what I did."

"And yet, here I am."

"Yes, here you are." His eyes were sad. "I'm sorry. I shouldn't have...I never thought I would—"

She reached out to grip his wrist. "It's okay. You don't have to explain. I understand."

"Do you, though?" He searched her gaze, his amber eyes piercing.

"Desperate times make people do desperate things. You needed money, and I needed a husband. You asked, I accepted. You said everyone has a choice in their fate? I chose *you*. I didn't have to, but I did."

"You didn't have all the information."

"I still would have chosen you," she whispered. She hadn't realized it until this very moment, but even this knowledge wouldn't have driven her into Alastair's arms.

Because when she looked at Merrick, she felt *something*. She wasn't quite sure what, but whatever it was gave her hope. And hope was a feeling stronger than anything else. Stronger than fear. Stronger than sorrow. Stronger than any curse or haunting could ever be.

Hope was a feeling worth staying for.

"If that's true, then you're mad." He snorted in disbelief.

She cocked her head, waiting for the sting of his words to hit. Surprisingly, it never did.

"I think it means I fit in here," she reasoned, smiling.

He laughed outright this time, shooting her a sidelong glance. "You fit in fine as frog's hair, right alongside the rest of us—the others crazy enough to stay."

"It would be nice," she said, trying to be brave, "to belong to a family again. To build my own family. With you."

He shifted at her words.

"You said we could have an honest conversation—"

"I did, and I meant it. You want a family, then?" he asked. "Children?"

"Of course. Don't you?"

The silence stretched, on and on.

"There is an expectation of course...that we would..." He gestured between them. "I mean, that's generally how things go...when people marry."

"You aren't the only one who's felt alone for a very long time," Margot murmured, looking at her hands, folded in her lap to keep from shaking. "And just because this house—*your* house—hasn't been happy for a great number of years, it doesn't mean we couldn't make it so again. Together." She raised her eyes to his, tentative. Hopeful.

"With children?"

With love. But she wasn't brave enough to say that. She bit her tongue, settling instead for a quick nod.

"I mean, if we did, I would love for...I would hope..." He grasped for words. "Perhaps, in time, we may develop feelings of fondness toward one another...but I don't expect that from you, not given our circumstances."

Fondness.

"I would happily settle, in the interim," he continued, "for mutual respect and friendship. I don't know about you, but I could certainly use a friend."

A *friend.* Her heart stirred as she recalled her father's words. *Friendship is a very good place to start.*

"Yes," she said softly. "Yes, I could use a friend."

"Well...well, good."

"And as far as children would go," she continued. "How, uh, might that happen?"

"Well, I imagine it would just...happen. If and when the time is right." Was that a blush rising on his face? A hint of pink tinging his sun-kissed cheeks?

"Right."

"Right," he echoed.

She looked expectantly at him.

He squirmed under her gaze. "Why are you looking at me like that?"

"I'm just trying to figure out how it's going to work, that's all. Have you ever...before?"

She thought again of him sneaking out at night and looked away, feeling foolish. For a moment, she'd almost forgotten. And that made her terribly foolish indeed.

This man was dangerous. In more ways than one.

"Never mind." She shook her head, precluding his answer. "You don't have to explain anything to me."

"Maybe I want to."

When she turned, he was looking straight at her, his amber eyes so focused, they burned. Blazing. Hot as fire.

She waited, trying to remember to breathe.

"Can we just...can we try something for a second?" He turned to face her, swinging one leg over the bench to straddle it. "Margot?"

"Yes?"

And slowly, so slowly, he moved his hand up her arm, over her shoulder, brushing her hair back from her neck.

"Can we try something quick?" he asked again, whispering now.

His hand wound its way fully into her hair. The other held her cheek. He was so close, she could see every eyelash. Every dimple. He waited.

"Yes." She gave permission.

Barely a breath later, his lips closed over hers.

It was strange at first, the feeling. Margot was self-conscious, paralyzed with the terrible fear of messing up. She stiffened, too wrapped up in her own mind to let him in.

Merrick pulled back, his eyes uncertain.

Now you've done it. A nasty voice spoke in her head. *You've gone and ruined it. Your one shot and look what you did with it.*

But he was still there, barely an inch away. Waiting for her.

She knew this was important. She shook her head, trying to shake off the fear. "I can do better," she murmured. This time, she leaned in. This time, she was the one to press her lips to his. She didn't think, didn't fight. She only *felt*. Moving her lips to fit his, feeling the rhythm. Leaning into it. The softness. His surety.

It felt *good*. Wonderfully good.

She wondered if he felt it too?

He gave her his answer by deepening the kiss, sliding both hands to her cheeks, dragging them through her hair. A quiet rumble of pleasure vibrated through his chest. She reached for his shoulders, grabbing on for dear life. As if he was the only solid thing in the world, the garden swirling and tilting around her. Disorienting.

If this be madness, then let it devour me.

When he finally pulled back, she was breathless and lightheaded. The way she usually felt just before she fainted.

The world kept turning, blurs of color in her periphery, but Merrick stayed still. And there were his amber eyes, pinning her down, centering her in his gravitational pull.

In that moment, all Margot knew was the somersaulting sensation soaring through her stomach felt like a heck of a lot more than *fondness*.

16

July 11, 1933

My dearest Margaret,
Wellness is a generality these days, but you may assume your
letters always find me so, made better simply by tracing the
ink of your words over a page. I feel your hesitancy through
that ink, daughter. You say the house is lovely—I confess relief
at your words. There were rumors, many years ago, but you
and I know a thing or two about gossip. Often malicious,
rarely true.
Perhaps you and your new husband have more in common
than you think.

Forever Yours,
Pa

W HEN MARGOT WOKE THE next morning, she no longer contemplated packing her trunk. Her kiss with Merrick had settled the matter. She was staying.

But.

But...

Merrick had conceded there was something unnatural about the house. Xander, Evangeline, and Ruth had all expressed fears of history repeating itself. Even young Julian, who hadn't lived through the events of the past, had extended his own vague warning.

Perhaps there was a curse, perhaps not. But *if* there was, Margot was inarguably the next target.

History repeating itself, she mused, dressing for the day. Did this only refer to the suicides? Or was there more at play here? Babette had reached out to Margot in her dreams. Had anyone, Eleanor perhaps, reached out to Babette?

There was only one way to find out.

And conveniently, the person who likely held answers had given Margot an open invitation to tea.

"So what'll it be?" Ruth's grin was playful as she invited Margot inside Hellebore House. "Doilies and fine china?" She gestured toward a curio cabinet, then lifted her opposite hand to indicate the sideboard. "Or shall we make a real afternoon of it and dip into the giggle water?"

Margot's experience with alcohol was limited, but judging from the impressive array of hooch on display—most bottles less than half full—Ruth was a connoisseur.

"Gin rickeys on the porch in the summer..." Margot eyed the bottles, trying to hide her trepidation. "Isn't that what you and Babette liked?"

A flicker of interest sparked. "We did."

"I see no reason to break tradition."

"Spoken like a true Dravenhearst." Ruth's eyes glinted with approval.

As Ruth prepared their drinks, Margot surveyed the selection on the credenza. She lifted a tall, rectangular bottle filled to the midpoint with a rich amber solution. The label was faded and peeling but clearly read *Dravenhearst Distilling*. In smaller print below came the year, 1912.

"Ah, Merrick's pride and joy, that is," Ruth said, nodding to the bottle. "It's from the 1912 collection, a particularly good crop of corn and one of Richard's more experimental mash bills. It was the first season Richard let Merrick do full tastings alongside him to decide whether the bourbon was ready to be pulled and bottled."

"1912?" Margot furrowed her brow. "But in 1912, Merrick must've been only..."

Ruth laughed. "Ten years old."

Margot dropped the bottle onto the sideboard with a clatter. "Started him early, I see."

Ruth waved this observation away. "Merrick had his first taste of bourbon slipped into his milk bottles. Helped with teething." She clucked her tongue and lifted her eyebrows. "He was a terribly fussy baby. Hopefully, it doesn't run in the family."

"Oh, I don't think we have to worry about that just yet," Margot replied, trying to keep her tone light.

"Mmm." Ruth raised a highball glass and sampled her gin rickey. She smacked her lips twice before splashing in an additional dollop of gin. "That's what Babette thought too, but she was late after only their first month of marriage. She miscarried the first, but it wasn't long before she was expecting again." She rolled her eyes, and Margot felt a frisson of anxiety at how cavalierly Ruth discussed another woman's fertility. "Merrick was born only a few months after their first wedding anniversary. Quite the fairytale, no?" But her eyes glittered with something that told Margot it hadn't been a fairytale. Not in the slightest.

She remained silent, accepting her glass.

"Do you want children, Margot?" Ruth's blue eyes were clear and piercing.

Margot took a sip, stalling. "I...well..." She licked her lips, tasting the tartness of the drink on her tongue. "We've only just wed."

"It can happen quickly."

"Well, yes. Yes, I realize that..." Her cheeks colored. She wasn't on even footing with Ruth, who talked about sex and pregnancy as casually as one might discuss a summer rainstorm. A single woman, yet far more confident and self-assured in these matters than Margot, a blushing virgin bride.

Ruth took a second sip of her drink. "Shall we take to the veranda?"

Margot offered a thin smile, grateful to let the matter drop. It would be highly embarrassing to reveal just how inexperienced she still was. Everyone expected something more from her. As a wife, and soon, probably, as a mother. It seemed important to be in on this secret. To be able to navigate the waters of womanhood with an ease that only came from experience.

Experience she simply didn't have.

Margot sniffed in frustration and turned her head. She gazed over the railing of Hellebore House and into the garden, which spilled over—fittingly—with hellebore flowers. She took a deep drink and closed her eyes.

Ruth settled on the porch swing with a soft creak. "I didn't mean to upset you."

Margot didn't open her eyes. If she did, she worried they would brim with tears. That was a weakness she simply couldn't afford. Not in front of a woman with as many hard edges as Ruth.

"Speaking of the past is...well, frankly, it's rather maudlin. Babette's marriage has no bearing on your own."

Margot's eyes snapped open. Ruth shifted on the swing but said nothing more, only began to rock slowly.

Margot pursed her lips, deliberating how much to share. In her experience, people tended to reward honesty with honesty.

"I've seen her," she whispered.

Ruth halted her swinging. "Who?"

"Babette."

"That's...not possible," Ruth said, shaking her head. "You mean Eleanor, don't you?"

"Why does everyone keep asking that?" Margot's eyes sharpened. "Did Babette see Eleanor? Did she talk to her, dream of her?"

Ruth swallowed nervously.

"She must've told you," Margot insisted. "You were her best friend."

Ruth sucked down the remainder of her gin rickey in one swig, then rose to her feet. "If we're going to talk about *this*, I'm going to need another drink."

"The dreams started a few weeks after we arrived," Ruth began, clutching her refilled glass. "Babette didn't...she didn't realize what was happening at first, didn't tell me about it until other things started happening too."

Margot leaned in. "Like what?"

"Odd things." Ruth furrowed her brow. "Things moving around her room, items Richard certainly wouldn't care to touch. A hairbrush, her perfume or paints, some clothes...dresses, I believe."

Margot held her tongue, though she was dying to ask about Babette's wedding gown.

"It would have been fairly innocuous if not for the dreams. She said Eleanor spoke to her, took her around the manor, showed her things at night. At first, I wasn't certain I believed her, but then she started *knowing* things, secrets about the house. About Eleanor.

"We ran around the manor playing detective for a spell. I wish we hadn't—there wasn't anything good to learn about Eleanor. Her life was full of sadness." Ruth shuddered. "She was plagued with miscarriages, six to be precise. One for each magnolia tree lining the front drive. She planted a new one after each loss. She was obsessive about children in a way that made Babette nervous. When she miscarried"—her eyes darted to Margot's, testing the waters—"Babette insisted Eleanor caused it, that it was her fault."

"Why did she think that?"

Ruth pursed her lips. "She drank something in the middle of the night. The cup was still on her bedside table when we found her in the morning. The physician said she'd ingested something toxic, and she lost the baby. When she recovered, Babette insisted Eleanor made her drink the tea, that she *wanted* her to miscarry, that it would make them better friends if she understood."

Margot read the doubt in her eyes. "You didn't believe her?"

"I certainly didn't at first. And Richard..." Ruth blew out a nervous exhale. "Richard was convinced Babette intentionally induced the miscarriage. He claimed she didn't want the child." She laughed bitterly. "Well, he wasn't wrong. That first pregnancy happened so quickly. She wasn't ready.

"After the miscarriage, Eleanor disappeared," she continued. "Babette didn't have any more dreams until she was expecting again, with Merrick. But things were very different the second time."

"How so?"

Ruth laughed again. "All you had to do was tell Babette she couldn't have something to guarantee she would make it happen. She *wanted* Merrick—possibly because Eleanor seemed determined she couldn't have him. It was a hellacious pregnancy, worse and worse with each successive month, until Babette was hardly herself at the end. I moved into her room halfway through, tried to keep her safe. She went into labor early, which was a blessing. As soon as Merrick was born, I moved out of the manor entirely. I'd seen enough." She looked straight at Margot. "If you came here today to tell me you've seen something, heard something, dreamed something, I'll believe you. I won't even be surprised. I stopped letting that house surprise me a long time ago."

"I've never seen Eleanor," Margot said, biting her lip. "But I've seen Babette. I've had dreams, and there's been some..." She trailed off, embarrassed to admit it, avoiding eye contact. "Sleepwalking. A few times. Some things moved around in my room as well."

Ruth's forehead creased with worry. "Margot, I don't mean to pry, but is there any chance you could be expecting? I only ask because that's when the visions, the *hauntings*"—she shivered—"started for Babette."

Margot vigorously shook her head. "No."

Ruth reached for her arm. "You can tell me. It's okay if you are, but—"

"I *can't* be." Her cheeks flamed with heat. "Merrick hasn't...we haven't..."

She couldn't finish the admission, but Ruth understood.

"Oh." Her eyes widened. *"Oh."*

Margot tightly crossed her legs, looking over the railing toward the rickhouses. "I mean, I'm sure we will..." she clarified, trying to hide her embarrassment. "We're just...taking things slow."

Ruth nodded. "Slow is good. If nothing else, I've learned a bit of caution with the Dravenhearst men is never a bad idea."

"Why do you say that?"

Ruth sighed, carefully considering her words. She tilted her empty glass, ice cubes rattling within it. "I think that may be a story for another day."

Margot rose to her feet. "It's one I'd like to hear. Same time tomorrow?"

17

July 12, 1903

Babs,

My secret recipe, as requested. Though I hardly foresee a reason you'll ever make these without me!

- Fill a highball glass with ice

- Add 4 ounces of gin (for those of weak constitution, 2 ounces will suffice)

- Add 1/2 ounce of fresh squeezed lime juice

- Top with (chilled) club soda

- Pinch of salt

- Garnish with one lime wheel

Yours,

Ruth

WHEN HE ASKED, MARGOT was on her third gin rickey of the day. She was downright giddy and giggly, very much not herself. That was how he got her to agree.

It was dusk, and she was hand-in-hand with Merrick, headed for the stables. Margot liked the feel of his fingers bound with hers. He was rubbing the back of her knuckles with the pad of his thumb, making tiny circles, and her world narrowed to that single contact point. The buzzing hum of the evening katydids droned around them, fuzzy and soothing.

"Looks like rain overnight." Merrick eyed the clouds. "We'll hurry. I only want to introduce you to Fox and Omaha. We'll be back to the manor before it storms."

"Fox?" She giggled, her head pleasantly light. Surely, anything named Fox couldn't be harmful. Foxes were tiny and cute, with pointed ears and whiskers.

"Yes, Fox. He won the Triple Crown three years ago," Merrick explained. "We retired him right after, turned him into a stud horse. Ruth thinks we'll make a good run for the Derby next spring with Omaha. He's still a bit green, but he's got Fox's stride and speed."

Merrick continued to chatter, full of excitement, and Margot nodded along. She was caught off-guard when they arrived at the stables. For a moment, she'd forgotten where they were headed.

Julian was exiting as they prepared to enter. "Mrs. Dravenhearst," he said, his lips curling in a slow grin. Margot was not above admitting he was quite handsome, particularly when he smiled like that, all dark hair and dimples. And that deep Kentucky drawl. "Well now, isn't this a pleasant surprise."

"Margot," she corrected, smiling back.

"And Merrick," her husband reminded, frowning with bemusement. "Just introducing Margot to Fox and Omaha. You headed home, Julian?"

"I am." He nodded toward the vicinity of Hellebore House and the woods. Perhaps he lived on the fringes of the estate like Ruth. Margot had yet to fully explore the grounds. "The horses are secured for the night. I reckon a storm is rollin' in—you two best hurry." With a cheeky wink at Margot, Julian departed.

"Come on, we'll be quick," Merrick said, tugging her hand.

Inside the stable, the smell of hay and horse was everywhere. She wrinkled her nose and held her breath, trying to keep the scent of manure at bay.

Merrick was talking, and she registered Fox's name several times as they approached a stall holding a towering, muscled bay stallion with a stark white blaze down his snout. He stomped his front hoof and nickered as Merrick approached.

Margot didn't like this, didn't like it one bit. Her heart rate ticked up. She couldn't make out Merrick's words; his lips were moving, but her ears were stuffed with cotton. Her mouth too, terribly dry.

She took a tiny inhale, just enough oxygen for subsistence as she tried to distance herself from the smell. It wasn't enough. A second tiny inhale. Her chest rose and fell, a fish out of water. Shallow. Gasping.

Merrick pulled her to a second stall. Another horse within, more chestnut than ruddy but with his own prominent white blaze. It was a leggy thing, very tall.

Margot placed a hand over her heart, hoping to steady it. She pulled subtly at her collar, seeking air. A flush rose on the back of her neck.

Distressing. So very distressing.

"Merrick," she panted.

"What do you think of him?" he asked, oblivious.

Her eyes latched onto the horse. *Remembering.*

"Strong," she managed.

She flinched, recalling in exquisite clarity the blunt force of hooves against her temple, how hard the fall had been. She began to sweat.

Merrick narrowed his eyes. "Are you okay?"

"It's warm," she gasped.

"You're rather pale." He stepped closer, and suddenly, there were two Merricks before her, wavering in her sight.

She reached for him, dots forming in her vision. She was going down. She only hoped the horse wouldn't get her, hurt her, when she went.

She didn't want to be afraid, but she was.

She didn't want to remember, but she did.

"Merrick?"

"Margot!"

She fell into darkness.

Margot's eyes fluttered open to dim light and a faint scattering of dust motes. The air smelled heavily of hay and musk. A horse whinnied nearby, and she instinctively thrust her arms up to protect her head.

Please, don't hurt me, she silently begged. She cracked open an eyelid, looking for Elijah. She had to get to him, help him. She struggled to get up. "Eli?"

"Margot?"

There was a man beside her. A man with tawny eyes. Worried eyes.

Not Eli.

She couldn't focus. She shoved the stranger aside, searching desperately for her brother. She'd seen him fall. She'd seen the horse towering over him before she'd been struck. Had heard the hoofbeats. She had to save him. She was the only one who could save him.

"Margot!"

Hands latched onto her arms, restraining her. Gentle yet firm. She traced them up to their owner. Golden and warm...bourbon eyes.

Merrick.

Though her heart continued to thunder, her mind slowed. She wasn't at Greenbrier with Elijah; she was at Dravenhearst Manor with Merrick. She was...

Margot looked around in confusion, saw the looming silhouette of a chestnut stallion over Merrick's shoulder.

Why in heckin' hell was she in the stables?

As she wiggled to rise, she realized the straps of her dress had been yanked down, exposing her chest and chemise.

"I'm sorry," Merrick murmured, looking away. "You were breathing strangely. I loosened it to try to help."

"It's fine." She made no move to cover the top of her exposed chemise. She was still feeling flushed.

"I'm going to get help, Ruth or Julian." Merrick stood. "I didn't want to leave while you were unconscious."

"Don't go," she said, reaching for him. "I'm fine. I'm sorry. I'm fine, really." She nearly choked on the lie. It tasted like the straw littering the stable floor, dry and coarse. She simply couldn't bear to be left alone with the horses, and she wasn't certain her wobbly legs would hold her if she tried to flee.

"You don't look fine."

She grabbed his hand and pulled him back to his knees. "Stay."

"What happened?"

"I just...started feeling strange all of a sudden. I told you, this happens occasionally." Actually, the more she looked around and breathed in the strong smell of horse, the more her claustrophobia returned. She closed her eyes against the onslaught, but then she heard a whinny.

Her eyes popped open, bulging. "I need to leave."

She tried to stand, legs trembling. Merrick's arms closed around her, forcing her down. "You just need to rest for a moment."

"No. I need to leave," she repeated. "Now."

His arms encircled her again, and she began to panic in earnest.

"Let me go!" she cried, clawing at his hold. Even as she fought, her legs buckled. Her neck pulsed with heat, and the room began to tunnel.

"Margot, stop!"

"Merrick," she gasped, desperate for air. "Take me out of here. Out. *Now.*" Her heart thudded explosively in her chest, and not enough oxygen, no amount of gulping breaths, could calm her.

She felt like she was going to die.

"Out," she barked, the single word harsh, expelled with a shuddering exhale. Her next breath hitched on the back of the last. And then the next. And the next.

He must not have liked the noise she was making, because he finally listened. Merrick scooped her up, tucking her against his chest. "Where?"

"Out," was all she could manage. She closed her eyes and buried her face in his shirt. Her next breath was filled with the smell of man. Smoky leather and oak-laden musk. She inhaled again, sucking down his scent like a woman possessed, filling her nostrils and her brain with it.

He smells like cedar and bourbon, she realized. *Like the rickhouses.*

The barn door opened with a whining creak. Then came the squelch of sticky evening air. The katydids buzzed loudly.

Merrick. Merrick. Merrick. She chanted his name in rhythm with his steps. Her heart slowed to match the tempo. Her hitching breaths gradually quieted, turning to soft, shuddering inhales.

Merrick's arms were taut and solid around her, so large they made her feel small. He kicked open the paddock gate and strode into the middle of the empty pasture. Finally, he came to a stop and laid her down in a patch of thick green grass. He grunted softly as he released her, his breath warm on the crown of her head.

Margot dug her fingers into the grass. She ripped out a handful and held it to her nose, breathing deep. In the absence of his overwhelming warmth and scent, she needed to be grounded by something tactile to banish the smell of horse from her mind.

Merrick watched her, wary.

She took a second sniff of grass, releasing an anxious noise, halfway between a sob and a laugh.

He sat beside her and rumpled his hair. His gaze darted sidelong to her, then away. To her, away. He was nervous, possibly afraid of her. Afraid of what she'd just done, showed him. Shame rushed in.

A tendency toward hysteria, the voices of a half dozen physicians burned her ears.

"I'm sorry," she whispered. She'd never wanted him to see it, how damaged she was.

"What the hell happened back there?" His words were demanding, but his manner wasn't. His eyes were wide, overflowing with concern. "Margot, one minute you were there with me, and the next, you weren't. And then you were...you were fighting me like a wild barn cat."

"I'm sorry," she repeated, feeling as small as an eight-year-old child. Now that she was out in the night air, exposed and illuminated by the soft light of the rising moon, she felt horrifically embarrassed.

"I'm waiting for an explanation," he said. Again, harsh words. But when she risked a glance at him, she saw tremendous softness in his eyes. She'd scared him. He was *worried*.

It was his overwhelming concern, concern in a place where she expected judgment, that unburdened her. She hadn't spoken of Elijah to anyone in years, had *especially* never spoken of what happened. Not beyond the initial recounting to her parents.

"I told you I didn't ride horses," she murmured, casting her eyes downward. "That was a lie. I used to ride all the time, and I was quite good. But I don't anymore. I don't...I can't be around horses. Not after what happened to my brother."

"Elijah?"

Margot's mouth went dry. *How did he know?*

"I've heard you say his name," Merrick said. "You said it just now in the stables. And I...I saw his gravestone at Greenbrier. His birthday is the same as yours." He didn't say what else he must have seen, Eli's death date.

"Yes, we are—*were*—twins."

He waited, digging his own fingers into the grass now. Fisting tightly.

"When we were fourteen, we went out riding together. We rode almost every day. We..." She swallowed. "He challenged me to a race."

His voice came to her, clear as day. *"Margot, catch me!"*

She was transported. Her lips formed the words, she heard them echoing in the night, as the scene played out before her eyes.

Elijah, streaking ahead on Cerberus, his dapple gray mount. His laugh carried by the wind to her ears. She hunched low over her mare, tucking in her knees and urging her to give chase. The sun caught her eyes, momentarily blinding her.

That was when it happened.

Margot saw a flicker in the grass. Cerberus did too. It was a copperhead, one that raised its head and hissed. Elijah's stallion jolted to a stop. Rearing, bucking. Her brother was thrown into the air. A scream rent apart the morning. To this day, she knew not whether the scream was Elijah's or hers. That was how it had always been between them—Margot had never quite known where she ended and her brother began. They were two halves of a whole. Two bodies, one soul.

Until suddenly, they weren't.

Margot slid off her mount as her brother tumbled to the ground, landing beside Cerberus's hooves. She sensed what was going to happen. She darted forward, knowing only she could prevent it, but she wasn't fast enough. Cerberus's hooves stomped down directly on the middle of Elijah's spine.

She would hear the resounding *crack* in her nightmares for years to come.

Margot continued to move, eyes only on her brother. Her *twin*. She didn't see Cerberus's rear leg kick, but she felt it when it slammed into her temple. She went down hard.

Head spinning.

Eyes blurring.

Heart breaking.

18

March 4, 1911 – June 3, 1925

Beloved Son, Dearest Brother—
Child of God who danced in sunbeams
Child of Earth who sleeps amongst clouds
On butterfly wings, be carried in
Be safe, be loved, be found
What we hold in our hearts shall never be lost
And you, dear child, sleep sound

—Tombstone of Elijah Greenbrier

I T WAS THE KIND of loss that fundamentally changes you. Changes the way your eyes see the world, the way your lungs draw air into your body. The way your very heart beats.

It was the kind of loss that rips through your life without warning, without apology, without sense. The kind that tears you apart from the inside out, creating tiny fissures everywhere, fault lines. And that's where the grief settles, into those thousand tiny cracks throughout your body. Weighing you down. Everything heavy. Everything aching.

Margot's legs grieved for Elijah with every step she took; sometimes it was easier to just stay in bed. Her mouth grieved for Elijah with every bite she chewed; sometimes it was easier to just skip meals. Her chest grieved for Elijah with every breath; sometimes she wondered if it would be easier if she just stopped breathing altogether.

She slept more.

Ate less.

Breathed less.

Took up less space, less oxygen. Margot let herself fade. For fourteen years, Elijah had been her mirror. She saw herself only through the reflection of his eyes. And when the mirror disappeared, she went with it. Margot was ripped asunder, a soul adrift.

She'd been drowning ever since.

After the confession spilled out into the night air over a horse pasture in the Kaintuck Bluegrass, she looked at the man sitting beside her. Her eyes wavered, brimming with tears. She refused to blink. For so many years, she'd hidden herself away. She hadn't said the words, hadn't known how to ask for what she needed...how to tell her own story. But here it was, out in the open. Taking up space in the distance between her and Merrick. Set free.

"For so many years, it was impossibly hard," she whispered, voice breaking, "to look anyone in the eye. To wonder whether, when they looked at me, they wished for *him*."

And there it was, the crux of the matter. The horrible, dirty secret she'd carried in her heart for years. If she and Elijah were two halves of the same soul, she was undoubtedly the lesser half. She alone had not been enough for her mother to stay well and alive. She alone was not enough for her father to trust with his business empire.

No, she had to be coddled. Married off. Protected.

Because she was weak.

Because a son would always be worth more than a daughter.

But Margot was *here*.

She was here, and he was gone. She was supposed to be living for both of them now, but she was too terrified to live at all. Not when every step forward was a step away from him.

Merrick shifted his weight in the grass. He was clearly uncomfortable and didn't know what to say. Margot had been here before. The impulse to shrink herself back to a manageable size, a neater package, was instinctive.

"You don't have to say anything," she said.

"I want to say something, but no words could ever be adequate." Understanding was carved into the somber lines of his face, in the arch of his downturned lips, in the frown lines of his forehead. Tremendous empathy resided in the expanse of his face, but it was the look in his eyes that spoiled everything.

Pity.

"Don't look at me like that," Margot whispered, half begging. She ripped out a handful of grass and swatted, throwing it senselessly at him. "The last thing I want is your pity."

He held quiet.

Margot brought her knees to her chest, wrapping her arms around herself. She gazed skyward, desperate to look anywhere but at him. Clouds rolled in overhead, beginning to obscure the moon. A single raindrop landed on her arm.

"What do you want from me then?" Merrick finally asked.

The question struck her dumb, for its answer was as vast as the cloud-shrouded galaxy above them. As unreachable.

"What do I want?" she repeated. Her crazed laughter shattered the night. "What do I *want*? Oh, I want a different life, a different past. I want to be sitting in this field with you to stargaze and talk and dream. Not chased here, fleeing my own ghosts. Having to be carried because my own two feet aren't strong enough to hold me up."

"What else?"

"I want to hear a different voice inside my head. Different stories. I want my family to look and see *me*, not 'the one who lived.' I want to change the song that's been playing on the phonograph for eight straight years. And I..." She faded, glancing away. "What I really want, more than anything in this world, is to not be afraid. To not be so afraid of who I might be without him, I stay frozen in time. I want to be brave enough to step forward, even if it means stepping forward alone."

His teeth bit into his lip, and something ripped free in her gut. Something wild with want. Being laid so bare before him...she was wild with the desire to be *seen*. Just this once.

"And I really," Margot huffed, "*really* want you to stop looking at me like I'm a wounded animal." A second raindrop landed on her bare shoulder. "I've had enough of those looks to last a lifetime."

"I'm not looking at you like that."

"You are."

He leveled her with a powerful stare, amber eyes pooling into her own. It was a different stare than she'd ever seen, one that made her toes curl. "How do you want me to look at you?"

She didn't answer. She turned away, grateful for the darkness. It hid the color in her cheeks. The desire swimming in her eyes.

Merrick scooted closer. He took her chin in his hand and turned it toward him. Rough skin, gentle touch. "How do you want me to look at you, Margot?"

He pinned her with his gaze. She couldn't have looked away if she tried. Her mouth opened, barely parted. "I just..." Her voice dropped to a whisper. "I just want you to *look*."

To see me and not turn away.

Several more raindrops fell, one grazing her cheek, dripping like a tear. Merrick thumbed it away. "Believe me, I'm looking."

She blinked once. Twice.

And then his lips were on hers. Her response was instinctive and immediate—*hunger*. It coursed through her with a rippling shudder.

She reached for his shirt, gripping it in her fist to drag him closer. His lips moved to her neck, beneath her ear. He nipped the lobe and tugged gently, eliciting a moan from deep in her throat. The carnality of the sound surprised her. Her cheeks flooded pink again, a voice in her mind telling her to be quiet and complicit and demure. To be *good*.

But he did it again, and she surrendered all pretense.

She wasn't quiet or demure or good. She wanted things that were very bad indeed. Starting with this hulking, beguiling man. He was everywhere, all fumbling hands, greedy lips, warm breath. He wasn't being gentle, and the realization made her feel strong. She was so very sick of being treated like a porcelain doll.

The rain fell in earnest now, speckling her hair, her dress, her arms. His fingers tangled roughly in her damp hair. His tongue slipped into her mouth. He leaned close, weight pressing, and she fell back in the grass, dragging him with her.

He tugged at her dress, pulling it down to fully expose her chemise. His lips dropped to her collarbone, vibrating against her as he murmured something unintelligible into her skin.

Her hands moved of their own volition. Moved over broad shoulders, strong arms, muscled chest. Margot couldn't explore all of him fast enough. She was shocked by her own fearlessness, by her mounting recklessness. Her fingers found his shirt buttons, began to work their way down.

He shrugged out of the shirt, and she pressed her lips against the dark hair on his chest. Her fingers streamed across the ridges of his back, growing wetter and wetter as the rain fell. A rumble of thunder boomed in the distance, and she pulled back, her mind hazy.

We should stop. We should go inside.

"Or we can stay outside and get very, very wet," he said.

She hadn't realized she'd spoken aloud. Her gaze darted upward, wanting to see his face, the look in his eyes.

Liquid gold.

Merrick's hands reached for her chemise, teasing the straps downward. "Tell me to stop," he panted. "Tell me to stop, and I will."

The question was there, right there in his eyes, but it meant nothing to her. Only his unvarnished desire mattered. The wanting inside her was ruinous.

"Don't stop."

The slide of silk, slithering down her body, clinging to the moisture coating her skin. Dragging. The reveal seemed infinite. Long enough for her mind to catalog a thousand tiny doubts. She almost reached for his hands and told him to stop, but then she saw the expression on his face as he took all of her in. The *reverence*.

Her doubts were silenced.

"I see you, Margot," he rumbled, hands digging in to grip her bare hips. "Every inch, I see you. And you are absolutely beautiful."

Merrick's fingers slid down her legs, hovering at the band of her thigh-high silk stockings. He played with the edge, softly sliding his fingers under, then out. Her leg trembled beneath his touch. Her hand moved down his strong chest, fingers trailing as gently as a whisper. Creeping closer, closer...

When she reached his waistband, she paused. His breath hitched.

That was all it took. She slid lower, taking him completely in her hand. Feeling his fullness strain beneath the fabric of his trousers, a fullness she sensed—distantly—belonged to her. It was both terrifying and thrilling.

He groaned, a strangled, desperate sound. Yielding more of his weight. Pressing into her.

"Margot..." he warned.

She began to work his belt buckle.

"Margot," he tried again. "We are rapidly reaching a point of no return. If you keep going, I don't know...I'm not sure I'll be able to stop."

She tilted her head, wondering exactly what he meant. What it meant precisely, if they didn't stop. Where, specifically, would he take her?

His belt was fully undone. Her fingers hovered, trying to decide.

"Margot." His hands folded over hers, stopping her. "I need to hear you say it. I need to know for sure. It's important to me."

"Just a little more," she panted, looking into his eyes, a little shy. *I want to know. I want you to show me.* "Please?"

"Just a little?"

He looked so impossibly good wet. Skin glistening, hair slick. A large drop fell from the tip of his nose to her cheek.

"Yes."

He guided her grip away from his waist. "Then let's leave my trousers on for now. Let me try something else..."

His hands were back on her, sliding up her leg. Past the stockings. Higher and higher until he was *there*. Slipping between her thighs.

Her head lolled back in the wet grass, unchecked mews spewing from her lips. His mouth covered hers, swallowing her cries. He smiled against her, his fingers continuing to tease.

"Do you like this?" he murmured between kisses. "Tell me."

"Merrick?" A breathless question.

"Tell me what you want, love. Just a little more?" His finger slowly plunged inside her.

She exploded into something wholly new, her eyes flying open in surprise. Her gaze swept over his face, but when he started to move—one finger deep inside her, another rubbing gently against her front—her lids slammed shut again.

It was all too much. She was feeling *so much*, couldn't possibly handle seeing right now.

No, she wanted only to feel.

To feel his roughened fingers against her, inside her. To feel his hot breath on her cheek, wet hair brushing her forehead. To feel the grass at her back, taste the rain on her lips, hear her own panting breaths rumbling in her ears, louder in her mind than the thunder in the distance. And then there was the pressing warmth of his body, shielding her from the storm overhead, drawing out an altogether different tempest from deep within her. One bigger than anything around them.

An unfamiliar sensation, hot and dizzying, began to build. No longer adrift in the terrifyingly wide world, she was anchored directly to him. Clinging to him. Crying out. Building, crashing, rising. Again and again.

"Merrick," she gasped. "Merrick!"

He bent down, kissing his way from her neck to her chest. His tongue circled her nipple, took it into his mouth, drawing an arch from her back and a cry from her throat as she surrendered completely.

She shattered beneath him as fast and hot and electric as a bolt of lightning across the sky. The world sharpened around her, then faded.

When her breath returned, Margot wasn't sure what to say. She trusted neither her voice nor words. She nuzzled into his damp neck, breathing in the smell of leather and bourbon. She wanted to get drunk on it. Drunk on him.

A lifetime of this, she thought faintly. That was what he could give her. What she wanted from him. Desperately.

He collapsed into the grass beside her, exposing her body to the full effect of the rain. She was pelted with it, drenched within a second. A shiver overtook her, but it started inside, not out. Misunderstanding, Merrick rolled back on top of her, taking the rain against his own shoulders again. She reached up, running her fingers through his dark hair to push it out of his eyes. She wanted to *see*.

Because the way he was looking at her...

She wasn't adrift. She wasn't wounded. She wasn't half of a missing soul. No.

Under the piercing clear gaze of his amber eyes, she suspected she was, for the first time in years, *whole*.

19

July 13, 1901

Darling,
I'm throwing a party tonight. Come.

Love,
Babette

S OFT GOLD LIGHT BEHIND slumbering lids. The tinkling of glassware, the gentle swell of laughter. A hint of smoke on the air. And somehow, her mouth. Full. Dripping with the taste of molten sin—sweet, decadent, and rich.

Margot opened her eyes to a new world.

She stood inside a high-ceilinged ballroom with mirrors along one wall. A shiny marble floor underfoot reflected light from the chandeliers. Romantically dim. Couches, wingback chairs, cushioned poufs, and curule seats were grouped in intimate bunches around the perimeter. In the center of the room, a dance floor emerged, filled with close-hugging bodies, moving together in a way she'd never seen before. Couples and clusters, skin to skin, swaying amorously to plaintive notes streaming from a single violinist's bow.

Margot shivered in the cold. Unlike the partygoers, who were dripping in extravagant Edwardian fashions, Margot was clad only in her nightdress with bare feet. The room, the *house*...she distantly registered it as her own. She'd explored this ballroom during her first days at Dravenhearst Manor, had wondered what lavish parties and secrets were locked inside its walls. The things this room must have *seen*...

Babette held court in the near corner, lounging carelessly on an ivory settee. Her posture was reminiscent of Merrick's rakish entitlement, the kind that only came with the certainty of absolute ownership. Ownership of the room, the people, the adoration, the subterfuge. She held it all in the palm of her hand.

Babette's red hair was unbound, tumbling in loose curls over one bare shoulder. Romantic and heavy. Her neck glittered with half a dozen strands of thick pearls and diamonds, and a glass of half-drunk champagne dangled casually from one hand. She wore a dress the color of a lemon drop, the skirt heavily embroidered with pink roses and violets. Butterflies hid amongst the flowers, their delicate stitched wings spread in flight.

Babette lounged alone, but the couches and chairs around her were filled with men and women in similarly opulent dress, all sharing space, rules of propriety forsaken. One man even sat on the floor, his legs stretched across the Parisian rug, head tipped languidly back on a velvet loveseat. His shirt buttons were half undone, exposing throat and chest, a woman's hand massaging through his hair. Margot flinched from the brazen display, meeting Babette's queen-like gaze instead.

She tipped her chin and smiled slowly at Margot, then raised a hand to waggle her fingers. A matching set of diamond rings—engagement and wedding bands—twinkled in the dim light.

Margot waited to see if any of Babette's sycophants would notice the wave, would look her way. None did. To all but the woman who summoned her, she was invisible. Margot drifted close to hear the swirl of conversation.

"...parties are terribly boring," a raven-haired beauty was saying, the one whose hands were knuckle deep in the floor lounger's hair. "Nothing like this." Her eyes darted around the ballroom. "You and Richard throw the most exquisite soirees, Babette."

"*Babette* throws the most exquisite soirees," her partner on the floor mumbled, eyes closed in pleasure. "Richard just foots the bill."

Babette tossed her head back and laughed.

A blonde whirlwind tumbled into the group. Margot saw her face first in the gilded mirrors on the wall.

Ruth, wearing a shimmering gown of powder blue. She stumbled through the array of poufs and chairs, falling comfortably onto Babette's settee, their shoulders colliding. She turned, lifting her legs to drape them over her friend's lap. Ruth's toes were scandalously bare, clad in neither shoes nor stockings. She reclined, laying her head against the cushions and fanning her face.

Margot registered this power move for what it was. None of the other revelers dared share Babette's space, breathe her privileged air. But Ruth had an open invitation.

"It's quite warm this evening," she pronounced. "I've overdone myself dancing."

Babette smiled and tickled Ruth's bare toes. "Who could blame you? Mr. Blanchard makes a fabulous dance partner."

"Yes," Ruth's reply was light, her smile mischievous. "I'll tell you a secret." Her eyes flicked merrily to Babette. "He's even more fabulous at necking."

Babette tipped herself sideways with laughter, swigging champagne and leaning into Ruth. "You mean petting, no doubt. Perhaps that's why you're so flushed."

The crowd hooted as Ruth sputtered.

"Which reminds me." Babette pushed herself onto an elbow. "Where *is* my husband? Richard?" She hollered his name, scanning the crowd.

"Speak of the devil." Ruth tipped her head as Richard stumbled into view, one arm slung jovially around another man's shoulder, the other clutching an open bottle of Dravenhearst Distilling bourbon. His shirt was undone nearly to the waist, exposing his chest. His dark hair was distinctly mussed, handsomely so.

"Richard," Babette called again, capturing both her husband's attention and that of half the room. "I love you!"

His answering smile was slow and charming. Wickedly so. His arm dropped from his friend's shoulder, and he pointed to Babette. "I love you too, Mrs. Dravenhearst."

Good-natured heckles rose from all four corners of the room, along with a certain amount of cooing. Margot was taken aback by the public display. This party was turning all she knew about polite society on its head.

"For heaven's sake, must you two always be so *loud*? All the time?" Ruth asked, dropping a hand over her eyes. "I think I've a headache coming on."

Babette grinned but didn't reply, only lifted her own hand to admire her wedding rings.

At that moment, a brown-haired man sitting alone in a fauteuil armchair rose to his feet and slipped away from the group. Babette's eyes followed his every move, her smile evaporating.

The man shouldered by Margot as he departed, his silver cufflinks catching the candlelight.

Racehorses.

It was all Margot needed to see. She followed the mystery man. He snatched a bottle of clear liquor from a mirrored serving tray en route to the exit, dragging a hand through his hair.

Soft footfalls gave chase. The man swung into a dark hallway and leaned against the wood-paneled wall with an immense sigh. He lifted the bottle to his lips and drank deeply. Misery radiated off him in waves.

In a flurry of skirts, Babette rounded the corner and barreled straight into his arms. She swatted the bottle away from his face and pressed her lips in its place.

The kiss lasted a fraction of a second, the man sinking briefly into temptation before rallying. He raised a gentle hand to push her away.

"Babette, stop." His brown eyes brimmed with hurt. "You don't get to do this anymore. It's done. You married him. I don't even know what I'm doing, coming to these stupid parties...I don't belong here. Not anymore."

"You always belong," she murmured, leaning into him. "Because you belong with me. Where I go, you go."

"Not anymore."

"Always."

The man sighed again, rubbing a hand over his face. "Not always. Not anymore," he repeated. "I'm going to ask Eliza to marry me."

"No, you're not."

"I am."

"No. You're *not.*" Babette pulled back to stare at him, eyes glittering dangerously. "She can't have you."

"Why not? Because you say so? It doesn't work like that."

"You love me."

"I do." The declaration was vehement—loud, sure, and quick. But it was tinged with pain.

Silence roared between them. Babette's chest rose, fell. She licked her lips.

"I do love you," he repeated, softer this time. "But you didn't choose me. You didn't love me, not enough to choose me—a poor farm boy—over your rich aristocrat. And now—"

"I'm late," Babette interrupted.

"And...*what*?" His jaw slackened.

"I'm late," she repeated, lowering her lashes. "Expecting a child."

"Congratulations." His response was dry. The set of his jaw stoic, though worlds broke apart in his eyes. "A Dravenhearst heir. I hope the three of you will be exceedingly happy."

"It might not be." Babette's teeth grabbed her lower lip. "It might not be a *Dravenhearst* heir."

"Don't do this." He shoved her away again, harder than the first time. She stumbled. "Don't you *dare* do this. You can't say these things, hold me captive on your leash. It's been months since we—"

"*Three* months," she said, righting herself and leveling him with an imperious stare. "You were in my bed two nights before my wedding. We both know it."

He was quiet for several long moments. "It doesn't matter," he whispered, chest caving, voice cracking. "It's his either way, Babette. You and I both know that."

Silence bloomed again.

"I'm going to marry Eliza," he finally said. "If I don't choose myself, my own chance at happiness, no one else will. You taught me that."

Babette clicked her tongue, displeased.

He reached for her cheek, two fingers brushing lightly across her skin. "I'll think of you often. Whenever someone pours a glass of his goddamn bourbon. Dravenhearst Distilling—my life's greatest curse."

She frowned. "I hate bourbon."

"I know you do. That's why this has never made a lick of sense. None of it has."

⤹

"I can't believe she showed you one of her Gomorrah parties." Ruth, shaking her head, was wide-eyed over her gin rickey the following afternoon.

"Gomorrah party?" Margot wrinkled her nose.

"Surely you know the story of Sodom and Gomorrah?" Ruth replied, waving the question away. "Sinful excess and whatnot."

"But that's...to host a party with such an indecent theme..." Margot tried to collect her thoughts. Sodom and Gomorrah were two notorious cities from the Bible, destroyed by God's hellfire and brimstone for their wantonness, for their surplus and indecency. "It's sacrilegious."

"Mmm, that's right." Ruth took a slow sip, then gave Margot an appraising look. "Merrick mentioned you were religious. Babette wasn't. She believed herself enlightened, a fierce apostate. And she loved irony."

"Clearly." Margot folded her arms, thinking of the half-dressed socialites she'd seen lounging in Babette's inner circle. Perhaps she should consider burning sage throughout the manor, a purging cleanse of sins long past.

Ruth laughed. "Oh, lighten up, buttercup. I'll not have your judgment here. What night did she show you? What were we wearing?"

Margot described Babette's butterfly gown, Ruth's powder blue dress.

"Oh, yes, I remember that party. It ended with a spectacular row between Richard and Babette. Is that what she showed you?"

Margot frowned. "No, that's not what I saw at all. She and Richard seemed quite happy. Boisterous, in fact."

Ruth's smile dimmed. "That's how they always were. Everything about their relationship was the loudest show. When they were in love and happy, it was larger than life, in your face. When they weren't happy...well, their fights were fierce enough to rock the foundation of the house. But they always came back together in the end."

Margot considered this. It didn't add up with what she'd seen. Both memories Babette had shared were focused more on the brown-eyed mystery man than Richard. Which was curious.

"She must be trying to tell you something with these dreams," Ruth mused. "And part of me has always wondered..."

"Wondered what?"

Ruth thinned her lips. "No, I shouldn't."

Margot gripped her wrist. "If it's peace she's searching for, I want to give it to her. The sooner the better." Because she couldn't live in a haunted house forever, and Merrick would never leave his distillery. She was sure of it. If she wanted to be with him, she had to free this house of its ghosts.

Ruth took a deep breath. "There was always something about Babette's death that didn't sit right with me. I knew she had bouts of melancholia, but at her core, she was fierce. Nothing made that woman shrink. Except...sometimes..."

"Sometimes what?"

"Richard. He had a power over her I never understood. The house did too, after we moved here. Theirs was a...volatile relationship. One that ended in tragedy."

"Are you suggesting Richard drove her to suicide?"

"Suicide? No." Ruth chewed her bottom lip. "I've always wondered if there was more to the story. If perhaps Richard did something to hurt her—in the heat of the moment, of course. He wasn't a bad man, but he did have a temper. It runs in the family, you know. In the bloodline. Bad blood will always out."

"What do you mean?" Margot shifted in her seat.

"Eleanor showed Babette things from her own marriage, things that warranted being leery of the Dravenhearst men. Looking back through the years, I've wondered if something happened behind closed doors in that house, in that marriage. Something I missed." She looked away, knotting her hands in her lap.

Margot's heart filled with sympathy. "You were an incredible friend to her. I've seen as much with my own eyes. Whatever happened, it doesn't rest on your shoulders."

"It's only…Richard was a different man after Babette's death. Maudlin, morose. He died a few years later, when Merrick was sixteen. Just wasted away. Guilt wears on people, you know."

Margot knew a thing or two about guilt. If Babette didn't commit suicide, if foul play had been involved in her death, it would certainly explain why her soul was restless. And if Richard *was* somehow involved…

Perhaps what Margot had mistaken as haunting and intimidation—the sleepwalking, the veiled threats with her wedding gown—was something else entirely.

A warning.

20

July 14, 1933

Dearest Pa,

*I understand the rumors of which you speak, and there is
history in this house, true. But I find myself growing rather
attached. It has not always been a happy home, but I'm no
stranger to sorrow. Perhaps there is common ground to be
found here.*
I think of you often. How do you fare?

Forever yours,
Margaret

"SO I'VE BEEN THINKING...ABOUT last night." Merrick lifted his
napkin and dabbed his mouth as he finished dessert.

Margot placed her spoon down. She'd barely stopped thinking about it
herself. Wondering all day on endless loop, *When can we do that again?*

"Which part?"

He smirked, leaning back in his chair. "Don't know. Which part have
you been thinking about?"

She blushed and looked down.

Merrick chuckled. "I was thinking about the horses, how you said you used to ride."

"Oh." Disappointment flooded her. Horses? *That* was the part of the evening he'd fixated on?

"I was wondering..." His gaze met hers. "Did you enjoy it? When you used to ride?"

"Of course."

She and Eli had both loved it. Sometimes when she dreamed at night, in the moment just before the dream turned into nightmare, she could feel the wind ripping through her hair. The sun on her cheeks, the bouncing rhythm of her body, attuned to her mount. And in those fleeting moments, there was joy.

Which made the ensuing sorrow ache all the more.

Merrick nodded, the set of his jaw tight. "I think you should try again. With me."

"No."

He lifted a hand. "Hear me out."

"No." She pushed back her chair. This wasn't up for discussion. Her fears, her *trauma*, weren't up for negotiation. She'd lived with this for years, knew exactly how to cope.

"Margot, please." He moved quickly, crossing the room to take her arm. "I'm only trying to help."

"Yes. You and every cockamamie physician east of the Mississippi." She reared back, yanking her arm free.

"I—what?" He blinked rapidly, confused.

Margot's eyes hardened. She lowered her voice to a near hiss. "You think I haven't tried? You think I haven't been poked and prodded and evaluated and *judged* by a million different men with a million different ideas on how to sort out what's 'wrong' with me?"

His mouth gaped.

"I'm done being someone's science experiment. *I* know what I need. You don't."

"I never said I did." His response was quiet but strong.

The sound of Margot's laborious breaths filled the room, echoing between them like cannon fire.

"You're protective of it because it hurts." His words came out slow and punctuated. "You clutch it close, like a wounded limb...because it hurts less if you don't use it, right? Avoidance consumes you. I'm not telling you what to do or how to feel, Margot. I'm speaking from personal experience. I know a thing or two about grief and trauma myself. I was the one who found my mother, hanging from the rickhouse racks in her wedding gown. I was eleven years old."

Margot's jaw slackened. He was the one who found Babette? At a younger age than she when she'd lost Elijah?

So much sorrow here, she thought, a wave crashing over her from head to foot. *So much unfathomable loss and pain.*

Merrick squared his shoulders. "I know how this works. I know about loss, about horror so great, you can never forget. You cannot shed it. You cannot leave it behind. You can only carry it with you. Forward."

She kept her voice soft, wanting to be kind, but she was unwilling to overlook his hypocrisy. Not whilst he challenged her on her own. "By sealing the rickhouse, never to return?"

"Yes, one of them, for a myriad of reasons. But I work in the other rickhouses every day. I push barrels down those racks every day. I walk under the rafters. Because one experience does not get to define who I am, where I live my life, or what I love. I will not give fear any more power than it already has."

"It's different," she insisted, shaking her head.

"It's not. I'm not asking you to ride the horse that killed your brother. I'm just asking you to walk into the goddamn stables and stand on your own two feet. Because you *can*."

"I can't."

"You can. I can help you. Come with me in the mornings. Sit in the grass and read a book while I ride. Just be there. When you avoid something, it festers. It causes greater pain. I don't like to see you hurting—when you hurt, I hurt."

Margot's lip trembled. Her voice, when it came, was small. "I don't want to."

He moved, crossing the chasm between them with a single step. When his arms encircled her, they were all-consuming. Warm and secure.

"Don't want to do it, or don't want to hurt?"

"Both," she whispered.

"Okay." He ran his fingers through her hair, down her spine. His palm splayed flat across her lower back. Steady and solid. "You're not ready now, but you will be. I hope you think about it. I hope you feel safe enough to try. Not *strong* enough—it's not a matter of strength. *Safe* enough. With me."

Her shoulders collapsed forward, yielding to him. "I will think about it," she promised, surprised to find she actually meant it.

Safe enough, not strong enough.

The distinction was quite revolutionary.

The vast majority of Margot's life had been spent locked inside her head. And it didn't often feel like a safe space. Maybe she did want to change. Maybe she *could*.

"Are you tired?" he asked, lips gently pressing into the crown of her hair.

"Yes."

"Then let's go to bed."

When he lifted her off the ground, when he tucked her into his arms and carried her up the winding stairs, she didn't feel weak. She felt cherished.

When he kicked open his door, when he laid her across his bed, she felt chosen.

And when he stepped back, shucked off his shirt and trousers, and dressed for bed directly in front of her—holding her eyes the entire time—she was aflame.

He disappeared for only a moment, passing through the adjoining door to retrieve a white nightdress. He undid the buttons on her back, kissing her bare shoulder. The nightgown went overhead, the day dress and chemise pushed to her feet. He pulled them off, his roughened fingertips just barely brushing the skin of her ankle.

When he pulled back the covers, when he curled his body around hers, wrapped his bare arm snug around her middle, she felt protected.

"Will you keep the ghosts away?" she whispered, her muscles growing loose, eyelids heavy.

"Yes, I promise. I will always keep you safe."

21

July 14, 1933

Mr. Merrick Dravenhearst,
Excuses, excuses. Case in point: you missed our last.
That's two strikes. You don't want a third.
Don't be late.

—A

T HE CREAKING OF FLOORBOARDS woke her. The slow, deep groans of a century-old wooden house resting in the still of night.

Margot didn't move, hardly dared breathe, but she did crack an eyelid. Merrick was there, at the foot of the bed. Slipping into a pair of pants. Tucking in his shirt.

He was dressing. Going out.

She could hardly believe it. Going out in the dead of night, while she—his wife—lay right here in his bed. After he'd *promised*, mere hours ago, she was safe with him.

Had this man no shame?

Merrick turned his back to her, sliding open a drawer with a whisper. He tucked something shiny into his waistband, shrugging into a jacket immediately after.

One breath later, the room was empty. His footfalls were soft, hurrying down the hallway.

When Margot exhaled, she breathed fire. She could almost see sparks and smoke curling from her nostrils. She sat up in bed, drumming her fingers on the mattress.

A liar. That was who she married. A liar and a cheat.

She continued the slow, rhythmic drumbeat of her fingers. She had options. Her mind cataloged them, increasing in order of escalation.

1. Pack her things this instant and leave.

2. Lie in wait to confront him upon return.

3. Storm outside right now and raise holy hell.

4. Look for his gun, every good Kentucky man had one, and...

And what?

The growl of the roadster roared to life, and suddenly, Margot was running. Bare feet. White nightdress. Hair unbound. Running through the halls of the manor, down the stairs, her nightgown ballooning behind her.

She flung open the front door just in time to see Merrick slamming the lid over the rumble seat.

"Merrick!" She flew down the steps of the portico, blinking in the harsh glare of the headlights.

"Margot?" He froze where he stood, one hand hovering over the storage latch.

She had half a mind to walk over and slap him. Hard, right across his obnoxiously handsome, stubbled cheek. She summoned every ounce of gumption she had, took four leaping bounds, then raised her hand to strike. "How dare you!"

His reflexes were like lightning, catching her hand before it landed.

"You filthy, rotten, lying piece of—"

"Whoa." He stumbled away from her. "Margot, calm down."

"Don't tell me to calm down," she shrieked, pointing an accusatory finger. "How could you? *Tonight*, of all nights. When you promised...you *promised* to stay with me. To keep me safe."

"Margot, I have an obligation tonight. One that can't be rescheduled." His tone was measured. Resigned.

"An *obligation*?" She laughed sardonically, tipping her head back. "Is that what you gentlemen call it these days?"

"Call what?" His brow furrowed.

"Stop acting innocent. I'm so sick of your lies. You've done nothing but lie to me since the night we met."

A thunderous scowl overtook his face. He turned his back on her, striding to the driver's door. "That's unfair, and you know it. I don't have time for hysterics right now. We'll discuss this in the morning when you're ready to speak calmly. And rationally."

Hysterics? Oh, this man hadn't seen hysterics yet.

Margot opened her mouth and screamed. It was shrill and feral, ringing out through the night.

It stopped him dead in his tracks, his shoulders hunching in a flinch. "Goddammit, woman. Are you trying to wake the entire Bluegrass?"

"Maybe if I scream loud enough, *she'll* hear me. Where does she live, your little harlot? Does she know you've gone and gotten yourself married? Or are you lying to her too?"

"Hold on." He turned to her, eyes wide. "You think I'm going to a *woman* tonight?"

"I've seen you," she hissed, moving along the body of the car opposite him. "I've seen you sneak out to meet her a half dozen times since our wedding night. Is nothing sacred to you? Not even marriage vows?"

He lifted a finger. "I've not broken a single vow I made to you."

Margot yanked open the passenger door. "Oh, really? Then I suppose you won't mind if I come along for the ride?"

"Margot, no."

"Go ahead, Merrick. Gas 'er up. Take me to where your little mistress lives. I'd love to meet her." She plopped herself in the passenger seat and crossed her legs. She wouldn't budge. He couldn't make her.

"I told you, there's no woman. Heckin' hell!" He ripped open his door, pausing to check his wristwatch. "You need to get out of the car. *Now.*"

"No." She folded her arms. He'd have to drag her out kicking and screaming—and oh, how she'd scream.

"Get out of the car, Margot," he bellowed.

She'd never heard him raise his voice like that, not to her. The look burning in his eyes was like kerosene, volatile and liquid. Rigged to combust.

She struck a match. "I won't."

He let out a scream of his own, raw frustration. "I can't bring you with me."

"You don't have a choice."

With another exasperated roar and glance at his watch, Merrick took his seat behind the wheel, slamming the door behind him. "Then you better hold on tight. We're running late."

As Merrick pulled out of the drive, the tires screeched. Margot was thrust backward, her hair blowing in the wind. He drove like a man possessed, whipping the roadster around winding country roads, fast and hard enough to make the rear tires squeal. Fishtailing.

She'd forgotten he drove like a maniac.

"How far?" She broke the silence.

"Fucking far," he grunted. "Get comfortable." He reached behind his back, tugging at his waistband. A silver-barreled revolver glinted in the moonlight. He rested it on his thigh.

"What is *that* for?" Margot asked, eyes widening with fear.

Oh God, she'd made a terrible mistake. He was going to kill her, wasn't he? Drive deep into backcountry and dump her body in a shallow grave. For the crows and vultures and maggots to find. Her bones would rot, grow mold, turn to dust. He was going to—

"You're asking the wrong questions," he snapped. "I would never hurt you. I don't have a mistress, and I'm sure as hell not cheating on you, Margot. I'm fucking celibate."

22

July 1933

Inventory reaching critical levels. Discounting Rickhouse One, only 2,000 barrels with usable product remain on the premises. It's hard to believe at our peak, we held 60,000.

—Excerpt, Dravenhearst Distilling Inventory Log, as maintained by Merrick Dravenhearst

A HALF HOUR OF silence. That was what followed his admission.

Celibate?

The word spun in Margot's mind, round and round. Perhaps she needed a dictionary. Perhaps the word didn't mean what she thought it did. It couldn't. Priests were celibate. He was a thirty-one-year-old atheist. With a *reputation*, for Christ's sake.

"If the gun makes you nervous, stow it in the dash," he finally said, breaking the standoff.

She hadn't been staring at the gun. She'd been far more focused on the crotch of his pants, actually. Wondering how on God's green earth this was possible...

A sign for the Indiana border flashed by, startling her. "Where are we going?"

"The 'where' isn't important, but I need you to give your word that when we get there, you'll stay in the car."

"Why?"

His grip tightened on the wheel. "Because I said so."

"I'm not a child."

"Really? You sure acted like one back at the house."

Margot sucked in her lips over her teeth. She deserved that. "If you would just tell me what you're doing, sneaking out like this multiple times a week, I wouldn't have to resort to *hysterics*." She spat out the final word, tasting the pain of it. Cataloged the dozens of times it had been used against her.

Merrick gave her a fleeting side-eyed glance. His shoulders softened. "I'm sorry I said that."

"No, you're not." She tipped her chin up and stared straight ahead.

"Yes, I am." He reached over to grip her thigh. "I'm sorry, Margot."

Three words. No excuses. Pure earnestness.

When she chanced a glance at him, his eyes were wide. Ringing with truth. They made her feel small. He was so much bigger a man than she'd ever expected. She, who had been unfairly judged all her life, had done the very same to him. A philistine, she'd called him. A rake, she'd assumed.

Celibate *and* an apology—one that somehow made a dent in the pain from all the times she'd never received one before? All in one night?

She cleared her throat. "I'm sorry I forced myself into your car like a wayward highwayman."

"A very pretty highwayman, at least. Nightdress and all." One corner of his mouth hitched up, the ghost of a smile.

"Will you tell me why I need to stay in the car?"

He sighed. "Because it's dangerous. The people I'm meeting...I'd rather not involve you."

Margot uncrossed her legs. Began to bounce a knee. Recrossed them.

"So will you?" he asked. "Will you stay in the car?"

"Yes."

His posture visibly relaxed once she gave her word. The remaining miles passed in silence.

Merrick brought the car to a stop on a desolate stretch of road just across the Indiana line, after pulling down a small embankment beside an underpass. There was another automobile waiting, a sleek black Duesenberg.

When Merrick shut down the engine, the Duesenberg flashed its headlights. Once, twice. Merrick flashed back.

"That's the signal," he murmured. "Stay put. I won't be long." He reached for the door, and Margot grabbed his wrist.

"You'll be okay, won't you?"

"I'll be fine." He offered a smile and tossed the revolver on his empty seat. "Look after that for me, will ya?"

She was sure he meant it to be reassuring—the implication he didn't need the gun—but she preferred he take it. Just in case.

Merrick moved to the back of the car, opening the lid over the rumble seat. He grunted and lifted out a heavy crate. Glass bottles tinkled within. He doubled back for a second crate.

Margot could hear everything clearly in the open-top roadster. Merrick's stilted footfalls as he walked. The *thud* and clinking of glass when he dropped the crates to the dirt. The ominous slam of two doors from the Duesenberg. The racking of a tommy gun—Margot both saw *and* heard that one. She watched, eyes wide with terror, as a shadowed hulking form laid the deadly firearm across the hood of the Duesenberg.

Two men crossed into no-man's-land to meet Merrick, strolling casually, hands in their trench coat pockets. The taller one wore a fedora and shoes so shiny they gleamed bright in the light of the moon. The squat one—Margot nicknamed him Beefy—slipped a pack of butts from his pocket and extracted one. Cupping his hand around his mouth, he thumbed a lighter for a spark.

"Antoni." Merrick inclined his head to the man wearing the fedora.

Margot stifled a gasp, recognition dawning. *Toni*. The man she'd encountered outside the rickhouses a few weeks ago. The one Julian had run off the estate.

"Evening, Merrick," Toni drawled. His sharp gaze flicked past Merrick's shoulder to Margot, dragging up and down her stiff form. "Out for a midnight drive with the missus, huh? How romantic."

Beefy chuckled and blew out a long drag, smoke curling skyward.

Merrick toed the nearest crate, rattling the bottles within. His voice came out gruff, all business. "Here's the hooch. Your usual. Cough it up."

Toni reached into his pocket and withdrew a thick wad of scratch. He started counting—a bit theatrically, in Margot's opinion. Her shoulders tensed, gut clenched with worry.

"So what's her name?" Toni asked, nodding toward Margot. "Heard through the grapevine you'd finally sold out for wedded bliss. Wouldn't have believed it if I hadn't seen it with my own eyes."

Merrick said nothing.

Toni extended the wad of bills but jerked back when Merrick reached for it. "I asked you a question. Her name."

Merrick scowled. "She's nobody. A farm girl from the Bluegrass. Real pretty," he emphasized the last words, as though they meant something deeper.

Margot's breath grew shallow. Like a hunted rabbit.

Beefy laughed, blowing smoke again before speaking. "That ain't what we heard. We heard you snagged yourself an *heiress*."

"Greenbrier, I believe is her family name?" Toni added. He flicked his eyes to Margot, sharing the joke.

Merrick chuckled. "A Bluegrass heiress is no comparison to Chicago money, to the empire Capone built. I've been keepin' my appointments, haven't I? Nothing about this situation has changed. Now pay up."

Toni fanned the money, tapping the stack of bills in his opposite palm. "I don't think so. Seems the terms have changed."

"This isn't a negotiation."

"Everything is a negotiation," Toni said. "You don't need our money anymore. Gone and got yourself a rich, respectable wife, you did. What you need now is our silence. And Cosa Nostra silence comes at a high price."

Beefy cracked his knuckles.

Cosa Nostra...dear god, the Italian mafia? Margot had heard all she needed. This wasn't going well. Terrified or not, she would have to do something.

The menfolk were focused on each other, busy posturing like the arrogant peacocks they were. Slowly, very slowly, Margot slid her left hand across the seat, fingers closing around the barrel of the revolver. The weight was solid and reassuring.

Just a Bluegrass farm girl, Merrick had called her. Why yes, in fact, she was. And every Bluegrass farm girl worth her salt knew how to shoot a gun. Her father had first handed her one when she was ten years old. The mechanics were simple—

Point, shoot.

"You don't get it, do you?" Beefy jabbed a finger into Merrick's chest, breathing cigarette smoke down his neck. "We could shut you down. Get you arrested..."

Margot quietly opened the car door and swung her bare feet to the ground. She was pleased to find her legs, though jittery, held strong.

Merrick whipped around. "Margot, get back in the car."

Yeah, get back in the car, you ninny.

She was glad her legs were braver than her mind. She began to walk, keeping the revolver close, tucked into the thick folds of her nightdress.

"We've not been properly introduced," she called in her best honeyed debutante drawl.

"Margot, back to the car." Merrick's eyes were accusatory. *You promised,* they told her.

She had, but that was before he needed her.

"Pleasure seeing you again, *Mrs. Dravenhearst.*" Toni extended his palm when Margot drew close.

"The pleasure's all mine."

In lieu of a handshake, she whipped out the revolver. She did it with gusto, shoving the barrel beneath her chin.

All three men stepped back in shock.

"Now that I have your attention," she said, "I do hope we can keep this brief. Blackmail is most uncouth, but my father is a brilliant negotiator. Taught me a thing or two, so we'll get straight to it. What's your price?"

"If it's intimidation you're after, you're pointing the barrel the wrong way, sweetheart," Beefy said.

She snorted and jerked her head toward Merrick. "He doesn't get a dime if I'm dead. And neither will you. My life is worth more than all three of you combined."

Toni smiled, then nodded at the gun. "That's a mighty fine bluff, Mrs. Dravenhearst, but somehow, I can't imagine a sweet woman like yourself actually pullin' the trigger. Suicide is a nasty way to go."

"Then you obviously know nothing about the Dravenhearst women. I'd be the third to go that way. I assure you, we have the balls."

Merrick choked.

"Now," she continued, "you can either take me up on it—in which case, I hope you're prepared to dispose of a body tonight—or you can name your price like civilized gentlemen. My pockets are deep, and I'm ready to negotiate."

"Burying bodies has never been a deterrent for us."

She was supposed to be intimidated; she wasn't. There was something quite freeing about staring death in the eyes. She'd been afraid of it, afraid of *everything*, for so long.

"Perhaps not. But I assume you usually bury bodies that aren't easily missed. You'll find I'm an entirely different breed. People will care, and they will look." She cocked her head. "Now, if you please, your price? A one-time lump sum to get you out of our lives for good. What'll it be?"

Toni and Beefy exchanged glances.

"Twenty-thousand dollars," Toni offered.

"Horsefeathers." Margot snorted. It was far too lofty a price. "Ten."

"Eighteen."

"Twelve."

Toni laughed. "Are we simply to meet in the middle then? We've got to come out on top, Mrs. Dravenhearst. We've a reputation to uphold. Sixteen thousand, final offer."

Margot narrowed her eyes. "Fifteen thousand, and I'll throw in tonight's loot, all the hooch." She kicked the box the way Merrick had, forgetting she wasn't wearing shoes. She bit her cheek to keep from crying out. *I think I broke a toe,* she inwardly wailed.

"Oh, we'll be takin' the crates." Toni glowered, his eyebrows low. "Make no mistake."

Margot cocked the hammer of the gun, her mind going curiously blank. "Do we have an accord?"

The two men stared at her. She stared back. She would not break.

"Deal."

"Splendid. Merrick, love? Help them load the hooch. You may sort out the sordid matter of payment amongst yourselves."

She stood by, continuing to press the gun to her jaw, while the men scampered. When it was time to go, she walked backward to the roadster, keeping an eye on the mobsters. Her arm ached from holding the gun so tightly.

"Just to reiterate. This is a *one*-time payment. I am not a bank from which you can make unlimited withdrawals. You've done good business with my husband, but Prohibition will be repealed before the new year." She parroted Merrick's words with feigned confidence, hoping they were true. "You've no more use for us."

"Agreed," Toni replied, swiping the tommy gun from the hood. "Pleasure doing business, Mrs. Dravenhearst."

Margot's answering smile was more grim than pleased. She yanked open the door and collapsed into the roadster. Lowering her voice so only Merrick could hear, she gave the directive. "Drive."

The engine turned over as he stepped on the gas. Only once they were on the main road and Margot was confident the Duesenberg was headed the opposite direction did she drop the revolver. Her fingers trembled violently.

"Jesus fucking Christ!" Merrick swiped the gun from her lap. "You cocked the blasted thing, be careful." He pointed the gun over the door and fired a round into the dark to release the hammer.

Margot jumped in her seat.

"You startle awful easy, given the show you just put on."

If she hadn't been looking at him to see the mixture of awe and jest in his eyes, she might've thought him angry.

She let out a nervous laugh. She couldn't believe she'd done that. *Her!* It was the boldest thing she'd ever done in her life. "I'm not certain what got into me. Burst of gumption, I suppose."

She was rather proud of herself.

"That took more than gumption, Margot," Merrick said, shaking his head. "That was insanity. You're utterly mad."

She'd heard the word so many times, in so many ways. Heard and thought it so often, she almost believed herself numb to it. But this time, coming from Merrick with appreciation and not condemnation, she considered it. Deeply.

You're mad.

For most of her life, she'd thought it an insult. Something marking her as "other." She wished to be rid of it, her quirks and follies. The strange way her brain sometimes worked, jumping to conclusions and making oddball connections. Riling herself into a panic, driving her to drastic ends. Seeing things that may or may not be there...

But who would she be without it? Truly?

Perhaps madness was in the eye of the beholder. A gift or a curse, depending on how it was used. Perhaps if she accepted it, she could learn to wield this part of herself. Like a weapon, she could sharpen it into something valuable.

"I'm not mad..." she said slowly. "I'm just a creative thinker."

"All the best people are. That was genius, love. I'm proud of you."

Madness and genius...

Margot tipped her chin skyward and let the wind tear through her hair. It felt like freedom.

Amazing how easily those two overlap.

When the sun came up in the morning, bathing her bedroom in an orange glow, Margot made another utterly madcap decision.

She pulled out the stack of legal documents from her father, specifically the marital addendum in the inheritance paperwork.

There was a blank line, awaiting her signature. She considered it, thinking hard.

If she wanted him all in, she would give the same in return.

What's mine shall be yours, she thought, meaning it.

Margot placed a pen to the paper and signed.

23

July 15, 1933

Dearest Pa,

~~I thought you should know~~

~~I know I wrote you only yesterday, but~~

~~I've decided to sign the marital addendum~~

—unfinished, from the desk of Margot Dravenhearst

M ARGOT WAS IN THE dining room, waiting for him. She'd been waiting all day, actually, but her husband had done a superb job of making himself scarce. Now it was suppertime—past suppertime, if the distant chime of the grandfather clock told her anything—and he had yet to appear.

Margot stood before the dining room windows, peering over the hill toward the distillery as dusk rapidly bled into night. She tapped her toe on the mahogany floor.

He was avoiding her.

They had things to discuss—bootleggers, celibacy, and inheritance law to start—and he was hiding like a child.

Determined, Margot turned on her heel and strode from the room. Down the hall. Into the foyer. She yanked open the door and stalked into the night.

The lights were on in the farthest rickhouse, Beau curled up outside. The dog lifted his head when Margot arrived, perhaps sensing danger. Dutifully, the pup rose and shook himself, then trotted inside behind her.

It was hot as hell in the rickhouse, the bricks retaining heat from the fading summer day. Margot's skin dampened with perspiration; her blood simmered in her veins.

Merrick stood at the far end of the aisle, his back turned. Five mason jars were lined up on a wooden beam, one that kept side-lying barrels in the rick. Two jars were empty, three held trace dregs of amber liquid. Bourbon.

Had he been down here drinking all this time?

She slowly closed the distance, watching Merrick work a cork stopper out of a barrel. He slipped a long copper tube inside the hole. His thumb moved atop the cylinder before withdrawing it from the barrel. Positioning the tube over an empty jar, he released his thumb, and a thimbleful of bourbon emptied into the glass.

Margot blinked, fascinated.

Merrick lifted the jar to his nose and sniffed delicately. He swirled twice, then turned the jar on its side without spilling a drop. Sniffed again.

Margot froze. There was something about watching him like this, his every move smooth and practiced. So focused he didn't notice her presence.

He tipped the glass to his lips and took a small sip, eyes closed. His throat bobbed on the swallow. The tip of his tongue peeked out through his lips at the end.

It's art, she realized, *the way Merrick tastes bourbon.* So reverent, it was near seductive.

She wondered, faintly, if his veins ran copper, blood tinted with bourbon. His eyes certainly did, those tawny butterscotch irises. When he turned those whiskey eyes her way, she was half convinced she'd summoned them.

"Margot?" He put the mason jar down, eyebrows raised. "What're you doing down here?"

She blushed, suddenly feeling like a voyeur who'd interrupted something private. By watching him taste, she'd invaded a sacred space.

"It's late," she murmured, stepping closer. Did she dare reach for his arm? "Your supper has gone cold."

"I'm sorry. It's been a busy day. I've been working in the stillhouse, getting the fermentation tanks clean and ready to run. Alastair's grain will be here by August, so I need to be ready to start making mash again."

"Bourbon mash? But it's still illegal."

"Won't be for long." He offered her a heartened grin. "Illinois, Iowa, and Connecticut just voted for repeal. The California and West Virginia legislatures have called for a vote in two weeks. That's fifteen states swinging from dry to wet. It's finally happening, Margot!"

"But not Kentucky yet." She hated to utter even a single word that would wipe the hope off his face, but she had to. Illegal was illegal. Had he learned nothing last night?

"Not yet," he admitted. "But they will. I've got to begin production. Even starting now, I have no hope of meeting the initial demand. I've sold off almost all my inventory over the last thirteen years. This is the only rickhouse with bourbon still in the barrels. I've been tasting tonight and—"

"Sold?" She had to stop him. "I think you mean *bootlegged*."

Merrick's mouth slammed shut, settling into his trademark scowl.

"We need to talk about last night, Merrick," she said. "I've been waiting all day to discuss it."

"What's there to talk about?" His eyes were flat.

"I think I deserve an explanation, don't you?" Surely she was worth that much to him.

"I didn't realize I had to run my business decisions by you." He dunked the copper tube into the barrel and filled a jar halfway with bourbon. He tipped it to his lips. There was none of the grace, none of the magic, she'd seen moments before. This was swallowing to get corked, not to taste. "If we're headed down this road, I'm going to need a hell of a lot more to drink."

Her curiosity got the better of her, and she ambled closer. "How does it work?"

"It's called a whiskey thief." He held the tube out for her inspection. "For thieving samples from barrels. It's simple—pressurized and released by your thumb."

"A whiskey thief...how appropriate," she murmured. "This is how you spend your days—drinking and thieving? No wonder you fell in with bootleggers."

Merrick leaned against a barrel, folding his arms. "I can't change the choices I made before you, Margot. My deal with Capone's men was struck more than a decade ago."

"A *decade?* Ten years of lawbreaking." The thought made her faint. "Weren't you worried about getting caught?"

"Not as worried as I was about losing the distillery. Bills don't pay themselves."

"What about a medicinal license?" He'd spoken of it the night they first met. She knew he had a deal with the George T. Stag Distillery, a perfectly legal one.

"That's a small loophole, not nearly enough to keep an entire estate afloat. It's the only reason I was able to keep my bourbon barrels here, though, rather than turning them over to the government when the Volstead Act passed." He sighed, running a hand through his hair. "It's very complicated, and the finer details don't matter—"

"They matter to me!" Her cheeks flushed, her voice rising. Beau startled at her feet. "Those men last night, those...*thugs*..." She spat the word. "They're dangerous. They could hurt you, *kill* you."

"Concerned, love?" He tilted his head, his scowl turning charming, almost mocking. "I'm touched."

"Don't do that."

"What?"

"You can't...joke and charm this away. I won't let you. This is serious, Merrick. You're done dealing with them, right? It's over?"

"Yes. Of course." His expression turned more sincere. He took both her forearms in his hands. "I promise. The debt is settled. No more sneaking out. No more bootlegging. Not ever again."

She searched his face for any trace of deceit, relieved when she came up empty. "Okay." She blew out a slow exhale. "Now, about the other thing..."

"What other thing?" But a flicker in his eye told her he knew. Or suspected.

He's going to make me say it. "You said something last night that surprised me." She waited again, hoping he'd speak up.

He didn't.

"Something about...celibacy?"

Every muscle in his body tightened.

"And?" He lowered his eyes, refusing to meet hers.

"And I...well, I wondered if...how..." She trailed off. This was so painful. "Is that a...a lifestyle choice?" *A permanent one?*

He laughed at her, ironic and bitter. It punched her in the gut, the tenor of that laugh.

"I only wondered because—"

"Because you want children?" he supplied, his eyes finally snapping to hers. Gold on fire.

"Well, yes...and..."

"And?"

And because I want you.

Margot licked her lips, tasting the words but refusing to say them. She hated him a little for expecting her to. She wanted him to say it first, to make her feel safe. He was usually so good about it, but not with this. Not with his heart.

"Why are you making this so hard for me?" Her frustration overflowed. The rickhouse was unbearably hot. "This is *your* issue. The least you could do is explain."

"*My* issue?"

"Yes. Yours," she said. "All red-blooded men have...needs. I've been wondering why you've barely touched me all these weeks. And now, come to find out—"

His lips slammed over hers before she could say another word. Hot and fierce. Demanding and powerful. Tasting like bourbon and salty sweat.

He sucked every ounce of oxygen from her lungs. Pulled her heartbeat straight out of her chest. Her pulse pounded in her temples. Dizzying.

"Yes, Margot." He pulled his lips away but drove her backward until her spine hit a rack of barrels. His chest rose and fell in a pant. "I have needs. Needs I've handled myself all these years. *Alone.* Needs I've been perfectly capable of handling, of controlling, until I met you."

She barely breathed. Lips parted, unable to speak.

"I saw you at those parties in Louisville, and you were..." His eyes glittered. He bit his lip. "You didn't see me, but I saw you. I saw you from the goddamn start! I was desperate—that's the reason I was in those ballrooms to begin with. But it was never about the money with you, not completely. Not for me."

"The Collingsworth gala...and the Feinstein's?" Margot asked, recalling the references he'd made the night they met. He'd known what she'd worn to both parties, right down to the pearl necklace.

"Yes." His gaze snapped to hers. "Yes. The most beautiful woman in the room both nights. How on earth could I miss you?"

"I—"

"You were never mine to have, Margot, but goddammit, I *saw you*. And now, after everything..." He groaned, a sound of the most tortured longing. "I want you so badly, I can't *think straight*. I've never...I didn't expect it, and I sure as hell don't know what to do with it...because I'm not supposed to have this. I made my peace with it decades ago, no more Dravenhearst brides." His eyes were wide, vulnerable. "No more heirs. No more goddamn *misery* in this godforsaken house."

Oh.

"But here you are," he continued. "Here you are, having no business wanting me or this twisted, miserable house...but somehow...somehow wanting us both nonetheless. Right?" Naked fear showed on his face now. "You do, don't you?"

"I do." She nodded. "I want you so much, Merrick. And you—"

This time when his lips closed over hers, they were positively aching. Tremoring with need. With hope and want. All of it and more.

"I want you," she breathed. "Please, let me have you. I'm begging."

His shoulders shuddered under her hands. "I don't know what I'm doing," he murmured. "I've never done this before."

"Please." Her fingers moved to his shirt, began undoing buttons.

"You should be running," he whispered against her lips. "Why aren't you running?"

She shook her head, her hands continuing down his shirt, revealing the smooth muscle and dark hair underneath. "I'm not going anywhere."

He groaned when she placed her palms flat on his broad chest.

"Your heart is racing." It was thundering, pounding relentlessly beneath his hot skin.

He took a shaky breath. "It's for you. It's yours. Black and mangled and cynical...and *yours*. If you want it."

She curled her fingers into a fist, nails gently scratching his chest. "I want it. I want all of it." *More than anything in this mortal world.*

The third time their lips met, there was no desperation, no aching, no questions. There was nothing but steady surety, smooth molasses on the hottest summer day, pouring languidly into each other.

Slowly, indulgently, Margot pushed his shirt off his shoulders. Her hands drifted over the planes of his strong back, then slid around to his stomach. Her fingers fluttered over the trail of dark hair there. Followed it down, down, down until she latched onto his belt buckle. He inhaled sharply.

"Should we..." He brushed his nose along her jawline.

She tipped her head upward, guiding his lips to the soft space beneath her ear. The skin there was damp with sweat.

"The house?" he asked. "My bedroom?"

"No. Here." Here in this rickhouse. In this place that brought him both the greatest love and deepest sorrow of his life. She wanted him right here, believing that together, they could bloom where he'd once bled.

She unbuckled his belt.

He lifted her, slamming her bottom onto a barrel. Her eyes floated to the rafters, sightline blurring, dizzy, with row after row of barrels. Her nose filled with cedar and oak. With the whisper of his sweet bourbon breath.

She closed her eyes.

He hitched up her skirts.

She spread her legs.

He was there, finally *there*, and she suddenly knew. The realization came from a distance—the hard, rigid pressure between his legs was meant for her. The barrel put them at the perfect height, his tip notching in her entrance.

Her eyes popped open.

"If it's too much..." His gaze flicked to her, watching every micromovement of her face as he pressed himself inside her. Deeper than deep, slower than slow.

"It's not," she breathed. But it almost was. There was just so *much* of him.

And that was what she told him, over and over again, when he began to move. That he was so much. Enough. Too much. Everything.

That she wanted him. Needed him. Now. Harder. More. With her. Deeper. Closer. Please. Now. Please. Please. *Please.*

Merrick let out an agonized, tortured moan. Began to move faster. With greater surety, losing himself within her. The intensity of his every thrust reached unbearable peaks, hitting a secret spot inside her every time...deep and true...

"Merrick, I...I'm..." He reduced her to impulse. Stole her words. Her rationality. Her sanity. He took it all. Robbed her blind.

A whiskey thief, indeed.

She couldn't fight it, wouldn't try. She surrendered herself, tipping over the edge. Spinning and reeling and clinging to his shoulders, digging in, crying out. She jolted when he found his release, emptying himself deep inside her with a groan. Collapsing onto her when it was over, his chest slick with sweat, melting into hers.

Hotter than hot in this hot as hell rickhouse.

Margot slowly regained her breath. She opened her eyes to a new world.

Merrick was there, waiting for her. Drinking her in.

"In case I haven't made it abundantly clear," he murmured, his chest rumbling against hers, "you are simultaneously the best and worst thing that has ever happened to me."

Her paranoid brain registered only one word. "The worst?"

"Yes. You've ruined me. Quintessentially and thoroughly."

She smiled, not the slightest bit displeased by his answer.

They stole back to the manor in the dark of night, exchanging secret, shy smiles, her hand clutched in his. A gentle breeze ruffled their hair, fanned their flushed cheeks.

The ebony stairs creaked under their feet. The hinges of his bedroom door whined. Springs groaned when he pulled her down onto his bed.

With him.

"Again," he told her, grabbing her wrists and pinning them to the mattress.

"Greedy," she murmured, lips fusing to his. Losing herself already.

Truthfully, she didn't think him greedy at all. Merrick didn't take anything from her she wasn't willing to give. She gave to him freely, by her own volition. Because she wanted to, wanted *him*.

He was her choice. An all-consuming fever dream of a choice, but *hers* nonetheless. And she would give herself to him again and again. A thousand times over in a thousand different ways. She'd give herself away.

For him.

24

June 19, 1870

Dear Diary,
I planted a magnolia tree today.

—*Excerpt, the diary of Eleanor Dravenhearst*

T HE BED GREW COLD in the night. It was either very late or very, very early. Still dark out.

Margot rolled over, reaching for him. Reaching to where he was supposed to be.

But Merrick's side of the bed was empty.

Her heart thudded painfully in her chest. She sat upright so quickly, the room swirled around her. Dizzying.

She rose to her feet and shivered. The room was ice cold, the door cracked open.

She knew he'd closed it before they'd gone to sleep. Before they'd made love in his bed.

"Merrick?" she whispered, creeping toward the hall. Her breath rose in a frozen cloud. "Merrick?"

The anxious and fearful part of her brain woke up fast. Surely he hadn't snuck out? Not again?

Not *ever* again. He'd promised.

Things were different now, weren't they? She was certainly different. With every step she took, she could feel the ache between her legs from where he'd been.

"Merrick?"

She reached forward, pushing open the door with a slow *creak*. He wasn't in the hallway, but someone was. Margot froze.

A woman. Dressed all in white. Turning the corner for the stairwell. Margot barely caught the swirl of skirts before she disappeared.

"Go back to bed." The familiar whisper raised the hair on the back of her neck.

Margot turned, expecting to find Babette, but the dark hallway was empty.

Where was Merrick?

She took off down the hall, heading for the stairs. She had to find him.

Her bare feet thudded on the carpet, slapped loudly on the wooden landing. She ran to the serpentine balustrade, looked into the foyer, and lost her breath.

There she was. The woman in white. Gliding across the floor.

She wore an ivory bridal ballgown, full and heavily skirted. Over her face hung a veil so long and thick it completely obscured her features and trailed to the floor, dragging behind her as she walked. Each step unhurried. Hauntingly staggered. Under her breath, the woman hummed. The echo resonated in the empty foyer, the tune familiar. An old children's lullaby.

Margot's veins ran with ice. When she blinked, there was frost on her eyelashes. She gripped the railing and descended the stairs, possessed by the sight of the woman in white. When she was halfway down, the woman disappeared through an archway.

Margot followed. Down the final stairs, across the foyer, into the hallway. The candles were snuffed out, fresh smoke in the air. It was pitch dark in the corridor, but a door was cracked open on her left. A door to a sitting room overlooking the front of the house, the magnolia trees.

Humming came from within, drawing Margot forward. She pushed open the door.

A small table was set. White cloth. China teacups.

And sitting there, right *there*, mere footsteps away, was a bride, illuminated by moonlight. A Dravenhearst bride, veil still covering her face.

"When the wind blows," the woman whisper-sang, fingers fluttering above the tea set, *"the cradle will rock."*

Margot suspected who she was, but she had to know. An icy fist of fear gripped her heart. Ruth was in her mind. Babette was in her mind. She was preternaturally afraid. Could barely get the words out. "Who...?"

The woman looked up.

"Who am I?" The voice was almost childlike, musical. Her head tilted, veil moving with it. "Who are *you*?" She lowered her voice, continuing to sing. *"When the bough breaks, the cradle will fall. And down will come baby..."*

"Margot," she whispered. "Margot Dravenhearst."

A sharp intake of breath, excited. The woman eagerly patted the empty seat beside her. "Margot *Dravenhearst*? Yes, of course you are. I knew it. I simply knew it. Come, sit with me. We have so much to talk about. Are you in love, Margot Dravenhearst?"

"Am I...what?"

"You look like you're in love." The words were fervent and wistful. "Tell me everything. You're going to have a baby, aren't you?"

Margot didn't answer. Her hand drifted to her stomach, eerily disengaged from the rest of her body. Like a puppeteer pulled her strings. The place between her legs was still sore and damp where Merrick had been mere hours ago.

"I know that look." The bride nodded. "You're one of us now. Just like you always wanted."

How did she...?

"Sit down. Please." She patted the seat again. "Have tea with me."

"Who are you?" Margot croaked.

"I'm Eleanor." The bride giggled, as though Margot was very silly indeed. The sound was high-pitched and girlish and wrong. So very, very wrong. "I'm so glad you're here. We're going to be the best of friends."

Margot awoke with a scream.

25

May 4, 1901

My sweet Babs,
I've dreamt of you for months on end. Today, the dream
becomes reality.
I wonder, do you remember the night we first met? You spoke
of horses with such passion, and I took the liberty of cheek.
"Why ride a horse when you can ride a bourbon maker?" Oh,
the way you laughed—that's the moment I knew you were
mine.

—Excerpt, a letter from Richard Dravenhearst to his wife on
their wedding day

MORNING SICKNESS SET IN quickly, and that was how Margot knew for certain. The words of a ghost could not be taken seriously, but her own body...quite another matter.

Quite an astounding matter, really.

The first time it happened, Margot was by the pasture at sunrise, watching Merrick ride. Her husband had cleverly extracted the promise shortly after bedding her—quite spectacularly—the night before. There had been a lot of that over the last two weeks, in every spare moment, in seemingly every room, on every free surface of the manor. A few more times in the rickhouses too.

The nausea crept up on her, an insidious knot in her gut as Merrick kicked his horse into a gallop. A twisting coil swelling into a wave and rising to her chest, then throat. Unable to be squelched.

When he noticed her distress, Merrick dismounted and held her hair back as she purged bile into the grass. He apologized profusely for pushing her, said if she wasn't ready...

"I'm ready. I'm fine." She was pathological, lying between heaves, waving away his concern, even as her eyes watered and her throat burned. She wasn't fine. She hated the sight of him astride Fox. Couldn't help but imagine him being bucked, thrown...that she would lose her husband to the same terrible fate as her brother.

But even with those terrible thoughts rattling through her brain, she knew they weren't the cause of the vomiting. She was pregnant. She knew it with a degree of omniscient certainty that sent shivers down her spine. The man holding back her hair was not only her husband, he was the father of her child. She was no longer just herself, just Margot. She was going to be a *mother*.

The sky overhead would never be the same again. Nor the grass under her feet or the hands tangled in her hair. Nothing was ever going to be the same again, because she, herself, was inherently different. The reason her heart beat and her lungs breathed...no longer for her alone.

It was as terrifying a revelation as it was awe-inspiring.

Ruth, who'd been training Omaha nearby, strolled over as Margot's nausea subsided. The expression on her face made it clear she, at least, was not there to hold back Margot's hair. She clucked her tongue, then pursed her lips.

Margot gave the smallest of nods. An admission a woman would always understand before a man. Merrick, bless his heart, released her hair and rubbed her back, oblivious.

As she wanted him to be. For now.

Margot sought out Ruth the next afternoon at her cottage. The two women settled on the porch swing, a faint scent of hellebore on the air. Ruth passed her a cup of tea, and Margot peered into its depths.

"No gin rickeys today?" she asked, her voice soft.

"I figured this particular conversation was better suited to tea."

Margot took a deep breath. "I think I'm...I might be..." She couldn't bring herself to say it aloud just yet, to speak the thought into reality. "I've met Eleanor."

Met her, seen her, been endlessly haunted by her for two weeks...same difference, really.

Ruth's teacup rattled when she placed it in its saucer. "Well, that's it then."

"What is?"

"You're expecting. I assume it's physiologically possible now?" She arched an eyebrow.

"Yes." Margot smiled softly, recalling last night's particularly adventurous romp. How Merrick had bent her over the dining room table. How her cries filled the room, giving voice to the wailing centaurs trapped in the coffered ceiling...

"Hmph." Ruth snorted. "That didn't take him long, now did it?"

Margot's daydream shattered. "He's not made me do anything I haven't wanted."

"Of course he hasn't, dear. He just doesn't understand the repercussions. Men never do." Ruth's gaze drifted toward the stables with a faraway look.

Margot didn't know what to say. She settled for the same as Ruth, watching Julian with faint disinterest as he led two colts to a water trough. From this distance, if she squinted her eyes just so, she could almost imagine he was Merrick, with his dark hair and sharp jawline. But Julian was a decade younger and lean, not carrying an ounce of extra body fat or muscle, the better to fly atop Omaha during training. Merrick was solidly built from his work at the distillery, with back muscles that rippled beneath her clawing fingers and abdominals that clenched deliciously when he moved above her. She closed her eyes, imagining the feel of his rough, calloused palm gliding up her thigh. The sandpaper brush of his stubble scraping between her legs...

"Children change everything, Margot," Ruth said, still looking at Julian and the horses. "And it starts well before they're born."

"I'm sure."

"Miscarrying her first changed Babette," Ruth continued. "Changed her in ways I didn't altogether understand at the time. She became a mother, but one without a baby. It pushed her closer to Eleanor and away from me. Then came the second pregnancy. Babette fought tooth and nail to bring Merrick into this world. She was already a mother the second time around, you see. Mothers will stop at nothing for the well-being of their children." Her gaze finally moved from Julian and the horses, latching onto Margot instead. "If you want this baby, you'll keep your distance from Eleanor. From Babette too. The Dravenhearst women have complicated histories with pregnancy, and misery loves company."

Margot shifted in her seat. She wasn't sure how she could possibly *keep her distance* from the Dravenhearst brides. Not when they burrowed like termites into her subconscious, welcome or not.

What she'd seen so far of the first Dravenhearst bride was a troublesome mystery. Eleanor could go from giggling one moment to weeping the next. And always, beneath everything, a compulsive need for closeness and reassurance. She attached herself like a barnacle, clinging to Margot with such fervor, it was sometimes difficult to rouse herself from dreaming. When she did, she often awoke with fingernail marks embedded in her forearms.

"Eleanor lost six children to miscarriage, you said?"

"Yes."

"And Babette just the first?"

Ruth bit her lip. "Well…"

"Well, what?"

"There was a third pregnancy," Ruth admitted. "Unplanned, mind you. Babette didn't enjoy motherhood in practice as much as in theory. She went to great lengths to prevent additional pregnancies, but about a decade into their marriage, there was a bit of a mishap."

"*Again?* Did she miscarry?"

"In a manner of speaking." Ruth crossed her legs, uncrossed them. She plucked at a gold button on her blazer. "The day Babette told me she was expecting was the day she died. She confided in me in the morning, and she hung herself in Rickhouse One that very night."

Margot gasped.

"I don't think she could face it." Ruth blinked furiously. "The house, Eleanor, even Richard—they'd all turned on her during her first two pregnancies. She wouldn't subject herself to that again. I don't know if she'd told Richard yet, but if she did…if she told him the same thing she told me that morning—that she wanted to leave…well, that could've done it as well, I suppose. That declaration would have made him rabid."

Margot was horrified. Struck speechless.

"Not to worry." Ruth patted the top of Margot's hand. A bit patronizingly. "Nothing like that will happen to you. Just steer clear of Eleanor and Babette. History does have a funny way of repeating itself here at Dravenhearst Manor." She chuckled weakly.

Margot didn't laugh. She didn't think she'd ever found anything less funny in her entire life.

The headboard slammed into the wall, keeping steady pace like a metronome. Tangible, auditory proof of her husband's feverish desire for her.

"Merrick, please," Margot gasped, arching her back, lifting her hips. Even when he was fully inside her, she wanted more of him. Always more. "I'm so close."

His fingers slipped between her legs, putting pressure right where she wanted it, *needed* it.

"Fuck," she cried, her vision blacking out. Her legs turned to jelly, her head lolling back on the pillow as she came apart. Merrick grabbed her right thigh, moving her leg over his shoulder to pull her slackened body closer. To angle deeper. Unfathomably deep. Three more strikes before he, too, found his release, crying out and collapsing forward.

"Fuck," she repeated, blowing out the word with a long exhale. She lifted her arm, heavy as lead, and dropped it over him, pressing his cheek to her breast and running her fingers through his dark hair.

"Such a foul mouth on you, Mrs. Dravenhearst," he teased.

"My husband is a terrible influence, I'm afraid. Positively uncouth."

Merrick rumbled with laughter before rolling onto his back. Margot snuggled into his chest. She sighed contentedly, long and slow as her eyes grew heavy with sleep. Was there a better way to drift off at the end of the day? She didn't think so. She wondered how she'd managed to sleep at all before Merrick.

Ah, that's right, she recalled faintly. *Laudanum.*

The bottle was still on her nightstand but gathering dust. Everything was different now. Sleep came easily, a natural extension of her consciousness. Naught but a crossing, easily made when she was so very warm and safe, slackened by satiation.

"I didn't know it could be like this," Merrick whispered.

Margot's eyes sprang open. The shift in his mood was evident, the words tinged with yearning and ache.

"Like what?"

"Like *this*." He gestured at the two of them, hopelessly tangled up in each other and the bed sheets. "I didn't know what I was giving up when I decided..."

"When you decided not to wed? To be celibate?" She wanted to talk about it, wanted *him* to talk about it. Desperately. She held her breath and kept her head buried in his chest. She didn't want to spook him with eye contact.

"Well, yes, *that*." His voice rankled with bitterness. "For me, the two are mutually inclusive. I'm not comfortable being vulnerable with just anyone, Margot, and I only make promises I can keep."

"I like that about you," she murmured into his chest. "Why do you say it like it's a bad thing?"

"Because it's a bit strange, isn't it? To prefer the company of oneself instead of others?" he asked. "It's only that...over the years, I've grown very comfortable being alone. I *like* being alone—I genuinely do. It's familiar. Reliable."

"You mean *safe*." She completed his thought, understanding.

"Yes. Safe, you could say. People are unpredictable, and I'm a creature of habit. In bourbon making, it's the uncontrolled variables that lead to destruction."

Margot realized what he meant and raised her head from his chest. Now was the time to look him in the eye. "I'm not going to destroy you, Merrick."

I'm going to love you. The words rose unbidden, sudden as a bolt of lightning. Images followed. An entire lifetime with him. A house full of children. A working distillery with barrels and bottles full of bourbon. Magnolias in bloom.

Her palm moved to her stomach, fingers splayed there. Seeing it. Believing in life and happiness and love, not destruction.

She reached for his hand. "I know what it feels like to be damaged beyond repair," she murmured. "I know why you like being alone. Because people can hurt." She took a deep breath. "But loving someone is not destruction. It's the beginning, not the end."

He stilled at her words. Didn't speak for several moments. "Loving someone, huh? Is that what's happening between us?"

She knew him well enough to hear the question within the question: *Are you in love with me? Do you choose me? Do you love me?*

Not yet, her mind said.

But we might, her heart answered. *We might very soon.*

She'd gone too long without answering.

He fumbled, trying to fill the gap himself. "You don't owe me anything, Margot. I don't want you to feel—"

"It took me years to realize this," she said, holding her gaze steady. She would not blink. She would not look away. "I would love my brother all over again, just to lose him. It would be worth it. I'd lose him all over again, just for one more day of loving him. Wouldn't you?"

He chewed on his cheek, considering this. "No."

"No?"

"I wouldn't." He looked away. "I...I don't feel the same. I'm sorry. My life, my losses—they're different from yours."

"Your mother?" Even now, while lying in bed with him, the specter of Babette loomed.

"I suppose. She wasn't much of a mother though." He looked away.

There was pain, so much pain, in his words. Margot's heart broke for him.

He took a deep breath before continuing, "She was just so damn unreliable. Maybe it wasn't all her fault. Ruth has told me, tried to help me understand"—he cut his eyes to hers—"there was more going on than I realized. Things with the house and my father...things an eleven-year-old boy couldn't possibly understand. But I don't forgive her. I don't forgive her for it, and I sure as hell wouldn't go back to love her harder. If I could go back, it would only be to tell myself not to walk into the rickhouse on that horrible morning, the one when I found her."

"I can't imagine—"

"No. You can't." His tone was hard now. "That's what I meant when I said my loss is different from yours. I feel very differently about it. Angry. It's been twenty years, and I'm still so goddamn angry." His hand ripped through his hair.

Margot wavered. "If...if that's what you need to feel, then—"

"I don't *want* to feel it," he exclaimed. "But I do. It's the only thing I feel when I think of her. She was always so selfish, even in death. She tried to ruin the only thing I had. The distillery is all I've ever had."

"I'm sure that's not true."

"It is. I sure as hell never had *her*. I'm not sure anyone ever did—me, my father, Ruth, all her stupid flings...no amount of love was ever enough. She sucked everyone around her dry."

"You knew?" Margot was aghast. "You knew about the cheating? You were just a child." She thought of the brown-eyed man in her dreams. Had that relationship ever died? Or had he simply been the first of many?

"Of course I did." Merrick laughed bitterly. "She didn't try very hard to hide it. Why do you think—"

"Did your father know?" Margot interrupted. This seemed a critical piece of the puzzle. It would certainly give credence to Ruth's theory about Richard. Give motive for violence, even murder.

"That he was being cuckolded?" His expression soured. "He knew, but he didn't do anything about it. He loved her too, loved her just enough to be afraid of losing her but not enough to make her want to stay. That's the worst way to love someone, I think. Loving them small."

"I see."

He shook his head. "I don't want a life that looks beautiful on the outside but rots on the inside. That kind of life falls apart when even the slightest bit of pressure is applied. Trust me, I know." His smile, when it came, was sad. "When the going gets tough, people leave. That's what they do."

"Merrick." She sighed heavily, thinking of her dreams, the pull of this family's ghosts. "What if there really is a curse? What if she didn't have a choice?"

"There's no curse, Margot. We *always* have a choice. She made the wrong one—a very weak and cowardly and selfish choice."

"Huh." She leaned back, eyebrows raised.

"What?"

"Nothing."

"*What?*"

"It's only...she has an awful lot of power over you. For someone you say was weak."

His jaw ticked, but he didn't reply.

"I've met your mother." Margot knew she was treading in dangerous territory now. "She wasn't weak, and she sure as hell wasn't a victim. Your memories don't square with mine. I think there's more to her story."

He gripped her face between two hands. "I don't want you sticking your nose into my family's past. No good can come from kicking that hornet's nest, and there's nothing to be gained from digging up ghosts."

"You'll never be free of her otherwise."

"I can be. I am."

"You're not."

He breathed heavily, her face still between his palms. Warm and steady.

"Besides," she continued, "there's no curse, right? So there's no harm in digging." She raised an eyebrow, challenging him with his own words.

"Right," he replied weakly.

"It's settled then. I'll give her your regards, shall I? When I see her tonight?"

He laughed mirthlessly, dropping a hand to cover his eyes. "Tell her to fuck off for me, will ya?"

"Ever uncouth, Mr. Dravenhearst."

"I think you'll find I can be all sorts of uncouth where you're concerned." He dragged her closer, close enough to press his lips to hers. To slide his tongue into her mouth. To slip his strong, broad thigh between her legs, applying pressure, encouraging her to grind down and ride. "Stay with me," he whispered into her lips. "Choose me, not her."

"Always."

26

April 5, 1873

Dear Diary,
I planted another magnolia today. That's two pairs now,
guarding the house. My babies take root in the earth instead
of my womb. Where they grow, even flourish.
I stand at the windows and wonder, "Why out there? Why
not within me?" What is wrong with me?

—Excerpt, the diary of Eleanor Dravenhearst

"SIT, SIT." ELEANOR FLUTTERED around the tea table, pulling out chairs and fluffing napkins. Her ever-present white veil dragged behind her, ghosting along the mahogany floor with a sinister whisper. "Please, sit. It's so nice to have all of us together, isn't it?"

Babette rolled her eyes. She leaned in the parlor doorway, wearing a dress of deep green. "I'll sit, but only if you remove that ghastly veil." She shuddered. "I'm not taking tea with Dracula's bride."

Eleanor froze. "I never take off my veil," she whispered. "You know that, Babette."

The second bride's mouth opened, a snide look twisting her beautiful face into something distinctly evil.

"Here, sit beside me, Babette." Margot slid into a chintz chair and patted the neighboring seat. She fought a shiver, pulling a blanket from the settee to wrap around her shoulders. Behind her, the windows were thick with creeping frost. Inside the panes, not out.

"Indeed, indeed. Sit and drink," Eleanor trilled. She settled on Margot's other side and began to pour. Smoke curled from the teapot, dewy steam collecting along the rim of the cup. "Tell us everything, Margot. Surely you've shared the news with Merrick by now? What did he say? How did you do it? Oh, did he cry when you told him he was going to be a father?" She propped her chin in her hand and waited expectantly.

Margot ignored the proffered cup of tea. The warmth felt delicious in her frozen fingers, but she didn't trust the brew for one minute. The story of Babette's miscarriage loomed heavy, and Eleanor's fervor about the baby frightened her. It was all she ever wanted to talk about.

"I've still not told him. The, er, time hasn't felt right."

"What could possibly be more *right* than a baby?" Eleanor wheedled. This too was a familiar refrain. "You're starting a family. There's no greater calling than children, Margot. No greater joy than motherhood."

"Is that so?" Babette plunked herself down at the table with enough force to rattle the teacups. "Is that why you offed yourself in the rickhouse, Eleanor? You were filled with *joy*?"

Eleanor slammed the teapot down, a large dollop sloshing out to stain the tablecloth. "Babette, *manners*."

She turned to Margot. Reached out to pat her hand. It felt like dunking her fingers in a bucket of ice.

"Babette and I have never seen eye to eye on this," Eleanor confided, leaning in. "But you, Margot...you're going to be a wonderful mother. You're going to be the best of us, I just know it. Drink up, dearie."

Margot continued to ignore the tea.

"How dare you." Babette kicked her feet up to an empty chair, lounging irreverently. "I was an excellent wife, a fantastic mother. Would have been even better if you'd left well enough alone. Ruined everything with your meddling, you did. Ninny."

Eleanor's hand flew to her chest. "I did no such thing. You were the one cavorting behind your husband's back. Really, Babette, do wedding vows mean nothing to you?" She ticked off the offenses on white-gloved fingers. "You *defiled* my house with your sinful parties. You made a fool of my beloved son, getting yourself in the family way not once, but *twice* by another man. Invited your degenerate, concubine friend—"

"You took my children from me," Babette bellowed. "I lost two babies and my life because of you." She grabbed her teacup so violently, a tidal wave spilled over the edge, soaking another section of tablecloth. "And your beloved, pious, perfect son loved those bloody Gomorrah parties as much as I did."

"When you've lost *six* babies," Eleanor said, her tone lethal, the tail of a rattler poised to strike, "you can come crying to me. And I didn't take your life or your second bastard baby from you, Babette. You've only yourself to blame for that."

The silence that befell the room was deadly, stretching for several long, uncomfortable moments.

It was broken by Eleanor's laughter, high and loud and altogether wrong.

"Oh, Margot." The bride dabbed her napkin at her veil, right at the place where her mouth should be. "I'm terribly sorry, dearie. What dreadful hostesses we are. We were talking about you and Merrick. Babette, wouldn't you love to hear about your son? How happy he is? How very much in love they are?"

"If my son had a half a brain," Babette replied, hands fisting in her lap, "if he loved her at all, he'd leave his blasted distillery behind and take her far, far away from here." She pushed back her chair and stormed from the room, slamming the door behind her.

"Don't mind her," Eleanor said, shaking her head. "She's never understood what it's like, the sacrifices women must make. When she came here, I thought we could be friends. The way you and I are." She nodded frenetically, veil flailing. "But she just doesn't have what it takes."

"What it takes for what?"

"To be a mother." Eleanor tilted her head. "She was a terrible mother, and she knows it. I'm sure Merrick has told you all kinds of stories. I certainly could. Drink up, dearie, your tea." She gestured toward the untouched cup.

Terrible mother, terrible woman—Eleanor's implication was clear. If a woman wasn't a good mother, what else about her mattered? Did anything?

Margot frowned. "About those stories, do you happen to know—"

"It started as soon as he was born. She refused to put him to breast—can you imagine? That's where the attachment issues began, mark my words. Right from the outset. You plan to nurse your own baby when the time comes, don't you, Margot?"

Truthfully, Margot hadn't given it a lick of thought, but she sensed implicitly only one answer was acceptable here. "Er, sure...but—"

"Aha! Because you understand." The shadow of Eleanor's lips twitched in a sanctimonious smirk beneath the veil. "You *understand*."

"I'm sorry." Margot's hands fluttered with her napkin, twisting it in her lap. "Understand what, precisely?"

Out of nowhere, Eleanor began to cry. Great, hitching sobs racked her body. "It's the best thing you'll ever do, you know," she said, between gasps. "Being a mother."

Gracious.

Margot leaned away, scooted to the edge of her chair. She was filled with aching sadness. Eleanor looked as frail as a baby bird. Thin wrists, shrouded face, heaving shoulders...if this was the portrait of motherhood, it was hardly a glowing advertisement.

"You've got to tell him." Suddenly, Eleanor lunged across the table, grabbing Margot's arms. Her nails dug sharply into skin. "Once he knows you're giving him a baby, things will be better. He'll take care of you."

Margot twisted in her grip and grimaced. "Eleanor, you're hurting me."

Her fingers clung tighter, rabid with fervor. A blotch of spittle stained the veil at her lips as she continued, "Once you become a mother, everything will change. You'll see."

"Yes. Yes, I do see," she lied. "I'll tell Merrick tomorrow."

Eleanor's claws softened, then released.

Margot exhaled shakily, rubbing her arms. "I'll tell him, but first I need to ask you about Babette. It's very important. Do you know the name of the man she was sleeping with? Was there more than one?"

"Oh, there were many playthings, but only one ever mattered to her." Her posture straightened, turning smug. "She never should have married my son, that harlot. Not when she'd already given her heart to another."

"Who was he?" Margot leaned back in. "Can you tell me his name?"

"Drink up, dearie. You've not had any tea."

"It's...it's gone cold."

"I'll pour a fresh cup then, shall I?"

Margot picked up an empty one, holding it obediently while Eleanor began to pour. "His name," she repeated. "Can you tell me his name?"

"They both loved horses, you know. They used to meet in the stables to screw there. She just couldn't stay away." Her voice was picking up steam with every sentence. "She was going to leave my son—leave her own son without a mother! Can you believe that?"

Suddenly, the tea overflowed the cup, cascading straight into Margot's lap. Scalding. Violently hot through the thin cotton of her nightdress. She screamed and leapt from her chair.

"His name," Margot cried, jumping away as tea streamed over her bare feet. She shrieked again. "Please, Eleanor, just tell me his name!"

"Of course, dearie." Eleanor tipped her head again, mouth agape. She continued spilling tea over open air. "No need to get yourself so riled. It can't be good for the baby. Your tea will help, drink up. Now let's see...the name...why, it's—"

"Margot!"

Her mouth was open in an ear-piercing scream when Merrick wrenched her from sleep.

"Margot, are you hurt?" He turned over her arms, checking, ripping back the blankets.

"Merrick?" Her eyes fluttered open with surprise. Eleanor and the tea party were gone. She was lying beside her husband in his bed. Her nightgown was dry, not soaked with scalding, potentially poisonous tea.

"Were you dreaming? Did they do something to you?"

It all came rushing back, and with it, the agony of how near she'd come. She'd been *so close*. The name, she was convinced, would unlock everything. And if she could unlock the past, she could set them free of it. All of them—her, Merrick, the house.

"I think we should go to Louisville," Merrick said, nodding as he came to the decision. His concerned eyes swept her face. "For a few weeks. I'll sort everything out. Julian can manage the distillery while I'm gone."

"Merrick, stop. Shh." Margot placed a finger over his lips. "I'm fine. We don't need to go anywhere. I don't want to go anywhere. And I don't want you to wake me ever again, not when I'm dreaming. You interrupted a very important discussion."

"You were *screaming*," he said, incredulous.

"I was fine. I'm more than fine, actually." She smiled softly and reached for his hands. "I have something to tell you."

She didn't know what possessed her, what possibly felt right about this particular moment, but something of Eleanor glowed in her chest, purring when the words came out.

"Merrick, I'm expecting. We're going to have a baby."

27

October 1933

Reopened the stillhouse and began making mash.
Three more states voted for repeal this week, twenty-five total
so far. It's finally happening! Barrel filling to begin within
the month.

—Excerpt, Dravenhearst Distilling Inventory Log as main-
tained by Merrick Dravenhearst

T HE INFAMOUS KENTUCKY HEAT didn't break until early October. Hot days and even hotter nights slipped into the crisp relief of fall. Alastair's first grain shipment showed up contaminated with weevils ("He's screwing with me," Merrick roared. "Trying to fleece me!"), and the second took an ungodly amount of time to arrive ("He's dragging his heels on purpose, the spiteful bastard!" "Yes, dear."). By the time Merrick was able to start making bourbon mash, twenty-five states had ratified the Twenty-First Amendment, seeking to repeal Prohibition.

"Mark my words," Merrick said as he and Margot walked down the hill together, "Kentucky will fall in line soon enough."

"They'd better…" Margot mused, leaves crunching underfoot. The trees behind Hellebore House were burnished with russet and gold. "Since you've gone and turned our estate into a bootlegging operation." She rolled her eyes. *"Again."*

"You'll feel differently in about ten minutes. That's why I'm bringing you down here." He smiled, full teeth and dimples. "Today, Mrs. Dravenhearst, is the day you fall in love."

"Really?" Margot replied, suddenly breathless, heart fluttering.

"With bourbon," Merrick clarified.

Was it her imagination or was there a teasing twinkle in his eye?

Merrick stopped outside a rather squat building at the outskirts of the distillery. He pushed the door open. "Welcome to the stillhouse."

The first thing she noticed was the smell, an overpowering mix of sweet and sulfuric, sharp on every inhale. A little yeasty and warm too, like sourdough coming out of the oven.

Then there were the vats, massive copper drums two stories high, and exposed pipes running every which way. Dominating the far corner stood a magnificent column still; its copper tower stretched to the ceiling with clear, churning distillate visible through small porthole windows running up its length.

"It's humid," she observed as Merrick pulled the door closed.

"That's the fermentation tanks." He rapped a knuckle on the nearest copper vat. "We'll start there. Come on." He vaulted up a set of rickety stairs to the second-story catwalk.

The pungent smell was even stronger on the second level.

"Bourbon mash," Merrick said, gesturing inside the nearest tank. "This batch is two days into fermentation."

Margot leaned over the rim. Inside, a golden mustard-brown mix of grainy soup bubbled softly.

"All bourbon mash has to contain at least fifty-one percent corn," he explained. "Every distillery has its own unique recipe. Corn adds sweetness, rye adds spice—that's a Dravenhearst family secret, most other distilleries use wheat—and barley acts as the chemical stabilizer. During fermentation, yeast converts grain sugars into alcohol." He reached for her hand, pulling it over the crust of the fizzing mash. "Feel that heat?"

Yes. Warmth radiated from the surface. She was mesmerized, staring into the vat. It looked *alive*. Bubbling like stew on a stove.

"Heat is a byproduct of the chemical reaction happening under the surface. The mash takes three days to ferment. And then..."

He dragged her back downstairs, pointing out the well draining the alcohol from the fermentation tanks, then the pipes straining and transferring the distillate to the copper still. His mouth moved a mile a minute as he explained the minutiae of the process. Tripping over himself, hardly able to get the words out fast enough.

So much knowledge, Margot thought, watching the glow in his eyes, the vigor with which his hands moved. *So much passion and precision and skill that's gone unused for so many years.*

It seemed, suddenly, a terrible waste.

Margot had never given much thought to the temperance movement. She grew up in a world of wets and drys, a world where Prohibition was the accepted reality. But here, standing in this stillhouse with Merrick, for the first time, she critically questioned that reality.

Thousands of lost jobs, he'd told her. Family businesses shuttered. Trade secrets forgotten. Decreased taxable revenue to the state.

It wasn't as simple as mere morality, the drys be damned. This was a *business*. A lifeblood and a lifeline. One Merrick had every right to stake his livelihood on.

Her husband didn't pause for breath until they settled before the column still. He exhaled slowly, eyes tracing the flow of the distillate as it moved up and down the tower. Turning to vapor and back, concentrating and purifying, readying itself for the barrel.

"I haven't seen anything distilling in here for thirteen years," he whispered.

"It looks like water," Margot murmured, just as riveted.

In silence, he wrapped his arm around her shoulders.

They stayed like that for a long time, watching the ebb and flow of the still. Mesmerized.

"That's my last name in there," Merrick finally said, pointing. "This is what it means. It's yours now too. For better or worse."

Margot nodded, understanding. It was profound, the way his sharing cracked open entire valleys inside her. Gorges. Eager to be filled, poured into, with more of him. She would never be full. Never tire. She wanted it all.

"You might not love it yet," Merrick continued, peeking sideways at her, "but you will."

Margot didn't reply.

She didn't need to. She was a hell of a lot closer to love than he'd ever know.

Anticipation was their bedfellow. Every day, they scoured the papers for news of repeal, for signs of weakening resolve amongst the Kentucky policymakers. Merrick stayed up late every night, making telephone calls to friends in the industry, rallying the troops.

"Last night, Colonel Blanton heard whiff of a state legislative hearing," Merrick said as Margot slipped into her bedroom to dress for church. "He's asked me to be there when the time comes. Together, we can talk some sense into those congressional bluenoses and put this ghastly decade behind us."

"Mm-hmm," Margot tossed back, distracted. She glanced nervously over her shoulder, having left the adjoining door open. Foolish. She rose on tiptoes to yank her wedding gown away from the doors to the balcony. The knots of the noose seemed especially tight this morning. Her fingers fumbled frantically. Merrick was still chattering away while he dressed, unaware.

"Come on," she muttered under her breath, nails picking at the rope. She sighed with relief when the bonds gave, releasing the dress into her arms. She clutched the gown to her chest and closed her eyes. "Babette," she whisper-hissed. "This little game is starting to get old."

Third time this week.

A chill at her shoulder. "Who says it's me?"

Margot whirled, expecting to see the socialite's specter lounging on the corner chaise, eyebrow raised. The picture was so strong in her mind, she was convinced for half a second she really *did* see her, but in a single blink, the image vanished. The chaise was empty.

Merrick's footsteps were on the move, approaching the door. Hurriedly, Margot balled up the wedding gown and stashed it behind her back.

Merrick leaned in the doorway, head tilted and arms folded, the buttons on his shirt only half done. "Well, what do you say?" he asked, smiling impishly.

"To...what?"

"To playing hooky from church today. So I can get the mash bill working first thing." His expression turned from playful to sinful, his gaze dragging up Margot's nightdress-clad body. "Although, I could be convinced to delay a few hours for a lazy morning in bed with you."

She laughed. "If you can delay your precious mash for a morning with me, you can delay for an hour of prayer. God doesn't ask much of us, Merrick."

He chuckled and raised his hands in surrender. Margot held the smile on her face until he moved out of sight. She strode quickly to the closet and strung up the wedding dress, then tucked it into the farthest back corner. Same as always, to no avail.

"This game is getting tiresome," she murmured again to Babette.

Tinkling spectral laughter answered, raising gooseflesh on her arms.

"I'm serious," she hissed, stomping a foot. "Leave it alone this time, goldarn it."

"Margot? Who're you talking to?" Merrick called.

"Go on," Babette whispered. "Tell him who haunts you, Margot dear. And in broad daylight? Tsk, tsk."

Margot swallowed hard. Closed her eyes again.

She was going mad, wasn't she? All of this was only happening in her head, wasn't it?

Not real, not real.

"No one, love," she called back. "No one at all."

The windows were open in the church house to let in the cool October breeze, but even still, Margot felt stifled. She'd worn a high-collared dress, and it scratched terribly at her skin. Tight and constricting.

Father Simmons was preaching, droning on and on, up at the lectern. *"And the Pharisees came to him, and asked him, 'Is it lawful for a man to put away his wife?'"*

Merrick's eyes glazed over where he stood. Just beyond him, in the pew across the aisle, lurked Alastair. He was staring intently at Margot.

Wrong. Wrong. Wrong. Her mind tolled like a church bell. A funereal echo.

Her fingers tightened on the wooden pew. Margot imagined her pallor turning green, tasted copper pennies in her mouth, the way she always did when a wave of morning sickness was coming.

Not now.

"*And he saith unto them, 'Whosoever shall put away his wife, and marry another, committeth adultery against her. And if a woman shall put away her husband, and be married to another, she committeth adultery.'*"

Margot's vision grew spotty. She couldn't tell if she was going to faint or be horrendously, embarrassingly sick.

She swallowed once, twice, three times, smacking her lips. She looked for an escape, but she was blocked into the pew by Merrick.

And across the way, Alastair. Alastair, who was frowning, all furrowed brows and sour lips. Alastair, who was turning in the pew, opening his mouth...

"Merrick?" She batted weakly at her husband's arm. "Merrick!"

He blinked awake. "What?"

"I need to..." She gasped, a hand fanning her face. "I think I might..."

With a single look at her, Merrick understood. He wrapped an arm around her waist, offering support. "Outside. Can you walk?"

She tried, letting him half guide, half drag her from the pew.

Gawking heads turned in their direction, but not even an earthquake could deter Father Simmons. He reached his climax with thunderous gusto. "*Verily I say unto you, 'Whosoever shall not receive the kingdom of God as a little child, he shall not enter therein.'*"

Margot's legs buckled. Her vision began to tunnel. She was going down. Here. In public.

Again.

Memories of shocked gasps and nervous laughter filled her ears. The church fell suddenly away, and she was back in a Louisville ballroom.

Wearing a white crepe Georgette gown and satin gloves pulled up to her elbows. A debutante set to make her debut.

Ready or not.

"The Texas Dip," her dead mother had hissed. Nineteen-year-old Margaret Greenbrier stumbled on wobbling legs. Alone, her mother buried barely a year ago. Ready or not...

She wasn't ready. They'd delayed a year for mourning, and even still, she wasn't ready.

She was lost. She was abandoned. She was *distressed*.

Margaret had begun to laugh. Hysterically. Her heart pounded, fierce enough to tear free from her chest and fly far away. It did. It had. Her heart had been wrenched free so many years ago, and Margaret was but a shell of herself, alone in a society ballroom in crepe Georgette.

Faces in the crowd blurred, jaws open, hands at shocked mouths while Margaret Greenbrier spun in the middle of the ballroom, arms out, crazed laughter bubbling free. She spun herself straight into a perfect Texas Dip. And after she rose on trembling knees, her eyes rolled back and she fainted.

At nineteen years old, she'd already lost so much.

But that was the day Margaret Greenbrier truly lost everything.

"My wife...Yes, she's well over two months along." Merrick's distressed voice floated overhead. "Yes, with child."

"Merrick?" She reached for his hand, eyes still shut.

"I'm right here, love."

Warmth. His long fingers twining with hers, easy as breathing.

She opened her eyes to bright sunshine. Haloing around his head.

"You look like an angel," she murmured, squinting.

"Did you hit your head on the way down?" He smiled. "I thought I caught you, but..."

She laughed, dropping a hand over her forehead. Embarrassment rushed in. "I'm so sorry—"

An unfamiliar low voice. "Oh, it's quite common in this condition, especially early on. Nothing to worry about, I'm sure."

Only then did Margot's focus go beyond Merrick, to two sets of peering eyeballs just over his shoulder.

"I, uh, was telling Dr. Smalls here about the baby. In case, well..." Merrick trailed off.

Her gaze flicked to the bespectacled man dressed in his Sunday best at her feet. She realized, a bit belatedly, he'd removed her shoes. Was checking the tops of her feet for pulses.

"Beg pardon, Mrs. Dravenhearst," he tittered, flouncing her dress so it covered as close to her ankle as possible. "Just doing a quick assessment. Your husband did the right thing, getting you out of the church. Mighty warm in there today for October. Seems you were overcome. Again, perfectly normal, given your condition." He nodded perfunctorily at her midsection.

Normal. That was a new one. It seemed pregnancy had its perks after all.

"Right," she replied weakly, moving to sit up. As she did so, her eyes landed on the second member of her rescue party.

Alastair.

"He helped me carry you out," Merrick murmured. "Managed the doors and such."

After Dr. Smalls finished his assessment, Margot was given a clean bill of health and orders to spend the day resting. The physician promised discretion and returned to Mass for the Communion Rite, but Alastair stayed behind.

Merrick cleared his throat. "Thank you for your assistance, Alastair. I suppose we'll—"

"You said she's expecting?" Alastair interrupted.

Silence. Stony, glaring silence.

The set of Merrick's jaw hardened.

Alastair broke the staring contest, his eyes softening when they moved to Margot. "Two months along?"

"Nearing three," she whispered.

His gaze darkened and switched back to Merrick. Full of judgment. Alastair rose to his full height. "You're a foolish, foolish boy."

"I am thirty-one years old, Alastair. Do not speak to me like a child."

"I will speak to you like a child when you act like one. You have no idea what you've done. The ghosts you've awakened—"

"What do you know of ghosts?" Margot interjected, her jaw dropping in surprise.

Alastair fell silent.

Margot licked her lips. "If you've something to say—something about Babette or Eleanor—say it."

"I only know the same as everyone else, everyone she loved. Ask Ruth. Or that butler of yours. Eleanor was before my time, but I knew Babette the same way the rest of 'em did. I'd tell you to ask your father, Merrick, but he's dead. Thank your stars for that, because he'd take your hind to the whipping post for this. That house is cursed. Dravenhearst marriages are cursed. Your mother—"

"Don't say one more word about my mother," Merrick rumbled. "You don't get to speak of her. Not in front of me."

Alastair stepped back and crossed his arms. Only then did Margot see it, at his wrists, silver cufflinks glinting in the morning sun.

A pair of racehorses.

"Oh my God." Her stomach bottomed out.

"If my parents' marriage was cursed," Merrick continued, "it was because of *you*. Neither ghosts nor hauntings inflict a shade of the damage adultery does. Remember it how you like, absolve yourself of the role you played in her death if you must, but I'll remember it how it happened."

Alastair grimaced. "Those wounds run deep, boy. I'm sorry for my role, but I wouldn't take it back. Same way you'd likely refuse to take *her* back." He nodded at Margot, then lowered his voice. "The die is cast. No turning back now."

"There's no curse," Merrick insisted. "I'll not be punished for the sins of my parents."

"No, you'll not be punished. Dravenhearst men never are." His gaze slid from Merrick to Margot. "But *she* will be. Mark my words."

<u>28</u>

October 8, 1933

My dearest Margaret,
I think of you and Merrick every day as I read the papers.
There are whispers in Louisville of a legislative hearing. No
imminent plans but very promising indeed. It's beginning.
I find myself keeping more to the townhouse as the weather
cools. I must confess, the crisp morning air does constrict my
stamina. Have the leaves begun to change in Frankfort? I
watch from the windows here, and I think of you, knowing
what I see is but the palest imitation of the beauty of the
Bluegrass in the fall.

Forever Yours,
Pa

ONE COULD ONLY RECLINE on stiff, upholstered sofas for so long.

Margot gave a dramatic sigh and flopped an arm over her forehead. Being confined indoors after a fainting episode reminded her of *before*.

She'd spent many years like this, moving from couch to couch, window seat to window seat, trying for invisibility. Because when one has a nervous breakdown amongst all of Louisville society, one has no choice but to vanish. She hadn't wanted to be seen anyway.

Things were different now. Now, spending even a single day with her feet up felt like a prison sentence. There was nothing to keep her mind off the melancholic letter she'd just received from her father. It wasn't so much the things he said, rather the things he didn't. The hints between the lines.

Keeping to the townhouse.

Constricted stamina.

The woolgathering reflections of fall in the Bluegrass.

She sighed again, louder, more drawn out.

"Gracious, Margot, I didn't peg you as one for lachrymose dramatics," Babette said.

Margot's gaze snapped across the room. Her mother-in-law's specter reposed on an adjacent chaise and mimicked Margot's posture—arm over her head, lips plumped in an exaggerated pout.

"Leave me alone." Margot harumphed, directing her attention to the magnolias beyond the window. A rhythmic, soft thudding sounded from outside.

"Goodness me." Babette smiled. "Aren't we keen to play the victim today?"

"I'm not playing the victim. I'm on doctor's orders for bedrest, and I'll not sit here to be your plaything. Not today."

Babette chuckled, eyes fluttering with amusement. "My *plaything*? Whatever has gotten into you?"

Margot's lips tightened as an insidious chill crept across the room. She thought of Alastair. Of Merrick and Richard. Of Eleanor. Even Xander, of what she'd begun to suspect might have happened between the butler and his former mistress.

So many people, she thought, staring Babette down, *who you've spun 'round and 'round in your web.*

Babette crowed. "Oh, I see. You learned something this morning you didn't particularly like about me. You've known it all along, Margot. I showed him to you myself. Do you think I'm ashamed?" Her brows dipped, the corner of her lip quirking. "I'm not."

"Maybe you should be."

"Maybe *you* are," Babette returned. "Maybe it's you who's ashamed. Because when you look at me, you recognize the darkest part of yourself. You recognize *desire*. Wanting to be wanted." She clucked her tongue. "Is he enough for you, my son? Of course not. They never are. It's *me* you want. My approval. My attention. My love. Same as all the others." She rose from her seat, prowling forward like a cat. Slinking. Margot couldn't tear her gaze away, for even now—especially now—the woman was so goddamn beautiful.

A frigid draft blew through the room.

"I don't," she whispered.

"You do. I wouldn't be here if you hadn't already been thinking about me." With each step closer, the temperature in the room plummeted further.

"Leave me alone," Margot said, voice shaking. She rose to go to the door, and that was when she saw it. Through the window.

Eleanor in her white gown and veil. Eleanor at the base of the nearest magnolia. Shovel in hand, digging.

Thud. The strike of metal meeting earth. A slithering whisper as the blade raised, dirt and pebbles raining to the ground. *Plunk.* Eleanor shucking the debris into a pile. *Thud.* The blade striking deep again. *Plunk.*

A hand clamped on Margot's shoulder. Ice cold. She screamed.

"She's digging for you, Dravenhearst bride," Babette whispered. Her fingers brushed the hair at the nape of Margot's neck. A chill ran down her spine. "For your baby. A place with all the rest."

Margot let out another frightened cry and ran from the room. Babette's cackling laughter echoed in her ears as she fled the house.

The sunlight was blinding but cleansing. Strong enough to chase away ghosts.

Margot leaned on one of the pillars on the portico, her arms cradling the imperceptible swell of her stomach. She could hardly be sure it was there at all—it was still so early. But she *knew*. She felt it, the precious, tiny life growing inside her. Early or not, she loved her baby fiercely. A piece of her and a piece of Merrick. Theirs and theirs alone. No one could take that from her. Not Babette. Not Eleanor. Not this house.

Could they?

She looked toward the magnolias, standing sentinel at the front of the property. Eleanor was gone. If she'd been there at all.

Margot raised a hand to her forehead, her mind racing. *Had* Eleanor been there? A veiled ghost digging a grave in broad daylight? It seemed unlikely.

It's getting worse. The phantasmagoria.

She shuddered, fingers knotting in her hair.

"Yoohoo!" Evangeline stood near the corner of the house, a pair of shears in hand.

Margot was so relieved to see another warm-blooded human, the menacing glint of sunlight off the blade was no deterrent. She strode toward the gardener.

"Need a hand?"

"Always," Evangeline replied, her throaty voice carrying over the hillside. "I've been trimming this morning and need to start my fall pesticide application this afternoon." Her grin was downright cheery.

"Pesticide?" Margot repeated, close enough now to fall into step. They headed for Evangeline's gardening shed.

"First frost will fall soon," Evangeline said, "which means outdoor critters will be wanting to come indoors where it's toasty. Can't have that, now can we?" She pushed open the wooden door and dropped the shears into a metal bucket full of gardening tools.

"I suppose not." Margot tried to peek inside the shed and caught a glimpse of drying herbs strung from the low ceiling and a workbench filled with glass apothecary bottles before Evangeline closed the door.

"Gloves." Evangeline plunked a pair into Margot's hands. "Don't want to be touching any of my special friends with your bare skin, sugar."

She led her to a small enclosure, popped a rusted key into the lock, and opened the gate.

"Yes," Evangeline breathed, eyes closing in pleasure as she gestured ahead. "This is where I keep my special friends, the ones I use for my herbals and poisons."

They sounded like two very different things to Margot, herbals and poisons.

Evangeline inhaled deeply. "Mmm, smell that? That'll be the hemlock." Her beady eyes popped open. "Musty."

Margot wrinkled her nose in distaste.

Evangeline guided her forward. "I'll give you a quick tour, shall I? Let's start with my purple lovelies—larkspur, foxglove, my dearest poppies." She pointed to each, tweaking the poppy with particular fondness. As her fingers drifted away, the flower heads bent, stalks twisting and stretching—unnaturally—toward Evangeline. As if she were the sun.

Margot's eyes widened, but Evangeline just laughed.

"See how well they listen, sugar? We reap what we sow. Now see here, a small crop of hellebore. Just a smidge, plenty more down at Ruth's cottage. Monkshood—careful not to brush up against that one. It'll stop your heart. Oh, and of course, my Witches' Bells. Beautiful, aren't they?"

Margot leaned close to examine the tilted heads, heavy and dome-shaped.

Evangeline pointed. "The greens are the ones you have to watch for, easy to mistake for innocent. Poison ivy—leaves of three, let them be. Belladonna, also called deadly nightshade, identified by the star-shaped pattern of the crown." She lifted a stalk, bending the five-pointed leaf toward Margot, a dark berry at its center. "A subtherapeutic ingestion causes hallucinations. A high dose is deadly." She dropped it and moved on.

Margot backtracked, pointed. "Why isn't the nightshade with your purples?"

"Clever girl. Because belladonna berries only turn this nice, bruising hue this time of year." She smiled. "Now be a dear and pluck a few hellebore petals, will you? And then, right by the gate, there's a bit of garlic from the summer harvest. Pull a few up for me."

Margot hurried to do as instructed. Once finished, Evangeline met her at the gate, her own fingers filled with purple flora.

Monkshood, Margot suspected.

They traipsed back to the gardening shed, where a single hanging bulb illuminated the dim space. A moth beat against it, plinking softly. The shed smelled of cedar and thyme with just a hint of something more darkly pungent. Perhaps turpentine?

Evangeline busied herself with a mortar and pestle, grinding up the harvested hellebore. She peeled back the garlic next, plucked out a few rotted cloves, then tossed two bulbs into a water-filled Erlenmeyer flask.

"I always have garlic percolating," she explained, grabbing another flask whose fluid was tinged yellow, two swollen garlic heads bobbing in situ. "We'll use these today."

It was fascinating to watch Evangeline, a mad scientist at work. Her wild gray hair shone silver beneath the dusky lightbulb. Her knobby fingers moved with precision, using pipettes to combine elements with accuracy. Four drops here, seven there. A single drop—that was of distilled monkshood. And all the while, Evangeline muttered softly under her breath.

"Is it a secret recipe?" Margot asked as they neared the end. Evangeline was bottling the finished solution now, oddly harmless looking. Near-translucent in its final form, just the barest tinge of yellow. Death disguised as innocence.

"Everything around here is a secret," Evangeline replied, giving a closed-lip smile. "Haven't you figured that out?"

Margot leaned in the doorway. "Will you share one with me?"

Her smile faltered at the edges. "Depends what you want to know."

"Why don't you ever go inside the manor?"

Evangeline's smile disappeared. Her face darkened. "Because it's a den of vipers in there, that's why. A pit of pestilence. Rotting, moldering legacies will cling to you like feral ivy, if you let them." She snorted. "Nothing natural, nothing *good*, survives in that house. You need to be careful, Margot. That woman has claws like you've never seen."

"What woman?"

"Babette." Evangeline's eyes narrowed.

"What did you think of her, when she was alive?"

Evangeline put the pesticide on her workbench. She made a great show of attaching an atomizer to the top of the glass bottle.

"She was the most beguiling witch I've ever seen," she finally said. She knotted her hands around the neck of the bottle, staring through the small window overlooking the manor. The glass was peppered with hairline fractures that rippled outward like spiderwebs.

"She could enchant a man with a single look. Women too. Babette didn't discriminate...she could make anyone fall in love in a heartbeat. She had the kind of charm that can't be bottled"—Evangeline shook her pesticide solution—"but was just as deadly. And she did it for her own amusement, the way a cat plays with a mouse before devouring it." At this, she cut her eyes to Margot. "That kind of power without conscience...it's lethal. She deserved what she got, in the end. You reap what you sow." She rapped the bottle twice against her workbench, nodding. "That witch had it coming."

"She killed herself," Margot replied uneasily.

"Oh, sugar." Evangeline's eyes sparked, conspiratorial. "I've never believed that, not for one moment. That woman was far too conceited to kill herself."

"Then what happened?"

"Eleanor's ghost remains here because she's grieving—yes, I know all about Eleanor," she said, taking in Margot's widening eyes. "She's a danger to others because she's a true threat to herself, consumed with heartache. Babette remains because she's vengeful. She's a danger to others because, even now, she enjoys breaking hearts. And she simply can't bear the thought that someone broke hers. Broke it beyond repair when they stopped it from beating."

<u>29</u>

September 1918

Second for you to remember—the Dravenhearst mash bill is your birthright, Merrick. Your blood runs 73% corn, 17% rye, 10% barley. This was my legacy.
Now it is yours.

—Excerpt, a letter from Richard Dravenhearst's Last Will & Testament

"At the risk of ruining a perfectly lovely evening..." Margot began, sliding a bare leg over Merrick's as they lounged in bed. A lit candelabra on his nightstand cast the room in flickering shadow. The tapers were nearly exhausted, short wax stalks that dripped and congealed down brass stems.

"Uh-oh." Merrick tucked an arm behind his head. "Have I done something wrong?"

Margot was struck dumb by the powerful curve of his biceps. He smelled like bourbon mash tonight—a little yeasty, a little sour, a little sweet...an unexpectedly heady combination. Her lips parted, words forgotten.

"Margot?"

"Yes?" She blinked, forcibly dragging her gaze away from her husband's muscles.

"You were saying something about ruining our perfectly lovely evening?"

"Yes. Right." She teased her fingers through the dark hair on his chest, delaying. It really was a most impressive chest, all swells and ridges. Highly distracting.

Merrick groaned. He reached to halt her fingers as they slid lower. "Love, what kind of ruining are you after?"

Against herself, she smiled. It would be so easy to forestall this conversation. She'd done so for more than a week. She leaned in to press her lips to his, but he pulled back.

"What's wrong?" he asked, his gaze searching. "I can see it in your eyes. What is it?"

She took a deep breath. "Evangeline told me something a few days ago, something Ruth suggested as well. I think we ought to discuss it."

"Okay." He shifted his weight, turning to give her his full attention.

"It's about your mother."

The tensing of his posture was immediate. Eyes, jaw, shoulders, chest, fingers...little ripcords tightening throughout his body. Pulling down hatches, guarding against the invitation of his mother into their bed.

"Is it possible," she said, the words coming slow, "she didn't kill herself?"

"What do you mean?"

"Is it possible her death came at the hands of another, not her own?"

His jaw fell open, closed. "That's impossible," he rasped, pulling back from her.

"Is it? Both Ruth and Evangeline said—"

"Said she was *murdered*?" His eyes were as turbulent as a storm.

"They've made it clear suicide was not in her nature. And the more I learn of her myself—"

"It was *entirely* in her nature," he cried. "I can very much promise you that. Spineless."

Spineless? Margot bristled. Suicide, she knew in her heart, was hardly a spineless act. It was an agonizing one. Merrick was hurting, but even still—

She froze, her own hypocrisy hitting with the force of a runaway cattle train. Why was she so quick to forgive, even *defend*, the Dravenhearst women for their agonizing choices...

But she was unable to do the same for her own mother?

Margot shook her head, scattering the ghosts. Right now wasn't about her. This was about Babette. Nothing added up. Stories conflicted. Her brain swirled.

Merrick—*She was weak. Unreliable, ultimately unforgivable.*

Ruth—*She was the brightest star in the sky, burned out too fast. A victim.*

Eleanor—*She was a sinner of the highest order. A bad mother.*

Evangeline—*She was a viper, a seductress. One who reaped what was sown.*

The truth lay somewhere in between. Surely it must. The only way to set both herself and Merrick free from this madness was to find it.

"Why are you bringing this up again?" Merrick asked. "Why can't you let it rest?"

Because what has died here refuses to stay dead.

She gritted her teeth against the admission.

"You told me not to wake you when you dream," he continued. "Why? You told me we can't go to Louisville. Why? Why won't you let me protect you? What is she telling you? What are *they* telling you? Why do you believe them and not me?"

"It's not a question of belief. It's a question of what's right. What if a wrong was committed here?" she insisted, trying to make him see. "A wrong so ghastly, it's cast a pall on your house, on your family. What if we can lay it to rest? What if our life together can't truly begin until we do?"

Merrick's hands moved to her stomach, cradling it. "Our life together *has* begun. You're the one clinging to the past, not me."

Margot joined her hands over his. "I'm just asking, is it possible..." She tried again, one final time. "Is it possible you've villainized her to protect yourself? Because it's easier? To hate her rather than to grieve her?"

His fingers spasmed over her stomach, but she held fast.

You must face this, she willed him. *If you face this, maybe I can too.*

The only sound in the room was his breath. Slow and deep.

"You were only eleven," Margot whispered. "There are different types of leaving, Merrick. It isn't always a choice."

"If she didn't do it..." he ventured, licking his lips. "That means someone else did. Who?"

There was no delicate way to say this. "It seems there are...a myriad of options. Your father—"

"My father *loved* her."

"Well, he wasn't the only one. There was Alastair, and there's an implication perhaps Xander—"

Merrick collapsed against the headboard, fingers pinching the bridge of his nose. "A myriad of options indeed. Her tastes were nothing if not eclectic."

Margot reached for Merrick's arm. "We needn't speak more of it tonight, but I thought you deserved to know." She squeezed gently. "You've carried a great deal of anger for a very long time. Perhaps there's more than one thing we need to lay to rest in this house."

"Perhaps," he whispered.

She looked back at him, into the eyes of this man who had sworn he'd never be a husband. Would never be a father. Who consistently gave her more than he'd ever taken.

She smiled softly. "We've turned each other's lives upside down, haven't we?"

"Right side up, I rather think."

Margot hadn't felt right side up in a very long while. "Hmm, perhaps that's why it feels strange?"

She meant the words as a joke, but he considered them seriously, for quite a long time before speaking. "You know how sometimes...you don't even dare to dream a dream? Because it's too big, too far out of reach, so what's the point in dreaming at all? It's not meant for you."

"I do." She had more than a few of those hopes and wishes herself.

"You and I are a bit like that. A dream like that coming true."

That was the moment Margot Dravenhearst fell.

The moment Margot Dravenhearst fell irrevocably in love with her husband.

30

October 14, 1904

Babette, ma petite amour,
Peacocks—these wild ideas of yours!
For you, my muse, I enclose a gown like no other. A visionary
dress for a visionary woman.
They won't be able to take their eyes off you...or their hands.

Your humble servant,
Jean-Phillipe

T HE LIGHTING IN THE boudoir was dim with a crescent moon rising beyond the French doors.

Babette sat at the vanity, the folds of her peacock-feathered gown cascading over the seat, trailing to the floor to coalesce in a puddle around her bare toes. She swept a plump powder puff across her face, dusting it pale and smooth. Turning her skin to porcelain.

"That's it then, is it?" Babette asked, dropping the puff atop its copper tin. "You've gone and fallen in love with him, given yourself away, just like that." She snapped her fingers. "You're foolish."

The sound cracked Margot's spine into a straighter position. "I'm foolish? For loving your *son*?" She bit down hard on the final word, her warm breath crystalizing in the frigid air.

"My son is a Dravenhearst," Babette snapped. "Pretty words drip heavy from their serpent tongues. Smart girls don't trade their hearts for words alone."

Margot walked to the settee, then settled there. "Perhaps you're jealous." She flounced her nightdress as though it was the finest gown of Parisian silk and Italian lace. "It's only natural, I suppose all mothers are. When their son gives his heart to another."

Babette popped her lips into a perfect O, painting them with a berry stain. "And he's told you so, has he? That he loves you?"

Margot opened her mouth to reply, then closed it.

"Oh, fledgling." Babette chuckled. The lid of an ornate jewelry box opened next. She withdrew a pair of canary diamonds and fastened them to her ears. "They're very good at this game, trust me. We must be better."

"Just because he hasn't said it, doesn't mean he doesn't feel it," Margot replied, uncertainty rising. Where was Eleanor when she needed her? Ever the romantic, surely *she* would understand. Margot looked left and right, searching.

"She's not here," Babette said, flouncing her hair. "Eleanor is dealing with her own ghosts tonight, the most pressing one shaped like the hulking Dravenhearst man warming your bed. You'll understand yourself soon enough. He'll turn on you. They all do."

Down the hall, the wail of a baby sounded—a toddler with a full set of lungs. Babette rubbed her temples.

"Babette!" Pounding rattled the adjoined bedroom door. "Babette, Merrick's crying."

"I have *ears*, Richard," she bit back. She lowered her breath so only Margot could hear. "That's what the bloody nursemaid is for."

"Babette." More pounding. The tenor of Merrick's cry rose to a fever pitch.

"I'm getting *dressed*," she shouted back, ripping a strand of pearls from the jewelry box and heaving them at the door. They landed with a startling rattle, the strand slithering like a snake as it settled.

A sigh through the wood, footsteps moving away.

Babette spun on her stool, wide eyes on Margot. Sweet eyes. Alluring eyes. She unfurled her fingers to reveal a pair of silk stockings. "Would you mind? I'd ask him"—she jerked her head toward the door—"but he's being a dreadful oaf tonight, isn't he?"

Babette lifted the hem of her feathered gown as though it was the curtain going up at the opera. She extended her pale, creamy leg—toes pointed—for Margot. Meanwhile, her fingers worried at her forehead, forcibly smoothing the lines. "If only he'd stop crying," she murmured. "Just once. For just one hour."

"You could go to him." Margot couldn't keep the judgment from her voice. "You could hold him. Dry his tears and rock him to sleep." *Mother him.*

"Is that what you think motherhood is? You imagine it like Madonna and child?" Babette arched an eyebrow. "You've much to learn. And learn you shall." She jutted her chin toward Margot's stomach.

"He's your son."

"Yes, he is. And when I first gazed upon his face the day he was born, do you know what I saw?"

Margot slipped Babette's toe inside the silk sheath, then unrolled it over her ice-cold leg. When she reached the top, unfurling mid-thigh and releasing as rapidly as she could, she looked at the ghost bride from beneath frost-crusted lashes.

"I saw what he would grow to be," Babette continued. "I saw a Draven-hearst man in my arms. A deadly one, just like all the rest. It's very dangerous to love a Dravenhearst...even more dangerous, perhaps, to be loved by one."

"What does that mean?"

The door swung open with a *bang*. Margot stumbled away from Babette.

"Darling! Your timing is impeccable." Babette lifted the remaining stocking for her husband. "Would you be a dear?"

"Merrick stopped crying," Richard said, frozen several feet away.

"Yes, Evangeline is with him. That's what we pay her for, after all."

He pursed his lips. Margot drifted nearer, curious. She'd never been this close to Richard. His dark hair, stubbled jaw—the resemblance was uncanny. But it was his hands that stopped her dead in her tracks. They hung loose at his sides, his fingers unfurled. The sheer breadth of them, the veins over knuckles, the shape and slender length of the fingers...

Margot had been touched by those hands. Merrick's hands.

Across the room, Babette smiled slowly, wicked with satisfaction. *Another Dravenhearst man...just like all the rest.*

"What *I* pay her for," Richard said.

"Semantics." Babette waved his comment away. Her hemline went up again, curtain rising. Bare leg, pointed toes. "Be a dear, won't you?" She offered him the remaining silk stocking.

Richard's scowl lifted in a grin. He dropped to his knees, planting a kiss on Babette's exposed knee. He rolled the stocking upward with practiced fingers, lingering over her thigh. Wrapping his hand around bare skin. Possessive.

"Not now, darling," Babette murmured. "Guests are arriving."

"There are always guests arriving," he said. "Always a full house. Maybe I want you all to myself tonight. I doubt they'll even notice."

"I'll be missed." She rose with a laugh, her exquisite gown falling to the floor. Curtain down, show over.

His scowl returned. Richard strode to the French doors, raising an arm over his head to lean on the frame as he gazed into the night. Lights shone on the drive—a few guests arriving in motorcars, more still in carriages. "What if *I* miss you? What if Merrick and I both miss you?"

A flicker in Babette's eye. Annoyance. "You have me all the time."

"Do I?" Richard continued to stare at the lineup of arriving guests. He took a deep breath. "Is Alastair coming tonight?"

Silence.

Margot sank back, blending in with the walls. She held her breath.

"Did you invite—"

"It's a party!" Babette threw up her hands. "Everyone between here and Louisville is invited. How should I know if—"

The speed with which he moved was astounding. Faster than a panther, he crossed the room in a dark blur and slammed Babette against the wall with the force of thunder, a crashing boom that rattled the whole house.

Margot cried out, but no one glanced her way. This memory would play on with or without her.

"Goddammit, Babette! You promised."

No quip came. There was always a quip, and that was what worried Margot the most. Not Babette's shocked eyes. Not the small gasp of fear betrayed by her lips. It was the loss of her voice.

"Tell me you love me," he pleaded, pinning her shoulders to the wall. A trapped butterfly. "*Only* me."

"Let go of me."

"Tell me he's nothing," Richard begged, shaking her. "Tell me you won't see him anymore. Promise me."

Babette raised her chin, a fierce glint in her eye. Margot knew the answer before she said it, saw the shape of the word formed by her lips.

"No."

Only the sound of breathing. Panting. Harsh. Guttural. Their faces mere inches apart.

"It's just a game to you, isn't it?" he whispered. "Me. Your son. Pieces on a chessboard."

"I prefer checkers."

"Goddammit!" He slammed her back again, and his hands flew to her throat. Squeezing.

Margot flew away from the wall.

"You are not to see him, not to look at him. Not to breathe air in the same room as him. I won't ask again."

Margot was at Richard's shoulder now, clawing. Trying to haul him away, but her fingers plunged straight through his suit jacket. Flesh moving through frigid vapor, nothing to grip.

Not real, not real, not real.

Babette was turning purple. It seemed very real indeed.

"Stop! Stop! Stop!" Margot screamed, slapping ineffectively at his hulking, transparent shoulder. Such a large man. Strong as an ox.

Strong in all the same ways as her own husband, she realized, stumbling back in shock. She'd never thought of Merrick that way before, in terms of the damage he could inflict.

But those hands...Merrick's hands...circling the pale throat of a red-headed woman...

Weak, fading, Babette struck. Her slap hit true, right across Richard's chin. It was enough to snap him from his stuporous rage. He released her, staggering away. Staring at his hands in horrified shock.

Babette crumpled against the wall, gasping.

"What have you done to me?" Richard whispered, fingers shaking.

Babette gathered herself and stood to her full height. Spine unflinching, eyes blazing. A single peacock feather slipped loose from her magnificent gown and drifted to the floor.

"I didn't know you had it in you. I'll admit it, you almost had me fooled," she said, fingers rising to her throat. "I wanted you to be different."

"Babette, I didn't mean—"

"You're exactly the same as your father," she spat. To hide her eyes—eyes filling with tears—she crossed the room to her vanity. Dug through her ornate box until she'd pulled a thick collar of jewels from its depths. Five strands wide. She slipped it around her neck, choker tight, to conceal the bruising already leaching through.

Richard fell to his knees. His voice was a plaintive whisper. "Babette."

When she turned, her eyes were clear, hard. She grabbed his cravat, yanking his head up. "You may be just like your father, but I am *nothing* like your mother. Make no mistake, I won't stand for it." She released him and strode to the door, pausing in the frame. "Lay a single finger on me ever again, and I'll do what she should have done. I'll kill you myself."

Margot gasped.

"Babette," Richard cried, rising to his feet.

They both followed the lady of the house into the hall, Richard storming, Margot fretting.

The hallway was dark and chilled. Margot shivered. Richard's specter blew straight through her, giving chase. Margot convulsed from the burst of cold. So sharp, so painful.

Babette rounded the corner, heading for the stairs. As Margot staggered down the shadowy corridor, raised voices argued on her left. A door swung open of its own accord, hinges whining. Slow. Light spilled into the darkness.

Margot froze as a fresh burst of frigid air exploded into the hall. Hesitantly, very hesitantly, she edged forward. Peered inside.

Eleanor was in the parlor. Eleanor and another dark-haired man. Twice her size with a scruffy jaw carved from marble. Long-fingered hands.

Another Dravenhearst man. Bearing down on her.

The smack of a backhand stole all the breath from Margot's lungs. The power of it so strong, it knocked Eleanor off her feet. She flew, tumbling onto a wingback couch. For the first time, she wasn't wearing her bridal gown and veil. Just a housedress. Simple. Pale pink. When she lifted her head, fearful eyes trained on her husband, Margot understood.

Eleanor's face, finally exposed, was littered with bruises. At the temple. Beneath her right eye. Fingermarks on her neck. Her cheek was bright pink, and what was pink today would be purple tomorrow.

The man grunted with exertion, then lumbered forward.

Eleanor's shriek was powerful enough to blow the door closed in Margot's face. She stumbled away. Running from the nightmare.

Another door flew open, to the right this time. Another scream.

Eleanor again. A blue dress and an arm across her throat, pinning her to the wall. Her husband's hand twisted in her hair, wrenching her face up to look into his eyes.

"Tell me you love me," he said.

Margot flinched away from the familiar words.

"I love you," Eleanor whispered, voice hoarse but earnest. Eyes shining with it, the terror and the love.

The door slammed shut.

Four more steps, another door.

Eleanor on the floor of a dark, empty nursery. Sobbing. Her fingers latched around the bars of a crib, clenching tight enough to splinter wood.

A kick to her ribs from a foot in shiny black shoes. "What good are you? What good are you if you can't give me a son? Locked in this room all day, crying. You take everything from me. *Everything!*"

"I'm sorry," Eleanor screamed. "I'm trying. I'm trying so hard. Please. We can try again. Let me try again." She spun, hands latching at his waist. Undoing his pants. "We'll try again."

The door blew shut. Margot ran. She wanted to close her eyes. She was almost at the end of the hallway. Only one more door. Only one more door to pass. Only one more door in this house of horrors.

It opened with a slow, ominous *creak*.

"No more," Margot whispered. No more windows to the past.

She didn't want to see, but she looked anyway.

A four-poster bed with bloodstained sheets. Eleanor, panting, sweaty, wild hair and even wilder eyes. Her husband at the foot of the bed. A physician crouched on his haunches, a newborn baby in his hands.

But the room was silent.

The room.

Was silent.

Margot covered her gaping mouth with a tremulous hand. The baby was blue and still. And far, far too small.

"My baby," Eleanor gasped, forcing herself upright. "Give me my baby!"

The physician looked at the Dravenhearst man beside him and shook his head. In that moment, the man was just a man. A man not yet a father. Not yet, maybe not ever. He crumbled, grabbing the bedpost for support.

"My baby!" Eleanor's voice was shrill, her hands extended. Grabbing. *"Please."*

The chill gripping Margot's bones was born of so much more than cold. She shook with it all the way to her core.

"Mrs. Dravenhearst," the physician began slowly, so very slow. "I'm...I'm sorry. Stillborn."

Eleanor blinked twice, uncomprehending.

"He's stillborn," the physician repeated, lifting the child.

"He..." the man-not-yet-a-father repeated, choking on a sob. *"He."*

"My son," Eleanor cried, reaching again. "Give him to me. It's all right. He'll be fine. I'll feed him...and then..." She hiccuped, tears beginning to fall. "And then..."

The physician shook his head.

"I'm his mother," she shrieked. "His *mother*. Give me my baby." She howled, a cry so raw, so feral, it crossed space and time, needling into Margot's brain. Every nerve connection shattering like glass.

Instinctively, Margot's hand flew to her stomach, caressing the spot where her own child grew. She couldn't breathe. Couldn't fathom...

There was only one thing she could do. She reached out and closed the door. Fell into it, eyes closed. Tears leaking.

This whole house was cursed. She understood fully now. Cursed in a way she couldn't ever hope to break. The cracks ran too deep. Sorrow baked into the foundation alongside the bricks. Blood sunken into the floorboards. Tears in the bedsheets. Heartbreak in the windowpanes. Babies buried under magnolia trees...

"Babette!" A voice thundered from the stairs, and Margot remembered.

She remembered giving chase. Remembered Babette with Richard's hands at her throat. Remembered a time when unraveling the mystery of the former Mrs. Dravenhearst seemed like the most important thing in the world.

The thing that would set her free.

Margot forced herself to turn the corner. Ruth stood at the bottom of the stairs in a gown colored like sunset, all fiery oranges and pale pinks, blurring and swirling, a work of art of a dress. She always looked beautiful, but tonight, she was a vision.

"Babette?" Ruth reached for her friend as she flew off the final stairs.

"Not now, Ruth," Babette snapped but didn't glance at her twice. Not at her beautiful dress or her concerned face.

Margot trailed behind the scene like a sleepwalker, the slumbering princess destined for the spinning wheel. Her feet led her to the ballroom, to Ruth's and Richard's sides at the edge of the dance floor. Shoulder to shoulder. A string quartet was playing, and there, dead center on the floor, was Babette in her magnificent peacock-feathered ballgown.

Dancing in Alastair Pendry's arms. Closer than close.

Margot was woozy with fear, dizzy with it as she looked sideways for Richard. His face was devastated, a man accepting lashes for a terrible wrong. There was no fight left in him, only defeat.

And beyond him, Ruth, her face twisted as if she'd tasted sour milk. Ruth, wrapping her arms tight around her middle, standing on the outskirts, watching her beautiful best friend at the center of the dance floor. Her eyes were aflame. Burning. Seething. Scorching. Boiling.

With *jealousy*.

Margot stepped back, her heart stuttering. She'd never seen Ruth's beautiful face twisted in such a way.

The strings played on. Resonate, thrumming. When Babette twirled by, she released Alastair and grabbed Margot. Their fingers joined, a ghostly connection, more whisper than flesh and bone. Margot allowed herself to be swept away.

"See how they watch us?" Babette murmured in her ear. She had no breath to warm the skin. Margot felt only cold. "See how they can't look away?"

Richard and Alastair stood on the edges, watching every move. Ruth too, her expression dull now. Resigned.

"I'm going to tell you the secret, fledgling," Babette cooed. "Men don't want a woman they already have. They're socialized to conquer. To chase. To *possess*. If you want a thousand ships launched in your name, it takes far more than beauty. You must be elusive. Unconquered and *unconquerable*. Only then will his heart be forever yours. Dance with another, he watches. Kiss another, he goes mad." With that, she leaned in and pressed her lips to Margot's cheek, ghosting over the skin, raising gooseflesh.

Margot's breath caught. Her voice, when it came, was high and breathy. "Sounds like a dangerous game."

Babette's eyes glowed with pleasure. She took her thumb and dragged it over Margot's lower lip, pulling. "Those are the only games worth playing. I've given you the secret. If you want to be wanted, you can never let him have you."

Margot's eyes were closed, but her feet were moving. Twirling. The fortissimo of the violin swelled in her ear.

Babette's fingers warmed within her own, coming alive. Two turns later, her chest bloomed with heat, the way it did after a sip of bourbon went down. Deliciously hot.

When she opened her eyes, it was like emerging from underwater, wrenching forcibly through the surface. A gasping breath, pulling fresh air into her lungs. A steady hand in her own.

And before her, his face.

Dark hair. Strong jaw. A Dravenhearst man. *Hers.*

"Merrick?" she whispered. She was engulfed by him, tucked into his arms. Dancing in a silent marble ballroom in the dead of night. A dozen Margots and Merricks—reflected in the mirrors—revolved in a close hold.

"Is that finally you?" he asked. "Are you back with me?"

"What happened?"

"You said never to wake you."

She swallowed. The edges of the dream were growing hazy.

"You said never to wake you," he repeated, whispering now, "but I couldn't stand it, couldn't bear to see you dancing without me. Who do you dance with, if not me?"

He dipped her slowly, bending her back. His nose grazed the soft skin of her throat.

"It was only a dream..." she told him as he raised her from the dip. "A dream, nothing more."

They stopped moving.

He dragged his thumb over her bottom lip, pulling. Eyes heavy-lidded with desire.

A shudder ran through her at the memory. *If you want to be wanted...*

"Dreaming or no," he breathed, "dancing is a dangerous game."

When he pressed his lips to hers, hungry and sweet, she could only agree.

A dangerous game indeed.

31

October 15, 1907

Darling,
Meet me in the rickhouse. I won't tell a soul.

Yours,
Ruth

MARGOT SHIVERED IN THE morning chill. Inside the pasture, Fox and Omaha trotted side by side, Merrick and Julian astride. The horses nickered, breath crystallizing in the air before their long snouts.

Ruth sidled up on her right. "Perhaps you'll come inside the fence this time?"

Margot didn't even glance over. She was riveted by Merrick, legs spread wide, thighs strong and tight around his mount.

Ruth fiddled with the latch, then swung the gate open.

Reluctantly, Margot dragged her gaze from her husband. She took a deep breath and entered the pasture.

"Come on." Ruth waved her hand and stepped forward. "Let's race them."

"Race?" Margot's voice shook. "I don't think—"

"Merrick!" Ruth flagged him over.

He brought the horse around in a slow trot. Ruth lined up the two stallions, side by side. She counted down.

When her hand dropped, Merrick's heels tapped Fox's side, urging him ahead in a sprint. Omaha remained still, ears pricking. Julian lowered his posture, bending forward. Just before his horse took off, he slid his eyes to Margot, warm with an easy smile.

"Go!" Ruth shouted, smacking the horse's rear.

And he was off, giving chase.

The hoofbeats were thunderous. Frozen dirt kicked up under horseshoes. Long stride after long stride, muscles of the beasts rippling...

Margot reminded herself to breathe. A tinge of lightheadedness crept in.

"He's gaining," Ruth said, smiling.

The words sharpened Margot's focus, honing her attention and keeping the dizziness at bay.

They *were* gaining, Omaha and Julian.

"Wow," Margot breathed, watching the horse close distance with every stride.

"We must always run him from behind," Ruth murmured. "Just like his father."

"Why?"

"It's in the blood," Ruth replied, shaking her head. "Fox was the same when he was young. Inordinately fast, but they lack focus, this bloodline. They're made to chase, to pursue."

Merrick doubled down on Fox, urging him ahead, but Julian pushed. Omaha tore up the ground, sneaking into the inside position as they rounded the final bend of the pasture.

"This is where he'll take him," Ruth said.

As the horses completed the turn, Omaha pulled ahead. Merrick laughed as he gave chase. The sound tugged at Margot's gut from all the way across the field.

Fear crept back in as the horses neared. Margot swore the ground shook underfoot with the vigor of their pounding hooves. Julian pulled Omaha up short, slowing him to an ambling gallop, then a trot. He thumped the horse's neck affectionately. Ruth strode over to meet the pair, rubbing and nuzzling Omaha's snout, offering praise. Behind the victors, Merrick slid to the ground. He pulled Fox by the reins toward Margot.

Instinctively, she stepped away and shook her head.

No closer.

Merrick stopped. Fox bumped his nose against Merrick's cheek, snuffling his ear. He reached into his pocket and pulled out a sizable sugar cube, offering it to his horse.

The move jarred a memory, the feel of Cerberus's soft lips against Margot's palm, nibbling gently at a treat. The velvet brush of his snout hit next, smooth and warm.

Something unexpected rushed in with the memory—love.

It hadn't all been bad. She'd always known it, but the final, horrific memory so easily eclipsed all those that came before. She bit her lip, wishing...

Wishing, wishing, wishing. She closed her eyes.

A breeze stirred the ends of her hair.

"Margot, we're flying!"

She almost smiled. Almost.

When she opened her eyes, Merrick was watching her. Under his gaze, she wanted to be worth more than her memories, to stand taller than them. His care, his *love*, did that to her. It made her feel brave.

This time, when the impulse to smile came, she gave into it.

"You lost," she called.

He smiled, unabashed. "I'm meant to lose. Fox is retired."

"Too many sugar cubes, huh?"

He laughed, then reached into his pocket and produced another. The horse snatched it with incredible speed. She giggled.

Merrick's eyes brightened, still watching her. He licked his lips, tilting his head.

"Would you like me to bring him over? To meet you properly?"

She shook her head. "Not today."

He nodded, and she saw the effort he took to maintain the cheer on his face. For *her*.

Her lips twitched again as she realized the words felt true in her gut before she released them into the world.

"Not today," she repeated. "But soon, I think."

It was so much harder to be hopeful inside the manor. So much harder to believe in something...*anything*. The future. In this house, everywhere she looked, Margot saw only the past. The stained-glass violets above the door. The candlesticks on the wall. Wailing centaurs trapped in the coffers. Dust-laden drapes over windows, blocking sunlight. Misery settled overhead like a blanket, stifling and heavy. Tight around her neck. Tight like a...like a...

"Noose, dearie?"

Margot startled, spilling a slosh of orange juice across the breakfast table. Eleanor stepped out of the shadows of the dining room, offering a thick coil of rope. Margot gasped, eyes darting from the apparition to Merrick, who raised his gaze from the morning newspaper.

"Everything okay?" he asked, waving Xander forward to assist.

"Y-y-yes," Margot stammered. Did he *see*? She was still there, Eleanor. Offering the noose. Margot couldn't look away, though her words were directed to Merrick. "Just an accident. Silly of me."

"That's what they said about me too." Eleanor nodded, tweaking the noose. Her voice lowered to a whisper. "Just an accident. Silly woman."

Margot's hand flew to her throat.

"Are you quite well?" Merrick asked, his brows lowering with concern. "You've gone pale. Perhaps you should eat?"

Did he *really* not see her? Hear her? Feel the insidious cold overtaking the room?

Margot tilted her head, chest rising in a muted pant. She licked her lips.

He stared back, waiting. So handsome. So innocent. So sane.

While she...

"I'm fine," she fibbed.

Lies, lies, lies.

Eleanor nodded again, sympathetically this time. "Best not say anything. Very tricky business, seeing things."

Merrick ruffled his newspaper. "Three more in the last week."

Margot swallowed. "Three more what?"

"States. Idaho, Maryland, and Virginia have all ratified the Twenty-First Amendment."

Eleanor stepped closer. Too close.

Leave me alone, Margot wailed, recoiling.

"It's all in your head, dearie. Only you can stop it. I'll save the rope for you, shall I?"

"No!" Margot snapped, thumping an arm down on the table.

Xander jumped beside her, where he was mopping up her spill.

Merrick lowered his newspaper again. "Margot?"

Heckin' hells. Now she'd gone and done it. Both men stared at her, expectant.

"No, uh, no thank you," she said, lowering her voice and her lashes. "Xander asked if I wanted a fresh cup of juice." *Lies, lies, lies.* "I don't."

To his credit, Xander didn't contradict her, merely inclined his head and resumed clearing the mess. But his lips puckered, and unease wafted off him in waves. Margot could taste it in the air; his fear was sour. Palpable.

He thinks I'm mad. She raised a hand to her forehead, eyes lifting skyward. Overhead, the centaurs silently screamed. *Perhaps I am...going mad like my mother. Is it truly the house? Or is it just me?*

It was, quite simply, the most terrifying thought yet.

By midday, Margot had taken to her bed. She could manage nothing more.

She needed to write to her father. It seemed pressing to tell him about the baby. If he was ailing, she wanted him to know. But the thought of lifting the pen, writing the words, feigning optimism...it was suddenly too much.

Her head throbbed. Her heart stuttered, heavy with exhaustion. It had happened this way before, in the Louisville townhouse. When the weight of living was simply too much to bear. When it was easier to reach for unconsciousness. To live there, safe in the in-between, where nothing was expected of her.

The balance was tipping, dragging her to a dark place. The dead outnumbered the living. She could feel them closing in.

Babette.

Eleanor.

Elijah.

Her mother.

She couldn't...

She simply *couldn't.*

Margot dragged the blankets up to her chin, late October chill seeping into the room. She needed to tell Merrick to turn up the heat in this frigid house. Winter was coming.

A floorboard creaked in the corridor beyond her bedroom.

Margot's head jerked up. She knew fear now, true fear. Knew enough to realize she should have felt it all along.

A whisper of skirts slithered outside her door, paused.

Margot tightened her grip on the blankets.

The knob turned in silence. Slow, teasingly slow.

The door cracked open. One by one, four translucent fingers gripped the edge.

No. Margot shrank back in bed. She didn't want them to find her, but they slipped into the room anyway, Babette and Eleanor. They said nothing, only watched. Watched her shiver beneath the blankets. Watched her bury her head in the pillow, exhausted, defenseless. Watched her eyes flick to the bedside table.

It was right there—the laudanum, dusty with disuse. She hadn't needed it in months, hadn't wanted it. For so long, she'd wanted only Merrick. This life with him.

This cold, haunted life.

Had she chosen wrong?

The chimes of the grandfather clock tolled. *Wrong, wrong, wrong.*

Downstairs, the centaurs screamed.

The bottle on her nightstand twinkled. Slightly blue, such a beautiful boozy blue. Margot knew precisely what it would taste like on her tongue. What it promised.

It whispered sweet nothings. Painted a portrait of velveteen oblivion. Of bitter sacred relief.

It whispered. Whispered, whispered, whispered.

And God help her—God forgive her mortal, weak, fractured soul—she listened.

Margot reached.

And she drank.

She didn't wake until twilight. Merrick roused her, shaking her shoulder.

"Margot, love?"

Bleary, she opened her eyes, blinking away the drug-induced slumber. Her limbs were torpid. Merrick's edges blurred.

Even hazy around the edges, he made her heart squeeze. She smiled. "Hi."

"Hello." He smiled back. The grin was indulgent. Irresistible. "Having a bit of a lie-in, are we?"

"Just a bit." She chuckled, feeling lighter simply for his nearness. "My...my head hurt, and the house is so very cold. Might we turn up the heat? We're on the heels of winter."

Merrick winced and bit his lip. "It's a large house, hopelessly drafty."

Margot frowned, not understanding.

"It's only..." Merrick swallowed. "It's very expensive to heat."

Ah. There it is.

"We'll get more blankets for your bed. And sweaters. I usually wear layers in the winter," he explained. "It helps."

Margot didn't want to wear layers. She just wanted the house to be properly warm, his pinchpenny ways be damned!

But she was too weary to argue. She yawned.

"Still tired?" he asked.

"It was only a short nap, not nearly enough." Half the day was short, no?

His hand slid down the blankets, warming through them to her stomach. "It's normal, I hear, in your condition. And you don't sleep well at night. Perfectly normal."

Normal. He thought her normal. Oh, she could kiss him for that.

So she did.

His lips were hot and soft. She sighed against them, wrapped her arms around his neck and tugged. She opened her eyes as he tumbled into bed with her.

Then she saw them.

Eleanor and Babette. Still there, in the corner by her vanity.

Watching.

Not real, she told herself. She blinked hard, hoping they'd vanish when she reopened her lids.

They didn't.

Merrick's lips found hers again. "Xander prepared dinner, but suppose we just..." His hand slid between her legs, wordlessly finishing his sentence.

She tipped her head back against the pillow, slack-jawed.

The room had been so cold all day, but he lent her his warmth. It seeped into her pores, lit a fire in her heart. An inferno crackled to life within her, brighter than the darkness in her mind.

She was normal, perfectly normal, and he wanted her. As his lips worked their way down her jaw, onto her neck, she opened her eyes again. Darted her gaze to the corner.

Still there.

His thumb grazed her nipple, tweaking gently through her nightdress.

"Merrick..." She was all sensation and very little thought, turning to putty beneath his hands.

He rucked up her skirt and lowered his head between her thighs, the breadth of his strong shoulders spreading her wide. His stubble scraped her sensitive skin, rough with promise. She liked him that way, just on the edge of rough, the promise of love lurking underneath his devastating power.

His possessive grip dented into her thigh. "Your fucking curves drive me wild, Margot."

She shivered and cried out when the warmth and surety of Merrick's tongue lapped her center.

"I want you," he breathed against her. Another slow, savoring lick. "I need you."

"Have me. Have me then. I'm yours."

A snort from the corner. Babette, not impressed.

Margot closed her eyes one final time, beyond caring.

Let them see, she decided. Let them see—if nothing else—she still had this. Him. They could take away everything else, but never him.

How truly cursed it was to be a Dravenhearst bride. And yet...

How truly blessed she was to be his.

32

October 27, 1933

Dearest Pa,

—unfinished, from the desk of Margot Dravenhearst

T HE SUN CAME UP in the morning. She walked to the pasture to watch Merrick ride. Went to breakfast with him. Kissed him by the front door when he departed for the rickhouses.

And then she stumbled, stuporous already, to her bedroom.

There wasn't even a question this time, zero hesitation. There was only the laudanum.

The laudanum and the voices in her mind.

"So much to learn, fledgling," Babette cooed.

"We'll stay with you, keep you company, dearie," Eleanor said, crawling into the bed beside her.

Margot reached, and she drank.

33

November 1, 1874

Dear Diary,
At church, it seems every woman has a baby on her hip. I stare
at them, like water in the desert.
I am not just thirsty, I am parched.

—Excerpt, the diary of Eleanor Dravenhearst

"TEA, DEARIE?" ELEANOR LIFTED the pot.

Margot's lips were dry. Steam curled as the veiled bride poured for her. She accepted the cup, a faint scratch at the edge of her consciousness. A niggling. The tea was delightfully warm in her frigid hands, but a warning stirred in her gut, hotter than a branding iron.

The baby. Merrick's baby. Her baby.

Hers to have, hers to protect.

Eleanor, she remembered suddenly, the name piercing through the haze.

Eleanor was not to be trusted. Not with this.

Margot pursed her lips and lowered the mug.

Babette exhaled softly in the seat beside her. Was Margot imagining the look of relief on her face? Her dress was pink and full of frills. She matched the tea doilies spilling over every surface. Doilies everywhere, sliding off the table onto the floor. Doilies sewn in as ruffles in Babette's skirt. Doilies folded into origami shapes and perched, hatlike, atop her red hair. Doilies raining down from the ceiling like snowflakes.

Margot replaced the teacup in its saucer. "I'm not thirsty," she lied.

"You're not today," Eleanor replied.

From beneath the veil, Margot saw the shadow of her lips twitching. A ghostly smile.

"You're not thirsty today. But you will be."

34

November 17, 1933

My dearest Margaret,
I've not heard from you in several weeks.
Are you well?

Forever Yours,
Pa

"A LETTER, MRS. DRAVENHEARST."

Margot startled awake. She was, inexplicably, in the solarium, standing before the windows. The midday sun scorched her eyes. She swiped furiously at them, thumbing away a layer of hard crust.

"From your father," Xander continued. "And a formal invitation for the legislature event has arrived."

"The what?"

Xander frowned as he handed over the correspondence. "The event next week. The lawmakers have called for a vote on the Twenty-First Amendment. Merrick has been asked to speak alongside Colonel Blanton at a dinner, on behalf of the state's bourbon makers."

She sensed from his tone she should know this; it had been discussed before. Margot hated that Xander, of all people, was currently more lucid than she.

"Right. That's right." She nodded and smiled, absentmindedly rubbing her stomach. Perfectly normal to be tired. Perfectly normal. "Thank you, Xander."

"Perhaps it's not my place," he said, folding his tremoring hands, "but are you quite well, ma'am?"

She forced out a chuckle and waved away his concerns. "Quite, merely tired."

Perfectly normal to be tired. Perfectly normal.

"Indeed. It's only..."

"Yes?"

"I know what it is to lose time, ma'am," he admitted. "I know what it looks like when it happens to others. It happened to someone else many years ago, the woman who was mistress before you, Babette."

A sour feeling invaded her gut. "Yes—you know all about Babette, don't you?"

Xander flinched. She wanted to take the insinuation back, but she didn't. His observation made her scared. And defensive. He was *noticing*.

And if *Xander* was noticing her failings, she was in real trouble.

"I wonder, does your wife know?" she asked tartly. "Does Evangeline know what happened between you and the former mistress of this house?"

Xander was silent for a long time. "She's shown you things," he finally said, his voice grave. "What has she shown you? What have you seen?"

Laughter pealed in the corner of the room. Margot cringed.

Babette, enjoying the show.

"I've seen everything," she lied.

Xander's eyes burned. She couldn't identify the emotion within. Fear? Guilt? Rage? All three could make people do terrible things.

"Does that frighten you?" she asked, tilting her head.

"No. No one believes a madwoman," he said.

"I'm *not* mad."

"You are haunted. It's more or less the same thing—I would know. I myself have been haunted for years." He spun on his heel to depart but hovered in the doorway. "She has power like you wouldn't believe. She made me do it."

"That sounds like an excuse." Margot narrowed her eyes. A man was just as culpable as a woman, no matter what the Bible said about femininity and piety, about filial duty. Load of hogwash.

Merrick and Babette's atheist ways were clearly rubbing off.

"A *weak* excuse," she added, staring him down.

"It is," he whispered, a shadow of regret flickering behind his eyes. There and gone.

He vanished into the depths of the manor.

Moments later, the conversation disappeared from Margot's mind altogether.

Eleanor was calling her for tea. She mustn't be late.

35

November 1933

Kentucky has called for a vote.

—Excerpt, Dravenhearst Distilling Inventory Log as maintained by Merrick Dravenhearst

A SWOOSHING WHISPER, THEN sunlight, bright against her sleep-crusted eyelids. Margot flinched away.

"Margot, love?"

His voice was the only thing able to penetrate the laudanum haze. She felt a cool brush at her forehead, sweeping back her tangled hair. The kindness in the gesture sent a bolt of heat straight between her legs. She opened her eyes, then screamed.

Eleanor lay beside her in the bed, phantom fingers brushing Margot's face.

"Margot." Merrick stood across the room, backlit by sunlight streaming through the window. In two bounds, he was at her side.

Eleanor vanished. Beau jumped onto the bed in her place, pawing maniacally at the sheets where she'd been. He snorted with displeasure.

"Margot, love," Merrick repeated, eyes wide with concern. "What's wrong?"

She shook the dust off her vocal cords. When her voice came, it was little more than a croak. "You...you startled me...that's all."

He frowned.

Margot waited. Already, mere seconds into consciousness, she was so tired.

"It's the middle of the day," he said, sinking to the mattress beside her. "Why are you still abed?"

"It's...it's normal..." she said, eyes filling with tears. "I'm just tired. It's normal."

His frown deepened, a furrow between his brows. He reached for her hands. "I think I should send for the physician."

She struggled. Suddenly, his grip felt restraining, not comforting. "No. It's normal. You said so yourself."

"I know I did, but that was weeks ago, love. Xander told me..." He trailed off, suddenly nervous.

"What?" she demanded. "What did Xander say?"

"I've been busier than usual lately, with the distillery and the upcoming speech for the legislature. I simply didn't realize..."

"Realize what?"

"That you've been in bed for weeks, all day while I've been working."

Weeks...is that how long it's been?

"I get up for meals." It seemed important to emphasize this. She was functioning. She was taking care of herself and the baby. She was fine.

"Yes, you do," he conceded. "That's why I...I didn't realize."

"Xander is exaggerating. We've had a tiff." They had...hadn't they? She couldn't quite remember though. Like smoke curling through her fingers, the memory came, then slipped away.

"Ruth hasn't seen you in weeks, said you haven't been visiting like usual. She's also concerned. Quite concerned."

Ruth—calm, capable, dependable Ruth—was much harder to explain away than the aging, half-senile manservant.

Margot shrank back from Merrick, making herself small, pressing her spine against the headboard.

"Don't call the physician," she whispered. "Please don't send me away. I couldn't bear to leave the house, to leave you."

"Who said anything about sending you away?" He reached for her again, trying to bundle her in his arms. Again, it felt restraining. Such large arms, capable of great force, great harm. Eleanor quaked in her mind.

"Let me go," she shrieked, kicking out. "I won't go!"

"Margot!" He scooted back from her, shocked. A new level of concern bloomed in his face. "Margot, you're...you're ill. I can't believe I didn't notice sooner. I failed you."

She began to cry then. He hadn't failed; she had.

"I don't"—she hiccuped—"want the physician."

He fell silent, watching her cry. Agony reared, his face crumpling like a little boy's. "I can't stand by and do nothing. I won't. I've made this mistake before, Margot."

Before.

Margot took a deep, shuddering inhale. She needed to say it. She needed to be brave enough, trust him to understand. No more hiding.

"Something strange is happening to me," she said slowly. "But it's not something a physician can help with, and you know it, Merrick."

He did know. Fear was written across his face, in every worry line.

"It's the house," she concluded. "Something in the walls. I already have sadness within me, and this house makes everything worse. It's untenable. It's swallowing me."

He didn't hesitate. "Then we'll go. We'll leave. Together. The legislative dinner is tomorrow in Louisville. We'll go, and we won't come back."

She nodded, relief seeping in.

When he spoke again, his voice was small. "Why didn't you tell me? Why didn't you leave sooner?"

Because leaving here means leaving you.

Of one thing she was certain, Merrick wouldn't leave his distillery. Not for long, at least. He would always come back to this place. If she couldn't find a way to be here, to live here with him, where would that leave them?

She avoided his eyes. "I didn't realize what was happening." It was only half a lie, better than most of the others she'd told of late.

"Really?" He tipped her chin up and took a deep breath. "Margot, did you maybe...did you stay for me?"

Naked vulnerability in his eyes, enough to take her breath away. This man who had been abandoned time and time again. Who never believed himself worth staying for.

There was only one answer. If anyone in this whole wide world deserved the truth, it was Merrick Dravenhearst.

"Yes."

His lips tightened.

"I stayed for you, and I would do it again," she said, trying for bravery.

She waited for the relief, for the love to sink in.

But it didn't.

His face collapsed in pain. He shuttered his eyes.

"Merrick?"

"You shouldn't have." He shook his head and rose from the bed, pulling away from her. "You stayed for me, and I didn't even notice you were hurting. I'm not worth staying for, Margot."

And with that, he departed the room, taking her heart with him.

36

November 22, 1933

Dearest Pa,

I'm sorry I've not written for a spell, but time has simply gotten away from me. I have exciting news—Merrick and I are headed to Louisville, planning an extended visit. In fact, I'll likely appear on your doorstep before this letter. This means I can share a secret with you, one I'll be telling you in person before you read these words—

Merrick and I are expecting a baby!

Due in late spring.

I can't wait to see the look on your face when we tell you. You're going to be a grandfather!

Forever Yours,
Margot

THE FIRST BREATH OF fresh Bluegrass air was as cleansing as a baptism. Margot filled her lungs, snuffing out the cobwebs. The dull ache in her skull lessened. The world outside seemed inherently brighter, lighter, as though a film over her eyes had lifted.

Why had she not merely stepped outside the ghastly manor sooner? Evangeline had warned her. Ruth too. How had she let herself be so overcome?

When Merrick closed the creaking front door behind them, she didn't look back.

Ruth waited for them on the portico, dressed in a gown of royal blue with white elbow-length gloves. Impeccably tailored in the fit, as always. The sun was setting over the hill behind her, illuminating a halo around her bright blonde chignon.

"They'll laugh at you," Ruth greeted Merrick, "for bringing an old spinster on your arm."

Margot scoffed. The words "old" and "spinster" were completely incongruous with who Ruth was.

"I want to see the look on Alastair's face when he sees you," Merrick replied. "When he realizes, not only is his inevitable fate to be properly walloped by a female equestrian come spring, but one who looks as stunning in a ballgown as you."

"Suave as always, Merrick dear." She tweaked his bow tie, adjusting it to her exacting standards.

Evangeline, Xander, and Julian stood alongside the roadster to see them off. A serving tray with six glasses rested on the hood. Julian poured from a bottle of Dravenhearst Distilling bourbon as they approached.

"A toast," Evangeline cried, clapping her hands together. "For good luck."

"I took the liberty of selecting a 1920 limited edition, sir," Xander said.

"A stroke of utmost brilliance." Merrick turned to Margot to explain. "Only ten bottles of this collection were ever made, pulled out of barrels in early January 1920, just before Prohibition took effect."

"Served neat." Xander handed the first glass to Merrick. "Precisely as you like."

Evangeline darted forward, a pile of leafy herbs in her hand. "With a sprig of mint"—she dropped it in before Merrick could protest—"for good fortune and prosperity."

Margot was handed a glass next, barely a splash of bourbon in the bottom—enough to taste but scarcely swallow.

Evangeline looked at her with significance as she handed it over. "Strong spirits don't agree with babes," she murmured.

Margot's hand drifted to her stomach. Nearly four months now. Hard to believe. She pursed her lips and stared into the soulless windows of the manor behind them.

A flicker moved in an upstairs pane. Her bedroom. A ghostly hand parting the gauzy curtains. A flash of red hair.

Margot looked away, not needing to see more.

Four more glasses were passed around, and Merrick lifted his in a toast. "To the beginning of the end of an era."

"Hear, hear!" Julian clinked his glass, the others tipping in to join.

Margot smacked her lips when the taste hit, her mouth flooding with flavor. Spice first, off the rim. A surge of woodsmoke—predominant but hardly unpleasant—and a whispering hint of caramel on the finish.

It tastes like Merrick's lips, she realized. A flavor she'd grown to love.

An acquired taste indeed.

Her husband withheld his own sip, watching her. A knowing grin quirked as he leaned in to whisper, "Notes of smoke and clove, upfront on your palate. With a smooth caramel finish."

She recalled the words with crystal clarity—they were the same ones he'd uttered the night they'd first met.

Merrick raised an eyebrow. "Do you still think me a liar, Mrs. Dravenhearst?"

In response, she captured his lips with her own, letting him sample the flavor off her tongue.

"Tastes even better on you," he murmured, pulling away to swirl his glass. He downed his bourbon in one smooth pull. He frowned at the sopping dregs of mint before delivering his verdict. "An abomination in an otherwise flawless drink, but the thought is appreciated, Evangeline."

It was time to depart. Margot slid into the shotgun side of the roadster while Ruth crawled into the back, settling in the rumble seat. She managed the maneuver with the dignity of royalty, not a hair out of place.

Merrick revved the engine and smiled, reaching for Margot's hand as he punched the gas. For the first time, she relished the fact that her husband drove fast.

"Margot, are we flying?"

Yes, flying. Flying far away from here.

As Merrick steered the car beneath the eaves of the magnolia-lined drive, Margot's eyes darted to Dravenhearst Manor one final time. The French doors to the upstairs balcony were open. Eleanor stood there, veil billowing in the evening breeze, ghostly hand waving. Babette was by her side, silent and still, her eyes narrowed, fox-like, on the departing vehicle. A predator watching its quarry escape.

Her lips didn't move, but Margot heard the woman's whispered promise in her mind nonetheless. Loud and clear, chillingly haunting.

See you soon.

37

September 1918

Third to remember—when you find yourself with a question, Merrick, and I am not there to advise, your blood holds the key.
Whatever the question, bourbon is the answer.

—Excerpt, a letter from Richard Dravenhearst's Last Will & Testament

THE ARRIVAL OF THE Dravenhearsts at Louisville City Hall would become the stuff of Kentucky legend.

Merrick's bachelorhood had been notorious, but it was not his arrival with a wife on his arm that society found most surprising. It was the prodigal return of Ruth Auclaire to the Louisville social circuit, a shock rippling through the crowd like a stone dropped into a placid lake. She took the room by storm. Engulfed in arms, exchanging air kisses and delighted exclamations of "Been too long!"

It was Ruth who secured Margot and Merrick two cocktail glasses within moments of arrival, a mixture of lemonade and sweet tea garnished heavily with mint and blueberries. Liquid courage was her gift, even when the drys made sure there was none to be found.

She winked as she passed Merrick a glass. "Pretend there's bourbon in it, dear."

Before she returned to the gaggle of adoring society friends, Ruth glanced at Margot and meaningfully raised her chin, tapping it.

Margot understood, lifting her own.

Trailing in Ruth's prodigious wake, Margot and Merrick were welcomed swiftly into the fold. Introductions swirled. The room was filled with balding, well-to-do legislators and the wealthy business elite of the state. Margot's stomach soured just looking at them, these powerful, privileged men who'd condemned her husband and so many others to years of struggle with a single stroke of their pens. Who held the authority, even now, to reverse it just the same.

Understanding the stakes, she lifted her lips in a practiced smile. Merrick turned on his Dravenhearst charm, his trademark scowl nowhere in sight.

"Yes, my wife," Merrick said, repeating himself when a legislator's wife expressed muted disbelief. "We wed in early summer."

The woman raised a pair of immaculately trimmed eyebrows and pursed her lips. "Did I miss the announcement? I don't recall seeing it in the paper."

She hadn't missed it. There hadn't been one.

"Oh, Isadora," Ruth called, swooping in from Margot's left. "Kindly remove the lemon from your mouth—that sourpuss smile favors no one. It's hard to believe, but bourbon makers, too, have wives at home and hungry mouths to feed. That's why we simply *must* talk about the economic repercussions of this blasted temperance movement." She steered the woman away, but not before Isadora reached out for one final piece of gossip.

"Hungry mouths?" Her eyebrows raised even higher.

"Yes," Merrick confirmed, a downright dastardly grin on his face. "We're expecting our first child in late spring."

"And we're clearly not above milking it for political leverage," Margot murmured in his ear, teasing.

"Come, Isadora," Ruth said, her voice fading as the pair departed. "Now, where is that husband of yours? We've business to discuss—the business of bourbon!"

"She'll have my job done for me by the end of the night," Merrick observed.

"Wouldn't put it past her." Margot sucked down a large pull of her drink and came up empty. Her eyes met those of a spindly man across the room, a man who'd clearly been watching her.

He wore a three-piece suit and a fedora.

"Another round?" Merrick asked.

She reached for his arm. "Merrick." She inclined her head toward Toni, who was chatting up sourpuss Isadora's legislator husband, looking all too comfortable amongst the society crowd. A wolf in sheep's clothing.

Merrick sighed. "I already saw him. He's been making the rounds, same as us."

"Why is he *here*?"

"He doesn't want Prohibition repealed—the mob makes a hell of a lot more money when hooch is illegal. Organized crime has backed the drys from the start, been filling their coffers every step of the way."

"That's horrific."

"That's politics."

Disquieted, Margot kept Toni in her periphery as Merrick guided her across the room to the bar.

"Looking for refills?" Alastair Pendry's booming voice startled Margot. He placed a pair of drinks on the counter in front of them.

"Alastair." Merrick's scowl reappeared.

"Dravenhearst." Alastair tipped his drink to toast. "To your good health."

Merrick begrudgingly tapped his glass, then raised it to his lips. "I'd hoped you wouldn't be important enough to garner an invitation tonight."

Alastair tossed back his head and laughed. "I've grown my farm into one of the top agricultural exporters in the state, and you don't think I warrant an invitation?"

"You could double your profits if Prohibition is repealed," Merrick replied, his tone light. "You've the highest quality grain in the state. You've already taken my order for mash. Others will follow."

Alastair tilted his head. "I make plenty of scratch, Merrick. I don't need a bourbon boom to pad my pockets."

"We're in a depression, the likes of which hasn't been seen before. The economy of the state at large—"

"Don't waste your breath on me, boy," Alastair interrupted, his voice hard. "If I had the power, I'd burn your distillery to the ground."

"That's why I didn't sell it to you." Merrick narrowed his eyes. "Five years ago, when you made an insulting offer to a desperate man."

"No, you had too much foolish pride for that. It's the Dravenhearst trademark, that ego of yours. Your father had it too."

Merrick shook his head, frustrated. "I'm done feuding with you, Alastair. No matter what you see when you look at me, I'm *not* my father. I have people depending on me now, my own family. If you'd open your eyes and look beyond my last name, maybe you'd see that."

With that, he drained his drink, berries and all. Out of the corner of her eye, Margot clocked Ruth beelining across the room toward them. For Alastair.

"Your family"—Alastair snorted and nodded toward the approaching Ruth—"is cursed. Riddled with predilections, with liars and sinners alike."

Margot frowned.

"*Adultery* is a sin, Alastair," Merrick said.

Alastair frowned. "You don't have to believe me, I'm sure you won't, but she was planning to leave your father for me, that final night. Ask your butler, he was in on it. She was expecting, and it was mine. She was *leaving*. For me. And she wasn't the only one—ask that horse trainer of yours too." A second nod toward Ruth. "Ask her about her own little bastard baby. There's more to this story."

Margot's jaw dropped. *Ruth's* baby? *What on God's green earth—*

"I already know about Julian," Merrick snapped. "I've always known."

Margot gasped.

"No." Alastair shook his head, glowering. "You have no idea. The devil is *inside* your walls, Merrick. You're protecting your 'family' from the wrong people."

"Alastair." Ruth at last entered their circle, her voice clipped.

"'Lo, Ruthie." Alastair inclined his head, his lip curling in distaste. "Long time, no see."

"The years have been...kind." Ruth's words sounded and tasted of a lie in the air.

"Far kinder to you, I reckon. Undeservedly so."

Ruth tapped her toe twice, a deadly staccato. "Merrick, perhaps you should take Margot for a dance? Alastair and I have much to catch up on, some lovely times."

Merrick acquiesced, guiding her away from the dueling pair.

"When is your speech?" She took his hand.

"A little under an hour, just before dinner is served. I'm giving the introductory bit, and Colonel Blanton will follow."

"Right." Margot released a shaky breath. "So we've a bit of time. About what Alastair said..."

"Which part?" Merrick's arms stiffened around her.

"About Ruth." She darted her eyes up to meet his. "Something about a baby?"

Merrick sighed. "Yes. Julian is her son."

Her son. "Why didn't you tell me?"

"It's not my secret to tell, particularly with the stakes as they are. She's an unmarried woman. We've kept it quiet—how in blazes Alastair found out, I'll never know."

"Who's the father?"

"I've no idea." Merrick shook his head. "She's never said."

They revolved slowly. Once. Twice.

"How old is Julian?"

"Nineteen, born in 1914. And to head off the follow-up, Nancy Drew, I don't know who the hell Ruth was seeing then. I was eleven, for Christ's sake, had just lost my mother. I don't recall ever seeing Ruth with a man, before or since. If she had a beau, she kept it discreet."

The song bled into a second. Margot's mind reeled.

All the time they'd spent together—all their talk of Babette and Eleanor, of motherhood, of that cursed house, and yet, Ruth had never once mentioned...

It felt like a betrayal. A deep one. She opened her mouth, then closed it when Merrick stumbled over her feet. She righted him and kept dancing.

A few seconds later, he did it again.

"Are you okay?" she asked.

He flashed an earsplitting smile. A very odd one. "You're pretty," he said, looping his arms around her neck. Margot staggered under his sudden deadweight.

"Merrick, what's wrong?"

"Nothing," he slurred, his hands coiling in her hair. His voice was off...his grip too. Fumbling, drunken.

She'd never seen him drunk, and he certainly hadn't been drinking tonight, save the single shot of bourbon at the manor. This was a dry event. It couldn't be that...could it?

She untangled his groping hands. Already, people were staring. Her gaze shifted through the faces in the crowd, halting at Alastair and Ruth. They were still huddled together at the bar, whispering fiercely. An empty glass rested on the counter beside them.

Merrick's glass.

Alastair!

The bitter old cad had given that drink to Merrick not fifteen minutes ago. Could he have laced it with something?

She turned back to her husband. His amber eyes were glassy. Frighteningly so. He leaned in to plant a wet kiss on her lips.

Margot knew she had to do something. He looked drunk. If people noticed, started whispering, it would hugely discredit his speech against temperance.

His speech. Oh, heavens!

An insidious flush crept up the back of her neck as panic set in. She panted, distressed.

No. Not now. Not when Merrick needed her.

She grabbed his hand and tugged. "Come with me."

He was hardly in a state to protest. Margot dragged him from the crowded ballroom into the foyer of city hall. There, she spotted salvation—a private bathroom, guarded by an attendant.

The beginnings of a shaky plan formed, only slightly compromising. She'd far rather compromise herself than Merrick. She stepped up on tiptoes to whisper, "Grab my backside."

"What?" Merrick's gaze was heavy-lidded, confused.

She gripped his hand and guided it to her rear. "Right there. Now kiss me."

She was pleased to find, if nothing else, he was a very obedient drunk. His lips pressed softly into her cheek.

"Merrick," she murmured, looking shyly at the uniformed attendant. "Hold on a moment, darling."

She flashed the bathroom attendant her most charming southern belle smile, then reached into Merrick's pocket for his billfold. Miserly as he was, it held but a small wad of scratch. She pulled out the lot and thrust it at the man.

"Take a smoke break," she commanded, channeling Ruth's haughtiness. "Fifteen minutes."

He snatched the money, watching them with amusement. "Yes, ma'am."

Margot pushed Merrick inside the bathroom, then slammed and locked the door. Before she turned, his arms were reaching for her, his lips pressing her neck.

"Merrick, no." She smacked him away.

"What?" He stumbled sideways, off balance. "But you just told that fella—"

"Merrick, there's something wrong with you. You're not well."

"I'm not?" He looked down at himself, puzzled.

"No. Do you feel...normal?"

He considered the question, tiny lines appearing on his forehead. "My stomach feels odd," he admitted. "And my legs are a bit funny...heavy."

"Merrick, I think Alastair put something in your drink. I'm worried." She started to pace, thinking furiously.

On the one-year anniversary of Elijah's death, Margot had found her mother on the floor of her parents' bedroom, passed out, barely breathing beside an empty laudanum bottle. A bottle that had been full mere hours earlier. When the physician arrived, he stuck a tube down her throat and sucked out her stomach contents, purging the drug.

Margot had gotten there in time to save her mother. Years later, however, history repeated itself. Empty bottle on the nightstand. A cold, still body in the bed. A hollow shell of the woman who used to be her mother. Margot hadn't found her in time. Couldn't save her. And she wasn't entirely sure her mother even wanted to be saved.

She blinked back tears, looking at her husband. *A curse on both our houses, not just his.*

But not one that would take Merrick away from her. Not today. Not while there was breath left in her body to prevent it.

Merrick doubled over, hands on his knees. "Margot," he groaned. "My stomach is twisting."

She had only one option. She grabbed his hand and tugged him forward. "This way."

She guided him on stumbling legs to the toilet, propping him against the porcelain. He closed his eyes and leaned back. His skin had gone pale, his breath shallow.

"Merrick, I'm dreadfully, dreadfully sorry about this," she said. "I do hope you'll forgive me."

Before she could give herself time to back out, Margot tipped his head over the toilet rim and jammed her fingers down his throat.

There was only one person Margot trusted inside the ballroom, one person she could count on to help her protect Merrick.

And she was currently in the center of the room, dancing a tango in Alastair's traitorous arms.

How on God's green earth had *that* happened?

"Ruth." She flagged her, pleased to see her friend had enough sense to abandon Alastair rather than bring the bastard along.

"Where's Merrick?" Ruth asked, searching the crowd. "It's almost time for his speech."

"He's ill. Someone spiked his drink. He can't give the speech."

"What?" Ruth cried, slapping a hand over her mouth.

"Shh." Margot quieted her. "No one can know. He looks corked. We can't have people talking. Pass along our regrets and give his notes to Colonel Blanton. Or get up there and do Merrick's part yourself. Please, it's such an important night for him...for all of us."

"Of course. I'll come up with something." Ruth's blue eyes hardened with resolve. "Just get him home and summon Dr. Smalls. Will he be okay?"

"I don't know," Margot admitted, turning to depart. Before she'd taken two steps, Ruth grabbed her arm.

"Who could have done this?"

"Alastair gave Merrick a drink shortly before he became ill."

Ruth's jaw tightened. "I understand. I'll handle it."

Margot had scarcely taken two steps when she was besieged once more.

"Mrs. Dravenhearst." Toni sidled up to her, tipping his fedora. He tucked her fingers within his own, lifting them to his lips for a kiss.

Margot's skin crawled. She would have to scrub the spot later with bleach. "Lovely to see you again, Antoni." She forced a perfunctory smile. "If you'll excuse me—"

He didn't release her hand. "Where's your husband run off to? I was hoping to catch up with him tonight, see if he'd reconsider our business relationship."

Margot held her smile in place. "I'm sure he's around here somewhere. If you would just release me"—she tugged her hand from his grasp—"I'll go find him."

Toni laughed. "You do that. Prohibition isn't going anywhere, not in this state. Bet he's realizing what a mistake he's made tonight. Mistakes sure can be painful, can't they?"

Margot froze, thinking of Merrick doubled over in the bathroom, his gut seizing in pain. What, precisely, was Toni implying?

She shook her head. No. Toni had been on the other side of the room all night. He had nothing to do with this.

"Have a lovely evening, Antoni."

Margot disappeared into the crowd, returning to the bathroom posthaste.

"It's me," she whispered, helping Merrick stand. "We're going home. Come on."

"Is dinner over?" he slurred, accepting her hand. His was terribly clammy, his pupils dilated. "Did I give my speech?"

"Yes," she lied. "All done. It's time to go."

With one wobbling step after another, they departed city hall. They'd parked the roadster less than a block away.

The roadster!

How had she not realized before? Merrick was in no condition to drive. Perhaps Ruth...

But Ruth was inside, salvaging their reputations and their livelihood.

No, Margot would have to do this alone. She gritted her teeth and assisted Merrick into the passenger seat, his head lolling back, eyes half closed.

There was no time for fear. None whatsoever.

Margot settled in the driver's seat and slid her hands over the wheel. It was larger than she'd expected, dwarfing her grip. The seat swallowed her, an imprint of Merrick's overly large body pressed into the cushions. She needed to sit up very straight to see over the dash.

Keys.

She fumbled for them, digging in Merrick's pockets.

Gas valve open. Gearshift neutral. Hand brake on.

She took a deep, nervous breath before adjusting the throttle.

Ignition.

The roadster rumbled to life, a metallic beast at her fingertips. Her feet scrambled forward to find the pedals. Her fingers darted over the wheel. She'd seen Merrick do it so many times. She knew how.

In theory.

Be brave, she told herself. She brushed a hand over the back of her neck. It prickled with heat, but Margot was determined. Her vision did not tunnel. Distressed or not, she was strong enough to do this.

She had to be.

For Merrick.

"Lord Jesus, protect us," she prayed, sliding the car into gear.

They lurched forward into the night. Lurched out of the city and onto winding roads, making wild but swift progress toward the one place Margot swore she'd never return.

Dravenhearst Distilling.

38

October 31, 1913

Jean-Philippe,
I've had the most bewitching dream and must commission a
gown.
Think...French Revolution.
Need I say more?

Yours,
Babette Dravenhearst

A FEW HOURS LATER, with Julian and Xander's assistance, Merrick was propped in bed with Dr. Smalls by his side and Beau at his feet. He was unconscious.

Margot's head was pounding, had been since the moment she'd walked through the manor door. Her limbs were heavy. Like she was sleepwalking through a nightmare.

"What did he ingest?" Dr. Smalls asked, checking Merrick's pulse.

"How should I know?" Margot tossed her hands up in exasperation. "I think someone slipped something into his drink. It could have been anything. I didn't see it happen."

"How long ago?"

She looked at the clock on the bedside table. "Perhaps three hours? Roughly. Again, I can't be certain."

Dr. Smalls continued his exam, unbuttoning Merrick's shirt. A red rash flowered across his chest. The physician frowned, then produced a tongue blade. He opened Merrick's mouth to peer inside.

"Dry," he pronounced.

"I took him to the bathroom as soon as I realized something was wrong," Margot explained, wringing her hands. "I forced him to vomit up as much as he could."

Dr. Smalls paused his examination. "Clever thinking," he murmured. "Resourceful."

"Check his pupils." She moved closer to Merrick's bedside. "There's something wrong with his eyes."

He lifted Merrick's lid. All black, no hint of gold. He shined a light over the dilation. No response. Dr. Smalls's face turned grim.

"Get me a basin, Xander," the physician instructed.

"What are you going to do?" Julian asked. He stood at the edge of the room, looking terribly out of place in the main house, with his muddy stable boots and rumpled hair.

"Purge his stomach again. He seems to be suffering from a drug-induced inhibition of his parasympathetic nervous system, leaving the sympathetic to take over unchecked. Hence the dilated pupils, dry mucous membranes, flushed skin, and exceedingly high heart rate."

"And is that..." Margot fumbled, trying to understand. "Is it dangerous? What causes it?"

"A number of agents could do it, I'm afraid. That's the difficulty. A bad batch of heroin or cocaine perhaps. I trust he doesn't—"

"No." She shook her head, shocked. "That's not...that can't be it."

"Well...there's atropine and hyoscyamine, both belladonna alkaloids. Jimsonweed or mandrake root extract could also do it."

Her mind shuffled through his list, tripping over a single word. One she recognized with creeping dread. "Did you say...belladonna?"

"Belladonna alkaloids, yes. Atropine and hyoscyamine." He looked closely at her. "Do you have reason to believe he's been exposed?"

"Not to those drugs, no." She wrapped her arms around her chest.

"The plant could do it too," Dr. Smalls said, zeroing in on her discomfort. "Nightshade."

A plant growing on this very estate.

Xander returned to the room with a basin. He froze in his tracks, hearing the word.

"*If* so..." she ventured, emphasizing the word, "could it kill him? Belladonna?" She remembered what Evangeline had said.

A high dose is deadly.

"It could," Dr. Smalls admitted. "Hallucinogenic in small doses, fatal in high."

Margot sank onto the bed beside Merrick. "Purge his stomach," she commanded, gripping her husband's clammy, limp hand. "Please. Do it now."

"He'll rest awhile," Dr. Smalls said, preparing to leave. "I'll return in the morning to check on him. I recommend you get some sleep as well. You've overextended yourself tonight, which is unfavorable, given your condition."

"Thank you, I will." Margot sighed, exhaustion creeping in. "Xander will see you out." She dismissed the physician with a wave of her hand.

"Reckon we shouldn't leave him alone," Julian said as the two men departed. "Should I stay?" He loitered in the doorway, uncertain, but Margot couldn't hold his eyes. All she could think when she looked at him was, *Ruth's son, Ruth's son.* Over and over.

She didn't blame herself for missing the connection. As fair and elegant as Ruth was, Julian was dark and flippant. Even now, he slouched rather than stood tall, taking up as little space as possible.

"No, I'll stay," Margot answered, already curling up in the bed beside Merrick.

"Are you certain? Dr. Smalls said—"

"I can rest here just as easily as in my own bedroom," she snapped. "With my husband."

"I'll be downstairs then. I'll post up on a couch in case you need me."

"There are plenty of bedrooms," Margot murmured, her voice heavy with sleep.

Merrick's skin was warm. His heart thundered in his chest. It sounded like the pounding hooves of a racehorse, barreling down the final stretch toward home.

Julian muttered a reply, but she didn't hear it. She simply drifted away.

In her dreams, Margot ran. She ran and ran and ran through the dark manor. Chasing the tail of a bridal veil. Floating down hallways, whipping around corners, always just out of reach, always just—

Her sleep was torn apart by a scream. Toe-curling, hair raising. Ripping her out of the land of the dead, back to the world of the living.

Merrick.

He sat bolt upright in bed, eyes open. His pupils were still eerily black. Soulless.

"Get her down," he said, pointing to an empty corner of the room.

"What?"

"Get her down!" His voice turned shrill.

"Merrick, what's wrong?"

"Get her! Get her!" His shouts rang through the room. He tried to rise.

Margot braced herself against him, holding him down. His body was uncoordinated and soporific, hardly at full strength.

"She can't breathe. Get her down!"

Margot followed the path of his eyes, seeing nothing but an empty corner.

Hallucinations, Dr. Smalls had warned.

Margot licked her lips in fear. "There's no one there."

"I see her. She's there. She's *dying.* We can still save her!"

Margot began to cry, big silent tears leaking out. She shook her head, climbing into his lap. "She's not there, Merrick. She's not. She died a long time ago."

"No. Please...*Ma!*"

She couldn't stand it. Couldn't bear it. No child deserved to see what he'd seen. No boy deserved to grow up as he had. No man should be, decades later, so haunted. She gripped his cheeks in her hands, pressing her forehead to his and staring deep into his wild eyes. She wanted to stop his hurt.

"Merrick, I'm here. It's Margot. I'm right here with you. What you're seeing isn't real."

Not real, not real.

He stared back, his gaze that of a hunted animal. "Your hair is red. Like hers."

"It is." She'd tear it from her head strand by strand if she needed to, if only to make that terrible look on his face disappear.

"It hurts my eyes."

It hurts your eyes...or it hurts your heart?

She swept her hand down his forehead, trailing gently over his lashes. "Close your eyes then. Close your eyes and go to sleep, Merrick."

"Will I get to see my mother?"

"Yes, after you rest." It was the most terrible and beautiful lie she'd ever told.

"She's sitting just over there, you know." He opened his eyes and pointed to the opposite side of the room. "Right there. She'll still be there when I wake?"

Margot startled...because she *saw*. In the corner wingback, Babette. Leaning forward with a hungry glint in her eye.

She swallowed hard. Hated the words even as she forced them out. "She's always with you, Merrick."

Whether I like it or not.

39

December 10, 1875

Dear Diary,
All that I am is blood and bone bound together with longing.
Perhaps that's the problem—perhaps life cannot grow inside
a person so ravenous.
I devour my dreams. I must not deserve them.

—Excerpt, the diary of Eleanor Dravenhearst

MARGOT WAS RUNNING THROUGH the manor on bare feet.

"Catch me, Margot! Catch me!"

His giggle just ahead, just beyond the next corner...she was so close.

She burst around it, reaching with both arms. For the dozenth time, they swung through empty air.

"Catch me, Margot!"

She spun, her panting breaths fogging before her. The hallway was frigid. Her mouth was dry, growing frost. Tiny, sharp crystals sprouted on her tongue.

She took off through the labyrinthine corridors of the house, losing herself. She knew the way...but also not. Hallways lengthened. Doors moved. Shadows shifted, staircases rolled underfoot. She stumbled more than once, bruising her knees, but she was homing in.

Behind the next door, Eli's laughter. She'd know the sound anywhere.

It had been so long.

She was positively parched.

She stepped forward and opened the door.

"Tea, dearie?"

Margot licked her lips and reached.

<u>40</u>

June 2, 1902

Dear Ruth,

*Keep this letter and show it to me if I am ever mad enough
to desire this again. To subject myself to such horror.*

*Horror, yes—a woman is never closer to the veil between life
and death than when she gives birth to a child.*

—Excerpt, a letter from Babette Dravenhearst to Ruth

A S DAWN APPROACHED, MARGOT awoke to blinding pain.
Violent cramps pulsed through her abdomen, ripples of sickening throbs. She knew it was wrong. Something was wrong. So very terribly wrong.

Wrong, wrong, wrong.

Her vision swirled when she opened her eyes. Merrick's lips were moving, but she couldn't hear his words. He was very pale. His eyes were hypnotizingly black, scarcely a band of amber peeping through.

She focused on the glimpse of gold. The light.

Far better, she realized faintly, *to look at his eyes than all the red in the bed.*

Another wave of pain. She gritted her teeth. It was agonizing, ripped through her heart as much as her body. She understood enough to know something was being taken from her. Something precious.

Before she closed her eyes again, before she gave herself to unconsciousness, she saw it there, on the nightstand. A teacup.

So that was it then.

She had failed.

⚘

A soft breeze tickled her cheek. A shower of white all around.

Blossoms. Petals. Raining down from heaven. The eaves overhead dripped, heavy with them.

She spun, floating dreamily in her cocoon. Blooms landed in her hair. Her lungs filled with the scent of honeysuckle sweetness.

Her fingertips curled open, stretching to catch silk.

A soft murmur of voices. So soft.

The breeze crested, tugging at the ends of her hair.

Margot slept.

⚘

"I will rest after she wakes. I have to know she's okay."

Soft buzzing filled her ears. Bumblebees in spring. Cicadas in summer.

A thunderously jarring punch, a fist hitting a wall. A tree falling in the forest.

A tree.

Falling.

Falling.

Falling.

"No. I'm not moving. Why won't she wake?"

Her eyes opened slowly, fluttering, and with great difficulty.

The room was dim, the bedding lavender. A hunched silhouette slumped on the edge of the mattress.

Margot shifted her weight. Her legs felt heavy and stiff.

Merrick's head popped up. "Margot?"

He was a sight—jaw unshaven, cheeks hollow, dark circles etched beneath his eyes.

"Merrick?" she rasped.

"I'm right here." He squeezed her hand, pushed back his seat, and called for Dr. Smalls.

When the physician entered, his face was grim.

"What happened?" she asked.

Merrick put his head in his hands. The knuckles of his right fist were bruised and swollen.

She dragged herself upright, leaned against the headboard. The slightest movement was tiring. A dull but persistent ache throbbed in her lower abdomen. She started to pull back the blankets; something wasn't right. Her stomach...it was soft and doughy, where only yesterday, it had been stretched taut. A barely there swell, but she'd been able to feel it. It had been there. She was sure of it.

"What happened?" she repeated. "What happened to me?"

Her memories were fuzzy. She grabbed for them as she'd grabbed for silk magnolia blooms in her dreams.

Sunshine and soft breezes and spinning, spinning, spinning beneath a canopy of white.

But before that...before...

She'd chased Elijah in her dreams. Through the house. Through this godforsaken house.

And in the end, on the nightstand...

She remembered the teacup.

And that was it. That was how her whole world ended.

In a blasted cup of tea.

She heard her voice from a great distance, reflected back to her as though shouted from the end of a long tunnel. "Merrick, did something happen to the baby?"

His face was still buried in his hands. He could do nothing but shake his head.

Dr. Smalls stepped forward. The look in his eyes was pitying. Hearing the words would make it real, but God help her, she didn't want to.

He said them anyway. "Margot, I'm so sorry."

"No..."

"It was a strenuous evening, very distressing...yes, distressing circumstances indeed. Perhaps they...proved overtaxing? It's impossible to know for certain. These things simply happen. We can't—*I* can't always explain them." He was wringing his hands.

Margot stared blankly at them, hearing only two words.

Distressing circumstances.

In those two words, Margot heard the echo of every single physician, the ones who had paraded through her life for years. They all stood before her now, their lips moving in unison. Voices raised like a chorus to the heavens, reading the words that would adorn her tombstone. That would sum up her entire life. That she would have to stand before God himself one day and answer to. They were all she was, the distillation of all her parts.

Prone to fits of hysteria.

Avoid distressing circumstances.

Avoid.

Hysteria.

Fits.

Distress.

Nothing would ever change. She looked at Merrick with longing in her eyes. She'd wanted to believe it could...that *she* could change. But no matter how many times she opened the music box, the same song always played. The ballerina spun the same way.

"It's my fault," she whispered. She drank the tea. Eleanor's tea, yes, but Margot's weakness.

"No." Merrick spoke into his hands, still not looking at her. His words came out muffled. "It's not your fault. It's mine."

She looked at him, her eyes brimming with tears. "I lost the baby?"

He didn't answer; he didn't have to. She was staring at her shrunken stomach and Merrick's bruised hands instead of his amber eyes, and all the blame, all the doubt, all the shame in this mortal world landed squarely upon her shoulders.

"I lost the baby," she repeated.

His hands finally dropped. His lashes were damp, eyes red-rimmed. "We lost the baby."

She shattered.

They spoke in the corner, Dr. Smalls and Merrick. They spoke about her, not to her. In low voices. Concerned head tilts. Small nods. They discussed her body and her mind and her failings. And most importantly, as always, "the fix."

Because broken dolls cannot stay broken. They must always, always be fixed.

How asininely enraging, she realized, her anger sharp enough to cut through her sorrow, a hot knife lancing through butter. How absolutely infuriating that they—these men—believed they could fix what was broken inside her. That they believed she needed fixing at all.

Because that was where the problem lay, where it festered.

Fix implied an endpoint. Like flipping a switch to bring a room from darkness to light. That wasn't how this worked. It wasn't how *she* worked. It wasn't how grief and sorrow and distress worked either. There was no endpoint to those demons. There was no "cure." This house was proof enough of that.

Margot wrapped her arms around her middle, forcibly holding herself together. If she let go, she would shatter all over again. Broken porcelain doll fragments would scatter across the floor.

She closed her eyes, feeling hopelessly tired. Today, surely, she'd earned sleep. And tomorrow?

Tomorrow, she prayed, she might be strong enough to rise.

The longer Margot slept, the deeper the house sank its tendrils in. Eleanor and Babette cuddled beside her on the bed, wrapping their arms around her. The women—the ghosts—were there instead of her husband.

"You're like us now," Eleanor cooed, petting Margot's hair. "We're the same, you and me."

Babette snorted in displeasure.

"I only ever wanted you girls, *both* of you," Eleanor continued, reaching out to grip Babette, the same as Margot, "to understand."

Oh, Margot understood. She didn't even blame Eleanor, especially not now they shared the same pain. The same loss.

No, Margot only blamed herself.

A wounded whimper escaped her, that of a kicked dog.

"Oh, dearie," Eleanor murmured, rubbing her back. "It'll be okay, you'll see. It's still the best thing you've ever done." Wet splotches appeared on the veil where her eyes should be. Tears, thick ones, streamed down her face.

Margot's lids drifted shut. She didn't want to talk. "What is?"

"Becoming a mother."

Margot stayed in bed for a week. Sleeping was so much easier than being awake; being with the dead was easier than the living. Merrick was aching, needing things from her...things she couldn't give to him, things he couldn't give to her in return.

Her husband visited dutifully every morning and every evening. He was distant and businesslike every time. Asked how she was sleeping, if her pain was getting better.

Which pain?

She didn't say that. He might understand, but he certainly didn't want to hear it. He could barely shoulder his own; she couldn't possibly ask him to carry her load too.

It became their own choreographed waltz. They skated across the surface, determined not to crack the ice.

Yes, I'm sleeping well.

Yes, the pain is improving.

Yes, I'm okay.

No, I don't need anything.

Exit.

Return.

Repeat.

Everything they didn't say hung so heavily in the air, it choked them both. But Margot clung to the steps of the dance nonetheless. She tiptoed around him, because to look into Merrick's eyes, to see his pain...it would be like surrendering herself to the undertow. She was just barely afloat. One single look, and he would drown her.

Her buoy in the storm was her bottle of laudanum. She clung foolishly to it instead of her husband, his distance a growing thorn in her side. An anchor tied to her feet. She wanted Merrick desperately, wanted him to crawl into the bed and just *be* with her.

And yet, she couldn't get rid of him fast enough when he arrived.

She didn't know how to ask for what she needed. She simply wanted him to know how to give it to her. He'd always known before, and it was the loss of her husband, more so than the baby, that hit like a freight train.

She was tied to the railroad tracks, being run over again and again. Every time the door closed behind him. Every night when he failed to come into bed with her.

Margot cried quietly into her pillow every evening, not wanting him to hear through the bedroom wall. She tossed and turned all night, imagining him doing the same ten feet away. She was a prisoner to her grief, and he to his.

<u>41</u>

November 27, 1933

My dearest Margaret,
I received your letter postmarked on the 22nd—a baby! Such
incredible news. I dropped the note in shock as I read. Happy
shock of course, but oh, I can't tell you what this means to me.
I must confess myself confused though, as you said you in-
tended to visit? I did wait several days before writing, but
perhaps you've been delayed. Please write back.
I would simply love to see you.

Forever yours,
Pa

THE ONLY THING THAT got her out of bed was when her wedding gown started to appear in the morning again. It was a hideously familiar game.

Draped over the chaise.

At the foot of her bed.

Trussed up on the vanity mirror.

Suspended above the French doors by the noose.

Margot tore it down every morning, bundled it beneath her mattress. Locked it away in her trunk. Ripped it to shreds with her bare hands. Even went so far as to emerge from the safety of her bedroom, carry the cursed gown to the sinkhole, and heave it inside. She weighed it down with a crumbling brick from Rickhouse One, and she stayed, watching until it vanished. Until she was certain it was gone. Swallowed by the earth.

And yet...

And yet.

The gown was there again the next morning. Strung up in her bedroom. Pristine and unharmed.

Distantly, Margot knew this wasn't right. *She* wasn't right, not in her right mind. When she looked in the mirror, a strange woman with hollow cheeks and frazzled red hair stared back. A woman who wasn't, *couldn't be* her. This was all happening to someone else.

Not to her.

She awoke as she did every night, to the cold.

Margot stirred, raising her boozy laudanum-drunk head. The room spun. She looked around, shadows shifting and curling in every corner. Undulating like living breathing demons, waltzing on air.

Margot slipped out of bed. The floor moved underfoot. Her steps were lilting. Tilting. A little bit jilting. She raised her arms and spun. She, too, could waltz like the phantoms in the manor at midnight. She, too, could hide in the walls, coming out to play in the dark. Dark like her soul. Dark like her heart. Dark like her grief.

She tiptoed down the hall, just three steps. She cracked open the door.

They hadn't made plans yet—it had been far too early. But this was where Margot had imagined her baby would go. Right here. Only one door away.

In the corner by the window, an empty rocking chair lurched. Back and forth, back and forth.

This is where the baby goes, Margot thought.

Should have gone. Would have.

The rocking chair halted.

Something frigid brushed Margot's fingers.

Eleanor materialized, a hairsbreadth away. She shook her head. "That's not where the baby goes, silly."

The bride tugged her arm, leading her through the house, humming and towing Margot along like a stumbling, sleep-drunk child. The tune on Eleanor's lips was familiar. Margot's own voice thrummed, joining in.

The front door opened. They went outside. Eleanor led her straight to the nearest magnolia. She pointed to the ground.

"*That's* where the baby goes."

The lullaby swelled in her ears. Margot dropped to her knees, pressed her fingers to the earth.

When the bough breaks the cradle will fall,
And down will come baby...

When she woke the next morning, there was dirt on her feet and dried mud under her nails.

"The legislators repealed Prohibition in the state of Kentucky yesterday," Merrick told her, hovering in the doorway. He didn't like to come into the room. He seemed scared to breathe the same tainted air as her. "Only three more states are needed to make the change nationwide, and votes are scheduled next week."

"What does that mean for you? For us?" Her toes itched under the sheets; the dried mud was cracking. She hadn't washed it off. Beau sniffed at the bedding, following the trail of evidence.

Merrick waited several long moments before answering. A muscle jumped in his jaw. "It means we're free."

Free.

Were they though? Margot certainly didn't feel like it. Merrick didn't look like it.

She picked at the dirt under her fingernails, ruminating.

He would never leave this place, not now when he could make bourbon again. It was the only thing Merrick truly loved. The distillery.

He'd never told her he loved her. Had never said the words.

Margot had never been more aware of that than she was in this moment, when she realized he was choosing the distillery over her.

He always had.

He always would.

When the knock came in the middle of the day, it was disorienting. Merrick only visited morning and evening. She only had to perform twice a day. There were no midday matinees. Those were the rules.

"Yoohoo!" Thudding echoed again at the door. "Knock, knock."

Beau rustled at her side, a low whine escaping his throat. The dog had taken to her bed with her over the last several days. His warmth was comforting, his growls even more so, keeping Babette and Eleanor away from her dreams.

One final knock. "Margot, sugar?"

She was stunned, recognizing the throaty voice.

But it couldn't be.

It couldn't possibly be...Evangeline?

The door swung open, and a pair of wide batty eyes peeked into the room. "May I come in?"

Margot nodded, too surprised to speak. Evangeline never came into the house. Not for almost thirty years, she'd said.

She clucked her tongue like a mother hen. "Xander said you weren't getting out of bed, but I hoped...I didn't want to believe him." She stopped beside the mattress, a small porcelain bowl in her hands. She placed it on Margot's bedside table, then looked around the room, peering into every corner. "Are you alone?"

Margot blinked twice. "Merrick only comes in the morning and evening."

Evangeline shook her head. "Yes, but are you *alone*? Or...?"

Ah. Margot understood. "No. They aren't here." She didn't want to say their names in case it summoned them. The ghosts.

Beau gave a low growl.

"Right, very good." Moving swiftly, Evangeline lit a taper and tilted the flame into the porcelain bowl. Its contents sparked, then caught aflame.

"What's that?" Margot asked, the bedroom air filling with the scent of herbs.

"It's a blend of lavender and sage to keep malevolence at bay, but it won't protect us for long." She thumped the bed once before dragging back the blankets, forcing the dog to leap away. "Get up, sugar."

"Up?"

Evangeline pulled her bodily from the bed and plunked her into the chair at the vanity. She lifted Margot's hairbrush, starting to work through the snarls. "You need to get dressed and get out of this house."

Out of the house? She shuddered at the thought.

The house—her bed—was safe.

"It's not. It's not safe, Margot," Evangeline said. "It won't be safe until the women here find rest, and I haven't been able to figure out how to do that in nigh on sixty years. All the lavender in the world won't bring them peace."

"What do you mean?"

She sighed. "It's quite a long story, sugar."

"I've got time."

Evangeline bit her lip, dragging the brush through her hair. "I was born on this estate. I worked in the main house as a girl, and Eleanor was my first mistress. She was a kind but nervous woman, married to a man who liked to drink bourbon more than he enjoyed making it. That man lived his life at the bottom of the bottle, and the drink made him...unpleasant.

"I was still a child myself when Richard was born. Eleanor was different afterward. She'd always been prone to nerves, but after a baby finally came, she changed. She stopped sleeping, would stand over the crib to guard the child through the night. She wore her winter coat in the heat of summer and walked the halls in her wedding gown. She attacked a nursemaid once, claimed she was plotting to kidnap the baby. It made no sense, the things she would say and do."

Evangeline shook her head. "Some women take to motherhood like a duck to water. Eleanor was a drowning cat, striking out and clawing anyone who came near. One evening, I came upstairs to light the fires. When I went to the nursery, Eleanor was dressed in her wedding gown, standing over Richard's crib with a blanket over his face. She was smothering him. I knew she didn't mean it...she would never hurt that baby boy. She'd kill anyone who tried. She quite simply *wasn't right*. I saw it in her eyes when I stopped her, the horror." Evangeline shuddered. "We found her in the rickhouse the next morning."

"Gracious," Margot gasped.

Evangeline helped Margot to her feet. She plucked a day dress from the closet. "Put this on."

Margot complied, mesmerized as Evangeline continued her story.

"Xander and I were childhood sweethearts. After we married, I was late several times, but I never carried a child to term. That was when I started seeing Eleanor again, during my pregnancies. I thought she was my friend. She was the one who showed me what Babette was doing..." Evangeline trailed off. "I never told Xander I saw him with Babette. Eleanor showed me, but the way she did it was needlessly cruel."

Evangeline looked away, blinking back tears. "I quit working in the main house the very next day. I was finished. The women in this house hurt, and so they like to hurt others. It's a vicious cycle, a circle with no beginning and no end."

"And now," Margot said, chewing her lip, "I've been hurt."

"You have. You are but a piece in their game, a projection for their own pain." She offered Margot her hand, and when she took it, Evangeline squeezed. "How are you truly doing, Margot? You can tell me, sugar."

"Not good," she squeaked.

"No? Tell me about it. Tell me everything."

And so she did. But Margot's story didn't start at Dravenhearst Distilling. It started so many years before, at Greenbrier Estates. With Elijah. She started with Elijah and ended with Merrick, bookending her losses. The story poured out of her almost like vomiting—once she began, she just kept going until it all came out. A total purge.

She spoke about shame and blame, how both rotted inside her. Festered. How it was her fault her brother died. How she couldn't save him from Cerberus's hooves. How it was her fault her mother faded, slipped away pining for her dead son, unable to see the living daughter right there beside her. How it was Margot's fault, yet again, her baby died. How loss simply followed her like a storm cloud. Battered her over and over again. Made her afraid to live, afraid of what came next.

Finally, she told her about Merrick. How he wouldn't look at her. Couldn't stand to be in the same room as her. How, by dismissing her grief, he dismissed her as a person.

"Where is he, Evangeline?" Margot wailed, swiping at her tear-streaked cheeks. It was fruitless—more simply fell in their place. "Why isn't he here with me?"

Evangeline produced a handkerchief and wiped away the tears. "He's sad too, dearest. And alone."

"He doesn't have to be alone."

"No, he doesn't. He's just trying to deal with it in his own way. The way men do."

She sniffed. "Well, his way is *stupid*."

"It is, isn't it? Men are like that sometimes. They do very foolish things that we—enlightened creatures we are—can't possibly hope to understand."

Margot cracked a smile. It felt like the first ray of sunshine breaking through a rainstorm.

"There you are." Evangeline wiped away one tiny tear that escaped.

"Thank you." She took a shuddering breath. "For listening."

The air was clearing; Evangeline's herbs had burned to ash.

"I think you need to tell Merrick. You need to tell him all the things you told me. It helps. Don't you feel better, sugar?"

"Yes," she admitted.

"You need to talk about it. These kinds of things, Margot...they either bring couples together or push them apart. I would know." She nodded. "We'll go outside now. It'll help. You need a clear head. And tonight, you'll talk to your husband. You'll figure out a way through this. Together."

Before they departed the room, Evangeline placed a bundle of herbs beneath Margot's pillow.

"Rosemary," she explained. "To keep the dreams—those women—away. It's not a long-term solution—everything wild dies in this house. But for tonight, it's a start."

Margot was waiting for Merrick when he finally crested the hill at dusk, returning from the distillery.

"You're out of bed," he said. His face was blank.

"I am."

Silence.

"How are you feeling?" he asked.

"Like horseshit."

Heavier silence, positively thunderous. Merrick looked at his feet.

"You look like horseshit too," she said. "Shall we go inside and talk about it?"

When he looked up, his expression said *no*. His lips were thin and tight, his eyes guarded.

That was fine. She would just have to be brave enough for both of them. She turned and walked into the house. He followed. She chose a side parlor for no reason other than it was nearest.

The room had the cluttered feel of a house that had lived too long, seen too much. Filled with the bric-a-brac of generations, bursting at the seams the way stuffing spools out of a torn cushion. Ceramic vases on the mantel. Crystal bowls on the sideboard. Taxidermy on the walls. Porcelain cats on the sill. Ornate plates on pedestals, a collection of antique glass bottles...trinkets upon trinkets upon trinkets. All covered in the dust of centuries.

Positively suffocating, this old house.

When she turned to Merrick, his arms were crossed. He looked like he was gearing up for war.

"I've missed you." She wanted to start with earnestness. She hoped it would dent his armor.

It didn't. He didn't even blink.

"It's been really hard," she tried again. *I've lost track of time. I've lost track of you. Of myself. All of it.*

"I'm sorry for that," he said.

Silence. A quartz clock ticked on the mantel.

Margot searched for words. "I'm sorry you can't bear to look at me." It's where her pain lived, in his dismissal. "I'm sorry you can't stand to be around me. It must hurt when you see me. You blame me. I blame myself. I'm sorry I lost the baby, Merrick. I'm sorry for all of it. But I—"

"Margot, stop." He raised a shaking hand. "Please just...stop. I cannot bear to hear you apologizing."

"I need to say it," she insisted.

"Then say it. Say the things you came here to say but leave the apologies out of it. Go ahead, break my heart. Do it properly. I can assure you, I've withstood worse."

"What are you talking about?"

"I don't look at you because I cannot bear it. I cannot bear to see you in pain, knowing I am the cause. I..." He gripped the top of an armchair, the press of his fingers denting inward. "I owe you my life. I was incapacitated, and you saved me. You were brilliant and strong and a little bit harebrained—all the things I love most about you. But it came at a terrible cost." He blinked and looked away.

"That's not why I lost the baby."

"You overexerted yourself for me. You stayed in this house for me. The fault lies with *me*. My family. My house. My wife. My child."

"Ours," she whispered, correcting.

"Mine," he huffed.

She swallowed hard. Even now, he refused to let her in. He was locking her out of her own loss. Removing her autonomy from her own choices. It was maddening.

"If I knew how to fix it, I would." He spread his arms, plaintive. "I would give anything to fix it, Margot, but I simply don't know how."

Her temper flared. There was that horrible word again, *fix*. It wasn't what she needed from him. Not in the slightest. And to hell with every man who had ever looked at her and tried.

"I am not broken," she murmured, her tone deadly. "I do not need *fixing*."

She picked up a crystal bowl on the sideboard and dropped it to the floor. It shattered magnificently, breaking into a thousand shards all over the floor, glittering like diamonds. Like the first frost upon the earth.

Merrick inhaled sharply.

She moved to the mantel, lifted a single finger and flicked. A ceramic vase wobbled once. Twice. It tumbled over and cracked into pieces.

"What are you doing?" He didn't move to stop her, only watched.

"You want to fix something?" She pointed at the floor. "Go ahead, fix it."

He furrowed his brow.

She picked up a ceramic cat. Lifted it overhead, smashed it to the floor.

"*That* is broken." She pointed again. "*I* am not. I'm not broken because I *feel*, Merrick. Because I hurt. Because I have a past that haunts me...the same as you. I am not broken, and I do not need fixing." She lifted a second cat and tossed it into the space between them. It exploded at his feet like a launched grenade. "Do you understand the difference?"

His chest rose, then fell. "I don't care about any of those things." He nodded toward the floor, littered with shards. "I never have."

She flicked her wrist, knocking an ornamental plate to the ground. It fractured. "Oops. What about that one?"

"No." He shook his head, taking a step closer. Glass crunched underfoot.

Margot swept her hand across the mantel, knocking a second ceramic vase to the ground. "And that?"

"Couldn't care less." He took another step.

She crossed her arms, halting her attack on his house. "It's nice to finally have your attention, Mr. Dravenhearst."

"Couldn't look away if I tried."

"Because I'm acting out? Because I'm broken?"

"No. Because you're crazy and brilliant and mad and beautiful...and right. Completely, wholeheartedly right."

"You brought me here, Merrick. You chose to offer, and I chose to come. You don't get to look away now, when you don't like what you see, when the picture isn't pretty and perfect. I won't let you."

He froze. "I told you to leave. To run fast and far."

"Those are the words of a coward."

He flinched.

"You want me to run because it proves you were right all along, that you're alone and unloved, and therefore, unlovable. It's an excuse. You excuse yourself from the hard parts, withdraw to prevent being hurt. But life is messy." She flicked her wrist, knocking another cat to the floor. "My heart may break, but I am not broken. I've never needed you to fix me, Merrick. It's not *fixing* I need." She took a deep breath. "I have only ever needed *you*."

"But why?" he asked, whispering.

"Why does the earth need rain?"

He smiled. A small one. Half a dimple.

"Why does your bourbon need the barrel?"

He grinned fully this time, big and wide.

"Some things," she finished, "are just supposed to be together. To make each other better. Stronger."

Merrick picked up the quartz clock on the mantel. He flipped it over in his hand. "If I could turn back time, I would do so many things differently. I would love you differently. Better."

She caught her breath at the words.

"I'm still learning." He glanced up at her before dropping the clock. It shattered at his feet, freezing time. "But I'm here, and I'm looking. And what I see isn't broken. It's beautiful."

When his lips closed down over hers, she believed him. She wasn't wrong. She wasn't hysterical. She wasn't weak.

She was none of those things so many men before him had told her, had made her believe.

Somehow, he'd seen. And in being seen—exactly as she was—he made her whole.

"It's not you, Margot, it's me. I'm the one who's mad," he murmured against her lips. "I'm positively mad for you."

42

December 2, 1933

Samuel,

I have taken the liberty of responding to your letter on Margot's behalf. It is with a heavy heart I share this news: we are no longer expecting a baby.

Physically, Margot is recovering and doing well, but you can imagine the strain this has caused us both. Your correspondence always means so much to Margot, but I simply could not bear for her to write this note herself.

I couldn't say it to you with honor and integrity back in June, but I can say it to you now—I'm in love with your daughter, Samuel. So although this letter shares great loss, it shares even greater love. I hope you find comfort in that. I certainly do, every day.

Both Margot and I hope we will be able to visit soon.

Sincerely,
Merrick Dravenhearst

I N THE DARK, DARK, dark of the moonless night, they came.

They came as they always did, amidst plummeting temperatures and the quiet slither of silk skirts. From his position at the foot of the bed, Beau growled.

"Look how she sleeps in his arms," Babette murmured, shaking her head.

"Look how quickly she forgives him," Eleanor added, tapping her slippered foot.

Babette, standing tall and righteous, crossed her arms. "We have to do something about this."

Margot rolled over and shivered, half awake and half asleep. The bedsprings whined. Her pillow smelled of Evangeline's rosemary.

"Love is blind," Eleanor whispered.

"Death is omniscient," Babette finished.

43

December 1933

My hand shakes to even write. On this day, December 5th, 1933, it is over at long last. The nation has spoken—Prohibition has been repealed.

—Excerpt, Dravenhearst Distilling Inventory Log as maintained by Merrick Dravenhearst

THE DAYS BECAME ROUTINE, tentative and new.

Margot went to the pasture in the mornings, where she stood and chatted with Ruth, watching Merrick and Julian ride. Ruth would speak of bloodlines and training but never ghosts. She didn't have to. They both knew they lived amongst them. What more was there to say?

At midday, Margot went to the distillery to help Merrick work. Julian was there for much of that as well, a star pupil under Merrick's tutelage. Some days they filled barrels, some days they made mash.

But most importantly, hour by hour, Merrick let her into his world.

"Ten percent of this product will be lost when we crack the barrel open to harvest in two years," he told her, grunting as he and Julian lifted, pouring clear distillate into a barrel. White dog, it was called at this stage. He'd taught her that only two days before.

"Six percent is lost to the barrel itself." Merrick ran a finger around the wooden rim. "I told you once, do you remember? It's called the devil's cut, the amount lost to absorption. It's a necessary evil, the devil's take. Gives the bourbon its color and flavor, pushing in and out of the porous wood. Loss makes it stronger."

Yes, she remembered. *Transformative loss. Strengthened by loss...*

When she looked at Merrick, she saw it. Clear as day. How his losses had sharpened him, same as the bourbon in his barrels. Aged him smooth. He was richer for it.

"The remaining four percent," he continued, "is lost to the air. Evaporation."

"And what's that called?" she asked, captivated.

He smiled. "The angel's share. The part heaven itself can't resist taking. What we lose never truly leaves us. Traces always linger—that's why bourbon warehouses smell as good as they do. It's in the air."

She inhaled deeply, agreeing. The air in the rickhouses went down sweet, a reminder with every breath.

It's his version of fresh baked cookies, she realized. Of coming home to bread warming in the oven. Most children loved their mother's baking, grew up carrying those smells in their hearts.

This was Merrick's home—the distillery, the rickhouses. The place that gave his life meaning, where he'd been both lost and found. No matter the personal cost, Margot wouldn't take him away from it, would never make him choose.

Every day, she found a way to stay. And every night, after they crawled into bed, to his credit, he always asked.

"Margot, should we leave? Should we go to Louisville?"

Her answer was always the same. "No."

As December unspooled under their feet and Prohibition was repealed nationwide, demand soared. Bourbon brands were being relaunched, but there was no triumphant return for Dravenhearst Distilling.

"There's no stock left," Merrick said, shaking his head. "I emptied all my barrels and pawned off my bottles to bootleggers. Demand is high, but we simply can't meet it yet. Bourbon takes time. It needs the barrel."

It was a very real danger, the threat of becoming obsolete. Run out of town by the big dogs who'd been sheltered by pharmaceutical licenses and never stopped producing.

Merrick was right. Bourbon needed the barrel, needed it for a minimum of two years. Margot could learn many things about the business, but she would never learn to turn ahead time.

"No," a voice whispered, raising the hairs on the back of her neck. Soft and tantalizingly smooth. "Not turn ahead, fledgling. Turn *back*."

Margot spun around, expecting to see her, but Babette wasn't there.

Something else was though.

Something else stood tall and proud in the midday Kentucky sun.

Margot gasped.

The solution was staring them square in the face. They traipsed in and out of the rickhouses all day long, all but one. The one frozen in time. Shuttered and locked, full of bourbon aged twenty years.

It was a little bit crazy, a little bit mad. All her best ideas were.

Rickhouse One.

"Let me get this straight," Ruth said, putting down her gin rickey with a *thud*. "Your husband was poisoned by an unknown assailant, nearly killed. You lost your baby drinking the tea of a certified madwoman. You continue to have dreams, continue to be haunted by the ghosts of former Dravenhearst brides. And not only are you not vacating the premises—which for the record, I wouldn't just vacate, I would run from screaming bloody fucking murder—you want to open Rickhouse One? The beating heart at the center of it all?"

Margot fidgeted in her seat like a child before a schoolmarm.

"Merrick is here," she said simply.

"Merrick is a *Dravenhearst*." Ruth narrowed her eyes. "They're not the racehorse you bet on, Margot. It's bad business, bad blood."

"How can you say that about him?" she cried. "Don't you care for him, after all these years?"

"Of course I do. But I can say it because I watched my best friend die for it, for a Dravenhearst. I'd prefer not to put another body in the ground for the same reason."

"I thought Babette was *leaving* Richard," Margot said, her tone sharp. "What really happened the night she died? You've never told me."

Ruth paled and fell silent.

"You kept secrets from me." Margot raised her chin. "You spoke to me so many times about Babette and motherhood. You made me believe..." She trailed off. She didn't want to get upset. She knew Ruth wouldn't value it. Ruth valued levelheadedness and straightforward discussion. No bullshit.

But Ruth's omissions felt like betrayal. Margot was tired of the secrets. Of having only half the story, never the whole.

"You've learned about Julian," Ruth finally said.

"Alastair told me."

"The same Alastair who probably poisoned your husband, had an affair with his mother, and has proven himself, time and time again, to be the catalyst behind dark events at Dravenhearst Distilling? The puppeteer behind the curtain, that Alastair?"

Margot had never quite thought of him that way. She disliked the man, but he seemed like a sideshow player, a foil to Richard. A lover of Babette. He was a supporting character, not the leading man.

"I will tell you what I know of that night in exchange for not telling you about Julian months ago." Ruth looked carefully at Margot. "But I don't much like talking about either. These are painful things you've come here to ask about today, Margot. Shameful things." She lowered her eyes, quite uncharacteristically. "I will tell the story once but never again. So listen closely."

Margot leaned forward.

"There was a party scheduled for that night, same as every other at the estate. A masquerade ball. Babette had been planning for months. She was going to dress up as Marie Antoinette, had a ballgown specially made. It had half a dozen layers, if you can believe it, and she planned to walk around handing out slices of cake all evening." She snorted in amusement, remembering. "She was always so terribly irreverent, which I simply adored about her. But when she found out she was expecting, everything changed.

"She was certain the baby was Alastair's, and it was the final push she needed to leave the manor. When the party began, Babette descended the stairs, not in her Marie Antoinette costume, but in her wedding gown. She pulled me aside and said she planned to tell Richard she was leaving him during the party. She was going to walk out of his house wearing the gown she'd married him in, wanted it to be the last thing he ever saw of her. She simply couldn't resist the irony."

Ruth's face darkened. "Just before midnight, she had a row with Richard, very public. Nasty. I can't remember precisely what was said, but halfway through, Richard had the grace to take her outside, away from prying eyes. They were out there for almost an hour, and Richard returned alone. He said she was leaving, and that was that. I never saw her again."

"What? That's it?"

Ruth nodded. "I always thought it strange she didn't come in to say goodbye. We found her the next morning in the rickhouse."

Margot's mind raced. "Did anyone besides you know she was leaving?"

"Xander knew," Ruth said. "He helped pack her bags and stowed them by the stables, waiting for her departure."

"Anyone else?"

"Alastair knew, of course."

"Was he there that night?"

Ruth frowned. "He wasn't invited. Richard would no longer welcome him in the house. But he was lurking outside, waiting for Babette. They planned to run away together that night."

Two men unaccounted for. Two men who were each potentially the last person to see Babette alive.

Margot drummed her fingers on her lap. "It could have been either one of them who harmed her."

"I've always believed it was Richard," Ruth said. "Merrick was right to lock up that rickhouse, mark my words. There's a malevolence living in there. Spirits are never stronger in our natural world than at the places where they lost their lives. No good can come from dredging up the past, Margot."

"I disagree." She straightened in her seat. "I think what's been buried and hidden here has long since rotted out. I think we tiptoe on decayed ground. The way forward is through, not around."

This house was like a canker sore—a living, pulsating wound that festered across generations. It had been bandaged for far too long. Cauterized but not cured.

Ruth paled. "You really mean to do it, then? You want him to reopen the rickhouse."

"I do. He'll turn a profit from the bourbon to secure our future, and I'll ferret out these final family secrets to set us free from the past."

Margot found Evangeline next. She was mixing elixirs in her gardening shed, humming to herself under her breath. Margot nearly turned tail when she recognized the tune.

Rock-a-bye baby on the tree top,
When the wind blows the cradle will rock.

Evangeline wore gardening gloves as she chopped a cluster of green herbs with a long-handled knife. Her fingers moved with precision, dumping the pieces into a pestle, preparing for pulverization.

"Remember when you told me I needed to talk about the things that hurt?" Margot asked, leaning in the doorway.

Evangeline looked up, startled.

Margot took a deep breath. "I think this entire family needs to do the same thing."

When she shared her plans to open the rickhouse, Evangeline smiled. Oh, how she smiled. The most beatific grin, larger by the second.

"It's the only way," Evangeline agreed. "Those women need to be set free. All of us do."

"You missed a bit there." Margot pointed, but Evangeline swatted her hand away.

"Careful, sugar. Not with unprotected skin. That there's belladonna cuttings."

Belladonna? Margot flinched back. "What are you working with that for?"

"What, this?" She tilted her head, amused. "I grind it up to make a tincture for Xander. For his hands. It helps with his tremors."

"But isn't it poisonous?"

"Not after I dilute it. If it's poison you're after, you want the berries. Those are the easiest to extract. Which reminds me." Evangeline picked up the knife and pointed it at Margot. "Have you been skulking around my garden in the evenings?"

"No." Margot frowned.

"I found the gate unlatched a few weeks back. And again only a few days ago. I always keep my special friends locked up tight. It's no place for midnight wandering. Very dangerous."

"I've not been inside," Margot said truthfully, backing away.

"All right, sugar." Evangeline nodded, satisfied. She plucked a few fresh leaves from her bundle and continued dicing.

A memory tickled, faint. Evangeline dropping green cuttings into a bourbon glass before a toast. The night Merrick was poisoned. Mint leaves, she'd said.

Margot watched the quick, sure slide of the knife. The flash of green underneath the blade.

But...no, it couldn't be. Margot turned to depart, shaking her head.

"You come back and visit soon, you hear?" Evangeline called. "Toodle-oo!"

44

November 23, 1913

Babette, ma petite amour,
Enclosed is what you seek—Robe a la Polonaise in the finest
silk. Six layers, eight bows, 327 diamond crystals, hand em-
bellished by none other than moi. A dress most worthy of my
muse.
But, darling, please—stay away from guillotines while
wearing House of Worth. That's hardly the publicity we're
after!

Your humble servant,
Jean-Phillipe

MARGOT PLOTTED AS SHE dressed for sleep. She made her selections with care, looking for lace and sheer silk. Merrick shared her bed every night now, but he didn't touch her the way she wanted. Not since the miscarriage.

A slip, she decided, in lieu of the long woolen nightgowns she typically wore in December. She would be cold—Merrick still refused to properly heat the house—but long johns would hardly do for the task at hand.

The blue silk slipped over her head with a whisper, clinging to her chest. She went to the vanity and unpinned her long hair. Extended her legs to pull on thigh-high stockings. The mirror shimmered slightly when she gazed into its depths. A shiver walked up Margot's spine, fluttering ice-cold kisses.

"Look how you've learned, fledgling," Babette cooed, reaching out to run phantom fingers through Margot's hair. "Tell me, what is it you want from him?"

"You'll catch your death," Eleanor shrieked, walking through the wall. "Gracious, cover yourself up, Margot, or we'll be putting you in the ground alongside the babies."

Footsteps sounded in the hall. All three women turned to stare.

"He's coming," Babette murmured.

Margot rose to her feet. "Leave."

Eleanor vanished.

"Shy, fledgling?" Babette asked, reaching for Margot's cheek.

She stepped back, not wanting to be touched. Not by her.

"If I get what I want tonight, you'll get what you want. Isn't that right?"

Babette tilted her head and sighed with pleasure. "Oh, yes, you've come along nicely indeed."

A shimmer in the air, and she was gone.

Two soft knocks on her door, then Merrick slipped inside. She was pleased when his eyes lingered, drinking in the shape of her curves. His throat bobbed hard on his swallow.

"Ready for bed?" she asked, drifting toward him.

The tiniest bite to his lip, so quick she almost missed it. She smiled and reached for the buttons at the top of his shirt. He'd already undone two. She brushed her fingers over the exposed skin of his neck, lazed down, slipping one button loose. Then the next.

"Uh-oh," he murmured, the sound a deep rumble in his chest. "What're you after, love?"

"Hmm?" she raised her eyes to his. Wide. The portrait of innocence.

He chuckled. "You want something?"

Yes. She caught her breath.

There was an ulterior motive here, of course. One he'd clearly seen straight through. But standing here with his fingers gripping hers, his soft eyes pouring into her own...

Margot wanted. Oh, how she simply *wanted*. It had come so easily once, easier than breathing, being with him. A magic captured, now lost. The miscarriage had taken more than the baby from them.

Margot's eyes searched his. "You don't touch me anymore."

He stared back. "I hold you every night."

"That's not what I mean."

"I know." Merrick's gaze traced her body, his longing evident but firmly leashed.

She moved her fingers to the next button. His hands met her there, gently halting.

"What do you want from me?" His eyes burned with the question. "You know I'll give it to you. You know I'll give you anything you want. Just ask."

She froze. She'd intended to ask about the rickhouse *after*. When he was love-drunk and satiated. Unguarded.

But suddenly, looking into the earnest lines of his face, the move felt cheap. She didn't want to beguile him that way. She looked down at her clinging slip, her silk stockings.

She wasn't Babette. She never wanted her husband to be a piece in her game.

Merrick sensed her hesitation. "I don't want secrets between us this time around, Margot. Just tell me what you need, and I'll give it to you. And then I'll take you to bed with me. Properly, if it's what you truly want." He eyed her stockings and smiled. Devious and promising.

Her stomach curled.

"Well?"

"I want to open Rickhouse One."

He barely missed a beat, didn't blink. "Why?"

She swallowed. "Because there's bourbon in there. *Good* bourbon. Twenty years old."

His slow exhalation was telling. His lips twitched, and the realization struck—this was not a novel idea to him. She hadn't shattered his world by asking.

Margot swelled with hope. "You're already considering it?"

"I am," he admitted, sitting on the bed.

"But...?"

"But I'm scared," he whispered. "Scared of what it might do. To you, to us."

"I'm not scared."

"Maybe you should be."

"I'm not." She sank onto his lap, straddling him.

He sighed, wrapping his arms around her. "At what cost, Margot?"

"What do you mean?"

"My distillery, my family name, my livelihood, my dreams...at what cost?" He leaned his forehead against hers. "There are days I think I would give anything, do anything...what were all those years of struggle for if I give up now?"

"So we don't give up."

"I know why I'm tempted to open the rickhouse, but why are you? Truly?"

"Because…" She sniffed, her eyes filling with tears. "Because the only way I can stay here with you is if I figure out what happened to the women who came before me. There's no room for me here, not while they haunt these halls."

"Then we'll go," he said firmly. "We'll leave."

She shook her head. "It's not that simple. You'll regret it. You'll resent me. The ghosts will live on. They'll drive a wedge between us, whether or not we're living here with them."

"I don't think—"

She placed a finger over his lips to silence him. "There's a way for us to have it all. We have to try. I'll regret it forever if we don't try. I think you will too."

Merrick's hands slid down her bare arms. He pressed a soft kiss to her knuckles. Over her wedding ring. He held there for a moment, breathing against her skin. "You make me want to be brave. Very foolish or very brave, it's hard to tell the difference sometimes."

"The two don't have to be mutually exclusive."

He smiled.

"We'll do it together. You don't have to face it alone," she said, raising a hand to his cheek, reveling in the rough feel of his evening stubble. She pressed her lips there, dragging them along his jawline, scraping.

He inhaled softly. His fingers curled into her hips.

"The thing that hurts the most, Merrick," she whispered, "the place where the pain lives? That's also the place where healing begins."

He shuddered at her words, his jaw tremoring.

She kissed him there again. And again. And again.

His hand moved to her cheek, turning her head. He captured her mouth with his own. She could taste the need on his lips, the desire. His length grew hard between her legs. She rocked into him, tipping her head back with a groan.

"Before we go further," he rasped, "I need to hear you say it."

"Say what?" she cried, breathless.

"That you're ready. I haven't touched you because I haven't known, not because I haven't wanted to."

"You could have asked."

"I'm asking now." His eyes were twin fires, golden embers.

She swallowed. "I don't want to carry a child again," she admitted. "Not yet."

"You don't have to ever again if you don't want to. I don't need a baby from you, Margot. I never have."

She held her breath, scarcely daring to believe him. All men wanted sons. All men wanted—

"I'll pull out," he continued, closely watching her face. "I don't need a baby. I only need *you*."

Unable to trust her voice, she nodded. Slowly.

"Is that a yes?"

"Yes," she murmured.

His hands hitched her slip upward, lips closing over hers. His fingers grazed the top of her stockings, then slid under her bottom, cupping her mere inches from where she wanted him most. She ground down on him, seeking pressure. He groaned, lifting his hips.

"More," she begged.

He undressed her, sliding her sheer slip over her head. "I want you to wear this to bed every night."

She grinned wickedly. "Only if you promise to turn up the heat."

Merrick gave a tortured moan, grazing his nose over her peaked nipple. "You know exactly how and when to gouge me, don't you?"

She was breathless. Could barely form words. "Consider it an investment."

"Meaning I'll see returns?"

"You will."

He smiled and gently nipped her skin. "Deal."

Even though Margot was positively aching for him, Merrick took his time. Refused to be hurried. He was slow and thorough, taking immense care.

It was a stunning way to be loved, really. Her world narrowed to only him, everything else blurring away at the edges.

Only him, only her.

His hand between her legs.

Her head collapsing back on the pillows.

His fingers inside of her.

Her panting, gasping exhalations.

His tongue, sweeping her entrance, tasting her, wetting her.

Her incoherent mewls, his name on her lips.

His hard tip, just barely pressing in. Spreading her.

Her nails raking his back. Hardly able to stand it.

"Merrick, *please.*"

He pressed deeper, deeper and deeper still. He buried himself to the hilt with a guttural groan. So big, so full...she could barely take all of him. When Merrick began to move, Margot was lost. Consumed by his slow, heavy thrusts.

He was the most ruinous flavor of madness. The kind she longed to drown in. Forever.

"Tell me what you need," he murmured, whispering kisses over her neck. "I'll give it to you."

"You," she breathed. "I have only ever needed you."

⋘

The house creaked in the night, resting on tenterhooks. Poised at the edge of a precipice. Wind rattled the windows. Mahogany floors groaned underfoot. Two marriages had come and gone under this roof. The brides still ghosted the halls.

There was always a penultimate night. The one before everything changed.

The wind blew.

Down the hill, the rickhouse waited.

Margot Dravenhearst slept on.

45

September 1918

And finally—are you paying attention, Merrick?—never forget your life is to be a labor of love. It's a marriage, you see. Between the barrel and the bourbon, cycling through the seasons together. High summer temperatures increase pressure, forcing the bourbon deep into the pores of the wood. Cold winters draw the bourbon out, bringing with it the rich color and woodsmoke flavor.
Pressure makes the marriage stronger. Pressure makes damn good bourbon.

—Excerpt, a letter from Richard Dravenhearst's Last Will & Testament

I T WAS A BEAUTIFUL December dawn. Frost across the pasture, grass dusted glittery white. The sky was bruised, overcast with swirling grays and purples. Pine and woodsmoke permeated the air. Horse hooves crunched softly on frozen shards.

Ruth's breath fogged as she barked orders.

Omaha chased Fox. Again and again.

Margot watched. She was not afraid.

When Merrick slid off his horse at the end of the morning, heading for the stable, she stopped him.

"Are you sure?" he asked.

"We're being brave today, aren't we?"

She reached. After seven years spent holding her breath, Margot Dravenhearst brushed fingers against death itself. Against the beast of her nightmares. It was softer than she'd expected. Warmer. She closed her eyes, remembering.

She exhaled.

"We'll need to be careful," Merrick said, standing before the chained doors. "The building isn't sound. Especially at the rear, by the sinkhole."

Margot nodded.

"I'll check it out first," he continued. "You wait here."

He pressed his palm flat to the door, leaning in, his eyes closed.

"Go on then," she whispered.

He didn't reply, but he opened his eyes. He gripped the heavy chains and produced a key. The *click* of the lock was grating and rusty. Louder still were the iron links when Merrick pulled, untangling the chains from the door. With a mighty clang, the shackles fell to earth, raising a cloud of dust.

After twenty years, Rickhouse One was finally free.

Ruth stood on the porch of Hellebore House. Watching. She shaded her eyes with her hand, blocking the sun. She would come no closer.

She knew better.

Margot did not know better. She followed Merrick inside.

The rickhouse creaked. Its frame shuddered with relief.

The third Dravenhearst bride had finally come home.

Tasting, tasting, tasting. That was what Merrick wanted to do. Rolling, rolling, rolling. He wanted all the barrels moved out.

The back wall of the rickhouse was crumbling. The foundation was not secure. There were several areas where sunlight shone through holes in the exterior. Spots of water damage too.

The rickhouse air was thick with angel's share, every breath woody and sweet. But a heavenly scent could not disguise the hell underneath. They would not linger here. They would get the barrels out. As many as they possibly could.

Today.

Julian was summoned. Xander too.

"You'll put him in an early grave," Margot told Merrick, watching the liver-spotted manservant roll barrel after barrel down the metal track between ricks.

"These barrels are relatively light. We'll be lucky if they're even half full of usable product. After twenty years, the devil's cut and angel's share rise higher than fifty percent. Higher still in the top racks, where aging accelerates due to heat."

"I see."

"We'll concentrate on the lower floors today, the ones with the highest yield."

Hours slipped away. Every barrel rolled was a grain of sand slipping through an hourglass. Time sifted and fell through Margot's fingers. There was a ticking in her mind, keeping time. Every second, relentless. Ticking.

Tick.

Tick.

Tick.

Counting down, she realized, raising a woozy hand to her forehead, damp with sweat.

Counting down to what? What would happen here when the sand ran out?

What happened here twenty years ago when the music stopped?

By the time dusk fell, half the rickhouse was emptied. Xander and Julian were dismissed.

The lower-level ricks were empty, ghostly bare save five barrels lined up on the floor. One from each level of the rickhouse.

Merrick handed Margot the whiskey thief, the long cylindrical tool used to steal bourbon from the barrels. The copper was dense in her hands, heavier than expected.

"Want to try?" he asked, pulling out the cork stopper in the nearest barrel.

She did.

He showed her how, his fingers gliding over hers. Less than a thimble-full of deep amber liquid in each glass. Enough to taste but not to waste.

Merrick lifted his glass, assessing the color. She held her breath, watching him. He sniffed gently. Swirled the liquid in the tumbler. Paused to smile at her. "Ready?"

"Ready." She gave a delicate sniff of her own. The scent of oak was undeniably strong.

"Twenty years in a barrel," Merrick said, reading her mind. "A long marriage."

Margot tipped her glass to her lips. A symphony of flavors exploded across her tongue. She was flooded with woodsmoke upfront, sharper than sharp. But its power dulled, settling into a wash of botanical liquid heat that finished sweet. Lighter and smoother than any bourbon she'd ever tasted. So painfully, beautifully smooth.

Merrick watched her, awaiting the pronouncement. She licked her lips, not wanting to waste a drop. Fiery warmth swelled in her chest.

"Well?"

"Smooth. Rich," she replied. The burn lingered. "I've never tasted anything like it before."

"It'll sell for a pretty penny." Merrick smiled. "There'll be nothing like it on the market, nothing to rival it."

He kissed her, slow and sure. She slipped her tongue in his mouth, gently grazing his teeth, tracing his lips.

"I love the way it tastes on you," he groaned.

She loved how it tasted on him too. She always had.

Margot ended the day with a smile on her face and bourbon on her lips. Determined once more that this family could bloom where it had once bled.

Margot waited until Merrick was sound asleep to make her move, for there was still one final thing she needed to do.

Her feet led her downstairs and across the foyer, one hand dragging along the ebony wood of the serpentine banister. Her fingers knocked the slats as one plucks the strings of harp. She paused at the small table that held the manor's telephone.

The stained-glass window loomed overheard, the violet flowers dark in the night. Inky black.

Margot reached for the receiver. The line crinkled with static as the connection was established.

"Name, please?" the switchboard operator asked, her tone pleasantly clinical, bored.

Margot's voice came out breathy and high, nervous. "Alastair Pendry. Frankfort."

"Hold, please."

Margot waited. Her grip tightened on the receiver.

"Hello?"

She took a deep breath. "Alastair, it's Margot Dravenhearst. Margaret."

A long silence. She imagined his shock at the other end of the line.

"Margaret?"

"Yes." She swallowed. "I have a few questions for you. I'd like to start with the simplest, if you don't mind."

Silence.

She'd take that as *no, he didn't mind*. He might in a moment though. The switchboard operator's night was about to get a whole lot more interesting, assuming she was still listening.

"There's no easy way to ask this," she said, chewing her lip. "Did you poison my husband?"

46

December 7, 1913

Jean-Philippe,
You've done it again. Truly, I've only one thing left to say.
"Let them eat cake."

Yours,
Babette Dravenhearst

T HE HOUSE ALWAYS CAME alive at night.

Margot awoke at the witching hour with a shuddering gasp, chest arching toward the ceiling. She tasted jasmine in the air. Light flickered beyond the French doors. Margot slipped from Merrick's bed and went outside.

She stood on the balcony in her nightdress, watching a streaming lineup of ghostly motorcars approach the manor, headlights circling the round-about, passing up and down the drive under the magnolias. The moon hung low overhead, as thin and sharp as the blade of a scythe.

Margot turned toward the house. The master bedroom was dark, but the companion suite was brightly lit. She slipped back inside through the other set of doors.

Babette was there, wearing a gown of ivory lace with a high neck and full voluminous sleeves that tapered at the wrist. Her hair was pinned up with two glittering diamond clips. A bridal veil tumbled down her back. She stared at her reflection in the mirror, one hand gliding over her stomach.

Without a backward glance, Babette strode to the door.

Margot followed.

The hallway was dark and impossibly long. Longer than it should be. Colder too. Jasmine hung heavy in the air.

Babette glowed ahead, her white bridal gown cutting through the darkness. Doors flew open as Margot passed, but she didn't look inside. The only memory she was interested in was the one unfolding before her—Babette's final night at Dravenhearst Manor.

When Margot reached the top of the stairs, she paused. Babette descended, her veil dragging two steps behind her. Richard, Ruth, and Xander all waited in the foyer, three pairs of eyes drinking in the Dravenhearst bride. Margot leaned over the ebony rail to watch.

A pair of hands gripped her from behind, startling her. She gasped, teetering. There was a perilous moment when her stomach spiraled, when her vision blurred, and she imagined the fall. How the air would rush as she plummeted...

"Babette!"

The grip on her shoulders was ironclad, pulling her back. She spun and saw the real Xander. Heavily wrinkled, hair white and spotty.

"Babette," he cried her name again. "I've packed and delivered your suitcase to the rickhouse. Everything is in place. Richard need never know."

"What?" Margot's brow creased. A shadow shifted over Xander's shoulder in the dark hallway. A pair of white eyes, low to the ground.

Beau. Muzzle down. Eyes sharp.

"I've done as you asked," Xander said. His bulbous blue eyes rolled about in his head, half mad. "We're even now." He squeezed her shoulders tight, just hard enough to yield pain.

Margot was locked in his talons like a field mouse. Prey.

"It's there," he repeated. "Inside the rickhouse, just as you asked. I'll not tell Richard where you've gone, and you'll not say a word to Evangeline about what we've done."

"Xander," she began. He was confused, though something about his words niggled at her.

His hands moved from her shoulders to the front of her nightdress, fisting there in his twisted grip. His eyes filled with tears. "Please, I'm begging. Set me free of you, Babette."

"I'm leaving tonight," Margot said, leaning into his delusion. "You'll be free of me."

"We should never have done what we did," he hissed, spittle flying. "I love my wife. I can't lose my wife."

"You won't." She could make the promise because she knew, twenty years later, it was true.

Yet Xander was still haunted. Still consumed by the memory of his mistake.

"Can you ever forgive me?" He closed his eyes, exhaustion seeping in. "I need...to be forgiven."

Margot's gaze softened. "Yes. You're forgiven, Xander. I forgive you."

His hands released her, and he stumbled away, mouth gaping. Fingers trembling. He raised his eyes heavenward. "Thank God. Oh, thank God."

Margot exhaled, stepping away from the railing. Beau slunk out of the shadows and positioned himself at her skirt. His warmth brushed her leg, reassuringly solid.

"We're even then," Xander said, straightening. "Your secret in exchange for mine. Your bag is at the rickhouse. Make haste and depart."

Margot froze, her brain finally catching up to her intuition. "Xander...the rickhouse? Are you certain?"

"Yes."

"The *rickhouse*, not the stable?"

"You told me the rickhouse," he said, holding firm. But his eyes were still crazed, eerily blue, flashing with the milky taint of cataracts. Margot didn't know if she could trust him.

Hadn't Ruth said the bag was delivered to the stables? And Alastair, on the telephone...he'd said he waited at the stables.

The *stables*, not the rickhouse.

"Xander, are you sure—"

He lunged, his hands twisting into her nightdress again. "The *rickhouse*." He shook her shoulders, enough to jar her head. "That's what you told me. Is this another one of your games, Babette?"

"N-n-no!"

"Do you want me to take you there? I'll show you. I've done as you asked. I only ever do as you ask."

"No." She wrenched away. She wasn't going anywhere with him, least of all the rickhouse. She turned and fled down the stairs.

Xander didn't give chase. He remained on the landing, watching her with those milky aged eyes. Beau was at her heels, stepping on the hem of her skirt.

"Go to bed, Xander," Margot called, trying to keep her voice from shaking. "You've no more business here tonight. Go to bed."

He melted into the shadows of the house and disappeared.

Margot drifted to the base of the stairs, gripping the newel post in her shaking hands. Overhead, the crystal chandelier swung like a pendulum.

The foyer was empty and cold, the veil to the past shattered. Babette was gone.

Margot's mind raced.

Xander had been insistent. He took her bag to the rickhouse.

Ruth had barely mentioned it in her recollection, but Margot was certain she specified the stables. And again, Alastair had been very clear on the telephone tonight, the meeting place was the stables. He was told so by Ruth herself when he arrived outside the party—she browbeat him away from the door, directing him to the stables to hide.

He waited there all night, Alastair did. Waited until dawn for a woman who never showed. Alastair, who swore on his parents' graves he had not poisoned Merrick. That he had nothing to do with Babette's death. That he'd lived with a broken heart for twenty years...

Margot rubbed circles over her eyes. When she opened them, weary, the front door blew unlatched in the wind. The chill of centuries blasted into the foyer. Beau yelped, pressing against Margot's legs.

"Shh," she murmured, bending to scratch the dog behind his ears. She peered outside and saw a woman running across the lawn, heading for the hill. A wedding veil fluttered behind her like an ivory parachute. When Margot passed over the threshold of the door, a shudder ran through her—the ghost of Richard, storming back inside the house, moving directly through her with tears coursing down his cheeks. Margot lost her breath. His crossing felt like being doused with a bucket of icy water.

The wedding veil disappeared over the crest of the hill.

Margot began to run. She had to see. She had to know. Paws thundered behind her—Beau, giving chase. Her white nightdress twisted insidiously at her ankles, threatening to trip her as she lengthened her stride. She lifted it to her knees, the skirt turning ominously silken in her hands. She pointed her feet in the direction she'd last seen the fluttering of Babette's veil.

Not heading for the stables, but for the rickhouse.

The rickhouse doors were cracked open, their metal handles covered with frost. Light spilled out in a single thin beam. Margot panted, pressing a palm to the door, followed by her ear. Trying to listen.

The night was silent. It answered no questions.

Margot knew fear. It twisted its snakelike tendrils around the hammering beat of her heart. Squeezing, telling her no. Telling her to turn back. To wake Merrick.

Whatever she did, above all else, *Do not go into that rickhouse alone.*

But never yet had a Dravenhearst bride been able to resist the pull of Rickhouse One.

A lantern cast flickering shadows on the wood floor. Margot's gaze lowered, and her hand opened in shock, dropping her skirt to the floor. The skirt that, horrifically, no longer belonged to her nightdress but her bridal gown. Margot wore silk. Silk where moments ago had been cotton and wool.

She caught her breath, a trembling hand raising to her chest. And then she heard it, just ahead. Beyond the first row of ricks—ricks that had been empty a few hours ago, now filled with barrels...blocking her view.

But she heard. Raised whispers.

And she saw. A pair of long shadows.

Ghostly black shadows on the wooden floor. Close together. Two people. Just beyond the first row of barrels.

Margot turned the corner.

Babette was there, pressed against a wooden beam by Ruth. Ruth, who had her hands in Babette's red hair and her lips on hers. Kissing fiercely.

"You promised," Ruth pleaded against her lips. "You promised me."

Babette pulled back. "You should know better than anyone not to trust my promises."

"You've always kept them to *me*. Always."

Babette licked her lips. "I have to go, Ruth. I can't stay in this house another day, not with the baby. Alastair loves me. He'll take care of me."

"I loved you before he did. Before *both* of them. We'll run away together, you and me."

Babette tilted her head. She brushed her fingers down Ruth's cheek, tucked a lock of escaped blonde hair behind her ear. "I know you love me."

"But?" Ruth's voice cracked.

"But he can give me more." Babette pulled away.

"He's not even here," Ruth spat, gesturing to the empty rickhouse. "He didn't come for you. *I* did. I came here with you twelve years ago, when you asked me, *begged* me. I'm still here, and now I'm the one who's asking. I'm asking you to choose me."

"He'll be here," Babette replied confidently. "He loves me."

Ruth flinched. Her black gown glittered in the lanternlight, and her eyes bled with betrayal. And pain, so much pain.

"Don't look at me like that," Babette snapped. "I owe you nothing, Ruth."

Her jaw dropped. "How can you say that? How can you say that after everything we've done, everything we've been to each other? A decade of our lives, Babette. It's been you and me from the start."

"I'm after a fresh start." Babette narrowed her eyes. "And I'm not taking anything with me. I don't *want* to take anything with me."

Ruth tipped her head back and laughed. The sound rang through the rickhouse, echoing amidst the rows. Margot recognized something very dangerous in that laugh.

Ruth moved forward, a steely glint in her blue eyes. "I could ruin you. You know that, don't you?"

"If you do, it will prove you never truly loved me. That more than being *with* me, you wanted to *be* me. Always clinging close, ingratiating yourself in my life. My circle. My world. Do you fancy yourself the next Mrs. Dravenhearst?"

Ruth paused and tilted her head, considering.

Babette chuckled under her breath. "Don't fool yourself. You could never carry it off."

"Looks like you're the one who couldn't, turning tail and running away," Ruth baited. "Your husband, your life—I could make it mine in an instant. If I truly wanted it. You have all of this"—she gestured at the distillery around them—"because I *let* you have it. And helped you keep it."

A flash of fire in Babette's eyes. "You didn't *let* me have anything. You have a place here because *I* allow you to stay. When I'm gone, you will be too. And unlike me, you have nowhere else to go."

"I always land on my own two feet, and they're strong enough to hold me up. But you?" Ruth's gaze darkened, twin irises of molten destruction. "You're a disgrace, a leech. Only as strong as the people around you, propping you up. Maybe someone *should* step in here and make things right. Maybe you've been the curse on this house all along."

Babette threw the first slap, stinging and loud. Straight at Ruth's cheek.

But then Ruth's hands were at her throat, wrapping around the heavy pearl collar of the wedding gown. Tightening. Cutting off air.

Margot opened her mouth to scream, knowing it would be fruitless. That what had died here could not be saved. "Stop! Stop it!"

Horrified, watching the color drain from Babette's face, Margot stepped back until her spine slammed into a barrel. A freestanding one, lined up in the aisle. She blinked, seeing the copper whiskey thief on top. The one she and Merrick had used mere hours ago. She blinked in confusion and looked up. All the barrels suspended in the ricks had vanished. The entire first floor of the rickhouse was empty.

The imprints of Babette and Ruth were gone.

Margot shuddered, nauseated by what she'd seen. She could not, would not believe it. Didn't want to. She had befriended Ruth. Drank tea and gin rickeys on her porch. Had been saved and reassured by her the night Merrick was poisoned. Trusted her...

No.

No, no, no.

She stumbled toward the rickhouse door. The weight of the past bore down upon her, threatening to snap her neck, to cut off her air supply. Margot couldn't breathe—

"Noose, dearie?" Eleanor appeared suddenly, offering a length of rope.

Margot reared back and screamed.

The door to the rickhouse opened with a pealing screech, revealing a tall, stately woman with immaculately manicured blonde hair.

Ruth. In riding boots and a tailored pantsuit despite the late hour. Older, wiser, and infinitely more composed than the figment Margot had just seen.

Infinitely more dangerous, she realized.

Eleanor vanished when the door opened, dropping the noose to the ground. It landed with an ominous *thump* at Margot's feet.

"Margot?" Ruth slid into the warehouse, her sharp eyes taking in the length of rope on the ground. "What are you doing in here?"

47

March 14, 1914

Richard,
No more avoiding me—I need to talk to you. Come see me in
Hellebore House.

Yours,
Ruth

L IKE A FISH OUT of water, Margot's mouth opened and closed. Open. Close. Open.

"Margot, what are you doing with that?" Ruth pointed to the rope.

Her mouth snapped shut one final time. *That looks bad. That looks really bad. Goldarn it, Eleanor.*

"What are you doing here?" Margot finally managed.

"I saw the light from Hellebore House. It worried me. What are *you* doing in here?" Ruth's eyes skimmed up and down, taking in the silk drape of Margot's wedding gown. "Dressed in *that*?"

"I...don't know," Margot replied, keeping her tone careful. Neutral. "I think I was...I was sleepwalking."

"I heard voices as I approached. Who were you talking to?" Ruth peered deeper into the rickhouse. As she did so, Margot spied Beau over her shoulder, nosing his way inside.

"Voices? I don't recall..." Margot wrapped her arms around her middle, sick with fear. "I don't always remember my dreams. I'd best return to the manor. Thank you for checking on me."

As Margot moved to step around Ruth, the woman grabbed her arm. Pincer tight.

"I don't think you should go up there at all," she said, her voice low.

Margot tugged gently, trying to free herself. "Merrick will be worried if he wakes..."

"Margot." Ruth's gaze softened. "I can't let you go back up there. Don't you see what's happening? What that house—that *man*—is doing to you?"

"I'm fine."

"I walk in on you in this godforsaken rickhouse, in the dead of night, dressed in your wedding gown with a noose at your feet, and you expect me to believe you're *fine*?" Ruth's eyes were wide. She shook her head. "Margot, you need to leave the manor. Immediately. You're not well."

"I'm not going anywhere." She thought of Merrick, sleeping soundly just up the hill.

"You're not in your right mind," Ruth murmured. "He's cast a spell on you. The whole blasted family has. The same thing happened to Babette. That's the real Dravenhearst curse. If you would just trust me—"

"Babette was *leaving*." Margot yanked her arm free. "The night she was killed. She wasn't bewitched. She didn't love Richard, not the way I love Merrick."

Ruth grimaced. "Margot, you don't. You don't love him. You don't know what you're saying."

"I *do*." She'd never been more sure of anything in her life. "I love him. And I'm not leaving him."

"You have to. Either you lose him, or you lose your life." She kicked the noose at their feet. "Don't you see? The whole damn bloodline is rotten to the core."

Margot inhaled, quiet and sharp, hearing the veiled threat in Ruth's words.

"I'll help you." Ruth lowered her voice. "I'll help you get out. The way I tried to help Babette. We'll go together, you and me."

"You didn't help her." The words escaped before Margot could stop them.

The air in the rickhouse chilled.

Ruth's jaw tightened. "What has she shown you?"

"N-n-nothing." Margot stepped toward the door.

Ruth exhaled through her nose, the snort of a bull set to charge. "What have you seen?"

If Margot ran now, could she make it? She didn't like her chances—Ruth was wearing pants and riding boots. She'd overtake her.

"I saw," she breathed, "that you once loved a Dravenhearst too."

Ruth froze.

"Loved her enough to stay." Margot's tone turned soft. "Loved her enough to build a life here, despite the odds. Despite what it cost. We aren't so different, you and me."

"You're more right than you realize," Ruth said, thunderclouds forming in her eyes. "You think you've got it all figured out, don't you?"

Margot's breath caught in her throat.

"But you've got one thing wrong, the most important thing," Ruth continued. "I didn't love a true Dravenhearst, not at first. I didn't know what it really meant to love a Dravenhearst until my son was born."

What? Margot stumbled back, banging into the door. It swung open, and Beau jumped away, melting into the shadows of the night. A scampering of paws and soft footfalls on earth. The dog was running away.

"You think you love your Dravenhearst husband?" Ruth's eyes glowed with feverish zeal. Bright blue. Glittering like sea glass in the lantern light. "That love is the faintest shade of what I feel for my son. Motherhood changes you. It changes you in ways you can't possibly understand."

Even through her fear, the casual cruelty of the remark stabbed deep into Margot's chest. The loss of her baby was still preternaturally fresh, and with four words—*you can't possibly understand*—Ruth ripped the wound open. Mercilessly.

Margot bled, hemorrhaged. The floodgates thrown open to every single casually cruel slight that had ever been said to her. A lifetime of brushes aside. A lifetime of being different, never good enough.

Not a good enough sister to keep her brother.

Not a good enough daughter to keep her mother.

Not a good enough mother to keep her baby.

A lifetime of losing where she'd only ever hoped to gain. To grow. To bloom where she'd once bled.

Margot's vision swirled. She lifted a hand to her forehead, covering her eyes. She didn't want to watch her vision tunneling. She didn't want to feel the flush at her neck, the sweat pouring down her back, her legs growing weak. How many times in her life had it gone this way? How many times had she let the ship go down without its captain?

Because it hurt. It hurt so damn much.

But then came a memory. Merrick's face. Listening to her words.

That thing that hurts the most, she thought faintly, *the place where the pain lives...*

What had she told him?

That's also the place where healing begins.

Margot dropped to her knees, overcome.

You don't get to bloom, to heal, until you *stop* bleeding. And Margot wasn't sure she ever had, not really. Hers was a blistering sore, an oozing canker she couldn't stop touching because she'd learned to love the answering throb. The pain was protective, kept her from getting too close, from gazing directly into the abyss of the mirror to stare down the ghosts within. From setting them free instead of holding on.

Margot's vision crystalized. Sharp and clear.

She alone could stop her own haunting. She alone could bury these ghosts.

Ruth yanked Margot's shoulder, trying to drag her forward. "Get up. Get up, Margot."

She pulled back, clinging to the door. "Julian's father...it's Richard?"

Ruth laughed, a bittersweet cackle tinged with both longing and regret. "I'd never slept with a man in my entire life, you know," she breathed, remembering. "I had dalliances, true...but Babette was an addiction, one I could never quit. After she died, this ghastly house..." Ruth shivered. "She was so close all the time, yet so far away. And Richard was here. The last thing she touched. The last thing she loved. He was all I had left of her. We slept together, only once, about a month after the funeral. But once was all it took. That's how it always is with those damn Dravenhearst men."

Against all odds, Margot smirked, thinking of herself. Of Babette. Of Eleanor. No, conception was never the problem in this house. Fruition was. Blooming.

"I tried to warn you," Ruth cried, her eyes widening, pleading. "I told you not to sleep with him. I told you not to love him. I tried so many times, in so many ways."

Margot gasped. "Did you...you didn't...you wouldn't..."

Ruth's eyes turned to steel. "There's nothing I wouldn't do. I think my darling, dearest Babette has already shown you that secret."

"Did you poison Merrick?" Margot asked, mind racing. Alastair hadn't been the only one who delivered drinks at the legislature dinner. Ruth had, at the very start of the night. Two drinks dripping with berries, purple and blue and round.

Evangeline's garden. The unlocked gate.

"I wasn't trying to poison Merrick," Ruth hissed. "I was trying to poison *you*. You and that blasted baby. Merrick has never been a threat to me, a threat to my *son*, until you came here. Merrick had promised—no more Dravenhearst brides, no more heirs. My son would have been given everything. My son's bloodline would be the one that lived on. This is *our* home."

"He's still a Dravenhearst," Margot said.

"He's *mine*. I raised him right."

Margot tilted her head, thinking of Julian's dastardly charming face. His dark hair and smooth-talking lips. His sweet smile. He didn't seem so different to her than any of the rest. No more or less deserving, certainly, than Merrick. Margot didn't know how she hadn't seen it before.

Or how Ruth didn't see it now. Amazing how mothers were deluded by their sons.

"What you've done is unforgivable," Margot whispered. No wonder Babette, imperfect though she was, refused to rest. There was so much betrayal here.

Ruth huffed, blowing away a strand of blonde hair that had escaped her airtight chignon. "We've reached an impasse, dear Margot," she said. "I tried to keep these secrets from you. I didn't want it to come to this, but you're so full of questions. There's only one left to answer." She glanced over her shoulder to where the rope lay coiled on the ground. "Are you going to come quietly, or will you go down swinging like the last Dravenhearst bride?"

48

March 15, 1914

Ruth,

I thought about what you said. I'll do it, but only the birth certificate. Not the will. I'll make private allowances, set up an account. I don't want Merrick to know.

We won't speak of this again; we're in agreement on that. Even still, I hope you stay. You and the child will always have a place here.

Hellebore House is yours.

Sincerely,
Richard

MARGOT WAS WELL USED to fighting—every day, a war of attrition against her ghosts—but never before had she truly understood what it meant to fight for her life.

Never before had she stared into the eyes of another human and known, with absolute certainty, they intended to kill her.

Ruth seized her.

Margot stumbled, battling over the threshold of the rickhouse, but the woman was *strong*. Ironclad grip born from holding reins. Powerful legs from riding astride. In the span of a single heartbeat, Margot knew she couldn't win this fight. Not this way.

No. Like everything else in her life, Margot Dravenhearst would have to work outside the confines of the box.

A secret smile rose to her lips as a plan formed. A little dastardly, a little mad.

Her favorite kind.

Ruth gave a massive tug, expecting counterpressure. Margot didn't give it; she capitulated, vaulting into Ruth's arms, gripping her.

"Please. Stop," she gasped, fluttering her eyes. "Please. I feel…"

Her eyes rolled back, and she faded to deadweight, feigning her own trademark—unconsciousness.

Ruth stuttered, then dropped her to the ground. Margot landed in a puddle of liquid limbs, one eyelid barely cracked, just enough to survey the scene.

"Well." Ruth brushed her hands on her pants and doubled over, catching her breath. "That was slightly easier than last time."

Margot withheld an angry shudder.

Ruth hooked her hands under Margot's armpits and gave a solid yank. Another. Dragging her lifeless body across the rickhouse. Moving deeper, toward the beams of the second-floor catwalk. Closer to the discarded noose.

Margot allowed it to happen, biding her time. She let her head roll, slack and heavy.

On the fourth pull, she was finally close enough to act. She was beside the first tasting barrel. She waited until Ruth turned to grab the length of rope. The rope that had ended the life of two prior Dravenhearst brides.

Margot would not be the third. She would, indeed, go down swinging.

Quite literally.

She moved. The copper whiskey thief was just there, atop the barrel. Solid and deadly in her hands. Margot gripped it tight.

And she swung.

She swung *hard*.

She swung with the fury of three generations of Dravenhearst women behind her.

She swung for Eleanor, bruised and battered, broken beyond repair.

She swung for Babette, betrayed by the hand of someone she loved.

She swung for herself, haunted by the past but no longer a prisoner to it. The master of her own fate at last. Strong enough to bear it.

Margot's arms rippled as she brought the whiskey thief down, directly onto the back of Ruth's head. The woman's hands slackened, dropping the noose. She crashed to the ground with a rippling shudder, then lay still. A tiny puddle of blood trickled to the floor.

Margot released a huffing exhale. She stared, cataloging the blood but also the shallow rise and fall of Ruth's chest.

Not dead then. Not yet.

A sharp clap pierced the silence of the rickhouse. A single beat. Another. And another.

The utterly hair-raising and altogether misplaced sound of hands coming together.

Margot tracked the noise to the shadows as she emerged. Tall, haughty, proud—Babette, still in her bridal gown. Clapping her hands for Margot. Slow and steady.

"Brava!" Babette cried, smiling. Full teeth. Gleaming eyes. "Oh, brava, Margot darling!"

Margot swallowed hard, her gaze flickering to the catwalk overhead, where another vision appeared. Eleanor sat on the overhang, dangling her legs in the open air. Her bridal veil hung down, flapping like a sail.

"How far you've come, fledgling. How far you've proven you will go for us." Babette prowled closer. "For your Dravenhearst sisters."

Margot didn't reply. She watched the faint rise and fall of Ruth's chest. Her breaths were growing less frequent. Death was coming.

Babette was inches away now. She brushed her knuckles down Margot's cheek. Instead of the usual chilling, phantom-like whisper, her touch was corporeal. Flesh meeting flesh, tinged with warmth.

Margot shuddered, recalling Ruth's warning. *"Spirits are never stronger in our natural world than at the places where they lost their lives."*

"There's only one thing left," Babette said, her full lips parting. She walked around Margot, dragging her fingers down and around her neck, pausing to whisper in her ear from behind. "You know what to do, Margot."

Eleanor giggled and dropped to the floor, landing with a solid, squelching *thud*. Fully human, the sound of that fall. No longer spirit, now flesh and blood, she crossed the floor and picked up the rope, the end sticky with Ruth's growing puddle of blood.

"One of us," Babette continued whispering, completing her circle. Her heels tapped on the wood floor, every step. She settled in front of Margot. "It's what you've always wanted, to be wanted. We *want* you, Margot."

She couldn't look away if she tried. Distantly, a ruckus rose beyond the walls of the rickhouse. A yipping. Very faint.

"Forever. With us." Babette took the rope from Eleanor and handed it to Margot. She reached out, curling Margot's fingers around it. "Once haunted, forever haunting."

There was a beautiful symmetry in that. Margot looked toward the rafters, noose in hand. The noises outside grew louder.

"That's it," Babette encouraged. "You know what to do. You've dreamed of it. You belong to us, Margot. Belong *with* us. With Elijah. He's waiting, only a crossing away."

Elijah.

A ripple passed through her, a sharp whip of pain. Her body was conditioned, so long a glutton for it.

But the pain was the place where healing began. The rope was in her hands, yes, but it was time to let go. Not hold on.

"No," Margot said, raising her eyes to Babette's.

"No?" Her beautiful face contorted into something ugly, something unforgiving.

"No."

The door to the rickhouse ripped open, slammed with enough force to nearly tear it off its squealing hinges. Merrick skidded inside, revolver in hand, Beau howling at his heels.

"Margot," he cried, gaze clocking the scene. Her wedding gown. Her grip on the noose. He raised a shaking hand. "No. Don't. Please. I love you. I'm in love with you, Margot. Please don't do this—"

"Do it!" Babette screeched, flying forward.

The gun fired.

Margot gasped and dropped the rope.

The bullet streamed by her, landing in the center of Babette's chest. Directly over her heart. Blood bloomed, spreading in crimson rivulets down the bodice of her wedding gown.

Merrick fired the revolver again. A second bullet pierced Babette's stomach. Then a third.

He can see her, Margot realized with shock. Finally. Here in the rickhouse.

Babette shrieked, looking at her son in disbelief.

"You're not welcome in this home anymore," he roared, the gun still raised. "I don't know how to possibly make it more clear."

"You can't kill what's already dead, son," she replied. Blood trickled down her skirt.

"I can sure as hell try. I *will* try, because you have no place in our lives." He reached for Margot, dragging her to his chest. "Your power here, your power over me, is gone."

Margot stared Babette down, tucked inside her son's arms. Gently, very gently, because his fingers were shaking, Margot pried the revolver from Merrick's grip. She pointed it at Ruth, who was lying a foot away, barely breathing.

"You can have her, a third Dravenhearst mother," Margot said. "But not me. She's the one you want anyway. The one who loved and betrayed you."

She fired the gun. More blood bloomed on the floor, and Ruth's labored breathing ceased.

Babette wavered, growing paler and paler with every passing second. She dropped to her knees and grabbed Ruth's hand. Her mouth opened, but whether to lament or lash out, Margot would never know. Before she could say a word, Babette vanished.

There was still one Dravenhearst bride in the room. Eleanor. Several paces away, hands pressing into the veil over her mouth in shock.

"Eleanor." Margot stepped forward, lowering the gun.

"I live here because I died here," Eleanor whispered, tilting her head to look into the rafters. Her voice was tremulous. "Not all at once, a little bit every single day."

"I know," Margot murmured. For Babette, she felt anger. Her haunting was selfish, righteous and power drunk. But for Eleanor...

For Eleanor, Margot felt sorrow. And beneath that, forgiveness. It was a release.

It's not your fault, nor is it mine.

Eleanor's gaze turned to Merrick. "Did you mean what you said—do you love her? Truly?"

Merrick didn't waver. "Yes."

Eleanor continued to stare. "More than a child? More than the drink? More than the distillery?"

"Yes."

"Prove it," Eleanor said, beginning to fade. "Prove it, and I will finally rest." She looked at Margot one final time. "Thank you for listening...thank you for listening and not looking away."

And then she was gone.

Merrick exhaled, long and shaky. He started moving, approached the five tasting barrels, lined up in a row. He dropped them to their sides, one by one, then grabbed the first and started rolling. The seams of wood leached something red and sticky from within, leaving a trail across the floor.

Blood.

"What are you doing?" Margot asked.

"What I should have done a long time ago."

Margot followed him outside, around to the back of the rickhouse. He slammed the bloody barrel into the dirt, just at the edge of the sinkhole, where the back wall was crumbling into the earth.

Four more rotting, rancid barrels rolled out, lined up.

Merrick called for Beau and tucked Margot under his arm. He walked them around the edge of the sinkhole, standing a safe distance away. He lifted the revolver, taking aim.

"Wait!" Margot cried, grabbing his hand. "There's still bourbon in there."

Half full, the upper levels...

"I don't care," he said. "I don't give a flying fuck about the bourbon, Margot."

She released his arm.

"As long as that rickhouse stands, those ghosts will be tethered to this place. It's where they died. Blood mixed with bourbon, that's the real family legacy. I should have destroyed it years ago. Should have faced it."

The *crack* of the gunshot rang through the night. The first barrel exploded, followed by the rest, blowing out the wall of the rickhouse. Flames reared, licking inside. The earth gave underfoot, the sinkhole expanding with the force of the explosion. Hungry.

They watched together as Rickhouse One was consumed by flames. As the shell of the building went up. As the fire engulfed the roof. As the walls caved in. As the sinkhole devoured the remains, the earth reclaiming all that was lost.

Ashes to ashes, dust to dust.

That which had once lived here—had festered within—was now, finally, dead.

49

December 19, 1933

My dearest Margaret,
Will you come home?

Forever Yours,
Pa

T HE LETTER CAME BY morning post. Margot recognized her father's shaky handwriting.

"What does it say?" Merrick asked. His lips posed the question, but his eyes knew the answer. He hadn't left her side since they'd watched the rickhouse burn the night before. He reached for her hand now, offering all he could give. All that he was, all of himself. For her.

Margot knew too. She didn't need to open the letter, though she did anyway. She knew it in her soul. She knew, and she was ready.

Finally.

"He's gone home to Greenbrier."

Home to die.

50

"He chose magnolias."

*—Samuel Greenbrier to his daughter Margaret on her
wedding day*

S HE'D FORGOTTEN HOW THE hydrangeas looked in the winter, how
they remained in full bloom, rotund, but turned brown and crisp.
How the heads would break off and blow like tumbleweeds around the
property.

It had been eight years since Margot last set foot at Greenbrier Estates,
and in her mind, the hydrangeas flowered always. Blue and soft, fragrant
and divine.

Like her family, preserved meticulously in her memory by the way she
dreamed of them, the way she wanted to remember them—in full color,
lovely, soft around the edges.

Memories didn't lie, per se, but they didn't tell the whole truth either.

There wasn't much time after they arrived, barely twenty-four hours. But it was twenty-four hours more than Margot had ever been given before, and she knew exactly what to do with them.

She was brave. She said the things she needed to say. She held her father's hand.

And when the time came, she didn't hold on, and neither did he.

Her father let go.

And so did she.

There was much to do in those first days, but she saved the most difficult for last. Margot had never been good at staring down the hard things, the painful things. There was sweet relief in avoidance, in circumnavigating pain. Numbing it.

But she wasn't going to live that way anymore. Margot was done granting power to ghosts.

The graves were surprisingly tidy, all in a row. Two old, covered with grass. In the spring, Margot imagined there would be dandelions, maybe chickweed and creeping violets. Maybe she would return when the ground thawed, bring flowers. Maybe plant some, dozens of them, herself.

She was avoiding again. She blinked once, long and slow, gathering courage. Then she opened her eyes and looked.

There was the third grave, freshly dug. A gaping, ugly hole in the ground. The place where her father's casket would rest on the morrow. No headstone yet, but it would come, would be here by spring.

Spring...when she might plant flowers...

Her eyes filled with tears.

She was the last remaining member of her family. There was immense, soul-crushing sorrow in that. In realizing she was all alone in the world. The people she'd started with had all, one by one, gone.

Merrick squeezed her shoulder. His timing, as ever, was impeccable. She leaned into him, against his full chest. His arms wrapped around her.

Not alone, she realized, closing her eyes again. Tears fell, dripping down her cheeks and onto the ground. Salting the earth where she stood.

The last Greenbrier, yes, but not alone.

"I want to come back in the spring," she whispered. "I want to plant flowers." To see blooms here.

"All right," he answered, steady. "Maybe hydrangeas?"

"I was thinking, actually..." She turned to face him, slipping her arms around his neck. "A magnolia tree."

"A magnolia?"

"Yes. To start."

His smile was a little bit shy and a whole lot hopeful. Margot watched her entire future open up in that smile, ribboning out before her like the tail of a kite in the breeze. Like a wedding veil streaming behind a bride in the wind.

Like magnolia petals falling to the earth in the spring.

Blooming.

Blooming, blooming, blooming.

Epilogue

Summer, 1935

"Margot, are we flying?"

—*Elijah Greenbrier*

"I'VE GOT ALL BREEDS and colors here, Mrs. Dravenhearst. Chestnuts and sorrels. Arabians and Friesians. Fine stallions all, would make excellent riding companions. Or perhaps you're after a broodmare, for that exceptional racehorse of yours?" The breeder opened the gate to the paddock.

Margot smiled lightly. A broodmare for Omaha? She flicked her eyes to Merrick in amusement. "No, I don't think so. Not a broodmare."

"But you do plan to breed him, don't you? With that bloodline?" The man whistled. "*Two* Triple Crowns? One by his father and one by him? Priceless stock, you've got."

"There are things far more important than bloodlines," Margot murmured, holding her palm out to a curious inky-black colt.

"Show us your best and brightest," Merrick said, gesturing ahead. "She's an excellent rider, needs a horse who can keep pace with her."

"Merrick." She shushed him, his sly undertones not lost on her. It was something incorrigible Julian might say. They'd been spending far too much time together since Julian moved into the manor a year ago.

Brothers, Margot mused. Smiling, because she remembered all too well what it was like to have one.

They wandered through the paddock for nearly thirty minutes, meeting different horses. Margot grew attached to a friendly sorrel the breeder called Scotch.

"Short for Butterscotch, you know," he said, rubbing down the horse's side. "Because of his color."

"Hmm, yes." She looked into the horse's soft brown eyes before turning away.

"What's wrong, love?" Merrick asked.

"Nothing, nothing...he's an excellent horse, I'm sure." She tapped her fingers against her bottom lip, still scanning the field.

"But perhaps not for you?" Merrick finished.

"Perhaps not."

Her eyes alighted on a lone horse across the paddock, a beautiful dapple gray, tied to a fence post. Margot changed course, her stride lengthening. "What about that one?"

"Oh, no, Mrs. Dravenhearst." The breeder shook his head. "You don't want her. She's a mare and not built for riding, poor disposition. She won't mate or breed either." He rubbed the back of his neck. "In fact, she's likely headed for the chop the day after the morrow. I've no use for a mare who won't breed."

"Oh, surely not!" Margot quickened her pace. "I want to meet her."

"Mrs. Dravenhearst—"

"I really must insist." She silenced him before turning to Merrick and muttering, "What *is it* with men and your obsession with fertility?"

He barked out a laugh and followed.

She approached the horse with care, not wanting to spook her. When the mare consented to let her rub her nose and neck, she turned to the breeder. "Will she take a saddle?"

"A...a saddle?"

"Yes, a saddle. For a rider."

"Well...I'm...I'm not sure. We've never tried. She's easily distressed, this one."

Distressed.

Is she now?

Margot bit her tongue to keep from sniping but couldn't keep her voice entirely free of sarcasm. She pulled herself to her full height, commanding. "Well, perhaps we should try, since she's otherwise headed to the slaughterhouse."

Every now and then, she noticed bits of Babette slipping through. She never minded when it happened. She'd purged Dravenhearst Manor of so much of her predecessor's influence, beginning with the stained-glass window in the foyer, where magnolia blossoms now glinted in the afternoon sun. But a few things were worth holding on to.

The man scampered away to find a saddle, sufficiently chastised.

"Really, Margot?" Merrick looked at the dapple horse with a critical eye. "This is the one?"

"Do you have a problem with her?" She turned to him, her tone still sharp.

He threw his hands up. "No, no problem."

"She's sweet." Margot continued rubbing her snout. The mare lazily closed her eyes, enjoying the attention.

And it turned out, she took a saddle just fine. Margot mounted with ease. It took a moment to settle, but the horse responded with proper encouragement. Together, they looped around the paddock. The wind in Margot's hair felt heavenly.

Flying...

Yes. It had taken years, but Margaret Greenbrier was flying again.

Dismounting beside Merrick, she handed the reins to the breeder.

"She's mine," she told him. "And since she's so worthless she was headed for the chop, I expect her price to be more than reasonable."

She winked at Merrick. *We Dravenhearsts do love to pinch a penny wherever we can.*

"Yes, ma'am." The man winced, leading the horse away.

"Wow," Merrick said, chuckling. "I'm impressed. I created a monster."

"Just you wait." She looked at him and smiled, her hand ghosting absentmindedly over her belly.

She hadn't told Merrick the news yet, but she would soon. Maybe tonight. She imagined the scene—handing him a glass of bourbon, sitting in his lap...

She knew, for certain, what his smile would look like. Full dimples. No reservations.

Because there was nothing to be afraid of this time around. Margot had slept soundly for over a year. The halls of the manor were quiet. The rickhouses too.

This time, the only monsters they had to fear were the ones they created themselves. Little ones.

Together.

Author's Note

This book began with a glass (or ten) of bourbon.

My husband is a whiskey collector, and a few years ago for his birthday, we traveled to Kentucky to explore the Bourbon Trail. I went into the trip with low expectations—I didn't particularly enjoy drinking the spirit, though my husband (like Merrick) continually reminded me that bourbon is "an acquired taste." He was right. I started that trip as a tagalong, and I finished it with a deep love of Kentucky, rickhouses, and the bourbon industry.

The first bolt of inspiration for this book came when we toured Maker's Mark Distillery in Loretto, Kentucky. At its core, Maker's Mark is a love story, one that began with husband-and-wife duo Bill and Margaret "Margie" Samuels. Bill came from a family with a long lineage of whiskey distilling and in the 1950s, he decided to produce his own brand. Bill was focused on his bourbon's quality and taste, whereas Margie knew a great product didn't matter if it didn't *sell*. She made branding and marketing her mission. Margie is the genius behind Maker's iconic bottle shape, its hand-dipped red wax seal, and she personally designed every label with calligraphy penned by her own hand.

Because of her ingenuity and acumen, Margie Samuels was the first woman to be inducted into the Kentucky Bourbon Hall of Fame, and I chose to name my main character Margaret in her honor. Whiskey is typically seen (and intentionally marketed) as a highly "masculine" product.

But after touring Maker's Mark, I was captivated by the idea of a woman's influence in the male-dominated field of distilling. Of bedrocking a love story within the labor of love that goes into bourbon making. I found the distillery setting to be a powerful vehicle and metaphor for which to base an epic romance.

A critical point of external conflict in this book is Prohibition and the Great Depression. Merrick's character gives a face to the distillers across the nation who were devastated by Prohibition. Only six distilling companies were allowed to continue limited operations under the Volstead Act, permitted to sell their product under medicinal licenses. In this book, Merrick partners with the George T. Stagg Distillery, managed at the time by Colonel Albert Blanton, to stay afloat. Readers who know their bourbon history may be aware that the George T. Stagg Distillery is now known as Buffalo Trace, one of the largest spirit-producers in the US today. Blanton's Single Barrel is one of their flagship bourbons, named in Colonel Blanton's honor.

Prohibition had far-reaching effects on both downstream and upstream industries running parallel to bourbon makers. At the same time as hundreds of distilleries like Merrick's were shuttered, thousands of breweries were shut down, and hundreds of thousands of liquor stores closed their doors. Upstream, barrel cooperages came under great distress and so did bottle manufacturers. Across the alcohol industry as a whole, it is estimated that approximately 250,000 jobs were lost. Entire communities in Kentucky and generations of trade secrets were forfeit when bourbon entered its "ghost era" in the 1920s. The loss of one's livelihood and heritage is no small matter. Merrick struggles against both the weight of carrying his family legacy and against the threat of its erasure for much of the book.

You can't talk about Kentucky without mentioning horse racing. I knew I wanted Merrick to be a horseman as well as a bourbon maker because...hello, sexy thighs and tight pants! Merrick's two prize-winning stallions, Gallant Fox and his progeny Omaha, are real horses from the same bloodline that won the Triple Crown in 1930 and 1935 respectively, though my story cheats Omaha's run by one year, implying a 1934 Derby debut. Both stallions had the distinctive white blaze down their snouts that is detailed in the book, and historical record reports the stallions were "chasers," just as Ruth describes. Theirs was as mischievous a bloodline as it was title-holding, with Omaha described by a famous horseracing broadcaster as "a big, leggy, green thing that invariably seems to get into a lot of trouble."

My greatest joy in writing this book was bringing Kentucky—a wholly underrepresented and rich setting—to life on the page. But the themes of this story and the characters themselves proved a great personal challenge. If Merrick is the face of a lost generation of tradesmen, Margot is the voice for all women throughout history who have been silenced and subjugated while struggling with their mental and/or physical health. At times while drafting this book, it was hard to separate Margot's pain from my own because I was drawing on my personal experiences with mental health and grief to create her character.

When I was twenty-one, I was diagnosed with anxiety and depression after a series of vasovagal fainting incidents. Much like Margot, I had reached a place of such tremendous repressed stress and unhappiness that it triggered existing predispositions in my physical health. I began fainting, fleeing the conscious world altogether, rather than face down situations I simply didn't want to be in. The details around Margot's fainting episodes in the book are drawn from my own lived experience, as is much of her evolving perspective on her mental health diagnoses and her journey to a more compassionate headspace. Knowing that my experiences are neither exhaustive nor universal, I did seek out sensitivity readers for the various identities contained within this book, and I committed to writing my characters with the utmost respect, intention, and care. Any errors made within the text are my own.

There is a dark history in our nation of overlooking, mislabeling, and mistreating women's pain. In this book, the "curse" or black stain on the Dravenhearst family begins with the first bride. In modern times, we would identify the end-stage of Eleanor's mental illness as postpartum psychosis, a condition that can develop after childbirth in which women experience mood swings, paranoia and delusions, hallucinations, and can ultimately lead to thoughts of harming oneself or their baby. Women with preexisting mental health struggles, including prior pregnancy losses, are predisposed to developing postpartum psychosis. The condition is fully treatable if identified properly and supportive care administered. Unfortunately, "supportive" care was so rarely given when issues of the mind were identified in women throughout history.

Much like Eleanor and Vivian Greenbrier, the label of "hysteria" is weaponized against Margot instead of identifying and addressing the root cause of her struggles. Throughout history, laudanum was often provided to women as a band-aid to cover a bleeding wound. But numbing the pain does not help someone heal. Margot's healing only begins when she is brave enough, and feels safe enough, to share the darkest parts of herself with Merrick. Speaking her pain out loud helps set her free instead of continuing to hold on. This is the gift therapy and/or a supportive partner or friend can provide.

I chose to layer themes of mental health into every page of this haunted and healing love story because I want everyone out there who is struggling to know they are not alone. Speaking up about mental health saves lives. Listening saves lives. Talk about your demons, learn how to coexist with them. The monster under your bed only has the power you give it. When we shine a light on it, when we look those demons in the eye, we take back the power.

If you are out there and you are struggling with your mental health, please know you are not alone or abnormal. Just like heart disease or diabetes, this is a medical condition that can be managed and optimized so you can live your life to the fullest. You are beautiful and wonderful precisely the way you are, but sometimes we all need a helping hand on our journeys, be that from a supportive partner, a trusted therapist, or both. It can feel so overwhelming, reaching out for help. So let me go first, let my hand guide you to a few places you can begin.

NAMI, the National Alliance on Mental Illness, has a number of resources, educational materials, and peer-to-peer support groups that can be found online at https://www.nami.org/.

In the United States, dialing 988 on your phone will connect you with the **Suicide and Crisis Lifeline**. They're here to listen and help.

The Trevor Project provides supportive services and crisis intervention specifically for LGBTQ+ young people. They can be reached at https://www.thetrevorproject.org/, and their crisis hotline is available 24/7 by phone call at 1-866-488-7386.

RESOLVE, the National Infertility Association, provides advocacy resources for those looking to support reproductive rights, and they also coordinate support groups and online communities for those struggling with infertility. They can be found at at https://resolve.org/.

Uniquely Knitted is a nonprofit organization that fosters community among those struggling with infertility. Their podcast Infertility Feelings can be found through Apple, Spotify, or YouTube. Thanks to the generosity of donors, they also run low-cost, six-week processing groups that teach evidence-based tools for coping with infertility. More information can be found at https://www.uniquelyknitted.org/.

You are not alone. Shine a light under the bed. Set your ghosts free instead of holding on.

Be well.

ACKNOWLEDGMENTS

When I'm not hidden away drafting books, I work in healthcare, and I must begin by acknowledging how important one particular patient population was in the creation of this story. Obstetrics patients everywhere, otherwise known as *mothers*...phew. Where do I even begin?

I go to work every day endlessly inspired by the conviction, heart, and bravery of women who have chosen the path of motherhood. I have shared your joy in C-sections when your baby takes their first breath. I have kept you safe during high risk, lifesaving procedures to protect your unborn children. I have held your hand when you are suffering a loss. Not a single day goes by that I am not utterly awed by the strength of those who have chosen to walk the path of motherhood.

In commending mothers, it is equally important to acknowledge those who are childfree, whether by choice or by fate. I stand in solidarity with you. I know the invisible struggle you experience every day when you are ceaselessly asked *when* you will have children—as if motherhood is an expectation, and you owe the world a justification for subverting. Because of the rampant pronatalism in our society, I agonized over the decision to set Margot on the path of motherhood in the epilogue of this book. Ultimately, in my heart, it felt right for the fruition of her character arc and her personal dreams. But a baby is not every woman's "happily ever after," nor does it need to be. One day, I am going to write a childfree manifesto and epic love story. And when I do, it will be dedicated to all of you.

The heart of this book was born from wisdom gained after years of therapy. To all the caring therapists across the globe who have reached out their hands to people who are struggling—what you do matters immeasurably. My every day is brighter, braver, and more compassionate because of you. Therapy saves and changes lives.

A most gracious thank you to the librarian of my heart, Agatha Andrews. This book would not exist without you, or at the very least, it would be a pale imitation of the final product. Everything I know and love about the gothic genre, I learned from you. I hope members of the She Wore Black Podcast community will southern gothic swoon with me over this story. I wrote it for all of you—gothic girlies unite!

To Kitty Yanson, my high school English teacher, who first put a copy of *Rebecca* in my freshman hands...and then wrote on my gothic heroine essay to come see her after class to chat. You set me on a path neither of us saw coming. Thank you for being the very first person to tell me I had the gift of words. I have carried your belief and early mentorship with me ever since.

My most heartfelt appreciation to the following authors who took the time to read *The Dravenhearst Brides* and shared beautiful blurbs of support: queen of gothic fiction, Paulette Kennedy; queen of the gothic whodunnit, Jess Armstrong; queen of historical romance swoon, Erin Langston.

All my love to CPs Christie Curry and Katrin Dreessen-Engler for being the first to tell me Merrick Dravenhearst—who gave me absolute *fits* while drafting and had me half-convinced he was no kind of romance hero at all—was unbearably sexy on the page and worth fighting for. I know I've said it before, but this book truly would not have gotten finished without you two. I mean it this time.

To the world class crew of beta and sensitivity readers who gave their time to this story and provided thoughtful, impactful feedback: Anne Alcott, Shayna Becker, Kimberly Lynn Hanson, Maren Jenner, Anne Knight, Celine Oliver, Hannah Sharpe, and Thea Verdone.

To my unparalleled team of Rachels—my brilliant editor Rachel Shipp and proofreader extraordinaire Rachel Fitzjames. In your hands, this book became what I always dreamed it would be.

A standing ovation to Austin Drake, who designed the jaw-dropping cover of this book. Thank you for going gorgeously gothic with me...and for giving Merrick the most iconic chest hair and sideburns imaginable.

For Trisha, brave and beautiful. She knows why.

For Tammy and Cindy, the mothers in my own life, who—to be clear—are nothing like the monster-in-law mothers in this book.

For my father, whose illness and decline I was grieving while drafting this manuscript. Dad, I gifted Merrick your pinchpenny ways and penchant for thermostat tyranny. Bone-chilling winters and sweltering summers in our drafty old house truly were character-building, in more ways than one!

To my pure-hearted protector, Bear. Just like Beau, you are always there to chase away my ghosts.

To my husband, for understanding that I have sadness within me, same as Margot. For loving me in every color I come in, from bright sunshine yellow, to pure magnolia white, all the way to the deepest bruising shades of blue-black. This story began with your love of bourbon and turned into my love letter to you for the countless ways you strengthen, support, challenge, and celebrate me. On good days and bad, in every color. Our love is my rainbow, guiding me through every storm. It is my barrel-aged glass of bourbon—deeper, more complex, and stronger with every passing season.

And finally, to my readers. You have always been the dream, one so far-flung and coveted I barely even dared to dream it at all. What a privilege it has been to share my words and stories with you! You've brought me more joy than you can possibly imagine. Thank you for making reality even better than my daydreams.

Looking for more of your favorite characters...?

Sign up for Lindsay's newsletter and receive a free BONUS EPILOGUE, told from Merrick Dravenhearst's point of view.

https://www.lindsaybarrettbooks.com/newsletter

ALSO BY LINDSAY BARRETT

Savannah Royals

ABOUT THE AUTHOR

Lindsay Barrett is a Maggie and RWA award-winning author who crafts dark stories with lots of kissing. An avid world traveler, most of Lindsay's writing inspiration comes from perpetual wanderlust. When she isn't snowshoeing atop glaciers in Alaska, drinking bourbon in Kentucky, or binge eating tapas in Spain, she can be found in her home state of Maryland, where she lives with her husband and their tiny titan (read: prince) of a rescue dog.